TIME'S F

Charles J. Schneider

TIME'S FICKLE GLASS

DOUBLE DRAGON

This novel is based on an extensively revised version
of the previously published novel

A PORTRAIT IN TIME

and represents
the prequel to:

THE ARRIVAL OF AN HOUR

O thou my lovely boy who in thy power
*Dost hold **TIME'S FICKLE GLASS** his fickle hour*

William Shakespeare
Sonnet 126

Dedicated to my father:
A man with an ever-artistic eye
who always knew how to tell a good story

Charles M. Schneider
12/22/1928 - 12/15/2008

FACT AND FICTION
IN ALL THINGS
'COURBET' AND 'CAILLEBOTTE'

Fact: *Jean Désiré Gustave Courbet (known by the second of his two middle names: 'Gustave') gained notoriety for his suggestive nudes—especially, his explicit depiction of an anonymous model's genitalia in his controversial erotic painting The Origin of the World, created in 1866.*

Fact: *Courbet's erotic painting entitled Sleep depicting 2 female lovers was the subject of a police report for obscenity in 1872. Sleep, Woman with Stockings (which shows a lascivious woman exposing her genitals), and The Origin of the World were all deemed inappropriate for public display and were thus banned from exhibition.*

Fact: *The Origin of the World was never viewed publicly until 1988. It is currently part of the permanent exhibition at Musée d'Orsay in Paris.*

Fact: *The model for The Origin of the World remains a mystery to this day, although long presumed to be one of Courbet's numerous secretive mistresses who doubled as artistic subjects, with the top contender until recently being Courbet's Irish mistress and model Joanna Hiffernan. Authorities now believe that the model may have been the Parisian ballet dancer Constance Queniaux: the mistress of Ottoman diplomat Halil Şerif Pasha (aka Khalil Bey) who actually commissioned the creation of the painting in 1866 by Caillebotte for his erotic collection of artwork. The same uncertainty exists surrounding*

Courbet's other nude models, whose identities were kept secret and never revealed, in order to protect their reputation.

Fact: *Not much is known about Courbet's personal life. He was never married but had a mistress with whom he had a daughter in 1847. This mistress left with her child in the early 1850's and Courbet never maintained contact with them after the separation. He had countless physical relationships with various women and could have very well had other illegitimate children with these other mistresses.*

Fact: *Courbet also gained notoriety for his political views during the rule of the Paris Commune. He was forced to flee France in 1873, in order to avoid a large financial penalty for the key role he played in the destruction of the Vendome Column. He resided in Switzerland until his death on December 31, 1877 of liver disease exacerbated by heavy drinking.*

Fact: *Courbet was an inspiration to many of his contemporaries and a laughingstock to others. He was openly admired by Ferdinand Victor Eugene Delacroix and James Abbott McNeill Whistler, and was a role-model and teacher to many younger aspiring Impressionists, including Edouard Manet and Edgar Degas. His relationship with Jules Joseph Lefebvre was likely antagonistic since Lefebvre was accepted by La Salon as a legitimate artist notwithstanding his propensity for painting semi-explicit nudes, and Courbet was not.*

Fact: *There were three Caillebotte brothers: Gustave (the oldest), René (the middle sibling), and Martial (the youngest).*

Fact: *Gustave was a famous painter, and Martial was a renowned photographer. Not much is known of René, who died suddenly in 1876 at age 25 of an undisclosed and mysterious illness presumably cardiac in nature. Given the artistic creativity of his two brothers, it is conceivable that he had similar talents as well, though never documented.*

Fact: *Gustave and Martial both inherited millions, and spent most of their leisure time collecting stamps and devoting their energy to their various other hobbies (music and photography for Martial; gardening, yacht building and collecting paintings for Gustave).*

Fact: *Gustave, although trained as an attorney and painter, gave up his professional efforts to become a recluse, dying alone in his garden when he was 46 on February 21, 1894 of 'pulmonary congestion'. The true cause of his sudden and unforeseen death is unknown, and could have very well been the result of foul play.*

Fact: *Martial lived with his brother Gustave in Hauts-de-Seine prior to Gustave's purchase of his country home that he named Petit Genevilliers.*

Fact: *Charlotte Berthier was an alias for Anne Marie Hagan: Gustave's long-time companion (from a lower class) and the eventual heiress of his estate. It is rumored that Gustave insisted that Anne Marie use the fictitious name in order to disguise her identity and distract attention from the fact that she had worked as a prostitute before becoming his mistress.*

Fact: *Marie Minoret was Martial's wife, and had tremendous animosity towards Anne Marie Hagan aka Charlotte Berthier, to the point that Martial's* relationship with Gustave was eroded by restrictions placed by his wife on how often he could see his older brother.

Fact: *Martial Caillebotte and Marie Minoret had two children: a son, Jean, and a daughter, Geneviève. Geneviève, rather than Jean, inherited the majority of unsold paintings in Gustave Caillebotte's collection from his estate. There is no evidence that Jean had been disinherited, in contrast to his fictional portrayal in this novel.*

Fact: *Gustave only painted two female nudes: <u>Naked Woman Lying on a Couch</u>, 1873; and <u>Nude on a Couch</u>, 1890. The brunette model for the first piece was anonymous and unidentified, while the second redheaded model is uncontestably a depiction of Anne Marie Hagan (aka Charlotte Berthier), pictured in the early years of her relationship with the artist.*

Fact: *Gustave painted a handful of male nudes— unconventional subject-matter at the time, leading to rumors that he was homosexual. His reclusive behavior and the fact that he remained a bachelor until his death added to this unfounded conclusion.*

Fact: *Francois Salle was a slightly younger contemporary of Gustave Caillebotte with only one notable painting of historically consequence, of a male model posing nude for a group of art-school students (<u>The Anatomy Class at the Ecole des Beaux Arts</u>, 1888). Gustave and Francois (or easily the male model) could have very well crossed paths given their interest in depicting the naked male form on canvas.*

Fact: *Gustave was an art collector and had a vast collection of Impressionist paintings. There is* *admittedly no documentation of whether or not he owned any Courbet pieces.*

Fact: *Pierre-Auguste Renoir (known by his second-hyphenated name 'Auguste') was a close friend of the Caillebotte family, spending much of his time with Gustave at his estate at Petit Genevilliers. He was the executor of Gustave's Will and the 'caretaker' of Gustave's vast collection of Impressionist paintings until they were eventually passed on to Genevieve Caillebotte: Martial's daughter, after Renoir's death. Caillebotte had donated these paintings to the French government, but Renoir was unsuccessful in his attempts to facilitate Gustave's wishes since the Republic, unbelievably, declined the generous bequeathal. Many of these paintings were eventually purchased by Dr. Albert C. Barnes of Philadelphia and reside at the Barnes Foundation Museum, including* <u>Woman with White Stockings</u>.

Fact: *Auguste Renoir was a womanizer who had affairs with virtually all of his nude models (including the infamous Suzanne Valadon). He eventually married Aline Charigot, whom he had depicted nude in some of his most famous pieces.*

Fact: *Erotic photography as a genre was conceived in the mid-nineteenth-century, and was practiced by the French portrait photographer Felix-Jacques Antoine Moulin, among others. In 1851 his explicit photographs were confiscated, and he served a one-month prison sentence because of the obscene nature of his nude portraits.*

Fact: *N-methylaminophenol (also known as Metol) is a developing powder used in black and white photography. It was developed in 1891, and was*

13

widely used in the late nineteenth and early twentieth century by both amateur and commercial photographers. Ingestion of even a small amount leads to the formation of met-hemoglobin in the bloodstream: a 'poisoned' form of hemoglobin that cannot bind oxygen. The disorder leads to rapid death by 'hematologic' asphyxiation.

Fiction: *Everything else*

PART I

MORE THAN A FEW DAYS
PRIOR TO ARRIVAL
APRIL 2 – JUNE 1, 1876

CHAPTER ONE

It was the last day of May in 1876 when the letter, marked with Switzerland postage, finally arrived. With a gracious "thank you" to her landlord for accepting the delivery while she was out, Nicole Bruante climbed the three flights of stairs two at a time up to her attic room and ripped open the seal. Sitting on the edge of her bed, she pulled out the single sheet of paper and breathed a sigh of relief when, after unfolding and reading his reply, she learned that the answer was 'yes'.

Just about two months earlier she had waited patiently in line behind a dozen other patrons at the Montmartre postal station to send off the written plea that she held nervously in her hand. Who would have thought that on that very day and as a direct consequence of mailing her letter, fate would put her into direct contact with the man who could help materialize her request into reality. As she had counted out the correct combination of hard-earned coins and placed them with a metallic jingle into the outstretched palm of the clerk behind the counter, she thought he looked familiar.

"Have we met before?"

He met her gaze with eyes a shade of blue that could easily be called lavender—which is when she immediately knew who he was, because only one person she had ever met had eyes of that color. "Yes, while you posed anonymously for my brother: Gustave Caillebotte."

She saw him study her name 'Nicole Bruante' printed on the return address while stamping the letter with an official posting date: 2 April, 1876. Now she was no longer anonymous…to *him*; but 'identity revealed' in this case was not necessarily a bad thing. René Caillebotte was someone she had actually thought about time and time again over the years since that artistic sitting, so she didn't mind at all that he now knew her by her given name rather than just an unnamed naked woman.

The only reason she hadn't recognized him immediately was the closely trimmed beard, and what appeared to be a year or two's worth of hair-growth tied neatly back in true bohemian fashion at the nape of his neck. "That was about…three years ago?" she offered—knowing exactly how much time had passed since she modelled nude for Gustave in 1873.

He nodded and blushed, looking away as much from embarrassment as from the task of placing her letter in a basket labeled 'international', which made her laugh out loud. "I'm really not shy about that sort of posing, you know. Otherwise, I wouldn't be *that* type of artist's model."

He looked back at her directly and smiled. He was the best looking of the three Caillebotte brothers by far, and someone she wouldn't mind getting to know better since her intuition told her he would probably be good in bed. He seemed to have the same idea. "Can we meet for a drink sometime, Mademoiselle Bruante?"

"Call me Nicole, please," she corrected him mildly—and that's how it had all started.

But it had *really* started, in a sense, during that nude posing in 1873 that had resulted in Gustave Caillebotte's tastefully-explicit depiction of her naked body, immortalized on canvas when she was 25, that he called *Naked Woman Lying on a Couch.* This piece had earned her a few months-worth of rent and food shortly after Jean Désiré Gustave Courbet—known as 'Jean' to her alone as their private 'pet' name, and 'Gustave' to the entire rest of the world: her ex-lover and the father of her dear Edmond—had fled to Switzerland to escape his government creditors. *Naked Woman Lying on a Couch* was the first and as far as she knew the *only* female nude in Gustave Caillebotte's growing portfolio of paintings…for a reason. Whether he realized it himself or not, Gustave was gay, and painting her nude was clearly a part of his ongoing cover-up.

She knew from the moment she had stripped off her clothes while he watched, his stare cold and unemotional rather than lustful, that Gustave Caillebotte was not a lady's man. In every previous circumstance, her 'big reveal' was an act that never failed to elicit a flurry of verbal compliments accompanied by a certain hard-to-miss stirring of 'male-desires-female' below-belt…but not this time. He had studied her with the analytic eye of a scientist viewing a specimen rather than as a potential courtier, even as he described the overtly

17

seductive pose that he wished her to assume—one which, under normal circumstances, would usually lead to a romantic or often blatantly sexual proposition that she would decide to either deflect or accept, depending on her mood and sentiment. She had just laid herself out on the living room couch in the apartment that he shared with his two younger brothers when René: the middle one, and Martial: the youngest, had barged one closely on the heels of the other through the front door.

Both men (or rather boys, since Martial was barely 20 and René only 22 at the time) stopped dead in their tracks. Gustave had 'pooh-poohed' their stuttering apologies with a dismissive wave of a hand, clearly unconcerned with their breach of Nicole's privacy and intent on mixing his paints, giving both of them ample opportunity to linger and gawk. Nicole had met their awestruck gazes—grey and lavender respectively—with unabashed but good-natured defiance, amused while at the same time thrilled by their lust-filled scrutiny which groped her vulnerable nakedness like fingers. She had to chuckle to herself when *her* gaze drifted southward to note that sure enough, *these* Caillebotte brothers were reacting to her suggestive pose in the usual heterosexual fashion.

It took Gustave a few days short of one month to complete *Naked Woman Lying on a Couch*, which was remarkably speedy artistry at least by Nicole's standards having been used to Jean's slow and meticulous style. This was long enough though for Martial to set himself apart from René, in the most unflattering of ways.

Martial was as socially awkward and clumsy as he was physically, sporting a pear-shaped body topped with a head (*and* mind) that resembled a cinder-block. He was the low-brow and bumbling representative of the sibling triad, with no sense of boundaries or self-insight whatsoever. It took him just a few days of wandering in to the living room as an openly voyeuristic visitor to brag about his photographic talents, sitting eagerly on the edge of an arm chair with his eyes roaming freely over her naked body like he owned her. He chit-chatted with her while Gustave worked, oblivious and maddeningly silent, about an idea for a photographic style that he called the 'body-scape' that involved erotic poses quite similar, and different, to the one she was currently executing for *Nude Woman Lying on a Couch.* His 'brainstorm' was to photograph the most intimate parts of a woman's anatomy, including all of the off-limit regions, in a bold and unapologetic way that would push the boundaries of the art-photograph firmly into the realm of 'explicit' but in the name of artistic expression. It was no surprise to Nicole at all when he proceeded to inquire, after mentioning the imagined series only a handful of times, if she would agree to be the starring model.

"No thank you," she had responded without even a split-second's hesitation—not because she couldn't use the money, and not because she was self-conscious about the type of explicit nudity that he had in mind (because God knows she desperately needed the first, and would in all likelihood have secretly enjoyed the second—given the fact that she had been the anonymous model for Courbet's *The*

Origin of the World depicting exactly the type of unabashed exposure on canvas that Martial had in mind on photographic paper); but because she didn't want to encourage Martial's rough-and-ready romantic aspirations, which were as unsubtle as Gustave's predilection for men rather than women.

While Martial could be likened to a bull-in-a-China-shop, Gustave was akin to the resident cat, rarely heard or seen while roaming the aisles and shelves, harboring a covert agenda that he shared with no one. Gustave gave the appearance of aloof and uncaring simply because he lived in his own little world where those on the outside were as irrelevant as insects buzzing around his head. There was nothing personal or malicious underlying his cold exterior—it was just who he was. While Gustave unknowingly insulted those around him by evading personal interaction entirely, Martial's brand of insensate disrespect took the form of exact polar opposite, inserting itself inappropriately into conversations and situations in the most intrusive and unsolicited way imaginable. She was happy to finish the job if only to escape those two, but in the process she had sacrificed the promise of something exciting and potentially meaningful with the third.

René was a different breed altogether. In glaring contrast to his brothers, he was dashing, handsome, and courteous. Although traversing the living room was a requirement for entering and exiting the apartment, his interactions with her were usually limited to eyes respectfully averted but for a brief glance and a nervous smile, which went a long way to peaking her interest and winning her heart in advance. She had always viewed him as out of reach though, mainly because she was a family employee of sorts…and a confidential one at that. She was not in the habit of getting involved with business associates although exceptions were occasionally allowed, as with Jean for the most poignant case in point; but at that point in her life, in 1873, her ex-lover's unexpected departure was still painfully fresh in her mind, which meant that she wasn't even *close* to prepared for another relationship that soon anyway. But now, three years into her life of solitude, a fortuitous meeting in of all places the post office had given them a chance to rekindle the spark that had briefly passed between them in that cramped and close-quartered bachelors' apartment.

She met him for a glass of wine that very night, where the conversation led them first to the recipient, and then to the reason, for her letter-posting that morning. She had to debrief him first on her stormy romance with the hard to understand and even harder to live with Courbet, and to quickly clarify what she knew might appear as a written correspondence between absent husband and pining common-law wife, which couldn't be farther from the truth.

"I'm still in touch with Jean only because of our son. He will never return to Paris, and has long since set me aside as a fond but distant memory from his forgotten past. I am over him too."

"I see," he said warmly, the hope nearly beaming from his purple-blue eyes.

She had then proceeded to tell him about her financial troubles, but taking caution to minimize the true extent of her desperation out of pride;

followed by an explanation of her idea that revolved around the paintings that she had stashed away at Jean's pointed request when he had fled in the middle of the night, in 1873. No one wanted any of his highly controversial nudes, especially *The Origin of the World* (a sensational piece for which she had posed when she was only 18, in 1866) but others as well including *Woman with a Parrot; Woman with White Stockings*; and *Sleep*: this last one actually being the subject of a relatively recent police report because it depicted two 'lesbian' lovers (actually, Nicole and a friend half-playing the part) enjoying a post-coital embrace.

Thirteen paintings, all of them secretly featuring *her* as the bold and uninhibited nude model, were either propped against the walls of her attic room or hanging, so that she could admire them whenever she pleased. Some of them were well known, while others were never-before-seen such as the nearly-finished but unsigned piece that Jean had been working on the very night he had been forced to flee that he had named *Waking Nude Preparing to Rise* even prior to its completion—the title penciled in with haste on the paper backing right before he rushed out the back door carrying his speedily-packed travel trunk. This one (his last depiction of her) portrayed her sitting, with legs folded underneath her on rumpled bedclothes leaning on an outstretched arm, with the other raised upward and bent as a 'cradle' for her head: turned to one side and slightly obscured in the shadow of early morning—the 'classic' pose presented in a way meant to represent a sleepy nude 'stretch' at daybreak.

22

The most notorious one of all and her very favorite: Jean's self-proclaimed masterpiece called *The Origin of the World*, shunned by *Le Salon* as a shocking pornographic atrocity—she had intentionally hung right next to her grandmother's crucifix on the angled wall at the foot of her bed, which was squeezed into the tiny window-alcove of her attic flat. The pairing of female anatomy with religious icon she viewed as a statement of sorts, her logic being that a woman's womb deserved just as much recognition as humanity's divine creator since life sprang from that earthly vessel at God's fertile command, placing both on equivalent footing. Hanging them side-by-side was actually an act of devotion and reverence rather than sacrilege, so that she could worship *both* life-giving entities equally, exactly as each so well deserved.

She explained how Jean had his own financial difficulties to deal with, but that she had reached out to him in that letter with the hope that he would honor his paternal responsibility to their son by agreeing to her plan. Edmond—who was now nine but was only six years old when his father left—was Jean's only minor-aged 'bastard' (how she despised that term). The rest of them had already reached or passed the age of consent including his daughter who was now in her early thirties, being estranged from 'Papa' at the tender age of three when her mother: Courbet's mistress at the time, had walked out on him due to her partner's infidelity, in the late 1840's. So, if she could only find a willing buyer for the shockingly erotic paintings that Jean had instructed her to hide away and keep safe, then she would give the proceeds once collected to her mother 'Elle' (short for Noelle) to use for her dear Edmond. He had by necessity been living under his grandmother's custody these last few years, since a tiny attic room and a mostly absent nude-model mother who barely had the means to support herself were less than ideal circumstances for raising a little boy. She felt in her heart-of-hearts though that Jean wouldn't refuse her, because after all their son's welfare was at stake and her plan would make hundreds of francs available for their mutual cause. That type of money would last for years and years if spent wisely in support of Edmund's upbringing.

René nodded his head in agreement and understanding, as if it was a predesignated signal for fate to step out unannounced from behind the shadows and join them, quiet and unassuming, at the table. At that exact moment (that she later recognized as one of her life's true inflection points), René looked across at her as fortune's spokesman and smiled knowingly. "I do believe I have a buyer for you, Nicole."

CHAPTER TWO

As it turns out Gustave Caillebotte was a collector. "His first passion is stamps, and his second is paintings—and I don't mean his own," René had explained. "All of his free time and disposable income are devoted to these two obsessions, and I'm sure he would jump at the chance to add thirteen notorious Courbet nudes to his already impressive collection of Parisian artwork."

"Twelve," she had corrected. "I will keep the unsigned one for Edmond since without a signature it has little monetary worth." *Waking Nude Preparing to Rise* was one of her favorite renderings of her naked body, which she would give to her son without sharing the 'secret' of the nude model's identity with anyone other than her mother. Nicole more than anyone, even while she would willingly agree to the most explicit and exhibitionistic of poses in private, had a keen sense of morality and propriety in family and public circles. In fact, she made sure that no one but the artists themselves and her closest confidantes were aware that she was the uninhibited *poseur* for countless erotic paintings created not only by Courbet but by other well-known Realists and Impressionists as well. Nicole had posed in daring defiance of societal norms—some during but most occurring *after* her affair with the much-older Jean...for Edgar Degas, Edouard Manet and even Jules Joseph Lefebvre: one of Courbet's most vocal critics in public and as close to an 'enemy' as one could get, which necessitated a great deal of secrecy on Nicole's part when she sat for his piece called *Reclining Nude* in 1868, when she was 20 years old. That's why her sittings for Gustave and everyone else had been anonymous, with the intention of separating the private person called Nicole Bruante from the potential public notoriety of her nameless nude-model 'persona'.

And then there was the sticky business of concealing Edmond's parentage, which became a more pressing necessity after Jean became a national pariah of sorts related to the fiasco with the Vendome column. Yes, it was common knowledge that Nicole had been Jean's mistress dating as far back to 1866, when she had first met him at the tender age of 18 answering an erotic modeling ad on a dare; but having his baby was *not* universally known, by intention. They had decided to keep her pregnancy a closely guarded secret since even in those early days Courbet was a lightning rod of unconventionality and neither of them wanted their child to be subjected to a decidedly negative 'bias-by-association'. Thus, when their son came into the world (conceived on the very day her posing for *The Origin of the World* was completed and born just nine months later, in 1867) they quickly whisked him away to stay with her mother, who was recently widowed (God rest her own dear Papa's soul)— which had been as convenient an arrangement then as it was now. Edmond had no idea who his father was or what his mother did for a living, and Nicole remained determined to keep it that way—at least for now.

Because later...*much* later, things might change. Future generations might actually appreciate rather than abhor Courbet's naturalistic view of the female body and uncensored depiction of sexuality which he (and Nicole equally) considered a representation of God himself: a symbol of the cyclical miracle of birth and regeneration that is conceived in masculine devotion to his feminine counterpart materializing in a woman's womb. Nicole had always shared in Jean's belief that the prudish concealment of human nudity actually cheapened the divine act of reproduction, whereas the honest depiction of 'Adam and Eve' portrayed as nature intended did just the opposite. This is specifically why she loved modelling nude; and proud as she might be of this philosophical statement, the world—and her little boy—were not yet ready for this degree of physical honesty.

But years from now, after both she and Jean were dead and gone, someone would read her 'confession' ingeniously concealed between the canvas and the backing paper of *Waking Nude Preparing to Rise*. This idea came to her suddenly, immediately after René's brother had confirmed his interest in purchasing her erotic cache but before Jean had given his permission for her to sell the sensuous paintings; so she had penned the letter straight-away, dating it *10 May, 1876*. Her hope was that Edmond, or his children, or his grandchildren might find it, folded over twice: a cursory explanation that Nicole Bruante had been the most prolific, 'no-holds-barred' nude model of her time; and that the secret paternal contributor to their erotically-inclined blood-line was the infamous artist and political activist: Jean Désiré Gustave Courbet, who had to flee Paris and France in 1873 to avoid ridicule and financial ruin. She and Jean's distant descendants would be able to 'fill in the blank' on their family tree, thanks to her clandestine foresight in hiding this message of disclosure in the family painting.

She often thought back on how it had all started. Posing nude began as a lighthearted whim centered on the thrill of exposure and the sense of freedom, independence and rebel-like rejection of societal conventions, but quickly became a serious vocation that instigated the beginning of a seven-year ever-volatile romance and tenuous domestic partnership with the father of Realism. That first sitting which had allowed her to play the only-partially contrived role of lesbian lover with her best friend Céleste had resulted in the highly controversial piece called *Sleep*, followed quickly on its heels by the even more shocking *The Origin of the World*. It was immediately after her final session for this latter painting had ended that Edmond had been conceived—on the very same posing-pallet and with Nicole maintaining the exact same open-legged position as she had for months-and-months, even before the last brushstroke on the eye-popping canvas had dried.

A few days after they had met for drinks Nicole saw René again, this time for an early dinner. "To say my brother is interested would be an understatement," were the first words out of his mouth. He went on to describe Gustave's collection as heavy on landscapes, cityscapes and domestic scenes, but pitifully sparse on depictions of unclothed models—boasting only a handful of August Renoir bathers and a few obscure nude pieces by Édouard Manet including a watercolor 'study' for his much decried *Luncheon on the Grass* that disgracefully depicted two naked prostitutes picnicking with a group of fully clothed gentleman in the woods.

Nicole giggled when that piece was mentioned. "The girl folded over herself in the background was certainly *not* a prostitute—at least in real life!"

"How do you know?" René asked with a quizzically raised eyebrow.

"Because the model was me! I was barely sixteen at the time I posed for that painting."

And so it was that Gustave, it turned out, was prepared to pay an unbelievable 500 francs for the dozen Courbet nudes in Nicole's possession, which was more than double the amount she had hoped to earn for the set; and after he learned that Nicole was one of the models for *Luncheon on the Grass*, he also offered a generous 'finder's fee' if she would give him a list of all the other nudes that she had posed for over the past dozen years, to help in his now-obsessive naked-genre acquisition efforts. His very own *Naked Woman Lying on a Couch* would in this way be joined by as many other pieces as possible, necessary to fill the gap in his collection—with a focus on populating the erotic portion of his growing assemblage of paintings with those pieces featuring Nicole as the model. The discovery of such an unlikely buyer for her cache *and* for inside-information was fortuitous, but would mean nothing in the end if Jean said 'no'. This fear was one of the reasons that the following two months would be consumed by sleepless nights; and the other had to do with her night-time pre-occupation with her new and, as she discovered, exceptionally talented lover.

Where Gustave excelled in painting and Martial in photography, René was a burgeoning sculptor. The job in the post office was temporary, just until he could sell some pieces and make a true living out of his passion. Since it seemed clear that he would never ask due to his highly developed sense of propriety, she had decided to offer. "In case you're interested, I'd be happy to pose for you."

His initial response was silent hesitation, followed by a quiet observation that explained his reticence. "You turned down Martial, so I just assumed..."

"Well, you assumed wrong," she interjected in a tone that sounded more irritated than she had intended. "Do you know why I wouldn't agree to be Martial's 'body-scape' model?" She paused for a moment just for effect, and then continued. "If you thought it was the *concept* that turned me off, then you'd be wrong again."

He nodded his immediate comprehension. "Martial can be a bit much. He means well, but just has no sense of boundaries. He's been like that as long as I can remember, even when we were children."

So it was settled. René, equipped with stone and chisel just a few short weeks after they had started 'seeing' each other, had set himself up in Nicole's attic apartment rather than in the shared Caillebotte-brother residence at *Hauts-de-Seine* since limiting her 'exposure' to Martial would be best for all involved parties. In any case, the bachelors' pad was even more crowded nowadays and was no longer the exclusive boys' club that it had been a few years before.

"Gustave has taken in a young lady of leisure, and he's preparing to paint her."

"Pictured in a nude scene?" If so, this would surprise her almost as much as the concept of a live-in prostitute, given her theory about Gustave's sexual leanings.

"Yes, and on the very same couch where..."

The almost comical pregnant pause meant that René, whose sentence seemed to have permanently trailed off, was at a definite loss for a polite way to say '...where you bared it all that first day I barged in to discover every man's fantasy lying right there in our communal living room, completely and unselfconsciously exposed,' so she pulled him gently and good-naturedly off his awkward hook. "I think you meant to say: 'on the very same couch where I was posing when we first made our initial acquaintance'"

"Yes," he confirmed, the wrinkles of strain on his forehead relaxing the very moment she rushed in to save him from what she considered to be a quite unnecessary sense of morality. It's not like modeling without a stitch of clothing automatically led to lascivious behavior, because it almost never did. He was still struggling with the dichotomy of Nicole's professional versus personal lives. "Her name is Anne Marie Hagan," he added, returning to the original topic of conversation. "Martial actually has quite a thing for her."

She laughed lightly. "Why am I not surprised!" Now it seemed was the perfect opportunity to fish. "But what about Gustave? Doesn't he have a 'thing' for her too?"

René waved the thought away. "I'll tell you a secret."

She *knew* it! "If you're going to say he's gay, don't bother since I suspected as much."

His eyes nearly popped out of their sockets. "How in the world did you know?"

Now it was *her* turn to wave his surprise away. "Women in general have an intuition about these things, and *my* sexual sixth-sense is particularly keen."

"But he has taken great care to conceal it!"

"I wouldn't worry. If he's gone so far as to take in a prostitute as a 'beard', I'd say his secret is safe. *Plus*, unless you've posed nude for him as I have, his lack of sexual interest in women really isn't that obvious."

"Meaning?"

"Meaning that there is usually a characteristic physical sign that one cannot ignore, whenever I strip and pose for an artist. Don't you remember *your* reaction when you stumbled onto that scene in the living room 3 years ago? *I* certainly do!"

His cheeks were suddenly rosy again. "Was it that noticeable?"

She laughed lightly and took his hand. "It was literally impossible to miss!"; *and* distinctly flattering to both of them, she added silently to herself.

For the next five weeks she had posed unmoving for him in her very own apartment, her skin itchy from lying exposed on a tattered wool blanket for so long; but her toils were duly rewarded with dinner in one café or another followed by hours of passion each night, both of them falling asleep afterwards on her squeaky cot. He had positioned her in the most intimate of poses with her head turned slightly to the side, and her expression behind closed eyes giving the impression of building ecstasy. Her flowing hair streamed over the edge of her left shoulder, chest and arm—arranged by René at the start of each posing in order to accent the rounded contour of the breast on that side rather than concealing it. Always the consummate gentleman even in his role of erotic artist, he politely asked her to position her arms on either side of her naked bosom with elbows pointing outward: a maneuver that functioned to accentuate their rounded fullness; while, at her own suggestion, her fingers strategically accented the identical 'pose' featured in *The Origin of the World*, which would eventually be indelibly reproduced in marble— being the last 'third' of a 4-foot sculpture of her head and torso ending abruptly at her upper thighs. It was the most poignant sitting she had ever experienced because it was shared with a man who knew her intimately that way, and with whom she felt sexually at-ease.

By the time Jean's affirmative reply arrived, her upper-half had been reproduced from the top of her head to just below her breasts and elbows, with stunning accuracy and what she considered lightning speed, given the unforgiving artistic medium. She marveled at how he had perfectly reproduced the generous swell of her exposed chest in a piece that he told her he would likely name *Reclining Nude Pictured in an Intimate Moment.*

As a masterpiece in progress and made of inert marble sat motionless on the floor in the corner of her apartment, Nicole realized that she had never felt more content. René Caillebotte was a man with whom she could easily spend the rest of her days, offering her devotion and stability in a world that until now had given her only chaos. Their romance had begun in earnest.

CHAPTER THREE

That very day, eight weeks after their accidental meeting in the post office on the last day of May, she excitedly informed René of the letter's arrival and the happy message that it contained, giving Jean's consent to the sale of his erotic paintings, to be used for the upbringing of his son: Edmond. The first order of business was to bring *Waking Nude Preparing to Rise* to her mother's house for safekeeping so that it would not be mistakenly taken with the others tomorrow to Gustave's apartment, in the horse-drawn hansom cab that René had arranged—bright and early. Her dear Edmond and a pang of guilt were waiting for her at the door.

She had been so preoccupied with her modeling and the lusty repercussions that she had inadvertently neglected her little boy. She hugged him tightly and then studied him lovingly at arm's length. "I've missed you, my little man," she said with a tear in her eye. "You are growing so tall."

"When can I see you?" he asked simply, the hope hiding somewhere behind an unusually stoic visage for a child his age.

When *could* she see him? Tonight, she and René had plans to celebrate with 'something better than wine' (as he had cagily put it)—well into the morning hours; and then tomorrow morning, they would load the paintings and a comprehensive list of her nude posings together into a hired carriage, drop them off with Gustave in exchange for more money than she had seen during the duration of her entire twenty-eight years, and then continue on to a "surprise location" somewhere far from the city in the countryside for a few weeks. "Maman's going away for a while, my love; but how about we have a 'date' when I return?"

Edmond nodded happily so she made arrangements with her mother: Elle for a mother-and-son rendezvous, at twelve noon on the third Sunday of June (the eighteenth) in *Place Pigalle*, where nine-year-old Edmond so loved to sail his fleet of toy boats. Some of them were colorfully painted and looked beautifully realistic, with intricate miniature sails, oars, rudders or *faux*-engines, sailing or floating on the rippling waters of the Square's central fountain. For the past year he had been allowed to meet his mother in various locations unaccompanied for their visits, but his grandmother was still the responsible party in charge of marking the calendar and making sure Edmond didn't miss any of his 'appointments' with the mother that he so missed and loved.

Pigalle was Edmond's favorite location for a rendezvous. He would stare with the wide-eyed and not-completely innocent interest of a boy who was still pre-pubescent but quickly approaching adolescence, at the scantily dressed dancers reporting for their shifts at one disreputable nightclub or another. Little did Edmond know that their bright and opulent costumes, which gave the misimpression of a flamboyant respectability, would be tossed to the wayside as soon as they eagerly stripped off their dresses to flaunt and sell their nude bodies inside. Nicole had (and never would) go that far, reserving her uninhibited sensuality for the private artist's studio rather than for a cheering crowd of goggling customers and potential after-show clients. So she would grip Edmond's hand tightly with combined love and motherly protection (which he still allowed, at least for now), leading him around the assembly of *Moulin Rouge* performers waiting outside the dressing room door for entry. Edmond, more now than previously, would eye them with the kind of distracted curiosity that Nicole feared would someday cause him to wander unawares out into the street and right into the speeding path of some rich man's hansom cab.

So it was that later that day after the evening shadows darkened into night, that she and René finished off the second bottle of celebratory wine and switched to absinthe. Their flesh-on-flesh exertion, exquisite these past few hours, had made her skin tacky and flushed so she reached over him across the narrow space of the bed, to open the squat and narrow window on the wall. As the moon rose and then started its descent just after midnight, the last day of May moaned and sighed, surrendering itself to the first day of June; while at the same moment Nicole pressed her breasts suggestively against René's muscular chest as an invitation for more—one arm propped on an elbow while the other jiggled the window upward. He helped her by wedging a rectangular block of wood under the bottom of the window frame, their mutual effort allowing a cooling draft of late spring air into the still-cluttered bedroom. Come the morning, all of the paintings would be gone, freeing up some much needed space in the stuffy attic studio.

Just as she hoped he would, René pulled her on top of him after they managed to secure the window together—his dark, shoulder-length hair tied back, its waves buried somewhere in her pillow; while hers, quite a bit longer, fell over her face and onto his with a gentle sweep of soft brunette fragrance, just as she had hoped he would. She lovingly stroked his closely-cut bearded cheek with her fingers; rubbed the broadness of his chest and hardening nipples with her palms; and gripped the firm and uncontestable proof of his growing love for her with her eager hands. What she felt underneath her said 'this is for you, and you alone' so she took him in, kneeling astride and sliding down until skin-touched-skin, waiting for more.

He handed her another glass, to fuel their repeated passion. "Where did you get it?" she asked, sipping the semi-illicit liquor from her glass, already stained red from a few glasses of wine. The absinthe, considered by most to be more of a drug than an alcoholic beverage, had already started to have its desired effect. She was more than a little bit tipsy to start with, and the slightly bitter burn of the hallucinogenic mixture in her throat began to seep into her bloodstream, fogging her vision and causing her to feel detached and disoriented. "It seems stronger than what I've had before," she managed to say, her words sounding far-off and distant, like they belonged to someone else, not to her at all.

"My friend Chloe knows someone who makes it," he answered, pouring her more from a flask at the bedside. "Rumor has it they added a healthy dose of laudanum to this batch. It makes it more potent."

She finished her glass followed by another; and then became intensely intrigued with her shadow on the wall, wavering in the candlelight with a movement all its own like it was a separate being. But no, its actions *matched* hers, she realized—its ups-and-downs asynchronous just a moment ago but now reflecting hers perfectly as they both busied themselves with another round of mutual ecstasy. She was on her haunches, the flat of her hands on his chest for support; and then before she knew it, her chest was lying directly against him—her stomach and breasts pressed heavily on his. René's inserted hardness bound them together as if they were one; but it felt much more like she was floating, on a boat on the *Seine* or far out in the ocean somewhere. They were both sliding and slipping towards the inevitable '*petite mort*' that she knew would grip them both again—both at once; and although it felt so very nice, something else was happening…something that wasn't quite right.

All of a sudden, and timed it seemed exactly to the comingling wetness she felt inside her, the surface of her skin burned as if she was some kind of a living fire, generating a cloud of heat that blew in from somewhere deep inside and emanated outward—a backdraft ignited by God knows what (the absinthe and the laudanum perhaps?). Her feverish and writhing body, which she found preoccupied much less than it should have been by the shuddering throes of another conclusion to pleasure, became encircled in a seeming dome of heat that she feared would utterly consume them…how could it not? It would leave a sizzling hole where they now lay, pulling her, the man, and even the painting hanging on the wall at their feet into a white void of nothingness. These were truly absurd thoughts; but that's when she looked over her shoulder, directly behind her and saw a terrifying glimpse of it: a swirling vortex, opening in the wall, or *no*—the painting, leading to white nothingness just as her premonition had imagined. Was this a hallucination? It seemed too real; or maybe a dream? Horrified, she could only pray.

Hot, empty, swirling, pulling, it was taking her now…taking *him*, taking them. They were levitated upward by a mysterious, supernatural force. Naked and wet with sweat and the dripping humidity of intimacy, they rose into the air pressed tightly together but just for a moment; and then in an instant they were moving backward as one, still joined at the midpoint facing each other, plunging feet first into the void behind—quick and unstoppable although it seemed to happen in excruciatingly slow motion. This couldn't be real, but she knew it was.

Mon Dieu, help me! She tried to resist, but she couldn't; she screamed, but no one heard. She saw the panic in his eyes, a fleeting gaze—and she felt it too. They were slipping—no, plummeting—backward, backward, backward…falling and tumbling and burning into the terror also known as *The Origin of the World*; falling, falling, falling, into the white light of a scorching sun, so brilliant that it threatened to blind her, and so white that she had to close her eyes.

And when she did, that's when it all turned utterly and completely black.

PART II

THE FIRST FEW DAYS
AFTER ARRIVAL
MAY 31 - JUNE 3, 2011

CHAPTER FOUR

The full moon posed in the night sky high above, while far below the sculpted outline of *Musée d'Orsay* reclined in the midnight quiet of the Left Bank.

It was the last few minutes of the final day of May, 2011. The interior of the museum could easily be seen through the line of glass doors where, in dimly lit isolation, a solitary security guard sat at his post in front of a curved array of video monitors positioned to the far right, at a ninety-degree angle facing the center of the entry-lobby. Directly behind him the security office, which doubled as a control room and kitchenette, slept in darkness awaiting the guard's thirty minute 'lunch'-break which would begin in a couple of hours at two a.m., at mid-shift. The lobby lay quiet now, but in the morning when the museum opened the growing lines of people would be directed to the left, where a new day of smiling ticketing agents would be ready to greet them behind the mahogany counters, also situated at a ninety-degree angle to the facing-view of the museum, such that ticketing and the security desk 'looked' at each other across the polished floor. Three million patrons a year would enter through those doors and wait patiently in the roped-off, back-and-forth queue until they were handed their time-stamped admissions ticket that would gain them entry to two levels of exhibit rooms, spread out in front of them over more than a full city block.

Gaspar Charpentier was young, his skin still vaguely blemished from the recent memory of adolescence in-between ten-day stubble, his dirty-blond hair cut short on both sides but stylishly left long and wavy in front, his murky grey eyes nearly glazed over from the monotony of scanning the screens in front of him. His six-month probationary period having just ended, he was less determined to perform his night-shift duties perfectly now than he had been, just a few months before.

He had been trained to examine the four video displays one-by-one in sequence, each of them split into quarters reflecting sixteen separate cameras trained on a different crucial section of the museum—and he had done just that at first, in accordance with the regulation book; but this highly repetitive obligation seemed stupidly counterintuitive to the monitoring system's built-in fail-safe of continuous recording, which would capture any movement on tape and store the night's history in a digital archive. Why in the world should he waste time duplicating a machine's efforts, when he could be otherwise engaged, on his phone playing games or searching the Internet for this or that with an occasional penchant for something 'not-safe-for-work'? He rubbed his eyes wearily, abandoning his half-hearted visual scanning task in favor of a more engaging perusal of *YouTube*.

The digital images were in many ways ancillary

technology anyway, taking a back-seat to electronic motion sensors attached to every piece of artwork that with the slightest displacement would trigger not only a museum-wide alarm and blinding emergency spotlights intended to illuminate the entire interior of the vast space housing countless of would-be compromised masterpieces, but would also send an immediate electronic alert to the adjacent police station only one block away. Because of this direct-emergency line 'coupled' to the artwork-connected motion sensors, and because the dispatcher could easily be reached either by means of a modern-day 'walkie-talkie' dangling within finger's-reach on a handy utility-belt in security-officer possession at all times, only one security officer was needed for the midnight shift. It was quite a different story in daytime though, when a virtual cotillion of security officers was positioned in almost every nook and cranny of the facility, eyeing the gawking art-lovers suspiciously in order to prevent damage should anyone try to touch.

Yes, the night shift was easy but boring, which is why he truly looked forward to the walkabouts that occurred every hour-and-a-half: a distraction that was even *more* welcome now that the special exhibit of nudes, about to open to the public, teasingly awaited his periodic attention. So it was that twelve a.m. took its time coming but finally gave him permission to trade the drudgery of monitor-duty for the much more exciting walk-around, which usually took thirty minutes at the most—but *this* midnight stroll would take him a bit longer, since he planned to spend some time 'admiring' a few choice pieces of erotic art in the most unconventional way imaginable.

As he had done at 10:30 before, he stood up and grabbed the bulky set of keys from its resting-place on the table-top in front of him and latched the key-ring to his utility belt in the unlikely event that they would be needed to access a variety of storage closets and little-used entryways; but unlike before, he hit the switch located on the table-top of the security desk, which would turn off all the video monitors such that he could thoroughly enjoy his art-lover experience without being caught on videotape. Yes, this was somewhat risky—but no one would ever know, since he would be alone in the deep interior of the museum enjoying his guilty-pleasure in the privacy of muted lighting and the anonymity of an impotently-deactivated camera system. Of course if any of the art-work motion sensors tripped, the manual camera shut-off that he had just activated would automatically override, and all of the video monitors would immediately re-start. He needn't worry about being caught on tape though, as long as he was careful not to joggle a painting or dislodge a statue; and there was little to no chance that his pre-planned activities this evening would cause any such disruption.

The idea had come to him suddenly on his walking rounds a few days into his two-week night duty stint last Monday, prompted by the overload of 'naked' that the special exhibit offered. It had taken five long days for him to steel the nerve, but tonight was the night and finally, he felt prepared and ready. The psychology was simple, hinging on a deep-seated but timid variety of exhibitionism that longed for full exposure but never dared to take it that far. By virtue of his employment in the most public of places but at a time when not a soul was around, he had been given the perfect opportunity to live out his fantasy of being naked in just such a place, but with the assurance of total privacy. The very act of imagining the group of shocked and outraged onlookers who weren't present but *would* have been if the time of day was noon rather than midnight only added to the thrill; and who could blame him for wanting to inject some excitement into his thoroughly boring personal and professional life? This would be an adventure in 'sensual' that with a little bit of imagination would check off a box on his list of what the conventionally-minded masses would consider 'the erotically deviant', but totally harmless since it would be executed in total secrecy.

He tightened and secured his work-belt, now heavier since he had attached the keys, feeling as he did so the tingle of expectation located somewhere below the buckle accompanied by some fluttering butterflies in his stomach. Next he double-checked the walkie-talkie on his right hip and removed the long, black flashlight on his left—clicking it 'on' to give him extra visibility in the dimly-lit museum interior. With the flashlight in his right he began the duty-driven portion of his walking-tour by descending a dozen double-wide stairs that led from the lobby to the centered sunken level of the refurbished nineteenth-century train station. It wouldn't be long before he stepped 'out-of-uniform' at the entrance to the special-exhibit galleries, where he would become a mere civilian heeding nature's call for nudity overriding the artificially-imposed prudishness of human society.

This lower lobby gave the impression of a smoothly chiseled marble channel when it had actually served as the gritty receptacle for the comings and goings of transport locomotives before the building was stylishly refinished. This depressed space was narrowed by four massive blocks of hollowed stone, two on either side, each containing exhibit rooms vaguely reminiscent of Egyptian tombs. All of these lower-level salons were devoted to permanent collections of sculptures, furniture, decorative arts, and photographs. He checked them with a quick sweep of his flashlight, just to make sure that each priceless piece was still there; and when this task was complete, he doubled back to re-climb the central staircase of swirled marble leading back to the lobby where he had first started out but now facing in the opposite direction, towards the front of the museum. He could see the boulevard through the wall of windows, dimly lit an incandescent street-lamp yellow.

Turning on his heels, he took a moment to admire the two upper-level corridors that ran lengthwise in parallel symmetry from the front of the museum to the back on both the right and the left sides, the smooth stone roofs of the sunken-level exhibit rooms ingeniously doubling as the floors for the ground-level catwalks. The inner edges of these 'in-duplicate' walkways extended like massive balconies into the vast space of the immense structure, above and below, that had echoed years ago with the whistle and screech of steam engines. The two imposing rectangles of polished rock on each side were connected in the middle by a narrow 'bridge' leading patrons back and forth to either side of the first-floor space; and, at the far end, by a wide flat platform that was home to a small sampling of the museum's collection of Rodin sculptures as well as a double service elevator that led to the museum basement and staff parking garage. The resulting architectural pattern as seen from his vantage point was an upside-down, squared off letter 'U' with a line crossing through its midpoint.

He climbed the right-side stairs of the inverted 'U' ('∩' as seen from the front of the museum) which would gain him access to the main complex of galleries occupying that first-floor level through one of many evenly spaced doors carved into the arching iron and steel wall of the former *Gare d'Orsay*. He paused for a moment before entering the permanent Impressionist painting collections located there, looking over his left shoulder across the chasm of the renovated train station to the other side, where he would find himself shortly. Some permanent collections and all the thematic, temporary exhibits were located over there, with the current offering being of particular interest to him personally since the unique artwork about to open on special display for the next few months was unusually 'titillating' in every sense of the word.

Tonight was no different than any other night on the catwalk, except that a very special treat awaited him very shortly, on the other side. His routine began as he entered through the nearest archway on the right catwalk, which led into eight rooms running parallel devoted to Cezanne, Van Gogh, Pissarro, and Gauguin, then moving forward to double-check the multi-million-dollar collection of Monet's water lilies and Degas' ballerinas. He patrolled past Lautrecs, Renoirs, and the works of artists he had never even heard of, exiting back to the right-side walkway and eventually picking his way through the miniature forest of sculptures at the far end of the museum, at the connecting-point 'base' of the squared-off '∩'. He maneuvered carefully through the Rodin masterpieces, passing the elevators onto the left arm of the '∩' where he would begin a back-to-front trajectory, which placed all of the exhibit rooms onto his right side. He took another moment to look and listen, confirming the eerily peaceful silence that stretched ahead of him and all around.

The rooms on the *left* catwalk, which were in reality partitioned into thirds, were a maze that had confused him at first, but now he knew where each entrance would lead. The first 'third' starting from the back consisted of three closely-spaced archways which he always reached first if approaching as he did now from the back, offering entry to a connecting zigzagging series of small-sized galleries. The wood-tiled floors of one room started where the other ended, and housed most of the museum's permanent collection of pieces by Mary Cassatt, Berthe Morisot, and Suzanne Valadon: a tribute of sorts to these three major female contributors to the Impressionist genre.

The second 'third' positioned in the center of the catwalk could only be accessed through a single extra-wide archway: 'number four' in his back-to-front travels on the left catwalk, leading into a straight line of varying-sized exhibit rooms numbering four in total but not counting an alcove room measuring approximately thirty x thirty feet square jutting off of the first-room gallery on the left side. These rooms, always devoted to special showings, were currently roped-off as the final touches were being made to the current offering: soon to be opened to the public, but fully accessible to the night-time security detail beginning last week.

Strolling through these four center-rooms plus one, a would-be patron would find him-or-herself eventually at a dead-end, although staff could exit through a private door marked as such, located in the corner of the last room providing mid-point access to a long perpendicular hallway of administrative offices stretching along the full length of the museum on the left side as seen from the front, behind the wall. This same hallway could be accessed from the inside of the museum at two additional locations: the first being from the front, right behind the ticket counters and the second being from the back, directly off the catwalk near the elevators. Entry or exit from the back of the building was also available from the outside, by way of an alarmed door and the very end of the administrative corridor.

The final 'third' of the left-side galleries could be entered through two closely-spaced archways: 'numbers five and six', located closest to the front of the museum. These archways provided entry to a single gallery with a high, vaulted ceiling—the place where *Musée d'Orsay's* largest permanent acquisitions were always on display.

He walked quickly through the first labyrinth of

left-catwalk galleries, eager to reach the middle galleries that housed the special exhibit of Courbet, Caillebotte and various other Realist and Impressionist pieces that the museum staff had been busily assembling behind archway number four over the past month. The exhibit's coordinator: Susanne Bruante had taken pains to insure that the security force and the docent staff alike understood the value of the extraordinary exhibit during an information session provided by the most desirable single woman on the entire museum staff. He had taken a seat as close to his fantasy-lover as possible, a few rows in and on the aisle so he could view her from behind as she passed by.

She was gorgeous, perhaps in her mid-thirties, although she didn't look it. She had actually smiled at him as she passed his third row seat, her perfume and her dark hair trailing over her shoulders. He had watched the sway of her hips from behind with carefully-concealed lusty excitement, and how the smooth lines of her tight skirt seemed to caress her curves with an obscene intimacy. Rumor had it she was sleeping with the museum director, but this didn't stop him from hoping.

"This is a one-of-a-kind gathering of Courbet's most erotic pieces," she explained, "some of them lent to us from other museums, and others donated for temporary display by the Caillebotte family."

"But I couldn't help but notice that there are other artists aside from Courbet represented in your exhibit," a tour guide commented; "and the pieces are not exclusively paintings."

"Why yes. That's because the common theme is the *model* as the artist's subject in this particular display, rather than the artist or the creative medium per se. You see, very little attention has been devoted, historically speaking, to the artist's model—although the most memorable component of these pieces, one could argue, is the 'subject' rather than the 'creator'. In addition, my theory is that the *same* model is pictured in *all* of these works which are dominated by Courbet as the core of the exhibit, but includes many other artists too—as you astutely noticed. I refer to this as my 'model singularity' theory."

The museum's Director of Acquisitions and Special Exhibits nearly bubbled with excitement at the opportunity to discuss her life's passion with the museum assembly. "The audio tour explains my theory that an anonymous model posed for *all* of the disparate artists in this special exhibit, as depicted in various mediums such as paint, ink, charcoal, stone and photographic silver emulsion. The taped presentation also details how we managed to assemble a significant portion of the spectacular artwork for this show. You see, many of these pieces came from the so-called 'lost collection' of about three-dozen pieces, stored away in a secret crawl space behind a 'trick'-panel in a closet beneath the main stairway, in Gustave Caillebotte's country estate: *Petit Genevilliers*."

She paused and then nearly beamed as she continued: "I shouldn't name-drop but facts are facts and I might as well share them with you now. Genevieve Caillebotte-Bruante is my great-grandmother; and it was largely through these family ties that I gained access to these pieces, discovered inadvertently during recent renovations.

All of the sequestered pieces were *nudes*—some of them surprisingly erotic for the time…created by Courbet, Manet, Renoir, Degas, Lefebvre and various other contemporaries including the Caillebotte brothers. A large number of them required restoration but for the most part, they were remarkably preserved given the conditions they sustained over more than a century. My ancestry extending back directly to Martial Caillebotte: the youngest brother, fortunately allowed the assembly of these incredible 'lost collection' pieces; while others were gathered on loan from other museums and family collections."

An impressed murmur issued from the crowd, followed quickly on its heal by a virtual squeal of excited commentary from one of the docents. "A secret room discovered in a family mansion!" she exclaimed. "That's like something straight out of a mystery novel."

"Yes; and of some particular interest was the discovery of the very curious and explicit 'body-scape' photographs sealed in an airtight metal canister attributed to my great-great grandfather Martial Caillebotte; as well as an erotic sculpture that we have concluded was created by the *other* Caillebotte brother: René, who died young. None of these have *ever* been on display, so it goes without saying that I want this unique assembly of paintings, photographs and solitary sculpture to take top priority in your security agenda."

"Don't worry, Mademoiselle Bruante," said the chief of security: Guillaume Laroche, a portly man with sleeked-back hair who sat perched at the edge of his seat in the front row eating up her every word. "Each piece is wired remotely to an alarm that will trigger with the slightest movement; and of course we have our state-of-the-art security camera system eyeing every corner of the museum for vandals or thieves."

Susanne had nodded her satisfied approval as she concluded her presentation, gathered her notes in a folder, and walked away; while Gaspar, with just as much determination now as the woman of his erotic dreams had had then, nodded purposefully, slipped his flashlight back into its belt harness since it wouldn't be needed in this wing of the museum, stepped over the rope prohibiting public entrance, and took off all of his clothes.

CHAPTER FIVE

Gaspar Charpentier's rounds over the past week had followed a routine that he would by design deviate from tonight, in order to accommodate his premeditated unclothed detour. He would normally linger for a moment in the first gallery, the largest of the series of four, examining the details of the paintings with lusty reverence including *Woman with White Stockings* which offered an explicit between-the-legs view of a naked girl putting her clothes back on, in an outdoor shoreline setting where one could well imagine that she and her lover had just been intimate. They were all nudes, some of them surprisingly explicit, but none more so than the piece that he loved the most hanging on the right-side wall of the 30 x 30-foot alcove, with entry gained by walking through an archway located immediately to his left, cut eccentrically prior to mid-point in the wall of the first exhibit gallery. That adjoining space would be his last stop tonight rather than his first so that he could examine Courbet's *The Origin of the World* up close and personal, bathed in the soft yellow light of recessed lighting.

His plan had until now involved the experience of nudity alone; but now that he was naked, the need for 'more' presented itself as a natural consequence of his naked endeavor. What could be better than using the most notorious erotic painting as the focus-point for the 'culmination' of his little adventure? Of course the classic erotic positioning of the model which showed off her most intimate body part in explicit voyeuristic fashion could be easily found these days in any of many popular men's magazines; but back then, *this* painting in particular (but all of the others in this special exhibit as well) must have had the entire randy male population of Paris elbowing their way to the front row of *La Salon* for an unobstructed view.

But he would have no competition tonight positioning himself front-and-center, deliciously naked, to perhaps spend a few enlightened moments enjoying this nineteenth century version of pornography controversially excused as art, exactly as he conjectured it was intended. And why not, after all? He was alone, naked, and surrounded by 'material' that could propel his creatively-conceived experience into the realm of the truly memorable. What did he care about theoretical critics (*out of site out of mind*) when he was here by himself and had free reign to do whatever he pleased without the risk of societal condemnation? He wasn't hurting anyone, which meant that his mini-escapade into the realm of the socially unacceptable could be perfectly described as 'no harm no foul'.

In his mind, he planned his fresh new strategy 'on-the-fly' and in the moment. He would maneuver around the podium which extended to waist-high, measuring approximately four-feet long and two-feet wide positioned in the center of the room: home to a life-sized top-half body-sculpture of a reclining nude, just installed today. The restored piece was completed from the head to beyond the navel but ended in abrupt transition to raw block-stone immediately prior to the below-waist naughty-bits, since the piece was unfinished. The model's head was turned slightly to the side, her facial expression behind closed eyes reflecting impending ecstasy; while the marble recreation of her flowing hair streamed over the edge of her shoulder, chest and ipsilateral limb, careful to accent the rounded contour of the breast on that side rather than concealing it. Her arms, completed to just past the elbow in close-to-midline matched symmetry, were positioned on the outer edges of both perfect breasts, pressing inward to accentuate their ample appeal. The 'V'-like trajectory of her limbs pointed downward, suggesting the artist's unconsummated intention to have the hands and fingers meet between the legs in the sculptor's portrayal of a most intimate moment.

And the title reflected that very ambition. '*This nude sculpture,*' the placard read, '*is known as Reclining Nude Engrossed in an Intimate Moment and was reportedly chiseled by René Caillebotte, the unknown middle brother of the three Caillebotte siblings who died suddenly in May of 1876 at the age of twenty-five most likely while he was working on it, explaining its incomplete state. René's premature death was most likely caused by the very same congenital heart arrhythmia that would later take his brother Gustave's life while he was planting flowers in his garden.*'

Gaspar had discovered on his earlier rounds that night that the newly ensconced marble-figure's face looked strikingly similar to the Assistant Director's. Fortuitously, the statue was conveniently situated in such close proximity to *The Origin of the World*, that he could easily refer to it periodically as he gazed on the painting's erotic focus—his back leaning against the podium as he faced the object of his lust. He could hardly wait now that this brainstorm had been integrated into his plotting, so he moved hastily through the first gallery and on to the second, stopping in front of another one of his favorites described on a placard that read: '*Naked Woman Lying on a Couch by Gustave Caillebotte, 1873'*. This painting pictured the same familiar-looking brunette who could pass for Susanne Bruante's twin, lying invitingly on a living room couch with both arms raised above her head to emphasize her busty torso and to provide a full-frontal view of everything exquisitely feminine, as seen from a perfect artistic vantage-point.

Although his deep-seated infatuation with the beguiling Susanne Bruante definitely played a part, there was no denying the striking physical resemblance of *all* of the artist's models pictured in the special exhibit to the sexy museum executive. He knew for a fact that he wasn't the *only* secret admirer to notice the uncanny resemblance, since he had overheard Chief Laroche verbalizing the exact same thing at the conclusion of his conversation with the Assistant Director of Acquisitions and Special Exhibits just a few days ago.

"Mademoiselle Bruante!" he had called after her just as she had started to purposefully walk away.

She stopped and turned back, pivoting on her sexy high-heels. "Yes, Monsieur Laroche?"

He approached her and spoke in a low voice, but still loud enough for Gaspar to hear. "I don't mean to be presumptuous, but I wonder if anyone has told you that your resemblance to the model in most of the special exhibit pieces is remarkably similar?"

She was anything but insulted, smiling widely as if the Chief had just provided additional evidence backing up a hard-to-prove professional-turned-personal theory—perhaps affiliated with the one that she referred to as 'model singularity'? "Well as you know, I *am* directly related to the Caillebotte brothers so who knows—I might very well share some common genetic material with their model as well." Her smile faded as the expression on her face became a touch more serious. "My family genealogy is convoluted and confusing, but may very well enjoy contributions from *other* nineteenth-century artists as well. You will have to wait for my fascinating presentation on opening night of the exhibit to hear some more about this."

She turned dismissively having admitted to something and nothing, sauntering past the grouping of monitors where Gaspar was strategically positioned to enjoy yet another view of heaven as she brushed past him and then up the far stairway to the left catwalk, where she would probably cut through the special exhibit gallery to admire her lookalike on the way to the back hallway and her private office. How he wished he could join her there instead of the museum's Executive Director for a mid-afternoon quickie.

Gaspar pulled himself away from the hypnotic draw of *Naked Woman Lying on a Couch* depicting Susanne's physically interchangeable relative, and continued into the third room: the largest, where he took in albeit briefly another scene portraying the Assistant Director's lookalike posing this time with another naked beauty in what the label identified as '*Sleep* by *Jean Desire Gustave Courbet, 1866*'. Slumber seemed the last thing in either woman's mind as they lay in a loving embrace either preparing for or recovering from a sexual encounter. But nothing could top what awaited him in the fourth room: the smallest of the four; because it was here that the exhibitors had decided to display the titillating collection of 'bodyscapes' accredited to Martial Caillebotte, although none of the erotic photographs had been signed.

He and his stirred masculinity marveled at the artist's use of shadows and a soft infusion of light to enhance the black-and-white compositions but only for a few seconds, feeling the pressing urge to back-track into proper position in the alcove room in order to bring his plan to the desired conclusion. The youngest Caillebotte brother—if he was indeed the photographer—had created a collage of artistically tasteful yet shockingly explicit shots of the very same body, it seemed, that graced the oil-on-canvas pieces hanging on the walls of the other three exhibit rooms and alcove. The model's face, seen in illusory profile or partly obscured by her dark flowing hair but still clearly identifiable, was a perfect match to Susanne Bruante's—at least in the erogenous backroom of his ever-excited mind's eye.

He viewed one after the other of the magnificently indecent photos, which would have caused an unprecedented stir if they had ever been displayed in the nineteenth century; and then with a cursory afterthought on the discreetly-placed door in the right-side corner leading to the back hallway of offices, posted with a softly-lettered sign that gently warned *Restricted Access, Staff Only*. His professional obligations now fulfilled, he padded hurriedly back on bare feet through the line of rooms and turned right, into the alcove room and then right again, where *The Origin of the World* was waiting for him located on the right-facing wall upon entering the exhibit room.

With a quickly beating heart, and barely believing himself that he was actually about to do this 'thing', he positioned himself between the podium upon which the unfinished sculpture was now displayed and the painting, leaning back and feeling the coolness of wood on the naked skin of his low back and buttocks—just as he had only moments ago imagined. He confirmed that with a turn of his head to the left he could gaze on the model's face, while straight ahead he could take in her unconcealed private parts.

"This won't take long," he whispered while executing his outrageous exhibitionist's fantasy; but just when his ecstasy had built to its foregone conclusion, the painting's surface started to waver like ripples in a pool, accelerating into a swirling vortex that abruptly exploded with movement.

"What the hell!" he exclaimed; but there was no time for him to ponder the cause, because something bulky shot forward towards him like a canon-ball directly out of the painting, and made instantaneous impact. He had had no warning, and no chance to escape.

In a fraction of a second and while the back of his head exploded with pain, his world turned utterly and completely black.

CHAPTER SIX

She awoke lying face down on the floor immersed in a groggy disorientation that was at first entirely devoid of identity or context. A vague noisy commotion, heard at first in the background of her mind but quickly pushing itself forcefully into the forefront, became more discreet and recognizable as a screeching alarm-bell that continuously reverberated in her aching head and seemed to penetrate into her muscles and bones. While her auditory senses were being short-circuited by this overpowering warning-sound, her tactile focus was unavoidably directed to the chillingly-direct feel of hard cold wood on her bare breasts and the remaining flat undersurface of her unprotected body. She realized immediately that she was completely naked: a vulnerable certainty that did little to dispel the overwhelming sense of uncertainty and panic that totally ruled the moment.

As she rolled over onto her back with a groan, she felt the chilling nothingness of air grope her anterior nudity while bright lights pinned her down with judgmental harshness, flat on her back and helpless. Her right leg throbbed and burned as if it had been sliced by a knife; and when she reached down to examine the injury by touching her outer-thigh with her palm, she winced with alarm as she felt a gash and the sticky wetness of blood. Her eyes watered with blurry adjustment, discovering that she was lying directly underneath a wide archway measuring about six feet across connecting two rooms. Something odd and significant had happened; and here she was thrust into the middle of it.

She sat up as quickly as she dared, propelled into slow-motion action by the blaring cacophony surrounding her. Blood from the laceration on her leg had trickled onto the floor and had been smeared by her body's readjustment upon awakening, the stinging pain of the six-inch slash—superficial but painful—competing with the constant ache from a large surrounding bruise that she must have sustained in a fall or, rather, a 'hard landing' that she could not recall due to her state of unconsciousness when it had occurred. The effort of transition from supine to partially upright caused a nauseating dizziness that threatened to lay her flat again; so in order to avoid this consequence, she slid back, the skin of her naked buttocks catching slightly on the hard floor—propping herself up against the archway-wall and sitting partially frog-legged for a moment, her palm pressed tightly against her right thigh to tamper the sticky ooze that still emanated meekly from the cut.

Looking down still, she watched the soles of her feet (which didn't feel like they belonged to her but to someone else instead) slide back and forth on slickly polished wood-like floors lacking even one knot or splinter, barely feeling the joints between the almost nonexistent planks since they had been installed so close together that the minuscule gaps between them were barely perceptible. Reaching back with one hand, her fingertips marveled if just for an ultra-brief moment at the smoothness of the plaster—or whatever material had been utilized to fashion the surface in such a way that it was devoid of a single crevice or ridge. She doubted that this type of 'high-tech' fabrication was even possible in 1876, leading her to postulate vaguely that the entire environment surrounding her was most likely a figment of her fertile, inebriated imagination created, no doubt, by drug and alcohol intoxication—because that particular recreation (coupled with some especially intensive physical activities, she abruptly recalled) had, according to her sluggishly recovering memory, occupied most of her evening prior to this odd awakening from unconsciousness.

Her gaze, until now, had been focused blurrily downward; but now she looked up, brushed some strands of hair wet with sweat from her forehead, and looked to the right, where she discovered the first of several rooms separated by archways similar to the one under which she was sitting. The large space was lit by lights that seemed to be powered by the supernatural...or more likely some kind of fantastical, 'futuristic' technology that her delusional mind had fabricated. But setting the mind-boggling concept of impossible lighting-sources and manufacturing aside, there was the equally-perplexing matter of interior decorating to reconcile. Oddly, the walls of the room were accessorized with paintings: *dozens* of them, swirling and colliding in her still-dizzied and doubled vision with their thematic focus revolving around the same privately-natural but publicly-unnatural state of undress as she. Although compelling, it seemed a peculiarly repetitive choice of wall embellishments for a private residence.

What is this place? The room was inexplicably

devoid of furniture except for two wooden benches located in the exact center of the space, giving the impression of resting-seats for observers of the artwork. This could only mean that the room was some kind of a showplace, with certain venues such as *The Salon of Paris, The Salon of Those Refused*, and *The Cooperative and Anonymous Association of Impressionist Painters* coming to mind. These were all events that would theoretically take place in rooms just like these where famous artists would show their latest efforts, in off-limit locations that she had never had the opportunity to see being only an anonymous model rather than someone important. This space was likely something akin to these places but located in some nether-world where lights burned without fuel and the flooring and walls were magically fashioned.

As her racing thoughts tried to rationalize the completely irrational, she repositioned herself, still sitting on the floor under the archway, with her left arm extended behind her for support and her legs folded underneath her now, rather than spread apart, with her head facing to the right. It occurred to her, abruptly, that her positioning resembled a pose— which made her laugh out-loud almost giddily at the irony since in this posture she gave the distinct appearance of sitting for just such a nude portrait, mimicking the artwork that surrounded her.

But wait—she *had*! In a flash, the memory of posing for the unfinished nude that Jean had called *Waking Nude Preparing to Rise* came to mind— along with many, many others painted not only by her former-lover and the father of her dear Edmond, but by countless of other Impressionists and

Realists, known and unknown, living and breathing and creating in the fertile Bohemian artistic community of modern late-nineteenth century Paris. A shiver of terror passed through her as she realized in a flash that many (no, *most*…or maybe even *all*) of the paintings within eye-shot depicted *not* just some random selection of beautifully uninhibited and anonymous models. No, as unbelievable as it seemed, these pieces seemed to portray the one and only Nicole Bruante.

So *where*, in a 'state of consciousness' sense of the word, was she? In contemplating her truly implausible surroundings, she came to the alternative conclusion that if she wasn't immersed in some kind of hallucinogen-induced storyline (which remained a distinct possibility), then surely she must be dreaming. She couldn't fathom how these familiar, private and highly personal pieces had been instantaneously and magically relocated from (yes, her *bedroom* in Montmartre, she realized!) to a legitimate place like this, especially when every artistic institution that she knew of had refused to display the shocking array of naked artwork surrounding her, *and* depicting her, because they were judged as deplorably unsuitable for public viewing.

Now she looked to her left into a much smaller alcove room, where Nicole was met with first one stinging slap in the face of reality, and then another: much more painful—in very rapid sequence.

Like magnet to metal, her eyes were drawn immediately to a painting that looked quite familiar, hanging like a center-piece on the right-side facing-wall of the smaller room, more-or-less directly opposite her but thirty-degrees to her left from where she sat in the threshold, leaning against the archway-wall—and displaying, of all things, a woman's genitals. This one, she remembered in a flash (and as her entire being's focus concentrated on it) was titled *The Origin of the World;* and instead of being on display here, it was supposed to be hanging on the wall at the foot of her bed, right beside her crucifix…at least until tomorrow when it was scheduled to be transported by hired carriage along with the rest of Jean's rejected masterpieces, to join a cadre of other paintings in Gustave Caillebotte's growing collection of artwork. This painting, she abruptly remembered, had opened up in a swirling vortex that had literally appeared out of nowhere, centered in Jean's ultra-realistic representation of her genitalia—while she and her lover had been engaged in an alcohol-and-drug infused moment of passion.

But then, something begged for immediate attention clamoring on the bottom-edge of her peripheral vision. While still struggling to process the madness that had transpired right under and in-front that very painting on her squeaky bed on *Butte Montmartre*, she angled her line-of-sight downward in response; and what she saw caused her to startle in shock—not just because the scene that faced her was nothing less than terrifying, but also from utter disbelief that she could have initially overlooked it.

There, not even twenty feet away from her, clustered in front of the right-side facing-wall of the alcove-room, were two naked bodies messily entangled—head-to-toe of one aligned toe-to-head with the other—with a cracked and fragmented

67

statue, and an overturned podium upon which the piece of artwork had presumably been displayed. She blinked twice, which seemed to clear her view into sharper clarity. The amount of blood pooling and oozing around the bodies combined with the ominous lack of movement made her feel sick, causing her to retch bilious green vomit onto the floor of the threshold; but this purging evacuation did little to settle her stomach, which still turned with horror and dismay.

Had that terrifying plunge into the depths of the erotic painting hanging simultaneously on walls over there and right here, carried her and René from that world to this one? He had been lying right underneath her on that squeaky cot when the abyss had opened, sucking them feet-first inside…which could only mean one thing. If René had been trapped just as she was in the same powerful current that had pulled her in and then spit her out again, into this strange and drastically unfamiliar place, then there was no avoiding the terrible conclusion that he was probably one of the motionless bodies lying lifeless on the floor to her left! *God no—no, no!*

She managed to stand on shaky legs and not-insignificant pain from the scratch and bruise on her right thigh, cognizant of the persistent alarm and feeling a growing worry that someone would soon answer its repetitive call. She needed to get out of here; but first, to confirm her suspicion and in dire need of 'closure' by confrontation, she simply had to get a closer look at the bodies. She limped into the alcove room, where she took in the fallen podium with still-attached plaque which she did not have time to read in-full, head turned sideways; but the most pertinent words and phrases, relevant to the tragedy laid at her feet and her own personal predicament, leapt out at her as if highlighted in bold: *…head and torso…unknown woman…Reclining Nude Engrossed in an Intimate Moment…René Caillebotte…died suddenly…1876.*

"That 'unknown woman' is *me*," she spoke out-loud, while stepping with growing strength in her legs but wavering courage in her heart over the three large fragments of the erotic sculpture. To her dismay she saw that René, who had '*died suddenly in 1876*', was in fact one of the bodies: crumpled sideways against the fallen podium, and literally swimming in the other man's blood.

She could only conclude that they had been propelled together, feet first and facing each other as she recalled their positioning at the moment of 'entry', out of the small erotic painting: he from the lower half and she from the top, despite the hard-to-ignore size constraints. By her estimate, the explicit up-close portrait of her unmentionables only measured two-feet across and a foot-and-a-half tall, which in normal circumstances would be a tight squeeze for even one person with a slim physique, not to mention two. But in this situation, which easily qualified as paranormal rather than normal, logic was firmly overruled by the inexplicable which she was grudgingly learning to accept as the norm.

So it was in this bizarre mindset that Nicole envisioned her naked body, feet first, being fortuitously vaulted directly *over* the sculpture sitting atop its podium—probably glancing over the top, scraping her right thigh in the process and sustaining the cut and the bruise, while the impact apparently altered her trajectory enough to propel her in a thirty-degree 'ricochet' over to the archway threshold rather than directly towards the opposite wall. She had landed, unconscious and largely unharmed, facing down and spanning the archway-threshold with her feet partly in the larger 'gallery' and her head and torso in the smaller display-room; while poor René's, being on the bottom, had been impelled directly, feet first as well, into the pedestal…or the other naked man…or both.

René's lifeless body looked grotesquely limp, as if all of his bones had been broken…perhaps even shattered. She noticed with horror the rag-doll positioning of his left leg, bent unnaturally backwards and almost completely hidden under his body, while his right leg crossed over his pelvis. His chest, flattened is if from some heavy weight or pressure, sloped downward from an abdomen that was bloated and distended. His head, horribly disfigured as if the internal contents had actually imploded, was angled in keeping with the downward slope of his shoulders and had been turned by gravity to the left. It seemed odd though that no blood or secretions trickled from his purple, lifeless lips onto the floor where he lay; and his back-end was clean and dry, with no evacuation of intestinal contents whatsoever. But why wouldn't the external positive pressure and/or the negative inside-forces, from whatever higher-power destroyed him, have extruded some of his body contents *out*; and why in the world was the surface of his skin so clean and pristine, without even a scrape or a scratch to bear witness to his supernaturally-traumatic death? The appearance of his body seemed to defy the rules of logic as she knew them.

She poignantly recalled his muscular chest and torso, now flattened and collapsed as if pulled in by a powerful inward pressure; his perfect legs; and his glorious manhood: now pitifully deflated by a tragically-premature demise. His body, once vibrant and full, was now limp and empty—somewhat like a bag of sand which had lost most of its grains by leakage; or a balloon that had been lessened by a slow but steady air-leak. But despite the inward injury that she equated with some kind of disintegration induced by something mysterious and evil, his outward body was oddly intact without a scrape, cut or bruise to give testimony to the violent exodus. Granted, the *other* body had likely tempered the impact; yet, one would expect some surface-evidence of being squeezed through a painting's 'travel-tunnel' if it could be called that, and then jettisoned out into this strange new world. For that matter, *she* had emerged remarkably unscathed, save for a bruise on her thigh that she had likely sustained when her body hit the floor; and her 'insides' had suffered little or nothing from the journey—in contrast to poor René.

What strange rules of 'engagement' imbedded in the painting had favored her and passed an unforgiving terminal judgment on him? Was it something in their 'make-up' or heritage? Or, maybe it was due to the fact that she was a woman and he a man? She looked down on him, his beautiful purple-blue eyes staring vacantly ahead in

71

a dead-man's gaze, with tear-streaked love and pity. She remembered those same lavender eyes so full of life and lust, telling her without words just a few minutes ago '*yes, that's what I want*' when she had slipped him—hard, urgent, and hot with desire—deep inside her while she urgently straddled him lying on top; both of them reaching the moment of climax just before the impassioned reality of the not-so-distant past became the nightmarish unreality of the present.

She studied the other man, lying 'toe-to-head' opposite René's 'head-to-toe' positioning given the feet-first mechanism of impact, for a brief moment before turning away. He was merely a boy, in his early twenties at the most, with a pale and scarred complexion that gave away the very recent scourge of acne—the blemishes partly concealed by a few days of unshaven stubble. He sported a thin and unconditioned body, grey eyes, and dirty-blond hair tangled and matted with his own blood: still oozing from a crushing posterior skull injury. He had likely been an innocent bystander, present at the wrong place at the wrong time; but, why in the world was he naked?

But now was hardly the time for piecing together multiple distressing puzzles. The alarm was still screaming and echoing around her; and in a moment, when someone answered its call, she would be discovered, completely nude, presiding over two dead bodies like she had been their executioner. *I need to get out of here fast,* she thought, moving quickly through the archway while wiping away the tears with her shoulder and forearm, out of the alcove room, and into the larger room.

The space in which she stood appeared to be connected to two or three more to her left, at least one of them larger still; and to her right, she could see a balcony of sorts that seemed to overlook a vast and high-ceilinged expanse. If she chose the left escape route, it could very well lead her to a dead-end where she would find herself trapped at the end of a blind hole like a rabbit; whereas if she turned right, she would be able to exit through a gigantic archway three times the size of the left-sided ones, risking full exposure to anyone entering the painting gallery in response to the alarm. She would have to choose the lesser of two evils, it seemed—so would it be left, or right?

Right she quickly decided, venturing out of the exhibit room at a cautious jog since she still felt off-balance, and maneuvering around a scattered gathering of clothes, shoes, and a utility belt with a ring of keys attached—the latter topping the pile that she assumed belonged to the naked 'bystander'. She ducked under a rope that served to ineffectively barricade the 'exhibit' rooms from entry or exit. This exercise found her standing frozen on the 'balcony', which was actually an open hallway that stretched like a catwalk along a massive, cylindrical, cathedral-like interior of a building that stretched lengthwise to encompass at least a full city block, and soared upward to a dizzying height.

What is this place? she asked herself, feeling tiny compared to the grand cavern made of glass, stone, and steel that surrounded her. The marble-tiled hallway on which she stood looked down on similar floors below; and above, an expansive steel meshwork formed an arch that, in turn, supported a ceiling constructed entirely of windowed glass, curving upward and across in an aerial semi-circle. She looked to her left, where a gigantic clock was centered on the lower end of a wall that was partitioned by an iron grid into fifty or sixty windows. There was no possible way this was an exhibit hall for one of the salons. It looked more like a train station—but where in God's name were all the trains?

The sound of many pairs of footsteps to her right jolted her back to her predicament. A quick glance toward the other end of the station revealed a group of five or six gendarmes, dressed in blue and hurriedly jogging up the nearby staircase. Perhaps they hadn't seen her? But just as this hopeful thought came to her, the lead officer looked directly at her and even from this distance she could see his eyes bug out, surprised no doubt by her state of undress.

"Hey you!" he yelled, his voice barely audible over the howl of the alarms. "Stop right there!" They quickened their pace which was enough impetus for Nicole to turn on her heal with a pounding heart, back under the dangling rope— dashing as fast as she could, veering around the dead man's garments and belongings, and back again into the first gallery.

Now she broke into a full run, passing innumerable nude paintings that all, with few exceptions, depicted an anonymous nude model that only she and the artists who had painted her knew as Nicole Bruante. She bolted through the facing archway into a second, somewhat smaller room

74

hearing the still far-away footsteps of her pursuers behind, the rapid click of their numerous heels on the marble catwalk growing louder as she imagined them soon rounding the corner in heated pursuit. She hoped that she was not heading toward a dead end, but as she passed through a third room: the largest so far (and unbelievably home to the painting of her and Céleste posing naked in post-coital ecstasy that Jean had called '*Sleep*') and then into a fourth: the final one…it seemed that she had.

CHAPTER SEVEN

She had hoped to be able to exit through a door positioned in the far corner of the room posted with a message that read: *Restricted Access, Staff Only*, although the tone of the signage suggested that she might not. As she made a beeline for this questionable escape route, she couldn't help but notice that the four walls surrounding her were devoted to photographic art rather than paintings. Oddly enough, the pictures matched exactly what she imagined Martial's 'body-scapes' might have looked like, if they had ever been created—using *her* as the model, judging from the shots that included her face as well as her body!

She was now viewing, in a blurred rush as she passed by, by all accounts and without question the project that she had flatly turned down: the same one which René had told her had never materialized because Martial had been dismally unsuccessful in convincing a model to pose with that type of explicit boldness for a camera. Why? Because doing so was *vastly* different than being the subject for a painter's less-true-to-life representation of naked female exhibitionism pictured on canvas, as measured in degree of realism.

Yet here was her face: pictured mostly in profile and 'painted' with artistic shadowing, or partially covered by a falling wave of brunette; and there were her breasts: full, round and accented on dual curved crescendos with uniquely generous rims of silky pink. And over there, she made quickly-passing note of a virtual reproduction of Jean's erotic masterpiece, strikingly mimicked in shadowed yet still embarrassing photographic precision to the point of qualifying as a cross-genre replica...except that the private parts were shockingly unobscured by hair! Making this area smooth and bare was not a practice that she condoned—or the vast majority of her contemporaries, for that matter.

But—where was her birthmark? For this representation of Nicole Bruante's anatomy to be certified as true-to-life, the small dark mole measuring about a quarter of an inch located on her right inner thigh dangerously close to unspeakably-personal territory would need to be present...but it wasn't. This tell-tale 'signature' of her erotic identity had been obscured in *The Origin of the World* and all of her other most revealing poses by nature's 'curtain': growing in curly, shadowed protection in the paintings, inks and charcoal drawings displayed behind and around her, but bared to totally nude by scissors and razor in this perfectly-angled photographic shot. Without the 'beauty-mark', the model simply *couldn't* be her; yet, with the exception of this physical omission, the woman displayed in every single one of these revealing photographs—unclothed and with her skin shaved smooth in every conceivable location including the unmentionable—could have easily been confused for her identical twin.

These thoughts literally raced through her mind at a speed that equaled her breathless sprint, which had finally led her to the point of either 'win or lose' with a simple turn of a door-handle. She had now reached destiny's doorstep, located in the right-side corner of the room flanked and surrounded by the perplexing series of nude photographs featuring her photographic doppelganger, and marked with a sign that said *Restricted Access, Staff Only*. She placed her hand on the latch and prayed for a miracle while at the same moment, from behind, she heard the security guards enter the first of the four galleries.

"Stop," the lead pursuer yelled again, but instead of complying she pushed down and meeting no resistance, scrambled through the opened door to the other side with a sigh of relief. "*Merci*," she whispered, pushing the door closed with her back and then pivoting around, searching for a way to lock it.

The door was unlike any she had ever seen, with a rectangular metal bar measuring two inches at the most positioned northwest on its rightward-pointing top-side and southwest on its bottom-left, using a compass face as a reference. Correctly assuming that it probably controlled a locking mechanism, she turned it easily in a counter-clockwise direction a full ninety-degrees, so that the top now faced left and northwest, and the bottom right and southeast. This would buy her substantial time if the gendarmes did not have a key handy, and quite a bit less if they did.

She stood more-or-less in the middle of a seemingly endless hallway that spanned the entire length of the long building, to her left and to her right as she faced the door she had just locked. Behind her, a line of doors most likely leading into offices stretched both ways, opposite the solid wall separating her and the hallway from the gendarmes and the interior of the painting gallery. She had gained a brief reprieve, but she didn't have much time. In a moment the men—who without question would throw her in prison for a variety of offenses including a double-murder, damaging René's partly-finished nude sculpture, and lewd exposure— would burst through the door as she stood there stupidly and apprehend her with victorious, unsmiling faces…but only if they had the key. She hoped to God they didn't.

She looked in a state of building panic up and down the hallway with her palms pressed firmly against the door, as if her 120 measly pounds acting as a barricade would prevent them from gaining hallway access. She immediately concluded that she should run left not right towards a metal-framed sign that glowed 'exit' in red, lit brightly from deep inside by the same unearthly means as everything else in this strange and impossible world. This way should lead her to the outside, in *back* of the building assuming her pursuers had spotted her a moment ago after entering from the front, where with a little luck she might escape.

The marble floor felt cold against her bare feet as she sped in a race against time, hearing even as she did so the sound of futile pushing and banging on the other side of the door accompanied by muffled curses. It was apparent they didn't have the key, thank heavens; but it sounded like they knew where to find it.

"Back there—on the pile of clothes!" she heard one of them say. "I think I saw a keyring." *Yes, that's right*, she recalled; there were in fact keys attached to the utility belt on the dead man's discarded clothes! It would take them less than a minute to run back and get them, and maybe another minute or two to rifle through the dangling offerings and try each one until they would eventually declare hit-and-miss victory—so she had better act fast. She was almost at the exit door now, which drew closer and closer as she ran for her life and counted down the distance with each panting breath: fifty feet, twenty feet, ten feet...*there*.

She stood in a defensive stance for a split-second, her naked back and buttocks pressed against the wall next to the heavy hinges of the exit-door, as she contemplated her next move. The door would open, she thought, if she pushed on a steel bar spanning its entire width; but before she rushed blindly into the unknown, she would take a second to evaluate what was on the other side. She peered furtively through a lengthwise window traversing the opposite side of the door confirming that exiting this way would in fact lead her outdoors, down a squat metal stairway and into a short alleyway between two buildings. Beyond, she would find herself out in the open on a wide street backlit what looked like a thousand lights. It was unlike any city that *she* had ever seen, including her much-loved Paris. Regardless, this was her way out to freedom...or was it?

Was this *really* where she ought to go? Thinking more about it she became acutely aware of the goose bumps covering her skin, produced by the chilly air playing on her vulnerable, naked flesh. 'Naked' was a big problem because it would draw unwanted attention, marking her like a target where even a small-scale search party would find her shivering in an alley or surrounded by curious onlookers. She needed to rethink her plan, and quickly. There was no time for hesitation.

She threw open the thick but seemingly hollow slab of metal, causing yet another alarm to sound just as she had hoped; but it would certainly aid in the deception that she had used this escape-route if there was some way to keep the door open. As if in answer to this thought, the door swung conclusively out to its full extent against the outside brick wall with a metallic clang and did not ricochet back to closed, apparently due to its not being hinged on a spring. She was in luck.

So it was that she retraced her steps in a mad dash, doubling back while trying one door after the other along the right-side of the long hallway hoping against hope that one of them would be open. If her plan to conceal herself in one of the offices was thwarted then she would find herself back in the showroom but at the other end of the catwalk, at the front of the building where she would have to scramble to find a storage closet or similar such nook or cranny in which to hide. This would be far from ideal but much better than rushing headlong into the wide-open where she would most certainly be apprehended the moment she set her naked feet on outside soil.

She ran down the hallway stopping at each door on the way, jiggling the doorknobs only to find much to her dismay that the first half dozen or so were all locked. It was not until she had just passed the midway point that she found perhaps the only unlocked one, strategically positioned just beyond the still-locked door to the display-rooms, in the exact opposite direction from her pursuers' likely trajectory towards the open door leading outside, where they would assume she had gone. Slipping inside, she closed the door quietly behind her and promptly locked it, crouching down with her back against it as if the non-existent bulk of her petite, nude body offered additional resistance to someone trying to enter. So she waited for a few minutes that seemed like an eternity, eyes closed with heart pounding until she heard the jingle of keys and the rush of heavy footsteps—six pairs at least—leading away from rather than towards her temporary sanctuary.

"The door is open; she escaped that way, to the outside!" It was the 'lead' gendarme—the same one who had ordered her to 'stop'—speaking to his compatriots. "She isn't wearing any clothing so she won't get very far."

"We'll alert all units on the left bank," another voice said. These words told her two things: first, that she was in Paris although her brief view of the city through the window and opened exit-way was unlike any part of the left bank that she was familiar with; and second, that the entire police force would soon be involved, which spelled major trouble for a certain naked, inadvertent interloper who would, if captured, be tried and convicted for horrific crimes she did not commit. Serious pitter-patter in the corridor outside indicated that perhaps another half-dozen officials: reinforcements to the original six, were busy organizing an *outside* search party, just as she had hoped. The alarms were no longer sounding, turned off as unnecessary since the hunt for her would continue outdoors.

Nicole breathed a sigh of relief into the silence surrounding her as she sat on the floor, wondering what she should do next. One thing seemed certain though: namely, that whoever worked here would find her in the morning and turn her in without asking any questions. So although she might be safe now, this refuge was, at best, only temporary which meant that she needed to formulate a plan…and fast.

The room was dark, but the light from a full moon shone through the window. As her eyes adjusted, she observed pushed against the wall to her right a desk littered with stacks of papers, a matching chair, and some adjacent bookcases; directly across, a large picture-window situated above an oversized leather couch; and to her left, the shadowy rectangular outlines of framed pictures hanging on the walls to the right of a double-doored wooden coat-closet, opened on the side nearest to her which gave her visible-access to a piece of clothing hanging inside. She was in an office where it was quite possible that the intensely serious business of planning the exhibits, acquiring the artwork, and balancing the complicated financial ledger in this surreal showroom might fall on the person who sat behind that very desk during working hours. Whoever he was, Nicole needed to make sure he didn't find her waiting like a scared rabbit in his place of business, come the morning.

The coat-closet and its inside-occupant would be her first destination. Afraid that if she stood someone might notice her through the facing window looking out onto a grand boulevard lit by gas lamps devoid of flames, she crawled on hands

83

and knees to reach her objective. What she found hanging on the hook was an overcoat appearing as if it had been placed there specifically for her; but unbelievably, there was more. Opening the right door and swinging this one and the left outward to their full extents, she concluded that the pair of boots that the owner of the office had left, along with the hat and maybe even the umbrella, could possibly come in handy as she started to formulate a strategy.

She would have to time it right, though. She just might be able to escape from the building before morning, her nudity hidden under a tightly buttoned coat, her feet no longer bare, and her face partly shadowed under a hat, stylishly tilted forward, strolling among other city dwellers with her umbrella shading her from the glare of the rising sun or the imminent threat of a thunderstorm. It would be risky, but did she really have a choice? She couldn't stay here, where her discovery in the morning was nearly guaranteed; and now that she had some clothes, her escape to the outside presented itself as the most logical choice.

She sat with her back against the wall next to the closet, determined not to sleep despite her exhaustion. All of her muscles ached, as did the bruise and deep scratch on her outer right thigh—no longer bleeding but crusted now with the drying evidence of a 'close-call' injury. She felt so utterly exhausted that she couldn't help but wonder how it would feel to stretch out on the couch and rest, but she willed herself to resist the temptation. If she gave in, she might very well sleep past daylight, losing her opportunity to sneak out before the office's resident came in. By now, a chill had settled on her like a sudden frost, so she pulled the overcoat from its hook, clutching it to her chest to cover her naked bosom; and as she did, she smelled a fragrance (roses and lemon perhaps?) coming from the fabric.

Suddenly she realized that the coat belonged to a woman...*not* a man! She reached for the boots, holding them up out of the shadows and into a shaft of moonlight. *Heels; these have heels! They must belong to a woman, too!* Chance had strangely led her into a hiding place where a woman's coat and boots were waiting to aid her in her escape.

Then it occurred to her: how could this office possibly belong to a woman? Women were employed, for the most part, as domestics, barmaids, or consorts, if their circumstances required them to work at all; but she had heard of women who were actually pursuing an education and a career. More than likely, though, the male museum administrator had entertained a mistress or a prostitute right there on his couch. After they had finished, the woman had probably left in a rush, leaving some of her things either accidentally or intentionally on his coat rack. Nicole grew even more curious to find out more about the person who had discarded her coat and boots in Nicole's temporary refuge.

She would start with the pictures hanging on the wall, just to the right of the coat closet. She didn't have far to crawl, standing up for a moment only, just long enough to pull the largest one off and realizing as she did so that it contained a photograph, set under glass She would need better light to inspect it though, directly underneath the window; and so it was with this objective that she traversed the hard floor barely cushioned by a thin carpet, making for an unforgiving but necessary journey on aching knees and with some stifled grimaces. Reaching the couch, she decided to use it like a table where she placed the framed picture flat on the surface for careful scrutiny. Tilting it toward the moonlight, her first attempt caught the reflection of the moon in the glass which was surprisingly bright, completely obscuring the photograph displayed underneath. After several hit-and-miss alterations of the angle, she finally got it right—and what she saw made her gasp, on two counts.

Certainly she must be on the throes of some sort of mentally-unwell delusion. One of the two individuals pictured in the photograph was a woman who looked disturbingly familiar and caused Nicole to conclude beyond the shadow of a doubt that she had crossed over the line into the realm of the insane.

"Impossible," she murmured. She recognized the mouth, the lips, and the smile; the hazel eyes; the dark hair; the line of the jaw, and the delicate nose. "It's *me*," she whispered, as implausible as it seemed. There must be some logical explanation for seeing her own face staring back at her in place of someone else's, although for the life of her she couldn't figure out what it was. But the unbelievable coincidence of likenesses didn't stop there, because the slim and distinguished looking man that her doppelgänger was posing with—well past middle aged, with a full head of carefully combed grey hair and a closely trimmed salt-and-pepper beard—was a dead ringer for her late, dear Papa: Jerome Bruante.

It seemed clear that denial in the form of continuing to chalk this all up to a bad experience with absinthe laced with laudanum or to an undiagnosed mental disorder would only lead to her capture, so it held to reason that a blanket acceptance of her circumstances, at least for the moment, would serve her much better as a survival tactic. Finding a name to fit the people in the photograph seemed as good a place as any to discard her head-in-the-sand mentality, so she crawled over to the desk, opening the center drawer partly upright on her knees where she encountered a jackpot of pencils and pens—along with a small cylindrical object that easily fit into the palm of her hand, fashioned with an unfamiliar material that was hard like metal or wood, but clearly wasn't either. She pushed on a small button and was startled to discover that in so doing, the gadget produced a thin beam of light. She added this hand-held 'candle' to her growing list of the unexplainable; but true to her new mantra of 'no questions asked' and throwing caution (and skepticism) to the wind she stood up, unconcerned for the moment about being seen from the outside, and beamed the light-source pointedly onto the desktop and *voila*: in an instant she was able to put a name to the female face.

"Susanne Bruante," she said out loud, reading the nameplate sitting right there out in the open just waiting for someone to discover it. She and the woman in the photo (who, as unbelievable as this might seem from a gender-perspective, was apparently the 'occupant' of this office) were relatives given their matching last name, which by way of family resemblances explained away their physical similarities…yet, identical? And how in the world could lightning hit twice, with 'twin' Nicoles and 'twin' Papas existing side-by-side in this alternative reality, just by happenstance? This seemed simply too far-fetched to possibly be real, but she reminded herself that she had just vowed to trade the counter-productivity of disbelief and for the practicality of blind faith; so in the spirit of shelving her skepticism, Nicole put on her detective hat in earnest and shone the portable lamp-light in an arc over the shiny lacquered wood surface, searching for more clues. On one side was a neat pile of papers sitting in an organizing tray topped with a small stack of opened mail, which she would get to momentarily; but on the other stood a desk calendar, propped up and opened to the last day of the month of May…*2011*!

2011? She stifled a gasp but couldn't suppress the vocal surprise. "But it's 1876, *not* 2011!" she blurted out. This was the shock of the evening, but it also went the farthest to explain her unique predicament. If this was the future: a reality that she must accept to survive even though common sense told her otherwise, then the mechanism of her transposition was, without argument, the painting. The hole that had opened in it must be some kind of 'time tunnel' with a connection between past and future, with a powerful current that for unclear reasons she had been able to withstand…but René had not.

Tears welled again in her eyes as she thought of

his limp and overly-flexible limbs attached to a body that seemed as if it had been crushed—virtually imploding from the inside, lying at this very moment out *there* with his tragically lifeless body being poked and prodded by coldly inquisitive gendarmes. He would sadly be put to rest in an unmarked grave somewhere in a 'future' Paris where none of his living relatives would even be able to say their last farewells.

Nicole grabbed the stack of letters and sat 'Indian-style' against the desk with her legs crossed, shining the light on the small pile of evidence that she fanned out directly in front of her on the floor. As she pulled her leg underneath her she felt her thigh sting and throb, reminding her of the cut which she touched with a grimace…feeling the moist stickiness of new bleeding. Running like a rabbit from a pack of hungry dogs must have re-opened the scratch so she pressed her palm tightly against it to quell the lightly trickling stream.

Most of the letters were addressed to Susanne Bruante, Assistant Director of Acquisitions and Special Exhibits at a place called *Musée d'Orsay* (*this* place, she assumed—which finally affixed a label to Nicole's place of translocation); but near the bottom she found one that wasn't. The address given on this particular envelope ('*Susanne Bruante, 14 Avenue Georges V, Nombre 3B, Paris France*') simply *had* to be her place of residence…and that's exactly where Nicole would be heading next.

And soon, she contemplated, because it might not be safe to wait until daylight. The policemen had seen her standing on the catwalk, and if she looked exactly like Susanne Bruante who's to say they hadn't recognized her? And if they had, where would the search party look next when they came up empty-handed outside? Right *here*, in the Assistant Director's own office, of course! Suddenly Nicole's cozy sanctuary didn't seem quite as safe as she had thought, just five short minutes ago.

She would wait a bit longer, but not too long. Her timing must be perfect. If she left before the searchers gave up outside, they would apprehend her shortly after her exit from the building; and if she waited until the police re-grouped indoors, they would either discover her hiding here, or detain her in the hallway as she tried to make her way out the exit door and down the shallow stairway to the alley leading to the street running parallel to this side of the museum. Her window of opportunity might be very slim indeed.

She crawled back to the couch, retrieved the picture, and made her way back to the coat-closet wall she stood again and hastily replaced the photograph. She crept over to the coat rack again, stepped partly inside closing the right-sided door half-way so it would obscure the view from outside the window and dressed in the overcoat, boots, and hat. Then she sat against the wall right next to the door, umbrella in hand, to wait—not too long, but just long enough.

She prayed that her intuition would tell her when the time was right.

CHAPTER EIGHT

It didn't take Detective Michèle Crossier long to pull on a pair of jeans one leg at a time over her sleepy, until-recently-under-the-bedcovers nudity and slip on a t-shirt hastily over the unencumbered swell of her buxom chest. She had discovered that having only one layer rather than two between her come-hither body and the eyes of potential beholders led to more 'productive' interactions, in the right setting and circumstance of course. This tactic served her well not only in her personal life, but also in the workplace since her profession was overwhelmingly dominated by men. It only took a hint of enticement that in truth she almost never had to take to the next level of 'engagement' in order to get what she was after, whether it be a file, a piece of evidence…or an assignment.

The eagerly-informative phone-call a few minutes ago from the blue-eyed but otherwise nondescript police dispatcher who always hoped for 'more' from her (largely because she always gave him special attention in the little-did-he-know insincere flirtation department) corresponded with their arrangement that she would be his 'first call' when any provocative case of special interest came up. Yes, her dutiful puppy-dog dispatcher had gotten her out of her comfortable bed at the ungodly hour of 1:30 a.m., but it wasn't every night that an art museum security breach occurred resulting not only in destruction of a priceless piece of artwork—normally considered the 'main event'; but also in a sensational double-murder—by *far* the crime of the day and prompting the early morning involvement of homicide.

There were, in addition, some unusual components to the 'break-in' that peeked Michèle's attention not the least of which was the fact that *both* of the male corpses were starkly naked…and so was the escaped 'intruder': a totally unclothed woman who seemed to share Michèle's titillating propensity for nudity and who very well may have been the perpetrator of the crime. In addition, these events had occurred smack-dab in the middle of a special exhibit at *Musée d'Orsay* that held a special 'familial' interest to Michèle since one of her direct but distant relatives had actually been a contributing artist.

To remind herself of the 'principle' that guided such an early morning summons, she pulled from her top nightstand drawer the letter of promotion issued just over a year ago describing her transfer from the ho-hum Fraud division to prestigious Homicide. She kept it at her bedside for easy access—not only to 'gloat' but also to remind herself that she was in the business of breaking records.

For instance, she was the youngest graduate in police academy history. She was also the individual who had been promoted more rapidly from uniform-class to lieutenant within the *Police Judiciare* than anyone else in recent memory, and one of only a handful of women who had been 'accepted' into the elite male-dominated club known as Homicide. She had her sights on eventually becoming the Chief Inspector; and the first step towards that lofty goal would be to secure the role of 'lead detective' in a high-profile murder case such as this…and *solve* it.

With a self-congratulatory half-smile, she read the announcement over again, savoring every word and imagining that someday, after an accelerated series of promotions spurred on by her savvy talents, a similar memo would describe her ascent to the top of the *Police Judiciare*.

Monsieur Jean-Paul Golland
Juge d'Instruction
Police Judiciaire de Paris (DRPJ)
36 Quai des Orfèvres
75011 Paris

15 Mars 2010

Monsieur le Juge,

This notice will serve to inform you that Michèle Crossier, Lieutenant (first pay scale) with the Department of Monetary Fraud, has been granted her request for transfer to the Major Criminal Division, 36 Quai des Orfèvres. Her promotion to Inspector (second pay scale) with DCPJ Homicide has been approved. She has been instructed to report for her new duties on 25 Mars, 2010, under the direct supervision of Chief Inspector Xavier Deschamps.

Lieutenant Crossier has served the Fraud Division for the past six years, where her efforts were instrumental in the arrest of key individuals involved in La Banque Postale financial breach.

Congratulations to Inspector Crossier, and the best of luck in her new role.

Pour le Prefet de Police,

Luis Fleming
Prefecture de Police
1 Rue de Lutèce
75195 PARIS

As she put on a light jacket and slipped her police ID and her car keys into the pocket, she mentally reviewed the preliminary information circulating throughout the precinct, as told to her by her talkative, hopeful informant. The cameras had been manually turned off by one of the dead corpses before he had met his untimely demise; because, go-figure, the younger of the two naked murder victims was the *d'Orsay* night guard on-duty for the midnight shift, of all people.

Due to the fact that the video-feed was 'dark' at the time of the action, none of the obscenities, misdemeanors or felonies had been captured on digital media; but once the cameras started rolling again—brought to life either by the ultra-sensitive motion-activated sensors attached to a joggled painting or (more likely) the over-turned sculpture on its display case lying inertly on the floor right next to the equally-inert, unclothed and entangled male couple—they immortalized a dazed and confused woman, *also* naked, making her debut on film and presiding it seemed over the bloodied and battered corpses.

As her contact in the main office explained, the group of six responding police officers had initially spotted the beautiful mystery woman in all her

94

'nude' glory on the museum catwalk outside an about-to-open special exhibit featuring 'nude' paintings, sculptures and photographs from the nineteenth century—the 'nude' theme surrounding suspect and surroundings either purely coincidental versus not at all. How half a dozen professionals reinforced by at least another dozen, having the advantage of numbers and the combined years of training in this sort of thing, had incompetently allowed an unclothed, unarmed woman to slip away down a back hallway and out an exit door while they were in close pursuit was beyond her. The end result was that the 'criminal' was still on the loose in the city, posing more risk to herself than others in her current state of undress which Michèle imagined would draw unwanted gawking and even lascivious advances from any of a number of lecherous 'standers-by'.

The medical examiner's team, the chief of security for the museum, and Chief Inspector Xavier Deschamps had already been called; so she had best get a move-on if she wanted to secure the title of 'Inspector-in-charge' in this all-important case which might very well make her career. So it was that thirty minutes later Michèle approached the museum in her red Peugeot and made the turn down *Rue de Lille*, where two police vehicles sped past her going in the opposite direction, sirens blaring. They were part of the efficient and quickly mobilized search, and would surely find Mademoiselle 'Bare-It-All' shortly…if they hadn't already. The woman should be easy enough to spot and apprehend, her nudity sticking out like a sore thumb in a city that never slept—preventing her from inconspicuously joining the handful of pedestrians still out at midnight, walking back to their hotels or to the closest Metro stop. But perhaps not, if the woman had made a beeline to her own parked car, or to a waiting getaway driver's. This would either be a short night, or a very long one.

She pulled up in front of *Musée d'Orsay* a few minutes after two a.m. alongside a haphazardly-parked grouping of police cars and in front of a wide stone plaza, which was busy with a couple-dozen gendarmes. She unnecessarily flashed her badge since they all knew her (or knew *of* her), walking briskly through the front door: still propped open providing recent access, she surmised, for the carts, body bags and other various bulky equipment needed by forensics.

She nodded curtly to the 'uniform' positioned inside. "Where is the Chief Inspector?"

"He hasn't arrived yet," he replied, "but the head of museum security is here—in the control room over there, waiting for him." He tilted his head to the left towards a semi-circular desk lined with monitors that created a sort of barricade in front of a room that, through the open door, she could clearly see was home to a busy wall of instruments and digital equipment. This was actually perfect because now she could scope out the crime scene and question the coroner, preparing her case for lead-detective being first-on-the-scene and first-on-the-details.

Granted, Xavier Deschamps was a lame duck, retiring in only three short weeks after serving for more than thirty-five years on the Paris police force; but he was still in charge and she would have to play this carefully for him to give her this assignment. She was still the new kid on the block, relatively speaking—plus having an X chromosome didn't help matters; but he had been satisfied with her work the past year and she saw no reason why he wouldn't hand her a parting gift on his way out.

As she thought more about it, working with Deschamps like this, so close to his impending departure, couldn't be more perfect. He was a man with an impeccable reputation, whose opinion and decisions still carried a significant amount of weight in Parisian law enforcement and political circles. Rumor had it that his long years of service had made him weary and more than ready to cash it all in and relax for the rest of his days on a beach in St. Tropez. If she could just persuade him to give her control over a case in which he could never become fully involved, Michèle would be calling the shots and taking all the well-deserved credit, making a name for herself in record time—following her usual life's template.

Deschamps' replacement, currently the head of Internal Affairs, had been selected months ago, shortly after Deschamps had announced his retirement. The new chief was a woman—another plus in Michèle's book. All of these elements combined to create the perfect storm, delivering her a case that would never truly be Deschamps' or his successor's to close...but one that Michèle Crossier vowed to make her own.

"And where is the crime scene?" she asked the gendarme, leading to his reply: "I'll take you there." *I want this,* she thought as he led her up a short flight of stairs and to the left onto a catwalk

97

extending lengthwise through the building, *and I'm damn well going to get it.*

As they walked, she glanced over her right shoulder at the massive central lobby of the former *Gare d'Orsay*, the impressive *Beaux-Arts* train depot built between 1898 and 1900, finished just in time for the turn-of-the-century *Exposition Universelle*. Much of the original architecture had been preserved in the conversion of the station into a museum, including floors of marble and walls of granite and brick that reached upward on either side to support a complex grid of iron fingers cradling a ceiling constructed entirely of glass. They stopped in front of the special exhibit galleries, located through a large archway off the left-catwalk located midway between the front and back of the museum.

"In there, detective," the gendarme said, pointing diagonally to the left across a high-ceilinged room whose walls were adorned with nude paintings, towards a small alcove room busy with activity. Michèle had read with interest about the controversial special display and had actually planned on visiting it, but as a patron of the arts (and as odd as it might seem as an actual *relative* of one of the exhibit's nineteenth-century contributors) *rather* than in her capacity as a police investigator. You see, she was the great-great-granddaughter of Martial Caillebotte: the presumed creator of the infamous 'body-scape' photographic display that was featured in one of these very rooms; descended directly from Martial's disowned son, Jean, who was her great-grandfather.

"Thank you, officer," she said. "Please inform me when the Chief Inspector arrives." She ducked underneath a band of yellow crime scene tape, skirting around a pile of clothes with a utility belt planted on top to enter the first gallery, veering sharply left in order to approach a small archway eccentrically placed between the midpoint of the facing wall and the left corner. She walked briskly through, into a thirty-by-thirty-foot alcove room seeming exceptionally over-crowded with forensics personnel due to its small size. She made a beeline for the bodies, where she found the medical examiner and three assistants finishing their preliminary examination of the two naked corpses.

"Bonjour Michèle." Pascal Bernier, the Medical Examiner assigned to their Parisian division of homicide, looked up at her momentarily with a friendly grin of admiration since he was just one of the many in her professional circle that not-so-secretly longed for her 'unprofessional' attention. As he returned to his unpalatable task performed with another gloved member of his team taking samples from the younger man's genital area, she smiled internally to know that her reputation both as a no-nonsense law enforcement official *and* a highly desirable single woman clearly preceded her.

To be perfectly honest, she didn't mind the blending of her attractive attributes one bit—fully cognizant that part of her success so far, in this police division and her last one, was due to the fact that she was a young, sexy blonde. She had learned long ago that her good looks, coupled with an unmatched competence and a keen intelligence, could be used to her advantage—providing her with opportunities that other, less comely women would most certainly envy. Even if she was handed this kind of high-profile assignment in part because of her sex-appeal, it was *always* her intellectual abilities that ended up 'wowing' them in the end and earning her the respect she deserved.

At the same moment these self-congratulatory thoughts were passing through her mind and as Pascal and an assistant had just capped the last swab taken from the younger man's private parts (which were situated suspiciously close to the other man's face in respect to the two bodies' adjacent positioning), she looked down at both bodies and immediately felt sick. The victim whose sample-tube was currently being packaged was literally swimming in a pool of his own blood: the source being a crushing posterior skull wound, sustained she supposed from an impact injury delivered by a blunt instrument or from directed force onto an object located behind him…or both. She eyed the overturned podium and the split and fractured sculpture, surmising that the man had met at least the conclusion of his end via flesh-and-bone-meets-marble—a hypothesis that was confirmed when she noticed a smear of blood and the hint of flesh on the damaged piece of artwork.

And the *other* man, whom the crime scene investigators had pulled away from the coagulating pond of the other body's blood so that they could examine him better—well, she had quite simply never seen anything like it. The man's limbs were twisted, their positioning limp and unnatural—behind, across, and under his body, like a malleable bag of flesh without a skeleton. Had his bones been crushed? It looked like it, and by the same mechanism, no doubt, that had caused the collapse of his well-muscled ribcage and the partial implosion, albeit bloodless, of the lower half of his skull and jaw.

Pascal, noticing what must have been an obvious change in her skin tone from fair and vibrant to green and peaked, seemed mildly amused—although beneath that playful surface demeanor he couldn't hide an underlying current of concern. "Wish you were back in the Fraud Division, Mademoiselle Crossier?" he asked with a disconcerted grin, standing up while peeling off his medical gloves and tossing the soiled latex into a plastic bag on the floor. He shook his head and displayed a more visibly troubled expression on his face. "This first corpse is a bloody mess but at least interpretable. This other one is quite a bit more puzzling."

"That's an understatement," Michèle replied, choking down her disgust with a shallow cough. She had seen plenty blood and guts over the past year, but nothing as unnatural and distressing as the bizarre injuries of the second victim.

"It seems clear that the younger man was forcefully pushed, either intentionally or unintentionally, onto the statue or podium resulting in a crushed and fractured skull," he continued. "But this other guy appears to have been crushed by an external force, almost like he was squeezed in a vice."

"I was thinking along the same lines," she confirmed. "Maybe an industrial piece of machinery?"

"Maybe; but a device of that sort with enough power to crush something—I mean *somebody*—of this size would be too large and cumbersome to transport here."

"How about a garbage truck? He could have been killed outside and then dragged in here."

"That would fit the bill except that so far we haven't identified any foreign material embedded in his skin, which is oddly devoid of even a scratch or a scrape. I've never seen anything like it."

"That's a problem."

"Yes it is, *plus* that fact that whatever squeezed him did so without causing him to burst. Forgive my crudeness, but one would expect extrusion of his internal body contents outward if we were dealing with a sanitation truck. There's no 'dirty trail' but beyond that, look at the body: it's pristine!"

Of course he was right but her mind kept running in the same thematic direction. "What if the perpetrator used a *portable* piece of equipment, dumping him here immediately after the deed was done, and then pushing or pulling the murder weapon away?"

"Shouldn't a portable device have left scratches on the floor?"

"Maybe not. A modern piece of equipment on wheels wouldn't necessarily leave any marks," she suggested, thinking about it some more. "How about an industrial trash compressor?" Michèle couldn't think of anything else large enough to crush a human being but still small enough to move back and forth and then out of sight.

He wrinkled his brow skeptically. "That sounds like a stretch to me, mostly because we have the same problem explaining why his skin is unblemished and unbroken; and all of his orifices are dry and clean, for God's sake!" He sighed heavily. "But you're the expert in that department so I'll leave the conjecture and hypothesis-proving to you. I should know more about the causes of death after I examine both victims more thoroughly in the morgue."

She looked around the gallery, thinking as she did so about the irony of it all. How bizarre that their investigation involved two unclothed victims and a naked escape-artist 'suspect' in a case whose drama had unfolded in an art gallery depicting nineteenth-century nudes. Some of the paintings were quite explicit, even by modern standards, especially the masterpiece staring them down on the facing wall—a blatantly erotic depiction of the female anatomy painted by Gustave Courbet, titled *The Origin of the World*.

"Whose clothes are sitting in a pile over there?" she asked.

"The exsanguinating fellow with the crushed skull. According to the chief of security who wandered back here a little while before you showed up, he was apparently the night guard *sans* uniform, which he tossed aside in exchange for 'naked'."

"The night guard!?" she exclaimed. Now *that* threw an entirely different light on the whole situation. He had probably let the other two in for a pretty kinky three-some, gone terribly wrong.

"Yes indeed. The other two undressed somewhere else because your officers haven't found a stitch of anyone else's clothing anywhere nearby."

"This *is* very odd." But now was not the time for speculation about who had been fooling around naked with whom, when she had more questions about the evidence collected so far. "Have you found any unusual biologic material belonging to *any* of the three?"

"Yes indeed. We just collected semen from the younger victim's genitals. You see, he was *covered* with it; and so was the floor." He looked down, almost as if he were embarrassed to say it in mixed company. "It seems he had a private 'explosion' occurring in a very public location, right before he met his end."

She simply ignored his discomfiture. "And the mystery-man?"

"There was semen coating the length of his penis, and some pubic hair."

"The woman's?"

"Potentially, given the brunette coloring. We'll do DNA analysis on what we collected to find out." He pointed over her shoulder towards the archway. "We found some small puddles of blood and quite a number of intact hairs with their attached follicles over there that I'm pretty sure belong to our female suspect, assuming she was sitting or lying on the threshold between these two rooms. Additionally, there was a trickle of semen in that location too, which has to mean that one or both men made a 'deposit' in the woman's, um…vicinity, either before or after she took a 'breather' there. We'll make a comparison and I'll let you know the outcome as soon as the results come out."

At that moment the gendarme who had escorted her to the crime scene just a few minutes before leaned over the restricted access tape and called for her into the gallery.

"He's here, Inspector," he announced, referring to Deschamps. "He wants you to meet him in the control room."

"I'll check in with you tomorrow morning," she told Pascale, winking at him flirtatiously, "but call me tonight if your autopsy reveals anything surprising."

She followed her escort down the stairs to the main lobby. "What kind of mood is he in?" she asked.

"He's not happy," the officer said. "You know as well as I do that he never reacts well to these middle-of-the-night call-ins. Good luck." He left her standing in front of the security desk and stepped back into his position near the front door with two other guards.

She shrugged. Luck was for people who didn't have the ability or the know-how to get what they wanted because they earned it. She definitely had the talent, and she knew how to use it. She could handle him, no problem—by taking the burden immediately off his shoulders. And this way, she was very certain, getting the 'lead' in this assignment would be a piece of cake.

CHAPTER NINE

Crossier navigated around a semicircle of four monitors aligned atop a broad, unmanned desk where the museum's night security officer, now lying dead in the special exhibit gallery, usually sat for real-time inspection of the video feed. As she entered 'security central' through the open door behind the monitor desk, she saw immediately that it doubled as a break room since a refrigerator, microwave and sink took up the entire span of the right-side. Over to the left, a long table was positioned against the wall which was home to a built in 'large-screen' that she surmised could bring up the recorded footage from any of the many cameras positioned strategically throughout the building—commanded by a sunken instrument panel centered on the desk-top surface.

One look at Deschamps and she knew that the gendarme wasn't exaggerating; the chief inspector was definitely not happy—not in the least. He was standing cross-armed, literally glaring at the security chief: a burly man with a stomach protruding onto his lap who was diligently occupied with the busy task of fiddling with the table-top controls while typing search criteria into an integrated keyboard. Early in his career, he might have actually looked forward to the occasional phone call in the middle of the night, but not now. She could well imagine that, after thirty-five years, dragging himself out of his warm bed in the dead of night to investigate a gruesome double-murder was no longer his idea of fun. Just three weeks until his well-deserved retirement, the last thing he needed was a new challenge, and Michèle was more than willing to unburden him from that responsibility.

As soon as he saw her, Deschamps demeanor brightened slightly, from hurricane to tropical storm. "It's about time we had a detective in the house. Since you were the first one here Michèle, you're in the hot seat," he growled, as if he was handing out a punishment rather than a reward. But the simple fact that he used her first name was a good sign in itself that his kettle wasn't about to boil. *Perfect,* she thought, *the case is mine.*

"Forensics are still hard at work collecting evidence, up in the main gallery, sir," she said, her tone firm and self-assured. She decided not to waste any time and dove head-on into the circumstances. "The victims are two naked males: one who appears to be in his early thirties with unusual bodily trauma that Pascal and I find very difficult to explain; and the other in his early to mid-twenties, who died of a posterior crushing skull injury caused, it seems, by forceful impact onto a marble statue and/or its podium. They were lying adjacent to each other, with very suggestive positioning."

"What exactly is 'unusual' about the older man's injuries?" he asked, ignoring the sexual commentary…for the moment.

"By all appearances, he seems to have been squeezed to death by some type of external force. I'm thinking that an industrial machine may have been involved in the process." Although there were serious flaws in this theory, she had nothing better to offer on short notice and at least this was something.

"Hmm, that's very strange."

"I agree. After we are finished in here I plan on returning to the crime scene for a more thorough assessment of the situation—with your permission, of course."

He smiled. "Of course. You've been with us for over a year now, Crossier. You seem ready and willing to take charge, so if you want it the lead on this case is yours."

Her mouth nearly dropped open. This was much easier than she thought it would be. *Saint Tropez must be calling!* she thought because usually anything and everything was an argument and a fight with the notoriously hard-to-work-with Deschamps. "Thank you, sir. I'm definitely up for it and look forward to solving this promptly for you."

He sighed. "Before my retirement would be good. I don't want something like this dragging on past my departure. It's not my style to dump a high profile case such as this onto my replacement's lap."

"I won't disappoint you."

"We'll see," he countered as she gulped mentally. "Tell me more about the naked woman that our uniforms seem to have incompetently allowed to escape."

At this point the security official, an overweight man in his mid-fifties, turned towards them and stood up, smiling lecherously at Michèle with crooked teeth before addressing Deschamps in a voice as oily as his hair. "I've found the starting point of the relevant footage depicting your 'streaker', detectives. Whenever you're ready I can run it for you."

Deschamps waved him away dismissively, replying: "In a moment, Laroche."

Michèle still had her audience, it seemed. "There were some drops of blood and strands of hair in another location in the same room, that Pascal feels certain belong to her. He promised a very speedy analysis. It's too early to tell if she was a perpetrator of the crimes, or another victim who was lucky enough to get away with her life somehow while the other two were being attacked."

"Has anyone located her?"

She shook her head, knowing from her contact in dispatch that she seemed to have disappeared, virtually into thin air. "She escaped through the back door of the east wing not more than a minute or two before our uniforms reached the same spot. You see, she locked the entry door into the hallway from the inside, and our uniforms had to double back and retrieve the keys from a ring attached to the dead security officer's utility belt." Luckily she had been thoroughly briefed on the details of the pursuit by her would-be Romeo in the precinct communications office. "A strong possibility is that she had a car waiting for her outside; otherwise, they would have apprehended her immediately. That door opens directly onto a six-step metal stairway and into a short alley that leads in one direction only—out to the street running parallel to the left side of the museum."

His frown of displeasure was so deep it threatened to become permanent on his face. "How many units do we have combing the seventh Arrondisement?" he asked, referring to one of

Paris's twenty administrative districts.

"More than twenty," she said, quoting the information her helpful blue-eyed friend had given her over the phone more than an hour before.

"Double that number," he said. "We have to find that woman!" He turned back to Laroche, ready now to talk video-feed. "Do we have any surveillance footage from the outside of the building? Maybe we can identify the car she left in."

He shook his head. "There are cameras in every gallery which unfortunately were turned off—intentionally it seems—by our late night duty officer; but unfortunately none outside."

"Damn it," he muttered. "She'll be impossible to find now, without an ID of her car."

"We still don't know for sure that she isn't on foot," Michèle responded. "There are plenty of side streets around here, and she might have slipped unseen down one of them."

"This area is very well lit, so if she isn't driving, she should be very easy to spot running around out there totally naked. Make sure we have officers on foot as well as in vehicles."

"Understood, Chief Inspector."

"The mayor will want answers, and quickly." He bit his lower lip: a nervous habit. This case was already getting to him. "A dead body found in one of Paris's premier tourist destinations will make the front page of more than just *Le Figaro*; and this type of publicity won't be good for business." She heard him curse under his breath before re-addressing Laroche. "You're on, Monsieur. Roll the tape."

Laroche swiveled in his chair to face them. "Even if the cameras are manually shut down as they were by poor Gaspar," he explained, "they'll automatically re-boot and turn back on if any of the motion sensors on the artwork is disrupted. My guess is that it was probably the overturned sculpture that did it."

"So what we will be seeing is the 'after-event' footage of the crime scene—correct?" Michèle inquired.

"Yes, unfortunately—because the cameras were dark during all the 'action'. Shall we begin?"

This was a rhetorical question because he already had one finger poised and ready on a computer key while Michèle and Deschamps moved in closer for a better view. He tapped it, making the large-screen come alive.

The alcove room was monitored by a single camera positioned in the corner where two walls (the right one: home to *The Origin of the World*, and the adjacent one located to its left: directly facing the entryway) met, pointed out towards the archway leading to the first exhibit room. There, lying on the floor flat on her stomach, they viewed a motionless naked woman—her body spanning the threshold with her bottom-half in the first exhibit room and her head and torso in the alcove room. Her shapely *derriere*, colored a gentle alabaster, curved round and smooth—tapering down the shadowy midline into highly personal territory unknowingly laid bare by unconsciously parted legs, visible perhaps to another camera angled voyeuristically in the other room, but not from this one. As the feed played on, she moved ever so slightly oblivious to watching eyes, and then raised herself onto her elbows just a few inches upward, as if she had just woken from a state of dense unconsciousness.

"Well she wasn't the perpetrator," Deschamps proclaimed. "If she was we wouldn't be watching her waking up like this. Was she drugged?"

"Very possible," Michèle agreed; "or else she's faking it. This might be scripted; it's hard to tell."

As everyone processed her comment suggesting that the woman could be an accomplice simply playing the part of a victim, left behind on-purpose just to throw them off, the woman rolled over; and after a moment or two of disorientation, she sat up—wincing from a gash on her outer right thigh that was still bleeding, her head down—and scooted over to the archway wall, leaning back on it for support. Then she looked up, and low-and-behold...her face—seen straight-on by the most discerning of visual technology—came into view as clearly as the unobscured salmon-pink caught on camera between her frog-legged positioned limbs.

"Hold on," Laroche exclaimed, freezing the tape.

"This isn't a 'porno', Monsieur," Deschamps chided. "Keep it moving."

"No, that's *not* what I'm looking at, Chief Inspector. It's her face! I *know* that face!

"You *recognize* her, Monsieur Laroche?" Michèle exclaimed. "Who is she?"

Laroche, propelled by the excitement of recognition, hastily entered a series of commands on the keyboard which immediately brought the woman's face into sharper focus and in close-up. "I can't believe this. It *can't* be true!"

112

"Out with it, man!" Deschamps insisted.

"This woman is the Assistant Director of Acquisitions and Special Exhibits: a museum executive named Susanne Bruante."

"Are you sure?"

"Positive. There is no question whatsoever in my mind."

Michèle glanced over at Deschamps and suspected from the look in his eyes that the same thought had just occurred to both of them. "Monsieur Laroche, we are finished here," she declared. "Now the Chief Inspector and I would like you to take us directly to Susanne Bruante's office."

CHAPTER TEN

Little did Nicole know that she had 'timed' her exit from the office perfectly, escaping just in the nick of time by the stroke of intuition's luck rather than because of any type of concrete forewarning.

A nondescript 'sixth sense' coupled with astute observation had served her well. Peering out of the office window, she had had a clear view of the street running parallel to the museum, which led to the left towards the front of the building, and to the right a little bit more than half a block, down the road and away from chaos. After a while, she could see the flashing lights and the uniformed men congregating to the left, which she interpreted as her cue; it was time. If the gendarmes who had been searching for her out there were preparing to come back inside (which she highly suspected) their next stop might be this office; and she had to be sure she wasn't in it when they raided her hiding-place.

Gripping the umbrella like a weapon, she cracked open the door, double checking to make sure that she had pushed the metal button on the office side of the doorknob back in, so that the door would remain locked after she left. If the gendarmes didn't have the key, maybe locking the door would slow them down, buying her more time to put some distance between herself and her pursuers if they thought she was hiding quietly inside. She poked her head out, just a little bit. The hallway, dark and quiet now, might soon be teeming with police again, so now was her chance.

She slipped out into the open and closed the

door as soundlessly as possible, hearing a soft but definite 'click' as it locked behind her. She moved cautiously toward the exit, her steps muted, careful to suppress the echoing tap of her heeled-boots on marble. She wanted to run, but she didn't, telling herself that patience was her friend and panic the enemy. Finally, she reached the exit door. Would it alarm again when she opened it? That would bring them on her for sure. Should she try to find another way out? That would be much too risky, she hastily concluded. *I just need to get out of here…now!*

She took in a breath, preparing herself for the door's triggered siren to give away her location, leading to a frantic chase that would last maybe a block or two—a taste of freedom that would inevitably end in her capture, she feared. *I have no choice.* She put her hand on the metal bar that she had pushed before, expecting resistance; but instead she found it lax and spent, resting flush against the door! It hadn't been reset, she realized, which meant that she could slip out quietly. Luck, so far, was on her side.

One gentle push, met with easy silence, and she was out, a solitary figure in a hat and coat, stepping carefully down the metal stairs until she reached the bottom. She crept alongside the building, hiding in the shadow of a short alley until she reached a shield of bushes near the street, steeling her courage for the next step. The lights, the activity, and the danger threatened from the left, so she would walk the other way, her leisurely midnight stroll offering a quiet escape that she hoped no one would notice. *There is no need to run, just take it slow and easy*, she thought.

She found her surroundings overwhelming, to put it mildly—because accepting the harsh reality of finding herself displaced almost a century-and-a-half into the future did *not* mean that her mind would also agree to take in the wonders *and* the horrors of twenty-first century Paris nonchalantly, and without a few amazed double-takes. She found herself faced with noisy vehicles of painted iron and steel that rolled down the streets of their own accord, and colorful lights at every corner that seemed to give instructions to the passing traffic. Since her survival depended on rapid adaptation, she couldn't waste her precious time trying to sort out the mechanism of her translocation or philosophize on mankind's amazing technological progress over the span of 135 years, so instead she resolved to remain focused on a plan rather than squandering her energy on things she could not change.

The street was clear, so she took a deep breath in and struck out into the open. One block, two blocks, three blocks, then ten…she walked without looking back, praying that no one had noticed her and that she was not being followed. A handful of pedestrians passed her going in the opposite direction, but none of them made eye contact, and none of them seemed the least bit interested in the woman disguised in beige, the collar of her overcoat turned up around her neck and the floral-trimmed fedora pulled down low over her hair and covered brow. Soon enough, she had left the commotion far behind; far enough, she finally decided, that it might be safe to rest. She sidestepped into a dark alley, nestled between a tavern with its lights still on and a closed café: the interior dark and sleeping. She crouched in the shadows with her heart racing, catching her breath and willing herself to stay calm so she could concentrate on the next step. *So far, so good*, she concluded, surprised that her improvised agenda had actually worked. *Not bad for an amateur.*

The city in 2011 bore no resemblance to the Paris she remembered, in her mind's eye. All of the buildings were gigantic, many of them soaring into the sky for miles it seemed, and the streets were cluttered with unmoving parked vehicles: the same ones that she had seen passing her in motion, some of them moving fast enough to rustle the bottom of her overcoat with their swirling, smokeless breeze. Where were all the carriages drawn by horses, in *her* Paris of 1876? Relegated it seemed to her very recent memory, *and* to the printed documentation that she guessed could be found in present day's history books—where mankind's distant reminiscence collided and intermingled in confusing disharmony with *her* not-so-distant recollections.

What should she do now, escaped from the perils of the exhibit hall but thrust unwillingly into the menacing dangers of an unfamiliar time? She fingered the envelope she had taken from Susanne Bruante's office sitting at the bottom of her overcoat pocket, wondering how far it was to *14 Avenue Georges V* and whether she should head north or south, east or west—a futile question, at the moment, since she lacked the most fundamental reference point to even determine these directions. She didn't know central Paris very well. Montmartre was her home, and without a map to guide her she was truly lost. She would have to stop a pedestrian—she had no choice; and so she walked to the end of the alley and watched for a reasonable candidate.

The street was deserted, and she thought it unlikely that anyone except drunks or vagabonds would be wandering the street at this time of night. She noticed an inn or tavern that appeared to be open, but she couldn't risk the public visibility by going inside, since there might be dozens of patrons still waiting for closing time and the last call for absinthe or a final glass of *Marc*. She waited outside; and after fifteen minutes or so, the door swung open, and two men in their early twenties stumbled out, arm-in-arm in a show of masculine affection that could only result from ingesting an excessive amount of alcohol. One of them laughed as the other finished a confused and slurred story about a barmaid and what she might look like naked.

They started crossing the street, so Nicole followed. It couldn't be more perfect. They were men, so she might be able to use her feminine charms to divert suspicion; and they were clearly intoxicated, enough so that they might not think it odd for a woman to be out and asking for assistance in the middle of the night. She unbuttoned the top of her overcoat to expose her *décolletage*, hoping that if she dangled a subtle enticement she might get what she wanted, quickly and easily. When they stopped at the intersection to argue about which way they should go, she approached them from behind and sidled up beside them.

"*Bonsoir,*" she had said, smiling. "You both

seem very happy tonight."

They gave each other a knowing look. She knew exactly what they had in mind, and she would play along until she got the information she needed from them.

"We could be happier," one said. "Would you care to join us?"

"Perhaps." She dug into her pocket and pulled out the envelope with Susanne's address printed on it. "Could you tell me first, please, how I might arrive at this address from here? I am scheduled to meet a friend there; but afterward, I would be pleased to come back and meet you."

They both nodded with enthusiasm. "We live right around the corner," the first one said, leaning close enough for her to smell the yeasty aroma of wine and sundry other *digestifs* on his lusty breath. "Your friend can wait. Why don't you join us now?"

"I am afraid not. He would be angry if I missed our appointment." She winked, with a tilted head and a smile. "When I am finished, I will come right back. Now, what about this address? Is it possible for me to walk to *14 Avenue Georges V*, or must I take a carriage?"

She could have kicked herself. What had she said? Those weren't carriages parked along the street; they must have another name; and now, the two men would suspect that she really didn't belong here. They looked at each other for a moment and then exploded simultaneously in a fit of laughter. "I get it," the first one said, wiping the tears from his eyes. "It's theme night, and the guy on *Avenue Georges V* asked for 'nineteenth century'. Will you do the can-can for him after you lose the coat?"

"Something like that," she replied, relieved. "I can dance naked for you, too; but directions first, if you please."

"It's not that far," the second one explained, eyeing her up and down with undisguised and impatient desire. "Walk fifteen more blocks down this street, then turn left on *Avenue Georges V* and follow it up the hill. '*Maison*' *14* should be five or six blocks from the intersection. The buildings are well marked."

"Thank you." The closest one tried to put his arms around her and steal a kiss, but she backed up a step to avoid the embrace. "Not now, *messieurs*; but I will be back, I promise." Then she turned and ran, as fast as she could, crossing the intersection diagonally to the other side of the street…and she didn't stop.

"Wait," she heard one of them call after her. "You didn't write down our address!"

They didn't try to follow her, but she kept running anyway, leaving three blocks behind her before she finally stopped to catch her breath. After that, Nicole made the rest of her journey slowly, sliding into an alley or pulling her hat down whenever she saw someone coming just to be certain, as she travelled deeper into her lookalike's territory, that no one noticed her. The last thing she needed was a nosy neighbor or a concerned friend cornering her in the shadows and asking questions she could not answer—being an entirely different person who just happened to look just like Susanne Bruante. Finally, the stealth paid off and she found herself standing in front of *Maison 14*.

What next? Either she would find Susanne here or she would not; and if she didn't, she would need to entertain the serious possibility that Nicole and Susanne Bruante were one and the same person. As crazy as it sounded, she was starting to think that maybe her life up until now in the 1800's had been some kind of intricately-conceived dream or delusion, and that her *true* identity—obscured by some strange amnesia induced by mental illness—belonged to this art exhibit hall executive whose residence was right here: on a fancy upscale street in a futuristic yet tangible Parisian neighborhood in 2011.

Perhaps right in *there*, lying in a desk drawer, she would find (after gaining access from the landlord or some other such individual of authority since, after all, she had 'lost' her key) a birth certificate, stamped and official, asserting the fact that she actually *was* Susanne Bruante...and also, specifically *because* of this validated disclosure of her true 'persona', that she was completely and certifiably 'nuts'. Nervous yet curious, and thinking all the while that her perceived state of consciousness and actual *existence* was being put to the test at this very moment, she climbed the half-dozen granite stairs that led to the landing. She tried the handle of the entry door and, disappointed, found that it was locked—which was no surprise but still, she had hoped for easy entry.

She peered inside, confirming what she already knew from the address on the envelope—namely, that *14 Avenue Georges V* was not a single-family residence since, if her 'relative' lived in an apartment designated as *Nombre 3B*, there had to be

121

at minimum two other apartments in the building representing *Nombre 1* and *Nombre 2*. The entryway led to stairs, flanked on either side at the bottom by two separate doorways that obviously belonged to two different apartments on the ground level—most likely *A* on the one side and *B* on the other. She glanced up at three stories of windows, quickly determining that the same arrangement applied to the two upper floors, which added up to *six* apartments in total: *1*, *2* and *3* multiplied by *A* and *B*; and sure enough, six names were listed on a gold-plated panel to the right of the front door, each one with a number and a letter assigned to it, and each one with its own polished call button.

This is very expensive, she thought—*far* above my means. She flashed back to the image in her mind of the little apartment on *Butte Montmartre*, comfortable enough but so plain and practical compared to what she imagined to find behind the doors to *these* fancy living-quarters. The shiny bronze plaque confirmed that *Nombre 3B* belonged to Susanne Bruante, just as the address on the envelope had claimed...and the call button promised to wake her. Nicole pushed it once, then twice; waited and waited; and then pushed it again, and again. Nothing—she wasn't at home.

So here Nicole stood on the landing of *14 Avenue Georges V*, without a plan and no further along in her hunt for a genuine identity and a 'confirmed' personality than she had been a few hours earlier while holed up in Susanne Bruante's office. She had counted on finding living-proof that she was Nicole Bruante rather than someone else—the incontestable human-evidence standing on the

122

other side of this door, groggy and irritated from being awakened from a peaceful sleep by the insistent buzzer. Instead, Nicole had been greeted with silence; so who *was* she really, and what should she do now?

If she looked just like Susanne Bruante—or worse yet, if she *was* Susanne Bruante; and if she were recognized at the museum while she was being chased, where would the police decide to search next, after coming up empty handed at the person-of-interest's workplace? It stood to reason that they would make a beeline to her place of residence; and here *she* was, standing like a sitting duck in front of what appeared to be her own apartment, just waiting for the gendarmes to round the corner and detain her, exactly as common sense would predict.

So where should she go now? For the short term, staying here was not an option; but long term? She had no clue. She had no money, no clothes except for a stolen overcoat, and no identity. Without these basics, how could she possibly survive? *Stop feeling sorry for yourself*, she thought. There would be plenty of time for that later, crouched at the far end of another alley somewhere, far away from the next stop in law enforcement's logical search for Susanne Bruante.

Nicole turned to leave, and that's when the yellow 'carriage' with the word TAXI displayed on its roof pulled up on the curb. A woman, stylishly dressed in a slim-fitting embroidered dress and matching shoes, got out, uttered 'thank you' as she closed the vehicle's door behind her, and turned to climb the landing-stairs. She was holding something up to her ear, talking into it as she walked.

"Of course I gave them his name," she was saying, her voice edgy. "I didn't really have a choice since I needed an alibi. The question now is whether he'll corroborate our midnight quickie or throw me under the bus." As she reached the landing, the woman glanced suspiciously at Nicole, who was standing off to the side next to the front doorway. "Can you imagine they thought I was involved in a *ménage-a-trois* taking place in my very own special exhibit hall of all places; and with the night-shift security guard (who, by the way, I would *never* in a million years even give the time of day let alone have sex with him) and some other guy, probably his lover, who were both found dead on the scene. How ludicrous to think I would sink that low and jeopardize my career with that type of lurid recreation."

Nicole sighed with relief as she recognized Susanne Bruante immediately, thinking: *Thank God I am who I am, rather than her!* So it was that Nicole Bruante found herself standing face-to-face with the woman pictured in the office photographs, her features unmistakable in the soft illumination of adjacent street-lamps tempered by the black-to-grey premonition of pre-dawn, leering back at her with undisguised annoyance like a distasteful version of Nicole's own reflection in a mirror.

Nicole pulled down her hat again to partially conceal the resemblance, thinking that gradual would work better than all at once in terms of the 'shock' factor. "I am looking for Susanne Bruante," she said, trying to buy some time while she figured out the best way to handle her visibly irritated virtual twin. "Do you know her?"

124

"I'll call you back in a minute," Susanne said in a low voice to the object in her hand, which she took from her ear and slid into a side pocket of her handbag. "Who's asking?" she answered, addressing Nicole in a none-too-patient tone of voice.

Nicole had one chance, and she made an instantaneous decision. She removed her hat, so that Susanne would have an unobstructed view of the astounding family resemblance.

"You should recognize me," she declared with a smile. "I am your sister."

CHAPTER ELEVEN

As Susanne Bruante stood on the front step of her flat at about a quarter to six on Wednesday, the first of June—having been nearly accosted by this woman with a very familiar face (*mine!*) dressed in even more familiar overcoat (*also mine!*)—she understood immediately why the police had come so discourteously to call a few hours earlier.

She had been awoken abruptly, at about three a.m., by the insistent buzzing of her door monitor. She thought at first that maybe it was Marcel, although she couldn't imagine why he would feel compelled to bother her here—because they both knew that her apartment was strictly off limits. Earlier that evening and extending past midnight, the Executive Director had enjoyed a quickie with his sexy, sinful subordinate in a hotel room not far from *Musée d'Orsay*, their rendezvous explained away to Marcel Lauren's unsuspecting wife as an unavoidable late night of work at the museum—a last-minute scramble, as it were, to complete an important project before a mandatory morning deadline. Unless they had been discovered, Marcel had no business on the other side of her front door; and even if his bags had been packed by an outraged wife and then thrown out into the street with the thud of finality, there was no way on earth Susanne would have let him in. Their affair, to her, had evolved, essentially, into a business transaction; and as such it should stay right where it belonged—namely, at work, or in a hotel room every now and then…but *not* in her apartment.

She didn't love him—never had and never would. Even from the very start, he was a mediocre distraction, a casual amusement, a temporary stopgap between countless failed relationships, and an eternally grateful recipient of her sexual acquiescence—the latter definition of their *tête-à-tête* an essential component of their relationship that she would never let him forget. One good turn deserves another, as they say, and she quickly learned that sleeping with the 'top dog' was an investment that could yield some very high returns.

Not only that, but the thrill of the tease, and the excitement of seduction, were simply too much fun. She loved the exposure; loved the attention he paid to her body; and loved the effect that her nudity always had on him, every time they met for a roll in the hay. The way he looked at her with undisguised lust reminded her of the days when she would routinely model, nude, for an art class or some amateur painter, her curves immortalized for hundreds of eyes to see when the drawings or paintings of her naked magnificence were exhibited in the university's fine arts show, or at some regional art festival. What a picture-perfect way to live forever, as a perpetually youthful model whose unchanging and unaltered image was captured on canvas for posterity's benefit. The *true* artist's model was someone Susanne had always envied. Perhaps in another life, she would live out that fantasy.

But the benefits of Susanne's periodic physical liaisons with Marcel were hardly one-sided. She surmised that, for her director, she represented a young and beautiful boost to his middle-aged ego—

a dangerous and invigorating contrast to his stagnant thirty-year marriage to a "boring and overly conventional" spouse. He had no intention of leaving his wife for Susanne, thank God, because even if he did, she would never consider marrying him. The only reason she hadn't broken it off by now, truth be told, was because of his position as *Musée d'Orsay's* Executive Director. She might be on top in the bedroom, but in the workplace their positions were painfully reversed. There was no conceivable way she could dump her boss.

The honest truth be told, Susanne had painted herself into a corner, although she would never outwardly acknowledge her mistake. One day, if her relationship with Marcel eventually ended, she ran the risk of losing more than just her special privileges. Regardless of who dumped whom, she would be the ex-girlfriend, a constant reminder to Marcel of his infidelity and a veritable thorn in his side that he would feel compelled, she felt certain, to remove. She might very well find herself transferred to some back office at Versailles—or worse yet, to someplace provincial like Lyon. He would call it a promotion, of course, the irrevocable scribble of his signature on the bottom of the transfer papers sending her away, problem solved once and for all.

That just wouldn't do. Susanne had other plans, and she kept telling herself that if she played her cards right, it would all work out. *Musée d'Orsay* was her life; someday, she would be the Executive Director—or at least, this was her plan. If she could keep Marcel close for just a little longer, he would get his hoped-for appointment to the Ministry of

Culture…and Susanne, being at the right place (naked in his bed) at the right time (whenever he wanted her within reason), would be the logical choice for him to recommend as his replacement. It was perfect, really. And so she diligently met him when he wanted her, even on short notice, biding her time and waiting until the moment when he would get his, and she would get hers.

"I'm coming, I'm coming," she had muttered under her breath, throwing off her comforter and sliding, sleek and naked, out of her sheets. She stretched, leisurely slipping on a sheer peignoir, arm-by-arm. She was in no particular rush; her after-hours caller would just have to wait. Unhurried, she walked on bare feet across the expansive master bedroom, large enough to accommodate two seven-drawer dressers, an armoire, a loveseat, and two chairs. Unintentionally picking up speed, she was in the long hallway now, the polished wood floors cool and smooth on the soles of her feet. To her immediate left, she passed a closed door behind which was a guest room that she used as a resource library and study; and then, nearly halfway to the other end already, she moved beyond another guest room on the right, its door partly opened.

The continuation of the corridor past the two extra bedrooms actually doubled as a full-length gallery displaying, on both sides, her own exquisite black-and-white photographs, conceived as her final project before completing her exchange year of college (majoring in Art History but 'minoring' in Visual Arts) at The University of Chicago, in the United States. It stood to reason that she would have some talent in photography, given her heritage. You see, her blood-line extended back directly to the noted nineteenth century 'father' of this artistic medium, Martial Caillebotte: the less-known and youngest of three brothers—the eldest being the famed Impressionist artist Gustave Caillebotte. Her Bruante great-grandfather (*another* Marcel, ironically) had married Martial Caillebotte's daughter Genevieve, in what was well-known in family circles to be a pre-arranged union contracted by the bride and groom's fathers for the sole purpose of consolidating a large contested inheritance worth millions derived from Gustave Caillebotte's estate. Martial's son, Jean, was a 'ne'er do well' and had been disinherited long before his sister had hit the financial jackpot.

Although she knew exactly where she came from on her maternal great-grandmother Caillebotte's side, Susanne's Bruante-specific lineage had much less certain origins. Why? Because of the anonymous identity of her great-great-great grandfather: intentional for sure but intended to hide who-knows-what, but nevertheless resulting in a non-informative 'blank box' sitting mysteriously like some secret nest on that branch of the family tree. She had a theory, based initially on intuition further instigated by a thoughtful examination of the special exhibit display, about who should be roosting in there. Until recently she had uncovered no hard evidence in support of this hunch, but all that had changed a few weeks ago due to an accidental discovery made by her Uncle Henri.

The photos lining her hallway were her favorite

series of male and female nudes that in her opinion rivaled the sensual 'body-scape' series, on display at this very moment in her uniquely-conceived special exhibit. After years of painstaking research conducted by Susanne and her team, they had come to the conclusion that the old, preserved photographs—discovered along with other priceless pieces of erotic art in a secret room under the stairs at Gustave Caillebotte's country estate—had likely been created by Susanne's great-great grandfather, Martial. They had made a great addition to her exhibit, and appeared to feature the very same model pictured in *all* of the Courbet pieces and the other sundry Impressionist and Realist artists—a painter's living and breathing subject who just so happened to resemble Susanne in every physical respect as well. This could not be chalked up to simple coincidence, Susanne had concluded—a contention that had fueled her model singularity theory *and* her search for a familial connection between herself and the posing nude. As she sauntered proudly past her photographic display while thinking of past, present and future, she finally entered into a sizable front foyer that offered access to the dining room and adjoining kitchen to her left, and to the threshold leading to a spacious living room to the right.

Her apartment was a contemporary flat on the top floor of a three-story former family mansion in the exclusive *Georges V* district. The renovation had resulted in six separate condominiums accessed via a central stairway—one apartment on each side of the stairs, on each of the three floors—and guarded by an electronic call panel. Her entry door lay straight ahead, leading out into the central stairway, flanked by a newly installed, high-tech audiovisual sentry positioned on the wall to the right, and a line of polished bronze hooks for coats and hats to the left. She pushed a button, and the monitor flashed on to the remote display of a face belonging to a very attractive blonde with her hair pulled neatly and professionally back, with blue eyes that challenged their visual target to 'try me' in both Clint Eastwood and Brigitte Bardot fashion equally.

"How can I help you?" Susanne asked warily, holding down another button in order to activate the audio.

"Mademoiselle Bruante?" the woman queried.

"Yes, I'm Susanne Bruante. And who are you?"

Susanne studied the heart-shaped face and the provocative lips parted slightly over a row of perfect teeth as the woman showed her badge to the video camera. "I'm an Inspector with the police. Please forgive the intrusion at this early hour, but I was hoping to question you about this evening," the blonde said, her face an unsmiling harbinger of something serious.

"About this evening?" Susanne's mind raced to put two and two together. Had something happened to Marcel? When he had left the hotel room first, leaving her behind for their usual sequenced departure so that no one would see them together, he had seemed just fine.

"I realize the hour is quite inconvenient, Mademoiselle Bruante, but if you would agree to come down to the station with me, it would make it so much easier to take your statement."

"My statement? I'll need a little more information before I agree to go anywhere with *anyone*, even the police, at this ungodly hour." She was an expert at 'cool, calm and collected' even as she reeled slightly inside with uncertainty. Had something terrible happened to Marcel after they had left the hotel—he first and she after; and was she a suspect because they had been seen passing indiscreetly in front of a nosey lobby-clerk who mentally took note of the temporal association? It would be truly ironic if her carefully planned affair ended up backfiring, landing her in jail rather than in the museum director's swivel chair—a criminal sentence substituted for the professional promotion she had hoped to eventually gain by sleeping with her boss.

"Let's just say that we think you might be able to give us some insight into tonight's incident."

"Whatever happened, I don't know anything about it. Can't we talk here?"

"It would be much better for us if you came down to headquarters given the...*sensational* nature of the circumstances. It won't take long."

They obviously considered her a person of interest in something indelicate. Abruptly, Susanne realized that inviting the police into her apartment had been a reckless and foolish proposition. Of course she had nothing to hide, but who knows what they were looking for and what they were after; and letting them into her place of residence to informally poke around just wouldn't do. Let them get a search warrant if they wanted—but for now, keeping the Trojan horse outside, on her doorstep, was *far* better than letting trouble in; and going down to the station rather than opening her door and asking for problems was a much safer strategy, so she decided to comply.

"Give me a moment to get dressed," she said. "I'll be down in just a few minutes."

"Take your time, Mademoiselle Bruante. We'll be waiting right here for you when you come out."

Susanne had no doubt in her mind, whatsoever, that they would.

CHAPTER TWELVE

Susanne had returned to her bedroom, slipping on a designer dress and a pair of perfectly matched pumps, and tossing her keys into her should bag. *I may as well look fashionable for the police lineup.* A moment later, she had descended the two flights of stairs to emerge at the building's entrance, where she was greeted by the unsmiling faces of one striking female detective and three mundane-looking uniformed gendarmes.

"This must be serious," Susanne said, gesturing at the gendarmes. "I'm neither armed nor dangerous, officers, so I don't think this kind of welcoming party is even remotely necessary."

"Our apologies, *Mademoiselle*; we didn't know who or what we would find when we got here, so we came prepared for the worst." The blonde held out her hand. "I'm Inspector Michèle Crossier, with the *Police Judiciare*. I'm in charge of this case."

The *Police Judiciare*? Everyone knew that the PJ, more commonly called '*the 36*', handled homicide cases. Had Marcel been murdered? If he had, there was only one reason they had come to collect her. It was obvious they must think she had killed him.

"Does it involve Marcel?" she had blurted out, without thinking. Immediately, she knew she had said too much. This business definitely spelled trouble for her, if she had been the last person to see the Executive Director of *Musée d'Orsay* alive.

"Who's Marcel?" Michèle asked, gazing back at Susanne with an inquisitive yet knowing look.

Now I've done it, Susanne thought. Maybe Marcel wasn't the victim after all; or maybe he was, and the astute detective was just playing her. She had best remain quiet from now on, until she learned more about what had actually happened at the museum.

"Just a friend," Susanne had responded, almost under her breath. She decided to try a re-direct. "Can we get this over with quickly? I have a very long day of work ahead of me, since we're about to open a new exhibit."

"I don't think you'll be going to work today," Crossier said, her tone noticeably less polite now than it had been just a moment ago. "*Musée d'Orsay* is a crime scene, Mademoiselle Bruante, and it will be at least a few days before it's open again to employees or the public."

A crime scene attended by the homicide division could only mean one thing. As two of the three policemen escorted her, one on each arm, into the back seat of a police car, Susanne concluded logically that someone had been murdered (maybe Marcel, but probably not given the fact that the police Inspector didn't even seem to recognize the first name of the Executive Director); and, with growing disquiet, that the police considered Susanne to be the prime suspect, for some unimaginable reason.

They rode in silence for a little while. "Where are you taking me?" Susanne finally asked, just to confirm what she already knew.

"Thirty-six *Quai des Orfèvres*," Crossier replied from the front seat.

Just as Susanne had suspected, she would be

questioned at the regional headquarters of the *Police Judiciaire* of Paris, commonly known as the DRPJ. Without traffic, the trip to the criminal investigation division of the *Police Nationale* didn't take long at all. It was 3:30 a.m. when the police car pulled up to the curb in front of the historic nineteenth-century building. She had never been inside the five-storied Napoleonic structure, the impressive granite home to more than two thousand detectives and gendarmes, all of them dedicated to solving the most serious and complicated felonies, ranging from sexual assaults to drug trafficking, kidnapping, monetary fraud, and of course homicide. Well, now it was her chance to take an intimate, too-close-for-comfort tour.

They had escorted her through the front doors and into a two-storied lobby that could easily be mistaken for the entrance to a museum. Crossier led the way across a polished marble floor, showing her badge to an officer sitting behind a security desk who clearly recognized her and nodded her through. They stopped in front of a grouping of elevators rather than continuing on through the hallway to a room that Susanne could see, through windowed double-doors, was bustling with activity. The sign above the door said '*Processing*'.

"So, we're not going in there?" Susanne said, trying to make her tone sound light even though her mood was dark…and getting darker.

"Not yet," Crossier said with unsmiling seriousness.

They took the elevator to the fourth floor, where the doors opened into a small lobby, manned by yet another gendarme who was sitting behind a smaller desk. The wall behind him offered Susanne the greeting she had expected: '*Major Criminal Division, Homicide*' it read. After another flash of her badge, Crossier led the way through an automatic door that opened into a room full of desks, some of which were occupied. "You guys work late," Susanne said. Crossier didn't bother to acknowledge the conversational comment.

They led her to the back, where Crossier motioned her into a dimly lit room. The detective followed Susanne in, closing the door behind them. A distinguished-looking man with a silver goatee, his head mostly bald and the rest shaved close, stood up from his seat at the conference table as soon as the women entered, the gentlemanly deference seeming contrived rather than sincere. Although he was probably in his early sixties, he was dressed more like a much younger man, entirely in black, right down to the tips of his impeccable Italian shoes. His trim and tall build helped to exude a robust air of no-nonsense authority.

"This is Susanne Bruante," Crossier had announced in a matter-of-fact tone, giving the man in black a knowing look. "She wonders if a friend of hers named Marcel was involved in the incident."

The older man nodded acknowledgement. "Have a seat, Mademoiselle Bruante," he offered, indicating with his hand a chair positioned directly across from him at the table. "I'm Chief Inspector Xavier Deschamps. Can I get you something to drink—mineral water, or an espresso, perhaps?" Once again, Susanne felt as though he was trying to disarm her with insincere politeness. His smooth

138

hospitality didn't deceive her.

"No thank you, Monsieur," she replied as she calmly took the seat across the table from him. "Why have you dragged me out of bed at three o'clock in the morning? Do I need to call my attorney?"

"That all depends on whether you're innocent or guilty." As Deschamps spoke, Crossier took the seat next to him. It was now most obviously two against one, and the odds did not seem to favor Susanne.

"Innocent or guilty of what crime?" she countered, knowing without even hearing his reply that the answer would be murder. "I have the right to know what you're accusing me of."

He took a pack of cigarettes from his breast pocket. "Do you mind if I smoke?" he asked.

"It's late, and I'm tired," Susanne replied with annoyance, quickly losing her patience as he lit up. "Could we please get on with the questioning? What, exactly, am I being charged with?"

"Nothing, yet," Crossier answered, picking up where Deschamps had left off. "Could you tell us where you were this evening from approximately twelve to twelve forty-five a.m.?"

"In a hotel room with my lover. Why?" Susanne had answered their first volley in this game of cat and mouse without hesitating, more comfortable now with the concept of defiance, given the fact that she clearly had an alibi at the hour the crime was committed.

The detective and the chief inspector exchanged skeptical glances. "Are you sure about that?" Crossier asked.

"Absolutely certain." Susanne crossed her arms and glared across the table at her interrogators.

"That's funny," Crossier explained, "because a certain museum surveillance recording that documented a portion of tonight's activities in the special exhibit galleries would argue differently."

"What in the world are you talking about?"

"The chief of d'Orsay security identified the woman on that footage as *you*, fleeing the crime scene and leaving two grotesquely murdered bodies behind. Do you still claim you were elsewhere?"

"Of course," Susanne answered, indignant. "It must have been someone who looked like me. There's no other explanation." She looked Crossier right in the eye, saying with her glance 'let's cut to the chase' and asking simply: "Who was murdered?"

Crossier and Deschamps exchanged glances again, this time with uncertainty. "We haven't been able to identify one of the victims yet—but the other one…well, he works at the museum so we're sure you know him…perhaps intimately."

Her heart dropped. There was only one person that she knew from the museum with whom, at the moment, she was particularly 'intimate'…and that was Marcel. But he *couldn't* have been in two places at once any more than *she* could have; so she steeled her nerve and did the same to her facial expression as she countered: "Out with it, then and enough with the cat-and-mouse. Who is he?"

"The night security guard—a guy named Gaspar Charpentier." The look on Deschamps face was almost triumphant. "He is your lover…*yes*?"

Her reaction came out as a snigger. "My lover?

140

Of *course* not! How could you *possibly* think a woman like me would *ever* be involved with someone like him?" There's no question her response was harsh especially considering the fact that the poor fellow was dead, but brutal honesty seemed the most expedient way to get her out of the hot seat and back into her warm bed before sunrise.

"Lover or no lover, you...*or* your 'lookalike' (the word was laced with skeptical sarcasm) escaped from one of the back doors after hiding in your museum office."

"You searched my office? Don't you need a search warrant to do that?"

"Your office at *Musée d'Orsay* is public property," Deschamps said with a shrug. "Monsieur Laroche let us in with the museum master key."

She *never* locked her office door; so already, Susanne knew something was fishy but she would play her cards close for now. "So tell me then, what did you find?" she asked, bracing for the worst but unable to imagine what the 'worst' could possibly be since she had spent the late evening and early morning hours in a hotel room with her boss insuring her professional future and then in her apartment sleeping off the sexual charade...and *not* in her museum office.

"We found some evidence suggesting that you had just been there and left," Crossier had explained.

Now the ridiculous was becoming downright ludicrous. "And how would you know that?"

"Because of a few drops of fresh blood, on the floor next to your desk—right where one would expect it to be if you were sitting in your chair

141

trying to regroup before exiting the back-door."

Susanne shrugged as if to say 'that doesn't prove anything' before saying: "That doesn't prove anything. I wasn't there so the blood must belong to someone else…like the woman you saw on the videotape that you say looks just like me. She must have been hiding in there."

"How, might I ask, could someone have gotten in without a key?"

"That would be easy." *Now* was the time to show her aces. "You see; I never lock the door to my office." It was true, she didn't. What was the point, really? All of the night personnel had a master key, so anyone who wanted or needed to get in would, whether the door was locked or not. Why make it unnecessarily difficult for the cleaning crew? She would always take important documents home with her in her briefcase, or else lock them in her desk drawer, which was accessible only with a tiny key that she kept in a side pocket of her purse.

Deschamps had nodded, taking another drag on his cigarette. "Well, we'll see when we match the blood with yours—assuming you will give us your consent to collect a DNA sample. But before that…let's get back to your alibi. Who, exactly, *were* you with last night?"

Marcel wouldn't like it, but she had no choice. "The Executive Director of *Musée d'Orsay*, Marcel Lauren." She let it hang there in the air, just waiting for them to react…because she wasn't quite sure if they were playing her. A multitude of possibilities lined themselves up in her logical mind like she was a case analyst in a best-selling crime novel.

1. They were being truthful about the second

body being unidentified due to disfiguring injuries, and it wasn't Marcel.

2. They were being truthful about the second body being unidentified due to disfiguring injuries, but the corpse was actually an unrecognizable Marcel. For this scenario to be true, the Executive Director would have had to have been killed shortly *after* he had left the hotel room—his body transported lifeless in a van or the trunk of a car to the museum loading dock with improbable lightning-speed, and then dragged into the special exhibit gallery.

3. They were lying about the body being unidentified and it was actually Marcel, dumped as if by magic in his very own workplace as a twisted message from the mob or another sinister organization angered by some deal-gone-bad or debt-not-paid.

She had no problem whatsoever in thinking selfishly about it, as this was her 'norm'. Behind door number one her alibi was intact and she would be free to go; but open number two or number three (as unlikely as these plot-twists seemed, unless some of the integral characters involved in the nearly-instantaneous 'body-transport' were actually time-travelers) and she was screwed.

"The executive director is your lover?' Michèle asked, raising her eyebrows slightly. The detective seemed mildly surprised at this divulgence but gave no indication that Marcel Lauren and the second body were one-and-the-same. Susanne breathed a quiet sigh of relief as the Inspector offered her paper and pen. "Phone number, please."

"He's married, so please be discreet when you

call him. This is his 'private' cell phone." Susanne scribbled a phone number on the piece of paper, all the while wondering how Marcel would react to receiving a phone call like this from the police in the middle of the night. Not well, Susanne felt sure; but if he was alive (and she was now quite certain that he was), he had probably been awakened already, informed no doubt—perhaps even in person, by museum security, or the police, or both—about the horrifying incident at 'his' museum.

The scene she imagined in her mind actually made her laugh to herself. Marcel was a nervous adulterer, always looking over his shoulder and covering his tracks with an alias, a pre-paid cell phone, and cash rather than credit card transactions. God forbid that his wife should ever find out about his secret trysts with a younger and much more attractive woman. She was a jealous spouse, and Marcel was a weak and timid cheater, who would never stand up and take responsibility for his allegedly justified infidelity.

She could see him now, startled out of a sound sleep as his secret cell phone called to him from the pocket of his pants, which she imagined he had hastily removed and folded neatly on the bedroom lounge chair before slipping quietly under the covers next to his unsuspecting wife. The pre-paid mobile was the only personal number Marcel would ever agree to give Susanne, and now his compulsive attention to discretion would come back to bite him. Susanne smiled to herself (she just couldn't help it) as she envisioned Marcel stumbling over his own feet in an unsuccessful attempt to retrieve the source of his marital destruction before the incessant ringing woke up the unsuspecting Jeanine, who would be snoring on the other side of their king-sized bed.

"Uh, Marcel Lauren here," she imagined him stuttering.

"Who is it, dear?" Jeanine might say, raising herself up on one elbow and squinting into the darkness. "I don't recognize that ringtone—did you change it?"

"It's the police," he would say, taking the call out into the hallway so his wife wouldn't overhear. "There's been a murder at *d'Orsay*," he would stammer, if he didn't know already; but Susanne wondered whether an explanation like that would fly, especially if his jealous wife crept quietly out of bed to listen to his conversation, ear to the door, as he gave his replies in a quiet voice just a few feet away. It depended, really, on what he would say to the insistent detective on the other end of the line, after all. "Thank you for informing me, officer," sounded just fine, but: "Yes, I was with Susanne Bruante at *Le Meridien Etoile*, stepping out on my wife from ten p.m. until one a.m." definitely did not.

Michèle stood up, leaned over the table and ripped the piece of paper off the notepad. "Thanks, I'll call him now." She gazed at Susanne with a slightly condescending smile. "And don't worry, mademoiselle. I'll be discreet."

A moment later, Susanne sat alone with Deschamps, who eyed her up and down, his face a mask that was difficult to interpret. What was his theory? Maybe that she had in fact been with

Marcel at the time of the murders, but at the museum rather than in a hotel room because he was her accomplice? "I wasn't at the museum, and Marcel wasn't either if that's what you're thinking. We had nothing to do with these murders."

"We'll get to the bottom of it," he had said. "We always do."

She felt sure they would. This Chief Inspector Deschamps, so cool and collected, seemed like the type of seasoned detective who always got his man…or woman. But Crossier, all business and the epitome, it seemed, of efficiency, seemed a bit young for a homicide detective and probably had yet to prove herself. A major case like this one would be the perfect opportunity for a woman like her to show her stuff, and even make a name for herself, perhaps at any cost. The drive to succeed and climb the ladder would motivate Crossier to get to the bottom of things all right, but Susanne would have to swim fast in order to avoid getting inadvertently caught in the indiscriminate dredge of the lake bottom.

Who in the world was the victim at *d'Orsay*, and who was the lookalike who had somehow stumbled into her unlocked office, leaving traces of someone's blood on the floor? This whole thing, bizarre and surreal, was troubling; but even more important, so very inconvenient. The museum wouldn't open again for days, and that meant her much-awaited presentation (scheduled for the evening of Monday, June 6) explaining her 'model singularity' theory and introducing some intriguing evidence surrounding the special exhibit and its relationship to her very own family, would probably be postponed.

The door opened, and Crossier entered. She answered Deschamps' questioning gaze with an affirmative nod and then squinted in Michèle's direction. "He confirms that you two were together from ten p.m. until one a.m. at *Le Meridien Etoile*, and agreed to come in first thing in the morning to give a sworn corroborating statement. I guess you're off the hook—at least for now."

If Deschamps felt any disappointment, he didn't show it. "You're free to go," he said, looking past her and gesturing subtly with a finger to someone who stood on the other side of the interrogation room window, "*after* giving us a DNA sample, if you please?"

Susanne stood and reached for her purse. She had nothing to lose and quite a bit to gain, since those drops of blood in her office were *definitely* not hers. "Certainly." The technician to whom he had signaled a moment earlier came into the room with a portable kit; and an hour later, Susanne Bruante stepped out of the police station and onto the curb, sliding into the back seat of the cab that the police had called for her.

And so it was that she now stood on the front step of her flat at 5:45 a.m. with the rising sun behind her and a woman that looked identical to her in front, claiming to be her sister. Sister or not, Susanne had found the naked woman in the museum (or rather, the woman had found *her*) without even trying.

147

CHAPTER THIRTEEN

Henri Bruante put his phone down on the workbench, right next to the open case containing some of his more delicate instruments. Many of the paintings he was hired to restore had foreign material imbedded on the surface, usually from careless storage practices; and *Waking Nude Preparing to Rise* was no exception. God knows how some of the dirt and residue, not to mention the strange fibers that further analysis surprisingly identified as hair, had ended up in this one; and it was taking significantly longer than he had expected, even with the miniature forceps, pick, brushes, and tweezers, to examine the surface and remove the debris without damaging, or even chipping off, the paint.

He had been working for two months by now on this unsigned family painting with its title scribbled onto the backing paper in fading pencil, but with indelible ink carefully traced over the original writing by one of his fastidious relatives with foresight enough to preserve the unknown artist's naming of the provocative piece. The nude painting was originally in his great-grandfather Edmond Bruante's possession but had passed through numerous generations to his sister Joelle. Now it belonged to him, since Joelle, sadly, had succumbed about a year ago to a stroke.

Joelle had been generally uninterested in art and particularly indifferent to 'worthless' family heirlooms; but despite her disinterest had exhibited an extremely territorial attitude towards her inherited possessions. Henri, a well-known and very talented art restorer, had asked her on many previous occasions if he could work on *Waking Nude Preparing to Rise*, but her answer was always 'no'. Now that the painting had been passed on to him due to his sister's death he could finally enjoy a project that he had been waiting for years to begin; and this one, like most of his others, required patience and painstaking attentiveness: both characteristics that he had learned to foster over the past four decades while he had worked as an art conserver.

Immediately after Henri had transported the painting safely to his home workshop, he had applied a layer of facing tissue to the surface in order to hold any loose pigment to areas where the canvas was torn or buckled. He had then taken the oil-on-canvas nude off its cracked and splintered stretcher, laying it face down on the lining table; discovering, then, that the backing had been papered over—a not-uncommon practice that normally wouldn't have made a difference in the process of re-lining. He had almost missed it, but luckily the uneven discoloration had formed the discreet outline of the letter, folded over twice, and hidden ingeniously a very long time ago between the canvas and the paper. Susanne had taken the letter for examination by historical experts and if authenticated, his intuition that one of the French masters had in all likelihood created the anonymous nude (*and* Susanne's suspicion that the model and the artist were *both* responsible for establishing the Bruante family line, late in the nineteenth century) would be confirmed.

Then it was on to the next step. After removing the paper backing and his unexpected find, it had taken him a full week to apply the heat sensitive glue, section by section, to the back of the old canvas and then roll it carefully onto a new one, already suspended on a modern frame loom. Eventually, the glue would secure the canvas, primer, and pigment as a new, completely bonded entity, but that took days. A full week later, after the glue had dried, he had finally been able to start the tedious process of cleaning and restoring the surface, removing the facing paper bit by bit as he worked on a single three-by-three centimeter section at a time.

He used the ground floor of his home in *Saint-Germain-des-Prés* for business first, and pleasure second. Like most art restorers, he was good at what he did because of his own intrinsic talent: oil painting, to be exact—his understanding of the medium lending itself to a profession that began after art school and was still going strong. Although it seemed like just yesterday, it would be forty-one years this year since he had opened his home business right after college, removing all but the load bearing walls on the ground-level floor of his newly purchased city home so that he could devote the majority of the demolished-then-refurbished space to *Bruante Art Restoration Incorporated*, his pride and joy.

Since he had also set aside the back end of the enormous room for his none-too-shabby artistic efforts, he found himself, from the start, spending most of his time downstairs in the wide-open and spacious studio, equipped with fluorescent warehouse-style lighting and concrete floors, stained over the years with splashes of white, green, and black from almost daily paint, solvent, and detergent spills. His living quarters up above (which could be accessed either by an interior staircase or via an outside one, to the right of the building, leading up to a side entry-way door) were modest and slightly cramped; but he didn't care. The three rooms on the second floor, including one that had been converted into a kitchen and a dining room combined, were more than adequate for him to take his meals and to entertain the rare visitor; while in the top room, on the third level (really the attic) he would take his nightly rest, sleeping six hours at the most, always up before the crack of dawn, answering the call of his workshop below, where he would routinely get started with a cup of coffee while the rest of Paris slept.

He didn't need much space, since he had never married and hardly ever had any visitors, except of course for an occasional nephew or niece, or now and then a lady caller. He spent most of his time either in his workshop or on jobs that required on-site attention—like the one he had just finished yesterday for *d'Orsay*.

Certain pieces were either too valuable or just too large and too heavy to be taken out; or, as it happened every so often, the restoration of a piece of artwork might require special equipment that Henri simply didn't have at his home workshop on *Rue du Bac*. Case in point was his contracted *d'Orsay* project, freshly completed: the sculpture in marble, part of Susanne's special exhibit attributed to René Caillebotte and soiled with time, being discovered along with a cache of other erotic pieces in the so-called 'lost collection'. This particular piece, standing about two-thirds of the height of an average-sized man, weighed much-too-much to transport off the premises; but more importantly, Henri had needed access to the portable high-pressure submersion tank in the museum basement to restore it properly.

And so, for the past eight weeks, he had worked on the Caillebotte: his professional obligation, for three or four afternoon hours each day at *d'Orsay*; and on *Waking Nude Preparing to Rise*: his personal pleasure, first thing every morning in the workroom of his residence, until just after lunch. The completed sculpture, cleaned and fully restored just a few days ago, had been installed yesterday on a pedestal in the alcove room of the special exhibit gallery, right in front of a more-noteworthy Caillebotte's sensual masterpiece: Gustave's *The Origin of the World*—ready for opening day of Susanne's 'model singularity' exhibit.

Always an insanely early riser, he had already started where he had left off the day before when his cell phone rang, just before 5 a.m. He had *Waking Nude Preparing to Rise* secured on one of his oversized easels so that he could inspect some of the more problematic areas with a rolling spotlight mounted on top of an optical magnifier, its focus repositioned just a moment ago on the model's auburn hair, brushed in with bold strokes by the artist to cover the rounded top of her left shoulder and the front edge of her arm—extended out and back to support her sitting position, legs folded underneath, on rumpled bedclothes bathed in the

152

suffused light and dappled shadow of early morning. The caller ID told him that his niece was on the line, so he took it after the first ring.

"It's early for you," he spoke into the receiver, turning off the heat-generating examination light to give the century-and-a-half-old paint a breather. He backed up a step, admiring the unsigned and unfinished family cast-off again for just a moment—a beautiful brunette (who just so happened to bear an uncanny resemblance to the person he was speaking to right now on the phone), posing in classic nude-style with her head turned, cradled on the '*V*'-shaped elbow-bend of her raised right arm, intended to mimic a stretch after 'waking' from sleep, 'preparing to rise'. He heard Susanne take a deep breath in. Her calls were frequent, since he and his niece were close…by her standards at least; and he knew immediately from the tone of her greeting that he was in for an earful. She usually had some kind of drama to discuss with him, but he hadn't expected *this*.

"There's been a double-murder at *d'Orsay*, and I'll give you one guess who was just dragged into police headquarters for questioning as a suspect." If she had expected him to actually offer a conjecture, he had missed his chance because she continued to race on without taking a breath. "They still think I was there and had something to do with the crime, even with my alibi. The blood won't match, though. It's not mine, thank God."

"Slow down," he said, navigating around the end of the custom-made table that occupied the central space of his studio and extended from one side of the room to the other, spanning a length of at least eighteen feet. The workbench, if it had been used for a banquet instead of as the cluttered home for all of Henri's tools, supplies, and restorations-in-progress, easily could have seated twenty. "Could you start over, my dear? You're talking a mile a minute." He sat down on one of two utilitarian but decorative stuffed-chairs angled to partially face each other, positioned on either side of a small circular serving-table in the right-front corner of the room. From what he had heard so far on the other end of the phone-line, he was likely in for an earful so he might as well make himself comfortable.

He could hear her take in another breath and then let it out slowly. "Okay. Sorry, *Ton-Ton*." She occasionally used the traditional French diminutive for uncle that harkened back to their abbreviated relationship when she had been a little girl, but only when she really needed something. His niece was definitely a woman who could take care of herself, and she would never come right out and ask for help; but he knew her well enough by now to understand the implied meaning in this word choice.

Susanne, who was actually his great niece, was his nephew Didier's only legitimate child; and Susanne's childhood, from an emotional if not from a financial standpoint, had not been an easy one. The divorce had been anything but amicable, and her mentally ill mother—bipolar, with a touch of undiagnosed but inarguable psychosis—did everything in her power to keep the six-year-old Susanne away from her father, as well as anyone else who carried the Bruante name. Strong-willed and difficult to brainwash, Susanne didn't believe her mother's ranting accusations. At age sixteen, she took the matter into her own hands and embarked on a secret search for her father.

It hadn't taken her long to find him. He was still living in Paris, not even two kilometers from the house where he had endured co-habitation with her mother until he simply couldn't stand it any longer. A general internist-physician with a busy practice and a kind and gentle demeanor, Didier Bruante was nothing like the monster that her mother had described. Although Susanne had struggled to understand his passive acceptance of the father–daughter estrangement her mother had insisted upon, their two meetings went a long way toward reviving an affiliation that should have been permanently damaged by a decade of heartbreak.

It was ironic, really, that he had died just as Susanne's hope for rediscovering their relationship had started to come alive. He was walking to meet her for lunch, no less, immediately after making his teaching rounds at the hospital on a cold and frigid Saturday afternoon. The hit-and-run accident had killed him instantly, leaving behind a sizable estate that he had willed to Susanne as his sole heir, the money a poor substitute for an absent father, not even forty, who had now been taken from her for good.

A few years later, liberated by her mother's death from a stroke at an early age, Susanne reconnected with Henri too. 'Cher Ton-Ton', she used to call him when she was only four or five, in the days before her mother had isolated her from everyone who had been even remotely associated with Didier Bruante. Having no children of his own, Henri had adopted Susanne in spirit, hoping she might be the daughter he had never had; but Susanne was far too emotionally damaged to let anyone come that close to her.

Henri had watched sadly as Susanne moved from one relationship to another, always running before the roots of a romantic attachment could take hold, long before there could be any risk of being committed to anyone long term. It was painful for Henri to watch; yet oddly enough, Susanne seemed perfectly happy with her loveless existence, interspersed every now and then with a short-lived and superficial affair, often sparked by her nude-modeling side-line which would generate one flash-in-the-pan lover after another beginning as early as her college-years, at the University of Paris or in America, while she was an exchange student in Chicago. Now that she had graduated from post-adolescence, entering the work-force as a respected museum executive, her ever-therapeutic 'naked' hobby had taken a grudging backseat to a life that had become unhealthily focused, to the point of obsession, on her profession and career.

"Explain, now, about these murders and why they think you're involved," Henri said evenly, reaching for the cup of coffee, already growing cold, that he had left on the center-table next to the chair he now sat in, when he had begun his workday almost an hour ago.

"They came knocking on my door at about three and dragged me out of bed for questioning at the police station. Two naked men were discovered in the special exhibit gallery—both of them dead; one of them a security guard at the museum, who was killed after his head was applied to your

156

restored sculpture; and the other one unidentifiable due to what they described as very gruesome injuries. The cameras were off when the murders were committed but turned back on when the Caillebotte piece was overturned."

That sculpture, although unfinished, was a masterful and beautiful piece that had taken hours of painstaking attention to detail, to clean and restore. "Was the sculpture damaged?"

"It more-or-less fragmented…according to the police. I'm not sure if it's repairable, although I haven't seen it."

What a shame; but perhaps *d'Orsay* would hire him to fix it. After all, he was well-known as an expert in impossible reparations. "And aside from something criminal occurring in an exhibit that you designed and created, involving a piece of artwork that took me *months* to preserve—how are you even remotely implicated?"

"Because a nude woman was captured on the videotape footage fleeing the scene; and apparently she looks just like me."

He hesitated, but decided he had to ask. With Susanne, anything was possible. "The woman they saw on the videotape, Susanne, didn't happen to look like you for a reason, did she?"

"Please, Uncle Henri," she said. "I have an alibi."

"Well, that's a relief. Who?"

"Marcel Lauren."

"The Executive Director of *d'Orsay*?" He couldn't keep track of her fly-by-night affairs, and he had long since stopped asking. "He's married, Susanne!"

"It's nothing serious, just a pragmatic little affair that I hope will pay off for me big time, in the end." He heard her rifle through her change purse. "Hold on a second, I have to pay the cab driver." After a brief, muffled conversation, he heard her open and close the taxi door.

"Did you give the police his name?" Henri knew Marcel Lauren, since he was the person who signed Henri's paychecks whenever he was contracted to do work for the museum. *D'Orsay's* Executive Director would be none too pleased to have his dirty laundry exposed for everyone to see.

"Of course I gave them his name," she replied, picking up the conversation where they had left off. "They would have detained me if I couldn't produce an alibi. Apparently the woman they saw on the digital camera-feed could pass for my twin."

He heard some noise in a background, a woman's voice perhaps. "I'll call you back in a minute," Susanne said in a low tone; and a second later, the call disconnected.

He set his cell phone on the serving table next to the stuffed-chair he was sitting on. Should he just wait here for it to ring again? Unlikely. Susanne hadn't asked for his help, but there was no question in his mind that she needed it.

He picked up the phone again and slid it into his front pocket. He carefully covered *Waking Nude Preparing to Rise* with a sheet, just to make sure that no one could spot it from one of the windows. One could never be too careful—because he knew now that the painting was not only priceless, but also of huge significance to the art world as a lost-but-now-found Realist masterpiece. He felt certain that his sister Joelle would be stunned speechless from beyond the grave because he had more than enough evidence now, especially with the letter, that *Waking Nude Preparing to Rise* was probably worth millions.

After grabbing a light jacket, he set the security alarm by punching in a series of numbers and then stepped outside and triple locked the front door. He peered through the captain's window to the right of the entryway, just to double check. Satisfied that the painting was safe and sound, he put his hands in his jacket pockets and began the forty-minute walk across town to *Avenue Georges V*.

CHAPTER FOURTEEN

"You're the woman from the museum that the police are looking for!" Susanne declared in an accusatory tone tempered by a tentative sense of relief. The naked woman in the museum had somehow found her, which meant that Susanne was off the hook. *It couldn't be more perfect*, she thought, reaching in her purse, this time for her phone rather than her keys while thinking with pleasure that one simple phone call would do it, solving all of her problems in the blink of an eye.

"Wait." The woman was right in her face now, desperate it seemed to stop Susanne from making that call. "Look at me and tell me what you see," the woman insisted, grabbing Susanne's wrist to prevent her from retrieving her cell. She could see her, all right—bedecked in *her* hat: a unique, floral-trimmed fedora, available only by special order; and that wasn't all. The thief was wearing *her* coat, *her* boots—*and* her face, right down to the tiniest freckle.

"Please," the imposter said, and their eyes locked—identical shades of hazel, Susanne couldn't help but notice. "My name is Nicole Bruante. I think I am your sister."

The woman's manner of speaking was formal, proper, verging on ceremonial. Odd, how she used the antiquated pronouns—for instance, *vous* instead of *tu*. No one did that anymore. There was something very wrong with this picture...and also something very wrong with the woman standing in it, who claimed to be her sibling.

"I think not. I don't have a sister," Susanne said, indignant; but as she stood, face-to-face with this woman who could very well pass for her twin, she began to wonder.

"It is a long story," the woman said, looking furtively over Susanne's shoulder as if she were being pursued. "We should talk about it upstairs."

"I'm not so sure I want to harbor a fugitive." Sister or not, affiliating herself with a double-murder suspect was simply not on Susanne's agenda.

The woman stepped closer to Susanne. "I think it would be best for everyone involved if you let me in," she said, her voice steady but her speech rapid, giving the distinct impression of controlled desperation.

"And why is that?"

"Because I am very confused. I do not know what happened at the museum, but perhaps you were involved you, somehow. If the police find me, your name will come up." The woman who claimed to be named Nicole gave Susanne a knowing look. Yes, Susanne's name would come up—because this lunatic would make sure it did. "It could go very badly for both of us," the woman continued. "Do you really want to risk it?" Her eyes narrowed, emphasizing the threat; but her tone was distinctly conciliatory. "Please—I will explain everything upstairs."

Susanne took a moment to deliberate the pros and cons. She had a rock solid alibi, so anything Nicole said to the police about her wouldn't carry much weight; but still, explaining away their association, now that Nicole had made contact,

161

might not be that easy. Susanne didn't need any more trouble with the police than she already had, and any further implication in the *d'Orsay* incident could create a mess that would take considerable time to mop up. For the moment, damage control was the name of the game; and there was no question about it—letting Nicole in would achieve just that.

Susanne put on her best look of concession. "All right, I'll let you in, but you have to promise to behave. Turn out your pockets, please. I need to make sure you aren't carrying a weapon."

Nicole pulled out the lining from the two front pockets of the overcoat, proving to Susanne that she wasn't armed. Susanne nodded. "Now do the same for whatever's underneath."

"There is nothing underneath. I am naked. Do you want me to show you?"

That was odd, to be sure, but Susanne wasn't one to judge too severely when it came to the lack of clothes. She had done her share of figure modeling, and she was the first to admit that she liked the feel of nothing at all between her skin and the outside world. "Keep it on," she replied. "We'll save the peep show for later."

Nicole moved aside, but then made sure she was the first to enter when the keycard tripped the electronic lock to open. "Third floor?" she called to Susanne over her shoulder as she started up the stairs.

This Nicole had chutzpah, Susanne had to give her that; but admittedly, if their roles had been reversed, Susanne would be doing the exact same thing. She couldn't help but admire the girl's

162

audacity. "First door to the right. I'd tell you to let yourself in, but I have the key," she added sarcastically.

As she trailed a few steps behind her determined lookalike, Susanne came to the smug conclusion that her chess pieces were lined up, prepared for 'checkmate'. In a moment, she would have the unsuspecting Nicole cornered in familiar home territory, and the game would be hers. It definitely worked in Susanne's favor to have Nicole continue to believe that her couched attempt at blackmail had actually worked. The longer Nicole erroneously thought that she had the upper hand, the better. This would give Susanne more time to work out the best timing for her phone call to the police. Kudos to her.

They reached the top of the stairs, and Susanne opened the door. "Make yourself at home," she said, leading Nicole to the right and into the dining room. It couldn't hurt to give the impression of hospitality, to keep Nicole's guard down; plus, befriending a crime scene eyewitness had certain advantages. Nicole would probably be able to provide some very useful information that might go a long way toward explaining exactly what had happened at *d'Orsay* earlier that morning.

"I think we got off on the wrong foot. Why don't we begin with a fresh introduction?" She offered her hand. "I'm Susanne Bruante. Who, exactly, are you again?"

"I told you, I am Nicole Bruante. You and I share more than just a name, I believe. We are related, I am sure." The girl persisted in speaking her antique version of the French language. This

163

much, at least, didn't seem contrived.

"I thought you said you were my sister?"

Nicole gazed back at Susanne defiantly. "Look at yourself in the mirror, and then take a moment to look at me. How could we be anything but sisters?"

Nicole had a point. Unrelated people sometimes looked the same, but to this extreme? Could they *really* be sisters? She didn't know much about her father's personal life, either before or after his association with her mother; so theoretically, Susanne could have a multitude of half-siblings out there, just waiting to be discovered. Henri, being the self-designated family historian, would probably know. She'd call him back in a little while and find out.

"I can see the resemblance as well as you can," Susanne replied nonchalantly. She had moved from the foyer into the dining room, making a beeline for a liquor cabinet standing against the far wall. It wasn't even close to cocktail hour, but she could sure use a drink. "Would you like a drop of brandy, or a glass of wine?" This time, her offer was genuine, more or less. Susanne had nothing to lose and much to gain by appearing hospitable.

"No thank you." Nicole pulled out a chair from the dining room table and helped herself to a seat. She looked exhausted: a woman who had unquestionably been put through the wringer. Whatever had happened at the museum, even Susanne the cynic could see that Nicole had been on the receiving end, rather than the delivery end, of something terrible. Yet one could never tell; appearances were often deceptive. Lucrezia Borgia had fooled everyone too.

"How about something non-alcoholic?"

"Some water, or a café, would be nice."

Susanne poured herself some sherry into a wine glass and set it down in front of the seat directly across the table from Nicole. "I'll be right back," she said with a disarming smile.

Susanne pushed her way through the swinging door that led from the dining room into her kitchen, all granite and marble and equipped with the latest equipment incorporated tastefully into the floor plan. Feeling hungry herself, she decided that it couldn't hurt to offer Nicole some food. She found a fresh baguette on the bread shelf, some *Brie* and *Camembert* stacked neatly in the back of her refrigerator, and a bowl of fresh fruit, just replenished, on the center island. A moment later, she returned to the dining room with a heavily loaded tray.

Susanne sat across from Nicole and watched as the woman helped herself to the food and drink with measured restraint. She was obviously parched and most likely famished but seemed determined to disguise any sign of weakness. She picked some cheese from the tray, sliced a pear in half on the plate in front of her, and carefully poured some ice water from a pitcher into the crystal glass that Susanne had just retrieved from the china cabinet.

"You must be hungry," Susanne commented, watching Nicole's mannerly efforts with a half-smile that she managed to hide behind her glass of sherry.

"Mostly thirsty," Nicole admitted. She drank the water in gulps, despite herself. After Susanne had let her indulge herself for a while, she decided it

165

was time to get some answers.

"So, what happened at the museum?" In her usual fashion, Susanne got right to the point. The time for small talk was over.

"I am not sure," Nicole answered. Susanne studied the woman's face, which no longer wore a mask of defiance. Perhaps she was ready to come clean.

"What, exactly, do you mean?"

"I think I was knocked unconscious. I do not remember anything, not even being hit in the head."

"You must remember something."

Nicole shook her head. "Nothing. It is all a complete blank."

The way her gaze deviated down and to the side, without making eye contact, made Susanne suspect that Nicole was not being entirely truthful. But she wouldn't get far with the interrogation if she accused the woman of being a liar—getting her defense up from minute 'one'. "Let's back up, then. Where were you right before the incident?"

"I told you; I do not remember anything."

Amnesia? Possible, if she had really sustained a concussion; but more likely she was just faking it. "You know your name, though," Susanne pointed out, still the unwavering skeptic.

"True, but that is all. I have no idea where I live, what I do, or even who I am."

Was she telling the truth? She seemed sincere, but Susanne had learned, over the years, to trust no one, and she wasn't about to start now. "How did you end up here, then?" Susanne asked. If Nicole had truly lost her memory, then how in the world had she known where to look for her long lost sister? *Let's see how you answer this one.*

"When I was trying to escape from the museum, I hid in the first office I could find that was unlocked." She shrugged. "It was yours, believe it or not. I know it sounds as if I am lying, but it is true. I saw your picture on the wall and recognized the resemblance between the two of us immediately." She pulled an envelope from her pocket, tossing the evidence on the table in front of Susanne. "Here, look for yourself. I found this on your desk. Your address is on it," she explained with finality.

Susanne picked up the letter, appearing to confirm the plausibility of it all with a subtle nod of concession. She still had big-time doubts, but she would continue to string Nicole along so she wouldn't let her guard back up. The fact remained that Susanne never, ever locked her office door, which meant that Nicole could have very well ended up in Susanne's office by accident—a pure coincidence, plain and simple.

"What about the two men?" Susanne asked, moving on to another line of questioning. She felt as if she were the detective now, and Nicole the suspect: guilty as charged.

"I knew one of them, but not the other. The moment I gazed upon his face, I had a flashback." She looked down, embarrassed. "I think he shared my bed."

Susanne laughed; she couldn't help it. "There's no crime in that, unless you killed him afterward." *Got you, Nicole.* "I assume you're referring to the security guard? His name is Gaspar Charpentier, in case you forgot. Was he your lover?"

167

She shook her head. "No, *that* one was not my lover; but I think the other one was. And no, I did *not* kill either of them." Now the tears started rolling. "You should have seen his body. It was so beautiful before the...*accident*. He must have been crushed by something very heavy. Never could I have done such a thing." Just at that moment the overcoat slipped over Nicole's right leg, revealing a large bruise and a jagged cut that was traced with coagulated blood, located on her outer thigh. So *that* was the source of the blood-drops in her office that the police had referred to and that, at this very moment, they were probably testing for a DNA match.

How had Nicole gotten into the museum? What had happened to her unfortunate friend, *and* the night guard whom she claimed she didn't know? How had she been injured. And, last but definitely not least, who the hell was she? Susanne would get her answers, by God, starting with the last question first. She walked over to the credenza and picked up her landline.

"What are you doing?" Nicole asked. She seemed oddly fixated on the phone, almost as if she had never seen one before.

"Calling my uncle back," Susanne replied. "I have a feeling that he'll know who you are."

His mobile phone only rang once before he answered. "I'm downstairs," Henri's voice said. "Why don't you buzz me in?"

"Downstairs?" Susanne repeated, surprised.

"I thought you might need my help," he said; "so here I am."

CHAPTER FIFTEEN

Henri waited for the click of the lock, its mechanism remotely tripped by Susanne upstairs, allowing him entry into the softly lit stairway of the condominium. He took the ten steps or so that led to the first landing, then another ten in the reverse direction to floor one, repeating it again until he reached the third floor. He didn't have to ring the bell, since Susanne was waiting for him, standing partly in the hallway, one shoulder and a leg in the door threshold to prevent them from being locked out. It looked almost as if she might not let him in.

"I have a visitor," she said immediately.

"The pragmatic affair?" he asked, wondering why she would care if he met yet another one of her easy-come, easy-go love interests…even if *this* one was her boss.

"No. She says she's a Bruante."

Now that was unusual. In general, Susanne didn't care one iota for family—with the exception of her recent art-history research into their 'celebrity' heritage, and a grudging fondness for her great uncle. Susanne had adopted Henri as a surrogate father of sorts, whether she cared to admit it or not, after Didier had died suddenly. Having been unable to cultivate a meaningful relationship with her own father, she had half-heartedly nurtured a tenuous emotional bond with her great-uncle. She still played her cards close to her chest, and refused to let him entirely in, but it was something. In reality, Henri was the closest thing to a father that she had ever had; and by the same token, she functioned in some respects as a daughter to him. Regardless, hosting a relative would be drastically out of character for his niece, even if it *weren't* well before seven o'clock in the morning. Had one of Susanne's cousins come to call, perhaps? They were plentiful, but he couldn't imagine any of them fraternizing with his niece at any hour.

"Are you going to let me in so I can see who it is, or do you want me to guess?"

"She was waiting for me outside when the taxi dropped me off. She's the woman the police confused with me—the suspect from the museum. Imagine, she fell right into my lap! I'll be off the hook the minute I turn her in."

"Hold on, Susanne. Didn't you say she was family?"

"Yes—or at least she claims to be."

"Well if she is, you can't just throw her to the dogs." This was just so typical of Susanne. Henri had learned to overlook her selfish side, choosing to focus instead on her other qualities. She was an astute art historian and scholar, with a master's degree that had focused on the pre-Impressionist Realist movement; a skilled photographer, who had chosen to put her talent aside, for better or for worse, in order to focus on her successful career as a museum curator; a one-time figure model: a beautiful woman who had posed nude in her student days, not that long ago, as a hobby, when she probably could have made it a vocation of sorts if she had just set her mind to it; and (as Henri had to keep reminding himself) a good person he believed…deep down. It wasn't Susanne's fault that her childhood had been emotionally troubled. Henri

170

was, if anything, patient; and he had never given up on his complex niece. "Did she kill anyone?" he asked.

"That's hard to tell. She says she can't remember what happened—some kind of post-traumatic amnesia, she claims. I'm not sure I entirely believe her."

"Let's go in, then, so I can see for myself. If she's a Bruante, chances are I'll recognize her."

"You'll recognize her, all right," Susanne commented under her breath, stepping back through the doorway with Henri followed close behind, wondering what in the world she had meant by that. They passed through the foyer to the right and there she was, sitting at the dining room table with her back facing the entryway; and Henri abruptly understood. She was a dead-ringer for Susanne.

Hearing them behind her, the doppelganger turned her head and shifted in her chair so that her body faced him in profile. The overcoat she wore, draped loosely over her body and falling to the side so that her right leg was exposed, did little to hide her apprehension or her injury: a jagged gash lined with dried blood that slashed through a large bruise on the outer aspect of her thigh. He could tell immediately that she was trying to put on a brave face; but that face, at the moment, had turned a few shades paler than ashen accompanied by an expression that seemed to harbor a spark of recognition that seemed to mirror his.

"It's you!" The woman pushed the chair back abruptly to stand, grabbing the edge of the table weakly for support but then her eyes visibly rolled back in her head. "I feel so dizzy, all of a sudden,"

171

she murmured; and in the blink of an eye, before Henri could move, she was on the floor.

Henri ran to kneel beside her, reassuring himself with two fingers on her neck that she had a strong pulse. She hadn't hit her head on the table, thank God. "Help me move her over to the couch in the living room," he said, all the while wondering if he and this woman had perhaps met before, explaining her reaction to seeing him. Was she a second or third cousin once or twice removed, who had met him once when she was a child? If they had had contact, it was not anytime recently because in her present state of maturity, there is no way that Henri could have overlooked her striking (no...*identical*) resemblance to Susanne. Well they would know soon enough, once they revived her.

Susanne took the woman's feet while Henri lifted her off the floor with two hands hooked under her arms. "Do you know her?" Susanne asked as they managed to half-drag, half-carry their unconscious guest through the dining room and foyer and into the living room. He shook his head. "No; but she certainly seemed to recognize me. We can explore this topic further once she wakes up; but the pressing issue right now is this gash on her leg. Do you have a first aid kit? If we don't tend to it, it might get infected."

His tone was more than a little bit accusatory so Susanne didn't argue, fetching the kit from her bathroom with sheepish obedience. "Can't you see this woman has been traumatized?" he said harshly when she had returned. "She needs a bath, food, and a warm bed. If you're still thinking about turning her in, you can do it tomorrow."

172

Susanne's face blushed red. "I hadn't decided about that one way or the other, *Ton-Ton*. I wanted your opinion first."

Henri took a deep breath to calm himself. Susanne had called him, after all, and she usually followed his advice when she bothered to ask for it. "Well, my opinion, since you've asked, is that we should try to avoid drawing premature conclusions. I can tell you right now, Susanne, this woman is no murderer. With this monstrous bruise and the fresh laceration, I'd be willing to bet that she was another victim…and one who barely escaped with her life."

"I don't necessarily disagree. It's just that her story sounds so outrageous. She actually thinks she's my *sister*, Henri. You and I both know that I don't have a sister."

He paused for a pregnant moment and then said: "Actually, Susanne, you might." He had never told her, because she had never asked; plus, the embarrassing incident was nothing less than a family scandal. To Henri's knowledge, Didier had never even been in touch with his child, conceived when he was a minor—the result of a shocking affair with a household domestic.

Susanne looked back at him, dumbfounded. She opened her mouth to say something, but nothing came out. This was the first time that Henri had ever seen Susanne at a loss for words.

"Her name was Monique Montague," Henri explained to his speechless niece as he sat down on the end of the couch in the empty space just beyond Nicole's still-motionless feet. "She was a maid, living in the servant's quarters on your grandmother's estate—a beautiful woman, in her late thirties or early forties when your father became involved with her. He was only fifteen years old at the time."

Susanne was still in shock. "Your grandmother, God rest her soul, was furious when she found out about the pregnancy," he continued, using this rare opportunity to provide an explanation without being interrupted by his customarily mouthy niece. "My sister and Monique were roughly the same age, and her son: your father, was an underage teenager. Your grandmother made certain—with money, legal maneuvering, and more—that the scandal would remain a secret forever. She drew up the papers and had Monique sign a no-contact agreement—in exchange, of course, for a sinfully large sum of money."

Henri remembered that day, when Monique had been quietly escorted into the Mercedes that had pulled up in front of the family mansion. Henri, fourteen years younger than his sister Joelle, and only three years older than her favorite son, had really been more like a brother to his nephew Didier. Henri had known about his nephew's affair, and in truth he couldn't really blame him. Monique would be difficult for any man to resist, at any age.

"Did he love her?" Susanne finally asked.

Henri shook his head. "I don't think so. Honestly, I don't recall any tears that day my sister had her taken away."

"What about the baby?"

Henri shrugged. "My sister had a very strong will and was very persuasive, to say the least. Monique and her unborn child were sent away, their memory swept under the carpet. We never heard

174

from her again, which was my sister's intention precisely. I don't know for sure if the pregnancy came to term; and if it did, the child may have been a girl...*or* a boy. You definitely have a sibling, Susanne; and it *could* very well be her." He nodded in the direction of their still-unconscious 'relative'.

Susanne regained her composure as she thought through this information. "So, Nicole could very well be my older half-sister," she said quietly, almost to herself.

"Is her name Nicole?" Henri asked, his curiosity piqued.

"That's what she said. Nicole Bruante."

Interesting. Nicole was a family name belonging to Susanne's great-great-great grandmother. "I'll do some investigating," he promised. "With a little luck, I can probably find out what happened to Monique and your father's illegitimate child." He nodded at Nicole, who had just started stirring. "I think it's very possible, Susanne, that you've just been reunited with your long-lost half-sister." He shook his head in quiet disbelief. "My God, Susanne—you and she are identical. If someone told me that you and she were twins who had separated at birth, I wouldn't pause even a moment to doubt it."

He saw Nicole's eyes flicker open. She slowly raised herself up on one arm into a sitting position on the couch, her legs folded under her to the right, with her left arm extended backward onto the armrest for support. Then, turning her head painful to the right side, she rested it in the crook of her other arm that she had raised and bent at the elbow—positioning it in such a way behind her

175

head that she could rub the back of her aching neck with her palm. The way she was sitting looked oddly like a pose; and it was then, in an instant, that he knew why the scene looked so familiar. As Henri sat on the edge of the couch in Susanne's apartment, he found himself staring at a bizarre modern day replica of *Waking Nude Preparing to Rise* featuring a perfect replica of the painting's model; but rather than naked, the 'living' artist's subject right next to him was dressed in an overcoat as her sole piece of outer-wear instead.

Nicole sat up completely, immediately breaking her pose; but even with the change in position, Henri's strange feeling of déjà vu couldn't help but linger. Henri had originally been drawn to *Waking Nude Preparing to Rise* when he saw it as a child, hanging forgotten in a back hallway of his sister's house. When he asked about the model, Joelle shrugged.

"She is someone unknown, painted by someone equally unknown." It was only later when his great-niece, Susanne, had replaced the flirty innocence of her adolescence with the full-grown piquant of truly stunning womanhood that he had noticed the resemblance; and now, one falling domino had toppled the entire circular line in one brief instant. The model in the painting looked identical to Susanne; the model in the painting looked identical to Nicole; Susanne and Nicole looked identical to each other; and all *three* women—two from the twenty-first century, alive and well and staring each other down at this very moment in the very same room; and one long-deceased from the nineteenth century but forever alive as the subject of a

176

mysterious painting—could easily pass for sisters in-triplicate.

"What happened?" Nicole asked, rousing Henri from his philosophical ponderings. "My head is pounding."

"You passed out," Henri said. "How do you feel?"

"Dizzy."

"Nothing some rest can't cure," Susanne said, almost dismissively. "I'd like to introduce you to my Uncle: Henri—but maybe you know him already?"

Nicole looked confused. "I am not sure what you mean."

"When you saw me walk into the room, you said: 'it's you' as if we had met before," Henri clarified. "Have we?"

Nicole looked down, either from embarrassment or as a way to avoid eye contact— he wasn't sure which. "Oh, that. Well, I saw a picture of you when I was hiding in Susanne's office, so…that's what I meant."

Henri nodded, satisfied. So they did *not* know each other. "It's very nice meeting you, Nicole. I'm here to help figure out who you are."

Nicole looked up and made eye contact with a gaze that seemed intelligent and sincere. "It is a pleasure making your acquaintance as well," she replied, using the formal *vous* rather than the familiar *tu*. It was strange, Henri thought, that she would choose such an outdated grammatical convention. That old French linguistic standard had died out long ago; and for someone of Nicole's generation, using the overly polite form of the pronoun "you" was almost unheard of.

"We'll talk some more and figure everything out; but first, let me tend to that cut on your leg. Afterwards, I'm sure that Susanne would be happy to show you where you can clean up and then sleep for a while." He gave Susanne a look that clearly transmitted the message: *Treat her nicely or else.*

Susanne nodded her understanding. A few minutes later, after Henri had put a dressing on Nicole's leg and Susanne had shown her to the guestroom and bath, Susanne sat down next to Henri on the couch. "So, what do you think?" she asked, keeping her voice low.

"There's no question about it. She's a Bruante, all right. She looks just like you."

"My sister?"

"Maybe—or your half-sister's daughter, which might fit more from an age-perspective. Nicole looks to be in her twenties at the most, whereas Monique's daughter would be well into her forties by now. But who knows; the gene for surprisingly youthful appearances has blessed many members of the Bruante family, including you." He got up and headed for the door. "Whoever she is, I intend to find out before nightfall."

"Where are you going?"

"To the Office of Public Records. Give me a few hours."

"Are you coming back?"

"Of course." And, Henri felt certain he would have some answers when he returned later.

178

CHAPTER SIXTEEN

Dr. John Noland always had a mild case of the jitters before addressing a crowd, but this time it was worse than usual. Usually, his audience consisted of scientists who could easily understand the technicalities of his theories; but this time, he would be speaking to a group of popular journalists and television personalities with minimal, if any, scientific background.

He had never really been subjected to public scrutiny, but things were different now. Mathematical formulas scribbled on a blackboard and discussed with excitement amongst the scientific elite were one thing, but the actual transfer of genetically altered rodents between two distinct *Time-Shells* was quite another. His successes were a subject of discussion now in the trendy fringe press, the laughable exaggerations making the tabloid headlines now on a regular basis. This was his chance to set the record straight, so he had cautiously agreed to this unconventional forum, taking place immediately after his keynote lecture at the International Convention of Astrophysics in London, a televised press conference that would reach the masses on not one but two continents.

He had a script, of sorts. Questions had been distributed to the invited participants in advance, but there would still be ample opportunity for the wild-card query or the off-base comment. The answers he had prepared were consciously dumbed down, with all equations and most of the mathematical and astrophysical terminology simplified to make the explanations of his experiments more accessible to the lay public. It would be tricky to pull off, to be sure; but if he could, he might be able to stifle the crazy rumors that had been propagated by the very same people who would be attending the taping.

They led him to a table in front of the crowded room and had him sit in front of a microphone. He poured himself a glass of water as they rolled a television camera through the standing-room-only crowd and into position just a few yards from the table and slightly to his left.

A London newscaster, the host of a tabloid-style morning show, got up from his seat next to John at the table and made an animated introduction while standing at a podium. He was used to hearing his degrees and credentials listed chronologically, followed by a summary of his most important achievements, but this time there was none of that. Instead, he learned that he had just made *The Sun's* top ten list of the world's most eligible American bachelors; that he would be turning forty this October, but not to mention it because he was touchy about his age; that he was not only the youngest, but also the best looking, faculty member at the University of Chicago to ever be promoted to full professor; and that he had toyed with the idea of sending himself instead of a lab rat into the future.

After a few "*jolly good shows*," one or two "*smashing, old chaps*," and a handful of "*bloody amazings*" Tony Briggs finally finished, turning to John with a smile and an exuberant two thumbs up. "You're on, mate," he said, the cockney seeping ever so slightly into his incompletely tutored accent.

What had he gotten himself into? "Thank you, Mr. Briggs," John spoke into the microphone. This was going to be interesting.

Returning to the table, the newscaster sat back in his moderator's chair as if he were about to watch a fireworks display. "First question?" He pointed to a woman with her hand raised, sitting in the front row.

"Julia Wellington, *The Daily Star*. Is it true that the old adage referring to time as a river is actually true?"

She had asked one of the scripted questions, so this one would be easy. "Yes, in fact that is true. And believe it or not, the 'now' that you and I are currently riding in is very similar to a boat. This boat is actually a self-contained, positively charged *Time-Shell*, which is traveling along a magnetic river that we call the *Stream* toward a negatively charged pole. The positive end of the magnet reaches backward into the past and pushes us forward, while the negative end stretches ahead, pulling us into the future."

He took a sip of water, which gave the female journalist sitting in the front row just enough time to ask for clarification, tongue in cheek. "You contend, then, that we're riding in a solitary bubble, floating merrily down some kind of a cosmic energy river? Next, you'll be telling us that mermaids are guiding us, and that Neptune is the oarsman."

He ignored the laughter. "This is no fairytale," he said with a tolerant smile. "As it turns out, ours is not the only *Time-Shell* floating down the *Stream*. There are countless other *Time-Shells* lined up ahead of us and behind us—an infinite number of them, actually. The presence of many *Time-Shells* rather than just a solitary one is actually what allows the transfer of an object either into the future or into the past. We have incontestably proven their existence, not only with our calculations but by validated experiments."

The moderator pointed to another journalist, sitting toward the back. "Next question, please, for Dr. Noland?"

"Robert Morrow, *The Independent*. This is more of a direct follow-up," admitted the journalist, a young man dressed in denim jeans and a polo shirt. "What, exactly, is in these *Time-Shells*?" This one was not scripted, but it didn't matter. It dove-tailed beautifully with the previous one.

"Our mathematical models and observations indicate that each *Time-Shell* is an exact replica of every other, existing however in a different point in time, at a different location on the *Stream*. Imagine billions and billions and billions of *Time-Shells* traveling together in single file down the *Stream*." He looked at his watch to enhance the drama of the example he was about to provide. "At the same moment our *Time-Shell* passes some imaginary signpost for this exact moment—4:17 p.m. on June first in 2011, according to my 'timepiece'—another co-existing *Time-Shell* located exactly ten years ahead of us passes the marker for 4:17 p.m. on June first, in the year 2021; and the one ten years behind us passes the 4:17 p.m. marker on June first in 2001. If we were able to jump forward to the 2021 *Time-Shell*, we would find ourselves there, ten years older. Similarly, if we jumped backward into the

2001 *Time-Shell*, we would encounter the younger versions of ourselves from a decade before. As our *Time-Shell* moves ahead, so do all the others. When our *Time-Shell* located in 2011 eventually reaches the point on the *Stream* ten years from now, in 2021, the *Time-Shell* ten years behind us in 2001 will take its place in our current year—2011."

The moderator pointed at another member of the audience, her hand raised. "Carrie Johnson, *The Morning Star*. So how, exactly, is an object transferred from one *Time-Shell* to another? We're all wondering, I think, if you and H.G. Wells both use time machines." Her comment elicited some hearty laughter from the back of the room, which he once again ignored.

"The *Stream* is normally a perfectly linear electromagnetic field, with no waveform or curves at all. We can produce connections, however, between *Time-Shells* by forcing the *Stream* to buckle into peaks and valleys, called *Wave*s, which bring two *Time-Shells* into close approximation. So far, we have discovered only two ways to create *Waves*. One method is to use a Magnetic Field Generator Plate, while the other involves the use of a naturally occurring hormone called chronotonin."

"This plate of yours sounds like the transporter pad on the Starship Enterprise," Ms. Johnson quipped—resulting, of course, in more laughter. This *Morning Star* reporter was a real comedian.

"Hardly," he replied, trying to keep his cool. "Our Magnetic Field Generator Plates are strictly used to study the physical properties of the *Stream*. Our Time-Transfer experiments on mice were conducted with no machinery whatsoever. Sorry to disappoint all of the Star Trek and H.G. Wells fans out there." Now it was his turn to enjoy a chuckle or two.

He knew exactly where to take this next. "There are certain physical laws that control the pairing of *Time-Shells*, and whether a connection between them is made at all. First of all, when *Waves* are created in the *Stream*, *Time-Shells* always orient to each other with remarkable chronological symmetry. In layman's terms, this means that when a *Time-Shell* on the upslope of one *Wave* lines up with a *Time-Shell* on the downslope of another, it will be the exact same month, day, and time in each Time-Shell, but in different years. For instance, if it's 7:30 a.m. on Christmas Day in 1925 in the *Time-Shell* on *Wave* 'One', it will be Christmas Day at 7:30 a.m. in another year, let's say 1955, in the *Time-Shell* on *Wave* 'Two'. This is called the *Rule of Chronologic Symmetry*. Is everyone following me?"

He looked out into the audience and saw about half of the heads nodding in acknowledgement. The others were staring back at him blankly. Oh well, he would simply have to leave the slow ones behind. "Okay, then. Next, according to our formulas, we believe that once an initial connection is established between two *Time-Shells*, the same two *Time-Shells* will always find each other, again and again and again, whenever a geographically appropriate buckle is produced in *The Stream*. This process is governed (we believe) by a time-space mathematical law called the *Rule of Recollection*. And finally, last but not least, something called a *Common-Object* must be present in both *Time-*

Shells to function as an alignment post, of sorts, on both ends. We call the opening that forms between two *Time-Shells*, anchored at both ends by a *Common-Object*, a *Virtual-Hole*: interchangeably known as a *Time-Tunnel*."

"Question, on the left?" the moderator interrupted. John had admittedly gotten a little carried away with his scientific soliloquy—part speculation, but mostly fact, as laboriously demonstrated by their chronotonin experiments.

"Jamie McIntosh, *The Scotsman*. What exactly do you mean by a *Common-Object*?"

"A *Common-Object* is something inanimate that's present in both *Time-Shells*. It can be anything, really—the same dresser, table, boulder, or tree, for instance, as long as it exists in repetition, as a constant variable, in *Shell* after *Shell* after *Shell*. In our rodent experiments, the *Common-Object* that we selected was an antiquated penny, minted in 1926, which we place in the mouse's specially manufactured, body-sized cage. Old objects are required as a duplicated anchor on opposite ends of a *Time-Tunnel*, for the obvious reason that they must be present in a multitude of *Time-Shells* in the past to be used as a 'connector'."

A multitude of hands were in the air now. "Over there, on the right side," Briggs said.

"Ian Canter, *The Sun*. Could you tell us about your *Time-Transfer* experiments with mutant mice, minus all of the scientific jargon?"

This question was another scripted one, which would lead to the most exciting topic on the media-agenda. "Certainly; except that a tiny bit of 'scientific jargon', as you put it, is unavoidable to help everyone understand—so will you humor me while I give you a mini-genetics lesson as background? Nothing too complicated, I assure you."

"Go right ahead, Professor," interjected Briggs, ever the moderator, giving his permission.

"Every one of us has two copies of every chromosome: one set inherited from our mother and the other set from our father. The chromosomes that determine gender are 'X' and 'Y'. *Men* have an X chromosome passed on from their mother and a Y chromosome that comes from their father, making their sex-chromosome 'genotype' *X-Y*; while *women* have an X chromosome inherited from their mother and another X from their father combined to make an *X-X* combination. Does this all make sense to everyone?"

The response was a roomful of 'yesses' since, after all, this basic principle of 'boy versus girl' genetic make-up was common knowledge to anyone who had ever taken high-school biology. "Great" he continued; "so, let's get on to the fun stuff. My colleagues and I have discovered a gene located on the female X chromosome—present not only in humans but also in other mammals such as rodents—that encodes for a hormone called *chronotonin*. When this hormone is produced in excessive amounts due to a certain genetic mutation, the elevated blood levels above a threshold amount create a chemical 'aura' of sorts around the mutation-bearing animal that can induce a 'buckle' in the *Stream*."

The quiet in the audience was almost eerie. He had their attention, all right. "We've created

186

genetically engineered mice that have an activating mutation in the promotor region of the chronotonin gene, resulting in these animals producing higher-than-normal levels of this hormone. The amount of chronotonin produced depends on whether the mutation is present on one chromosome versus two, with *twice* the levels for females with mutations on *both* X chromosomes compared with those with only *one* mutated gene (or in males who have only one X chromosome to begin with). In addition, and quite interestingly, chronotonin production by the mutant gene is also 'revved up' significantly by certain...*environmental* conditions."

"And what, exactly, are those 'conditions'?" This prompt came from Ian Canter, the journalist who had asked the original question about John's experiments.

"Well, it seems that in animals harboring this mutation, their chronotonin production is increased linearly, three-fold, when they are sexually aroused; but *logarithmically* by ten-times-ten-times-ten when they are exposed to certain hallucinogenic compounds. When we inject a psychotropic mixture into these mice, the female 'subjects' with two gene mutations produce an inordinate amount of hormone creating a potent chronotonin 'halo' surrounding them that facilitates *Wave* formation in the *Stream*, opening a *Virtual-Hole*, or *Time-Tunnel*, between two separate *Time-Shells*. Female mice with only one gene mutation or a male mouse with an affected X chromosome (making them the equivalent of a 'single-gene-mutation-female') develop a halo as well but not to the degree necessary to open up a *Virtual-Hole*. We will

187

discuss the limitations of having only one versus two gene mutations in a moment."

"So what happens to the animals after they open up a *Time-Tunnel*? Do they simply disappear?" This time it was Tony Briggs, beginning to step somewhat out of his role as moderator in asking this pointed question, with reporter-like insistence.

"Funny you should ask. The animal disappears, but not permanently. The reason for this, we think, is because of a phenomenon that we have termed the *Boomerang-Phenomenon*."

"Could you please explain?" Briggs said. The entire room was now giving John their full and undivided attention. You could hear a pin drop.

"First, the animal produces an electromagnetic halo that won't dissipate until hours later, when the hallucinogen is out of its system. Second, the animal is trapped within its custom-made cage, which is transported—or rather, 'sucked' with the animal through the *Virtual-Hole* created around the penny that we place inside, kind of like water being pulled violently through a drain. If the transported mice were able to remove themselves from the cage, putting a safe amount of distance between themselves and their *Common Object*: the penny, we believe that the *Virtual-Hole* would close. But since they're trapped in the cage, in such close proximity to their *Common-Object*, their chronotonin halo keeps the *Virtual-Hole* wide open. The result is that the mice disappear, but they return almost immediately to our *Time-Shell*, like a boomerang. If we don't remove them from the cage right away using a robotic arm that keeps a safe distance between researcher and rodent-mutant, they will keep traveling back and forth continuously, kind of like a ping-pong ball, until the hallucinogen finally wears off."

"Is this back and forth time-travel harmful to them?" the moderator asked.

"Eventually. Let me say first that the mice with two gene mutations are not only capable of opening up a *Time-Tunnel* with their super-high chronotonin levels, but they also enjoy a considerable degree of chronotonin electromagnetic halo-related protection from the *Virtual-Hole*. They can go back and forth once or twice without too much of a problem; but after three round trips, they demonstrate behaviors that are indicative of central nervous system damage such as confusion, loss of balance, and seizures. After four round trips, they show signs of brain ischemia which manifests with stroke-like symptoms; and after five, they die. They never develop any signs of internal physical trauma, though—unlike some of our *other* rodent subjects."

"Are you referring to the mice with only *one* chronotonin gene mutation?" It seemed that Briggs had taken over the questioning now.

"I meant the *non*-mutated mice, primarily; but also the animals with only one gene mutation, that travel like stowaways with another double-mutated mouse."

"Can you extrapolate?"

"Of course. For the mice with a single mutation, their chronotonin halo cannot open a *Virtual-Hole*, even with the additional stimulation of hormone production caused by exposure to hallucinogens, because the chronotonin levels are simply not high enough. However, the chronotonin 'emission' (which I should say is not insignificant in these rodents but just not above the necessary threshold to induce a *Wave-Buckle*) *does* provide some protection for them against the crushing external force of the *Time-Tunnel*—if they happen to be sucked into a *Virtual-Hole* as a passenger of sorts, along with the double-mutant mouse that generated the 'connection'. It's fascinating, really. The protective effect is extremely variable and unpredictable from subject-to-subject depending, perhaps, on other genetic factors that we simply haven't been able to identify yet. Some of these animals make it through okay, while others…well, they suffer the same fate as the mice without any mutation at all."

"What happens to these *normal* mice?"

"They die instantly because they don't have an electromagnetic shield around them, in contrast to our mutant rodents. As I alluded to a moment before, the external pressure force within a *Virtual-Hole* must be substantial, because of how the normal mice meet their end."

"What do you mean?" the moderator asked.

The room was deathly quiet; waiting. "It's a horrible thing to see." John shuddered as he flashed back to the image in his mind of the limp and lifeless rodents. "They look as though they've been squeezed by some kind of powerful vice; but strangely, none of them exhibit any external evidence of trauma, in contrast to what one might expect."

"No blood or guts?" someone called out, hungry for something especially sensational to

190

report on.

He needed to choose his words carefully because the autopsies, which reflected some kind of bizarre implosion-like injury, were simply too gruesome for prime time. Describing every bone as "pulverized" and every organ as "liquefied" to a roomful of vulture-like 'yellow' journalists would only serve to agitate the anti-science radicals who might argue that his breakthrough technology would best be abandoned—his gene-splicing equipment, pharmacologic solutions and data-sheets summarily confiscated and destroyed because of the potential danger his findings posed to society. He would have to keep it vague yet intriguing, at least for today.

"Sorry to disappoint you; but the answer is 'no' to even a drop of blood or an inkling of guts." Should he say more? The lengthy pause as he pondered his next words unintentionally electrified the already-sensational atmosphere even further. "Let's just say that from the inside," he finally went on, "the unprotected animals are...*terminally* damaged; but on the outside, they look untouched, without even a single bruise, scrape or scratch."

It seemed to go over reasonably well, until the entire back row of participants stood up, holding various signs that said things like: '*Lab rats have rights, too*'; '*Mutated mice deserve better*'; and '*Put the scientists in cages instead*'. He hadn't counted on animal rights activists attending the press conference; and apparently Tony Briggs hadn't either.

"Alright then," the newscaster said, standing up quickly. "That will be all for today. Thank you, everyone, for attending." Obviously wishing to avoid bad press as much as John did, he whisked John off in a rush out a side door, clapping him on the back while at the same time pushing him along, saying: "Good job, Professor. You did well for your first time."

Maybe so; but his first time would also be his last. What had he been thinking, putting himself and his theories out there for all the 'crazies' to distort, twist and deform into something sensational, scandalous, and horrifying? He must have been crazy himself when he had agreed to this venue. "Right," was all he could manage to say, shaken up by the last few seconds of his presentation.

"How about being a guest on my show next week?" Tony Briggs pulled out his phone from his breast pocket, opening the calendar *app* with a forefinger as they walked. "Would Thursday work for you?"

"Thanks, but no thanks."

From now on, John Noland decided, science (especially *his* science) would, by hard-learned necessity, be left exclusively to scientists.

CHAPTER SEVENTEEN

Nicole woke up between sheets that felt cool and soothing against her naked skin. Susanne's hand was on her arm. "Henri's back," she was saying. "You should get up now."

Nicole's sleep had been solid, dreamless, and densely disorienting. "Where am I?" she asked.

The look that Susanne gave her seemed to say: '*you've got to be kidding me*'. "In my flat, in central Paris."

Then it all came back to her in a rush. "Oh, that's right." Nicole repeated '2011, *not* 1876' in her head a few times before she asked: "What time is it?"

"4:30 in the afternoon. You've been asleep all day."

The sleep had been recuperative, for her body *and* her mind. The pain from her bruise and laceration on her right leg had lessened considerably; and where her thinking had felt fogged and sluggish before, her thoughts were distinctively clearer now.

Susanne had some clothing in her arms. "You can wear these," she said, putting them on the end of the bed. "I'm sure they'll fit you."

"Thank you," Nicole replied politely.

Susanne shrugged. "It's the least I can do. After all, you're probably my sister."

After Susanne closed the guest room door behind her, Nicole sighed. She and Susanne were related, but they weren't sisters. This bold declaration along with the claim of complete amnesia were ploys—plain and simple, intended to buy her more time. Yes, it was true that she didn't *really* know how she had gotten here, mechanistically; and yes, she continued to actively question her own sanity and felt unsure of what in her past was really true or simply delusion—rationalizing that these uncertainties greatly justified the little white lie of memory lapse. She would know soon, depending on how her 'relatives' decided to handle her shortly, if she had to keep playing the part of a forgetful victim of physical and mental trauma for just a few more hours versus several more days.

One thing was certain, though: she would have to play along with the sister charade for quite some time. Why? Because the only thing standing between her and the gendarmes was Susanne; and the only thing preventing Susanne from giving her up was the concept of sibling fealty. It had worked so far, so why tip over the lifeboat?

Nicole didn't quite trust Susanne…not yet, but her intuition told her that she had an advocate in Henri: a man who, she hoped, shared more than just identical appearance to her late *Papa*. She and her father had been very close, sharing secrets and a similar life philosophy; and she hoped that Henri was a man cut from the same family cloth. Her hoped-for relationship with her father's lookalike aside, the brief interaction between he and Susanne told Nicole immediately that 'niece-respected-uncle' immensely, to the point that Henri's opinion carried an enormous amount of weight in every aspect of her life. Having Henri on her side would definitely tip the scales in the right direction such that if Nicole could win *him* over, then Susanne might eventually follow—but not now. It would work best, she knew, if she promoted the sister–sister relationship, at least until Nicole herself got her bearings. *No one* would ever believe something so fantastic as time-travel without proof; and until Nicole had some, she would hold the secret close.

She picked up the trousers that Susanne had called 'jeans'. Nicole had never worn trousers (they were for men, not women) but here, those rules apparently didn't apply. Susanne was right, they fit perfectly, and so did the lavender chemise that, curiously, had no sleeves or neck, leaving her arms and the upper part of her chest completely bare. She slid her bare feet into the open toed sandal-shoes that Susanne had left at the foot of her bed, and then took a moment to look at herself in the full-length mirror hanging on the back of the guestroom door, astonished by the end result. In her 'former' life, she recalled the headache of corsets, linen stays, drawers, and stockings; but not here, where people apparently didn't mind showing some skin. That suited Nicole very well. She turned from side to side, admiring her reflection, giving herself a quiet nod of approval when she noticed how the tightly fitting denim hugged her hips and showed off the lines of her shapely legs. She could definitely see herself becoming quite fond of the liberating simplicity of this unfamiliar attire.

She found Susanne waiting for her in the foyer. "He's in here," she said, leading Nicole to the dining room, where Henri had laid out some papers on the table. "We'll have some food in just a few minutes. Can you wait to eat?" Susanne was cordial enough; in fact, just a trifle *too* cordial. Nicole was willing to wager that Susanne had been pressured by Henri to be tolerant and hospitable. Nicole, it seemed, had Henri to thank for her brief respite from pursuit; and just as she had suspected, it was Henri whom she must court in order to win Susanne's guarded confidence.

Nicole nodded. "I am fine for now," she replied. "It helped me very much to rest."

Henri had pulled out two chairs on one end, positioned in front of a stack of papers. He smiled at her, his face warm and so heartbreakingly familiar. She *so* missed her dear *Papa*. "Why don't both of you sit down," he said. "I'll show you what I found."

Nicole took a seat at the table on the left, and Susanne sat down next to her. Henri stood between the two women so he could point out some of his discoveries, which he proceeded to lay out in front of them. "Let's start with this birth certificate." He had taken if off the pile, placing it face down on the tabletop. As he started to turn it over, Susanne gave him a sidelong glance.

"How did you get this so quickly, Henri?"

He grinned. "I have a contact in Public Records. She had quite a thing for me, a few years back." He slid the certificate, which was now face up, right in between them; and there it was, plain as day—the name written neatly on the official birth record.

"My sister's name is Nicole?" Susanne asked in disbelief.

I'm not her sister, Nicole thought; *I can't be!* At the moment, she couldn't help but think that this whole thing seemed nothing short of far-fetched. She passed her hand over her forehead, as if the action would wipe the confusion from her mind. Was she going mad? Had her previous life in the nineteenth century actually been some kind of complex delusion, experienced while in the throes of mental illness? This entire situation seemed completely crazy; and now, she didn't know what to think, except that her memories from the past twenty-eight years would not agree to just lie down and submit to the strong arm of a piece of paper.

"*Was* Nicole," Henri answered, sadly. "She died two years ago, of breast cancer." Nicole couldn't help but breathe a sigh of relief. She *wasn't* going crazy. "But it doesn't end there," Henri said, sliding yet another birth certificate their way. "Nicole Bruante Montague had a daughter, named after herself. It's a confusing coincidence, but this 'other' Nicole would match your age (mid-twenties, I'd say?) much closer than Susanne's older sister, who would have been nearly fifty years old by now, had she lived. This would make you Susanne's niece, and *my* great-great niece."

"This whole thing, especially the identical name 'thing', seems *extremely* improbable," Susanne commented dubiously.

"What's so improbable, really, about a family member being named after a beloved or respected relative…*including* a parent?" Henri replied matter-of-factly. "It happens all the time in *plenty* of families; so honestly, I don't see why you're questioning that it happened in ours." He turned to Nicole, having dismissed Susanne's incredulity with his unflappable logic. "Now that we know something about the presumed 'you', Nicole, I've filled in this part of the family tree."

"Well, all this proves so far is that she's a liar," Nicole said, while Henri took the thick stack of papers sitting on the table in his hand, unfolding a complicated chart that he had handwritten on more than a dozen industrial-sized sheets of white paper, attached one to the other. The final product was a complicated diagram that extended across and down to fill up the entire sixteen pieces of paper, combined together four across by four down, taking up half of the dining room table's surface area when it was finally spread out. "She's *not* my sister, as she claims to be."

"She's confused, Susanne. Just because she got the name right but not the generational-relationship due to shock and head-trauma means nothing." He turned towards Nicole and motioned towards the bottom of the chart. "Here you are, Nicole. I wrote your name and your mother's, in the right places on the family pedigree: Nicole Bruante Montague, and Nicole Élise Montague."

Susanne looked skeptically at the new entries, entirely unconvinced. Nicole didn't blame her because she herself wasn't convinced, either…for a good reason. She was fairly certain, despite her reflections about her doubtful sanity, that she was not the 'Nicole' that Henri seemed to think she was; she just *couldn't* be.

"According to this chart," Nicole noted, finger on another box, "Susanne and my mother have the same father."

"That's right, Nicole. Your grandfather, as well as Susanne's father, was Didier Bruante, my nephew. We were very close in age."

Nicole traced, with the same finger, the line from her supposed-grandfather that led to her supposed-grandmother. "My 'grandmother' was someone named Monique Montague? Do you know anything about her, Monsieur Bruante? I cannot remember anything about her." *This* much was true at least. She didn't recall anything at all about Monique Montague because Nicole still clung to her vivid memories of being someone else's child: born in 1848.

Her curiosity was sincere though, in part— because she couldn't rule out the possibility that she might actually *be* Nicole Élise Montagne, awoken abruptly from some kind of incapacitating stupor or daze induced by God knows what weird variety of mental illness? But also, her questions served the distinct purpose of buying some time to inconspicuously study the family tree with a focus on the *upper* portion, where she thought she had already found her true self on the top branch of Henri's family tree.

"Please call me Henri," 'Monsieur Bruante' said with a warm smile, responding to her formality with distinct 'familial' kindness as he launched into an explanation. "To answer your question about your grandmother, Monique was a maid in your grandmother's service with whom your underage grandfather became, well…*involved*. Your mother was the result." Nicole nodded, feigning interest, while her eyes climbed several generations higher up Henri's hand-written ladder. Didier's mother was named Joelle; Joelle's father was called Marcel; and Marcel's father was Edmond Bruante.

199

The Edmond Bruante *she* knew was 9 years old; and his mother…well, she knew *her* too, as well or better than she knew herself, because…

Nicole pointed at the name: a relative from nearly a century and a half ago. "Here is another Nicole," she declared, unable to prevent her voice from trembling due to the bizarre and troubling fact that she was looking at what she believed to be her very own past and future written down on paper and presented to her like a history lesson. "Do you know anything about *this* Bruante: Nicole Thérèse?"

She met Henri's gaze and their eyes locked, which is when she had the feeling that maybe the same crazy thought had occurred to *him*; a fleeting suspicion that the impossible might actually be possible, that he had dismissed because a more 'realistic' current-day contender had presented herself. Had he recognized her, perhaps, from an old photograph? The way he looked at her suggested 'yes'; but then again, she was still confused by this whole situation, and admittedly prone to misinterpret even the slightest change in facial expression.

He might not know me, she thought, *but I certainly know him—or someone who looked exactly like him.* His kind face, those empathetic eyes, the wild grey hair, and the closely trimmed salt-and-pepper beard… she could picture him, even now, in her mind, and she knew just where to find him on the family tree, one branch above her on the papers spread out in front of her. She reconfirmed for the fourth or fifth time that Henri, pictured in the photograph that she had stumbled upon in Susanne's office and now standing right next to her

200

in the flesh, looked exactly like Jerome René Bruante: her late dear, sweet Papa.

Henri gazed back at her with unmistakable affinity—the only person in this strange, new world whom Nicole could trust; her father's lookalike, the bizarre result of a family's genetic heritage, passed down through the generations to end up here. "She was your great-great-great-great grandmother, Nicole," he said, his gaze never leaving hers as if he was testing her; *challenging* her to say: 'no, that's not right—she's *me*'. "In all likelihood," he went on, "your mother was named after her, and you after your mother. Although your grandmother (my sister) prohibited your father, Didier, from ever meeting your mother *or* you, she wouldn't have been able to prevent him from suggesting a name."

He leaned over the pedigree, and put on his reading glasses. "This particular Nicole died young. Some kind of carriage accident, if I recall. She had a son named Edmond," he added, pointing to the appropriate box, "born out of wedlock. The boy's father remains unnamed: a family mystery." His eyes twinkled a little bit. "But Susanne and I think we know who should be written in—*don't* we, Susanne?"

"Yes, yes—he would be the *second* famous artist contributing to our noteworthy bloodline," Susanne said impatiently; and Nicole's heart leapt. That comment went a long way to bolstering her confidence; because who else could Susanne mean, if not her dear Edmond's father: Jean Gustave Désiré Courbet?

She had been concentrating on the Courbet-Bruante pedigree, over to the left; but now, as she

201

glanced over at the right side-branch of the family tree, her eyes widened—because, to her amazement, the name 'Martial Caillebotte' was written there. So *that's* what Susanne had meant a minute ago by 'second famous artist'. "Are we related to *this* family, too?"

"Indeed we are," Henri replied proudly. "The youngest son, a notable photographer, was your great-great-grandmother Genevieve's father."

"Can we please focus on *this* particular family member and leave the art history lesson for later, *Ton-Ton*?" Susanne interrupted, gesturing testily in Nicole's direction. "Is anything coming back to you now, Nicole? You'd think that *something* here—a name or a date—would jog your memory."

Nicole shook her head, trying her best to look confused although she really wasn't. "There is nothing. It is all a blank."

Henri was busy folding up the pedigree. "There's more," he said, slipping it back into his briefcase. "I found your address and phone number, Nicole."

Nicole understood the word address—but not "phone number." She would add that phrase to her growing vocabulary list, as soon as she found out what it meant.

"Now we're getting somewhere." Susanne stood up and retrieved something from her purse that Nicole quickly deduced was a phone. Susanne had been talking into this particular device right before their confrontation in front of the building.

"She lives just outside of Paris," Henri explained. He pulled a slip of paper from his pocket and handed it to Susanne.

"*35 Rue de L'Arbre, Croissy-Sur-Seine*," Susanne read. "That's not far." She glanced over at Nicole with a self-satisfied half-smile. "I could get you there in thirty-five minutes, without traffic; an hour and ten minutes, with."

"Not so fast," Henri said. "First, she doesn't have a key, remember? And second, we're not one hundred percent certain that *this* Nicole and *that* Nicole are one and the same person."

"That's why I intend to call."

"What if she lives alone?"

"Then no one will answer, but if she happens to have a husband, boyfriend, or roommate living there with her, then maybe someone will."

Susanne tapped the face of the phone, which appeared to be covered with glass, and then she held the device up to her ear. *Amazing*, Nicole thought; the small, flat box that Susanne referred to as a phone apparently connected voices, somehow. Nicole knew better than to show her ignorance of these modern contrivances, so she put on her best air of casual disinterest, pretending that all of this was completely normal instead of utterly bewildering.

Susanne tapped one foot impatiently for five or six seconds while holding the device to her ear. Nicole could make out a faint ringing sound, like a doorbell, coming from the phone. Then Susanne said, "*Allo*, is Nicole Élise Montagne there?"

Nicole heard a voice saying something in response, but she couldn't make out the words. "I see," Susanne said. "Can you tell me when you expect her to return?" Susanne nodded a couple of times, while the voice inside the box said something

203

else. "Well, this is a rather unusual situation. Would you mind if I put you on speaker phone so my friends can talk to you, too?" The answer must have been yes, because Susanne tapped the phone again and then put it in the center of the table.

"*Allo*?" a voice spoke out of the phone. It was eerie, Nicole thought; this disembodied voice—like someone speaking from thin air.

"Yes, we can hear you Sylvie," Susanne replied loudly. "Sylvie is Nicole's roommate," Susanne explained in a low aside to Henri and Nicole. "Sylvie," Susanne continued, her voice just a decibel or two below a shout, "my name is Susanne Bruante, and I'm here with my uncle, Henri, and someone who claims that her name is 'Nicole'; and that she's my sister…or some other version of 'related'. We think she might be your roommate. You see, she hit her head and claims to have complete amnesia for everything that happened before the incident. We were hoping you might be able to help us confirm her identity."

"Why don't you recognize your own sister?" the woman on the other end of the line asked, understandably cautious.

"Actually, not my sister; but rather, my estranged half-sister's daughter, which would make her my niece—although I'm skeptical. I don't recognize her because I've never met her."

"You said your name is Susanne Bruante?"

"That's right."

The phone was silent for a moment, while Sylvie tried to put two and two together. "Well, that makes sense, I guess. My roommate's mother had the middle name 'Bruante'."

"Your Nicole's late-mother and I are definitely half-sisters, although I never met *her* either," Susanne replied. "We have the birth-certificate to prove it. That's not the issue. We need to know if the woman sitting here, at my dining room table, is actually Nicole Élise Montagne, or an imposter instead."

Nicole didn't like the sound of that. Once Susanne discovered that 'that' Nicole and 'this' Nicole were two different people, it would all be over. In just a few moments, there would be nothing at all preventing Susanne from turning Nicole in.

"Do you think you can help us?" Susanne continued.

"Sure. Nicole is away on vacation, in Morocco. She won't be back until next week. I don't really see how she could be sitting there with you, when she's supposed to be someplace else."

"Do you think you'd recognize her voice?" Susanne asked.

"Probably."

Susanne turned to Nicole. "Could you say hello to your roommate, Nicole?" Susanne asked, not disguising her sarcasm.

Nicole cleared her throat. "*Allo*, Sylvie," she said loudly. "Something happened to me, I am not sure what, and I ended up naked in a museum. Does my voice sound familiar to you?"

The phone on the table didn't reply at first. "It *could* be you," Sylvie finally said, "but I can't be sure."

Susanne's face dropped. She was obviously on a mission to prove that Nicole was not who she claimed to be. "Does her voice sound familiar, or not?" she demanded.

"Kind of…"

Henri leaned over the edge of the table, speaking toward the phone. "Does your cell phone accept text photos?"

"Great idea!" Susanne exclaimed. "We can take a picture of Nicole and send it to you."

"Yes, that would work," Sylvie replied. She rattled off a number, and Henri wrote it down.

"We'll have to use my mobile to take the picture, so we have to hang up now, Sylvie," Susanne said. "Simply text message me a yes or a no, once you receive the image."

"Will do," Sylvie replied.

'Text message'. 'Text photo'. 'Mobile'—so many confusing terms! Nicole watched as Susanne grabbed her mobile—another name for a phone, apparently—from the center of the table and ended the call. "Good thinking, Henri," Susanne said. "We should have done this first."

Susanne pointed the phone at Nicole and pushed a button. Nicole heard a click, and at the same time saw a flash of light that made her see stars for a second or two. This phone was more than amazing—apparently it was a camera too. What else could it do?

Susanne tapped the screen again several times, looking back and forth from the device to the piece of paper with the number on it that Henri had written down. "There," she said with satisfaction, "it's sent. Now, for the moment of truth."

So the phone also was a telegraph of sorts, sending telegrams with photographs! Would the answer be yes, or no? Nicole felt sure it would be no, which meant that she would have to do some fast talking in just a few seconds, in order to prevent Susanne from making another phone call—to the police this time.

A series of beeps came from the phone, which could only mean that Sylvie had telegraphed her answer. Nicole began to tremble.

"Well, well!" Susanne smiled triumphantly. "Who are you, really, Nicole? Because according to this text message from Sylvia, you're definitely *not* my half-sister's daughter."

"She's not?" Henri asked, his forehead wrinkled in surprise.

"*Non*; not according to Sylvie," Susanne answered, "and I think she'd recognize her own roommate. I think a phone call to the police right now is probably in order."

"Wait," Nicole and Henri both said at the same time. They looked at each other, and there it was again—a kinship that simply had to be derived from common blood…and common 'ancestral' memories, if that was even possible.

"You can't turn her in just like that, simply because she isn't the Nicole we thought she was," Henri argued. "She could very well be, let's say, a distant cousin, for instance. Just *look* at her, Susanne. There's no question in my mind, she's a Bruante!"

"Who, exactly, are you?" Susanne asked, her eyes narrowing to slits. "Now is your chance to come clean."

"I will tell you who I am," Nicole replied defiantly. She had never been easy to intimidate, and she wasn't about to be bullied by anyone, especially her great-great-great granddaughter. "I am Nicole Thérèse Bruante," she said, her tone assured and surprisingly matter-of-fact. She pointed to the pedigree. "I am the *other* Nicole on that family tree."

"What?" Susanne asked in disbelief. "How in the world—?"

"Don't ask me how," Nicole retorted, "but it is true. I travelled here through time against my will— through a portal that opened up all of a sudden in a painting."

Henri's eyes widened, more from curious realization than disbelief. "Which painting, my dear?"

"Henri," Susanne chided, "you don't actually *believe* her!"

He interrupted Susanne by holding up his hand and looked expectantly at Nicole, telling her with a kindly glance to continue. "The one that nobody wants," she said, "called *The Origin of the World*."

"This would certainly explain a lot; and they *do* look identical."

"But we already *know* that Nicole and I look alike!"

"No, no—that's *not* what I meant, Susanne. I'm not talking about *you*." Susanne opened her mouth to say something else, but before she could utter another word Henri said: "I'll show you."

And a few minutes later, all three of them were on their way to his apartment, so that he could show them.

CHAPTER EIGHTEEN

Michèle Crossier sat in the hot seat, directly across from the Chief Inspector on the other side of his desk. She had gathered quite a bit of information in less than twenty-four hours; and although she couldn't help but feel proud of this accomplishment, the troubling inconsistencies were a nagging thorn in her side. Nothing added up. She already had her theories, but she couldn't prove anything—yet. With enough time though, she felt confident that she would. This was only the beginning.

"This is the preliminary autopsy report," she said, sliding a laminated folder across the desk for Deschamps to peruse.

He picked it up and thumbed through it quickly. "Can you give me a summary, starting with toxicology?" he asked, his attention still focused on the pages in front of him. He apparently wanted her to talk while he read.

"Our John Doe's blood alcohol levels were sky-high, as you can see; but there were also psychedelic and narcotic substances in his system too."

"Enough to kill him?"

"No, but enough to make him high as a kite."

"Odd that the murderer, if responsible for the narcotic component, stopped at sub-lethal doses. How about the security guard?"

"Not a trace of *anything*. It seems he was a tea-toddler—at least on *that* night." She paused and went on. "Since we're discussing the *easy* one, Monsieur Charpentier died of a skull fracture which was at least in part sustained on the facing-edge of the toppled sculpture. We know this because we found his hair, skin, bone and blood smeared onto the point of impact."

"Lovely."

"Just wait until we get to John Doe."

"Go on."

"The unknown victim's cause of death, as anticipated, was *not* quite as obvious as the night guard's, but I should say that our suspicion that he had extensive internal injuries from some kind of 'crush' trauma was right on target. I should add that our mystery-man had gotten naked *before*, rather than *after*, he was killed by this 'method' due to the lack of clothing fibers in his skin. If he had been wearing clothes when he was crushed, embedded traces of polyester or cotton would have been recovered from under the surface of the body, but the ME found nothing." She paused to take a breath.

"Go on," he said.

"Our 'John Doe', being completely disrobed (and his belongings stashed God knows where but definitely *not* on site at the museum) carried no identification, and his fingerprints and dental records have no matches in either the French or EU databases. Furthermore, he had no implanted medical devices or hardware anywhere in his body." *What a shame*, Michèle thought. Serial numbers on surgically placed health-care appliances often led to a positive identification through the patient's medical records.

Deschamps said nothing, only nodding as he flipped to the next page of the autopsy, studying Pascal Bernier's notations on page 4 or 5 while

210

Michèle continued with her summary.

"His skull was crushed but very cleanly, as if the positive pressure from the outside or negative pressure from within resulted in collapse and contraction of a brain that was volume-compacted…and, uh—" (she coughed uncomfortably) "—liquefied."

"Did you say 'liquefied'?"

"Yes although I wish I hadn't. His lungs were in a similar state of disintegration, as were his liver and lungs. The chest and abdominal cavities were filled with the by-product of this unusual trauma, mixed with blood. The inwardly directed pressure caused rents and rips in major blood vessels like the aorta, not only at the exit point from the heart but everywhere else, too."

"In other words," Deschamps interrupted, "his heart burst from being squeezed from the outside and/or pulled inward from the inside, and he bled internally."

"Something like that," Michèle confirmed; "but honestly, more than just the heart and aorta were damaged in *this* victim, and the mechanism of the trauma seems to defy the physical 'norms' that we are used to encountering. You see, the blood-filled organs were not the *only* casualties. Bernier said that every single bone in the poor man's body was literally pulverized. He'd never seen anything like it." She leaned forward. "But what's more, the amount of spillage was negligible—or should I say non-existent, in relation to the degree of internal trauma."

"What exactly do you mean by 'spillage'?"

"Bodily fluids, intestinal contents—you know,

211

that sort of thing. There was no blood or guts to speak of, extruding from *any* of his orifices. This is highly atypical for a body that has been crushed to death from an outside force."

Deschamps closed the autopsy report and tossed it nonchalantly onto the desktop, not because he didn't lack interest but instead because he had probably decided that he would learn much more by listening to Michèle's descriptions and analysis rather than reading the fine-print simultaneously. "What else?"

"Remember I said a minute ago that the ME didn't find any traces of clothing fiber embedded in the victim's skin? Well, that's not *all* he didn't find."

"Meaning?"

"Meaning that our victim couldn't have been crushed by something grimy—for example, a trash compactor. If he had, there would have been debris stuck to his hair and pushed into his skin. There weren't any particles like this on his body to speak of."

"What do you make of all this, Crossier?" Deschamps asked, tilting his head to one side while waiting for her to answer.

She had hoped he would ask. Michèle had a theory that she was eager to get out there so she answered without even a second's hesitation. "First, our victim must have been crushed in a tightly confined space. If his body was completely surrounded by the injuring device, more or less, that might explain why the contents of his body were contained inside, rather than being expelled forcefully outward. In order to explain the lack of

212

foreign material embedded in his skin, the machine in question would have to be easy to clean, with a surface that's amenable to decontamination after each job. I'm thinking that either a glass-like surface or something made of stainless steel would fit the bill."

"Do you have a specific candidate for this murder weapon in mind?" He obviously knew that she did.

"Yes, in fact I do." She put another folder on the desk. "Here's a picture of it."

He opened the folder. "What *is* this thing?" he asked, "and how the hell did you find it?"

"Monsieur Laroche, the chief of d'Orsay security, gave me the lead. I was thinking about a conversation I had with Pascale at the crime scene about the victim's injuries and what might have caused them, and I decided to ask Laroche about d'Orsay's industrial inventory. I asked him if the museum owned any permanent, portable equipment—let's say for restoring or cleaning artwork—that might be large enough to accommodate a human body. He told me to check in the basement, in the art conservation workroom; and sure enough, this is what I found."

"I'll ask you again: what exactly is it?"

"It's a size-adjustable, high-pressure submersion tank, used to remove rust and corrosion from sculptures and other similar pieces of artwork, composed of marble or metal. As you can see it is equipped with wheels to allow complete portability from its storage space in the basement, to allow it to be moved anywhere in the museum where it can be 'loaded' with the art work in need of cleaning." She stood and leaned over the desk, using her index finger to point out some relevant features of the piece of equipment on the image. "It's made of reinforced stainless steel. The dimensions can be adjusted depending on the size of the item that's being cleaned."

"How?"

"By extending or shortening the component panels and locking them into place with these corner latches. You see, the interior pressure jets need to be in very close proximity to the piece that's lowered inside in order to drive adherent and ingrained particles off the metal surfaces. This baby is capable of generating some extreme inwardly directed forces, especially when the unit is sealed."

"Hmm. So you're thinking the victim was stuffed inside this tank, on site at the crime scene?"

"Exactly, but minus the Sulphur chelation liquid. Do you see these connected rubber hoses?" She pointed again, and Deschamps nodded. "The rust removal agent is pumped into the tank after it's sealed, and the positive pressure generated by the associated air tank agitates the solution against the surface of the sculpture to remove any embedded material or corrosion. My theory is that our victim was rendered unconscious somehow, probably with an injectable drug—either downstairs in the basement, or upstairs in the special exhibit gallery; and then he was squeezed into the dry submersion tank. The tank was sealed; then the pressure jets were turned on."

"And the pressure jets acting on air itself rather than the chelation solution…"

"…would exert significant inward-directed

pressure on the external surface of the tightly 'stuffed' body with a force that isn't 'cushioned' at all by a surrounding liquid medium. I spoke to Bernier about it. He agrees that the victim's crush injuries could have theoretically been caused by this method, using a machine with these capabilities. What do you think? I know it sounds kind of far-fetched, but I think it makes sense."

Deschamps scratched his chin. "Maybe, but I'm not quite sure I buy it. Why would anyone go to such trouble, especially if they've already injected narcotics and could simply give enough to cause an overdose? Why not just get it over with using one simple method instead of two?"

"I haven't completely worked that out yet—except that maybe the killer was trying to make some kind of a statement with his choice of murder weapon. What if our mystery victim was an art restorer? In this case, killing him with a piece of art restoration equipment might strike an ironically appropriate chord in a certain type of sick mind."

"All right—now we're getting somewhere." The chief inspector offered her a rare smile. "I assume you've already asked forensics to check the inside of the tank for evidence?"

"Yes. I thought for sure we would recover something useful."

"But you didn't?"

"Unfortunately, no; but in my mind, at least, this doesn't rule out the submersion tank as the murder weapon since it could have been rinsed clean afterwards. What if our resourceful murderer transported the tank into the special exhibit gallery; killed our John Doe using the tank as a more 'meaningful' murder weapon than a knife, bullet or poison—right there 'on-site'; removed the body and left it at the scene of the crime, positioned in such a way with the other corpse so that it looked like they were romantically entangled, genitals in each other's faces, in life as well as death; and then moved the empty tank back to its storage spot in the basement, filling it with submersion liquid *downstairs*? It turns out the chelation solution composed of nitric acid, benzene, and acetone used in the corrosion removal process has the ability to emulsify oils and disintegrate proteins. Any hair, blood, skin, or fingerprints would be obliterated with even short-term exposure to this mixture. All our perpetrator would have to do is let the chemicals sit for a while before draining them, *et voilà*! The inside of the tank would be as clean as a whistle."

"Interesting." Deschamps drummed his fingertips on the table, his gaze resting on the contents of the folder. "How about the outside of the tank?"

"I've asked forensics to check for fingerprints, and to comb the entire workshop for pertinent evidence just as they have already done in the special exhibit gallery. I'll contact you immediately if they find anything at all of interest."

"Speaking of forensics," he said, leaning back in his chair, "do we have anything yet on the DNA analysis?"

"It's too early to have the *final* results, but I pressured Bernier for something preliminary at least as it relates to 'who' was having sex with 'whom' before, during or after the murders. Participant number one: the security guard. The semen all over

216

his genitals and stomach matched his own so he was either masturbating…" (she didn't skip a beat even while describing this most indecorous of activities) "…while enjoying the action happening around him as an observer, or alternatively he was part of the three-some and 'misfired' because his sexual interactions with John Doe, our naked suspect, or both were interrupted by the murderer. Participant number two: our mystery man. His own semen, containing viable sperm no less, was glazed onto his penis consistent with the expected distribution of his own secretions resulting from the in-and-out motion of sexual intercourse."

"So, he had sex with someone shortly before he died?"

"Exactly; and we have a good idea with whom. The forensics team recovered pubic hair dried into the semen on our victim's genitals, along with some epithelial skin cells, that matched not only the DNA extracted from the hair found on the floor in the archway, but the spilled blood as well. Not only that, but the trickle of *semen* located there—in the place where we know the naked woman was lying before she fled—tested positive as belonging to our John Doe. The droplet-distribution would suggest that his semen 'leaked' from her vagina…" (she remained unflappable even as she described the publicly 'unmentionable') "…at some point in time during or after being…*deposited*, indicating that they had sex together before John Doe was killed—either somewhere else or in that very spot with the security guard watching."

Deschamps' made the obvious connection. "Does the pubic hair on the unknown man's

217

genitals, *or* the hair and blood located in the museum archway, match the DNA sample we obtained from Susanne Bruante the other night?"

"A quick and dirty chromosome analysis confirms that the pubic hair on his penis and the hair discovered on the floor both belong to the same woman. The full genetic analysis will take another day to run to completion, but Bernier was willing to tell me that the comparison gene sequencing, so far, suggests a high concordance, although *not* an exact match, to Susanne Bruante's DNA."

"Concordance? Do you mean to tell me the woman our victim had sex with before he was murdered isn't Susanne Bruante, but someone *related* to her?"

"Apparently so." It was surprising, to say the least, and not so easy to explain. "I've been promised the full report by tomorrow morning."

"So our victim's lover, who was in the gallery and who is presumably one-and-the same with our missing naked 'suspect' who fled, is a Bruante." Deschamps frowned, as if trying to work out the different scenarios in his head. "What then are your conclusions, inspector?"

Michèle sat up straighter; this was her opportunity to impress the boss. "We should pursue Susanne Bruante's involvement further. Just because *she* didn't sleep with our John Doe in the museum but a relative *did*, does *not* exclude her as an accessory to the crime. Finding Bruante DNA on the body definitely *implicates* her, by way of family association if nothing else; because if she isn't our perpetrator, I'd be willing to bet she knows who was—singular less likely than plural."

"Your referring to other accomplices?"

"Exactly. It's very hard for me to imagine that two young and able bodied men could have been killed in such an efficient fashion by only one murderess. Most likely there were several people involved. Maybe our naked 'Bruante' was left behind intentionally, as a 'plant' to confuse us."

"How so?"

"Well, we have the toppled pedestal and sculpture triggering the alarm system to explain. If she had stayed behind specifically to do that, it would explain why the re-activated cameras didn't capture any of the gruesome action."

"But this makes no sense. Why bring attention to yourself when sneaking out under the cover of 'video' silence would be the better choice?"

"I'm not sure." At this point, honesty seemed the best policy. "But rest assured, sir—I'll get to the bottom of things."

Deschamps nodded. "I'm sure you will, Crossier. So, the first order of business is to assign a surveillance team tailing Susanne Bruante, if we think she was involved in some capacity. From the moment she leaves her apartment each morning until the minute she turns her lights out and goes to bed every night. I want to know where she goes, when she goes there, and who she goes with."

Michèle was one step ahead of him. "I thought you would ask for that, sir. I hope you don't mind, but I went ahead and authorized a vehicle dispatch and a personnel assignment, right before our meeting."

How would he react? She needed to be careful not to step on his toes, but at the same time she had

219

to prove to him that she had what it took to be the lead detective on a major homicide investigation. Of course she had the authority to order surveillance on a suspect, but this was the kind of thing that usually waited for the Chief Inspector's endorsement.

"Good." He actually gave her a nod of approval. *What a relief.* "I want another update by lunchtime, tomorrow." He picked up his phone and started to dial out—the signal, she gathered, that their meeting was over.

She got up and headed for the doorway; but before she reached it, he called after her: "Keep it up, Crossier."

"I will, sir," she called back over her shoulder. *I definitely will!*

CHAPTER NINETEEN

Susanne stood with Nicole in awkward silence, waiting for Henri to return with the box of family photographs. He was planning on using the uncluttered far end of his workshop table on the ground floor to display some selected examples.

"We can't do this up there," he had explained. Susanne was well aware that Henri used his dining room table on the first floor, up one flight of stairs, for many purposes, including a desk as well as a disordered filing cabinet. Piles of invoices, receipts, and other sundry paperwork were scattered and stacked here and there across the surface, to the extent that it could no longer be used for eating or entertaining, so using the workspace downstairs, on the ground floor, was really the only option.

"We might as well sit down," Susanne finally said. She took a seat in a wooden chair at the end of the extra-long table, and Nicole chose a metal stool, positioning it a good three or four spaces away. Susanne didn't trust Nicole; but judging from Nicole's distancing choice as it related to the seating arrangement, Nicole didn't trust Susanne, either. Maybe it was time to barter a truce.

"So you think you're a time-traveler?" Susanne knew it sounded ridiculous, but this was as good a place to start as any. She braced herself for some not-so-trivial small talk, but viewing it all with a grain of salt while she gathered some very questionable information.

Nicole shrugged. "I believe so. Nothing is familiar to me in this strange place, and all of my

221

memories seem so… *antiquated*, compared to everything I have seen here. I can think of no other explanation."

"What do you remember?" This would be interesting, if nothing else. Susanne would give this a little more time, at least until Henri showed them the pictures; but her skepticism was poised and ready. There was only one reason she had not turned Nicole in yet, and he would be back in a minute. Henri seemed convinced that Nicole was the real thing; so out of respect for her uncle and his oft-demonstrated intelligence, she would bide her time.

"A garret apartment, in Montmartre; artists— more than one; and memories that go on-and-on of a woman: me, posing for them in the nude. *Always* in the nude…" She had a far-off look in her eyes, as if the recollection of 'those days' (which, if her story was true, was not very long ago at all…in fact, only two days, to be exact) brought to mind both joy and sadness, at the same time.

"Do you mean to tell me that you were a nude model?" Susanne asked, incredulous. This was really too much. It was one thing for Nicole to steal Susanne's looks, but quite another for her to start encroaching on hobbies that, at least until recently, virtually bordered on a vocation.

"Yes, I was. I loved the exposure; I loved the way my body looked on canvas when the paintings were finished; and I loved what the artists and I created, both inanimate and living."

Susanne understood Nicole's love for exposure and the 'permanency' of having her naked body immortalized in a piece of art; but she couldn't fathom the love for something living…other than herself. "So, it sounds like your collaboration with some of the artists that painted wasn't limited to strictly professional. I take it that one or several of them 'knocked you up'?"

Nicole looked back at her quizzically. "What does this expression mean? I have never heard of the saying: 'knocked you up'."

"It means 'making you pregnant'. Did you have some children with some of your artist-admirers?"

Nicole smiled not-so-innocently. "Oh yes, I slept with many of them. It was Jean, though, who gave me my only baby: Edmond, just about 10 years ago by now." Well, 'Jean' was *not* the name of the artist that Henri and Susanne were on the verge of 'proving' as the father of her great-great grandfather, Edmond; so she mentally tabulated 'strike one' in this inning for the 'Nicole imposter' perched over there on her metal stool.

Nicole's smile faded and she looked down sadly. "I had hopes, though, that René would give me another; but he was killed…as you know." Tears started to trickle from both eyes. "It was horrible. The outside of his body was pristine—he didn't even have one scratch; but his insides…" (she looked down, emotionally overwhelmed) "…were gone, I think. His arms and legs were terribly twisted, like all of his bones were crushed."

Susanne was starting to feel the beginning of real compassion for the poor girl…*if* what she was saying was true and not simply a concocted fairy-tale. "So René was the fellow who 'travelled' here with you?"

"Yes."

"How about the other guy?" This would be a good test since the second 'victim' was a current-day museum employee whom Nicole, claiming to be from the nineteenth century, couldn't *possibly* know.

Nicole shrugged. "I did not know him. I think he happened to be in the way when we came out."

This was true; but why was he was standing there naked, right in front of *The Origin of the World*? Susanne vaguely knew the fellow and always thought he was a little 'off'. It wouldn't surprise her one bit if the sexually-deviant night-guard had stripped to totally nude and was getting himself off by viewing 1866's version of pornography. "Bad luck I guess, right?" Nicole did not respond so Susanne continued her information-gathering. "Was René an artist painting you?"

"He was not a painter, unlike his brother Gustave. He was a sculptor."

"Gustave?" Was she referring to Susanne's postulated great-great-great grandfather of 'Courbet' fame?

"Caillebotte." Nicole searched Susanne's eyes, perhaps for a reaction. "This is why I was so surprised to see the Caillebotte family listed on our pedigree a while ago, in your apartment. It seems that my grandson, Marcel, married Martial Caillebotte's daughter?" She shook her head. "It is so strange how life circles around. What an odd coincidence since I was involved with Martial's older brother." Very odd indeed, which only added to Susanne's continued and deepening skepticism. "He was very talented but so-far unknown; and now, he will *never* leave a legacy."

224

"This is truly a shame," Susanne commented, insincerely. Now it was *really* time to change the subject. "And your Edmond's father: this 'Jean'—was he a sculptor too...or a photographer...or something more traditional, like a painter?"

"He was a painter but had to leave many years ago, due to an unfortunate political incident coupled with his artistic...*inclination.* You see, his true love was erotic subject-matter rather than the pastoral landscapes that he was most known for." She took a breath in, visibly composing herself. "I could not take care of a little boy—not without money, and not without his father." A weaker person might have broken down, but this Nicole was tough, if nothing else. "He is better off without me, for sure—and will never know, if I can help it, that I work as a nude model. He stays with my mother, who dearly loves him and dotes on him; and keeps him protected from the life I have chosen. I—I see him when I can."

Did Susanne feel a twinge of sympathy? A little stab, maybe, she had to admit. Could Nicole be telling the truth? She sounded sincere. *But be careful, Susanne; it might be—no, probably was—just a scam.* Susanne had been a nude model, too, and it seemed an extremely odd coincidence that she and Nicole would share the same calling. It was entirely conceivable that Nicole was attempting to gain Susanne's trust by concocting a shared interest and by drumming up Susanne's empathy with an imaginative fairytale about the tragic separation of a mother from her son.

"But how did you get here? A door, a window—a rabbit hole?" Susanne asked, unable to

225

hide the sarcasm.

"It *was* a little bit like a hole." Nicole was actually serious; Susanne could see it in her face. She looked down, intently studying the surface of the table as she struggled to describe it. "I remember it was bright and swirling, empty and hot. It was a tunnel…a *wind* tunnel…that pulled me in—pulled *us* in at the exact moment that René's passion warmed me inside, taking us by surprise from behind. Just like '*la petite mort*', there was *nothing* I could do to resist the force that surrounded and joined us in that hopeless moment. It was much too strong to fight, sucking and drawing us both over the lip and into its center.

There was an even more distant look in her eyes, now. "I remember floating up, then rushing backward feet first, screaming—screaming and falling, tumbling into the whiteness. And then it was dark, all dark. I thought, at first, when it started to happen, that it was just the wine…plus something extra. You see, the two of us had been drinking a bottle or two of Bordeaux laced with absinthe and laudanum, so my head was spinning. But it wasn't the alcohol and drugs. It was *real*." She looked up, her hazel eyes locking on to Susanne's with convincing intensity. "It was real," she insisted. "I am *certain* that it was real."

It was real. Nicole spoke those words with such conviction that even Susanne, the ultimate 'doubting Thomas', imagined that her story might be true. Was it real? It couldn't be, and yet…

"I…" Susanne looked away. She had intended to say, "I'm starting to believe you," but the words just wouldn't come out. Would it be so terrible to let her guard down, for once? Why did she feel as if acknowledging Nicole's story as truth, however unlikely, was a sign of weakness? Yes, she was admittedly a defensive person—overly distrustful and exceptionally vigilant, but for good reason. She had learned, through personal experience, that trust led to heartbreak, and that it was safer to simply go it alone. Even the people who were supposed to care didn't. Case in point: look at her own mother, and even her father, who had left her not once, but twice: once in life and again in death. They had both had their own interests in mind, so why shouldn't *she*? Being selfish was necessary—a prerequisite for survival in this cold and lonely world. This hard-won philosophy had served her well so far, so why change it now?

When she heard Henri's footsteps on the stairway behind her, Susanne breathed a sigh of relief. His timing was perfect, saving Susanne from the need for further commentary. He was carrying a box, which he set on the table with a soft grunt. "It's heavy," he muttered.

Nicole walked around the table to stand next to Henri. "Have you seen pictures of me in there?" she asked.

"I do believe I have," he replied, acting very pleased with himself indeed. He started emptying the box of its photographs by the handful.

"They're all loose?" Susanne commented. "*Ton-Ton*, why haven't they been organized into photo albums or something?"

"Since when do you care about family matters?" he chided.

His comment was innocent, but still it stung.

227

Susanne acknowledged the reprimand with a grimace. "*Touché*," she responded grudgingly, knowing deep down that Henri was right. It wasn't entirely true, though. She cared for Henri; and Henri, the last time she checked, was a relative. He was different, though. He had no agenda, unlike everyone else she had ever known, who did.

It took a good half-hour for Henri to sort through the photographs. Nicole helped; and after a while, Susanne did too, although reluctantly. Finally, when they had picked out the relevant ones, Henri lifted the box containing the others out of the way and set it on the floor, arranging his samples in three neat rows in front of him on the table, with Nicole standing to his right and Susanne on his left.

The ancient photographs were no longer black and white, but aged by time to washed-out grays and faded browns. "It's a shame these were never preserved," Henri commented. "The images have faded in some of them, to the point that it's difficult to make out any of the details. You see, your great-grandfather and my father: Marcel Bruante, stored them in his attic; and when he died, they were passed on to Joelle being his eldest child—but sadly, she was the least willing of all of us to conserve our family history. I think it's too late to undo the damage, though; because photographs are not like paintings…they can't be very easily restored." He flipped over one of the photos. "Most of them aren't even marked, thanks to my father and my sister who both showed a very similar lack of interest in our family's history." He gave Susanne a sidelong glance and winked. "You have a lot in common with *both* of them!"

"Enough, *Ton-Ton*," she snapped, the sharpness in her tone a knee-jerk reaction to Henri's good-natured ribbing. He gave her a pained look that said he was only joking. "I'll help you put them in albums someday, all right?" she added hastily, the conciliatory offer her way of apologizing for her overreaction. Where had her sense of humor gone? The stress of the past few days must really be getting to her. When this was all over, she would definitely have to book herself a vacation—to someplace far, far away.

"All right." He nodded, her apology accepted.

Nicole pointed at a little boy in one of the photos, picking it up and speaking in a tone laced with sadness and conviction. "This is Edmond," she said. "He is my son."

Susanne and Henri looked at each other. "Is she right?" Susanne asked. "Is that a picture of Edmond Bruante?"

Henri nodded. "Yes, indeed." He selected another photograph that pictured the same little boy, about age nine, sitting on a woman's lap, and flipped it over to display the back. "Edmund Maurice Bruante," he read, "sitting with his *grandmère*." He pointed to the second name, running his finger across the words and the numbers as he read. "'Noelle Berthier Bruante, 1876.' Someone in the family wrote the information down on this one, but it's one of the very few with this type of annotation."

"That is my mother," Nicole chimed in, without hesitating. "She likes to be called 'Elle'. This was taken on Edmond's ninth birthday…just two months ago."

"Who is this?" Henri asked, pointing to a photograph depicting a man with a closely trimmed salt-and-pepper beard and a full head of unkempt grey hair.

"My father," she replied, "Jerome René Bruante." She gave Henri a keen look. "Does he look familiar to you?"

"Handsome, wasn't he?" He chuckled softly. "They always said I looked just like him, and I have to say I agree."

"Yes, very handsome," Nicole answered with a serious face, "and kind as well. He was always there to help, especially when times were hard for me. He's dead now though. He died when I was 21 years old, in 1869. I miss him sorely."

"I'm so sorry," Henri said, genuinely. After a polite second to allow his condolences to register, he indicated another photograph on the far right side. "And this beautiful woman?"

"Me, of course," Nicole laughed, her face brightening.

Susanne picked up the photograph and studied it with a critical eye. It showed "Nicole" standing in front of a studio landscape with an opened parasol balanced on one shoulder. She wore a below-the-knee dress, a ruffled shirt with a high collar buttoned in front, and lace-up boots, undoubtedly the height of fashion for the time. Of all the photos, this one seemed the clearest so far. Susanne looked back and forth, from the photograph to Nicole and back to the photograph again, making a careful comparison. Angled jaw—the same; mouth, lips, and smile—the same; dark hair, shoulder length, even down to the cut and style—the same; and body

230

type—the very same.

"We look alike, do we not?" Nicole commented, referring it seemed to both the photograph *and* her twenty-first century lookalike—declaring the similarities in her formal way of speaking that was actually starting to sound natural to Susanne, because she was getting so accustomed to hearing it. Nicole passed behind Henri and stood next to Susanne, giving Henri the opportunity to view them side-by-side and make a comparison. "It is interesting how appearances can be passed down through the generations, do you not agree? Henri looks just like my father; and you, Susanne…"

Susanne tried her best to make some sense of the utterly fantastic coincidence since there was no denying the affinity. "I have to say, the resemblance is truly remarkable," she finally said in the most objective voice she could muster, since honestly Susanne and Nicole could easily pass for twin sisters. Could she really be Nicole's—*what*, exactly? Great-great-great granddaughter? All of the evidence so far, unbelievable as it seemed, pointed to this bizarre conclusion; yet, Susanne would need something more than just photographs to accept the impossible.

Henri picked out three additional photos and lined them up in front of Nicole, near the edge of the table. "Do you remember when these were taken?"

Susanne listened, her skepticism lessened but by no means dispelled, as Nicole spoke. "I was about ten years old when this photograph was taken," she said, pointing to the first one on the left. It pictured her standing next to an old-fashioned

231

bicycle, wearing a frilly dress and with her hair tied back in a ribbon. "My mother brought me to a photographic studio to have it taken, and I remember being so very disappointed when I saw the image. I expected colors…" She motioned with her hand at the picture. "But, as you can see, everything came out in greys and blacks. I was wearing a lilac dress, and the bicycle was painted bright red."

Next, Nicole pointed to the second photograph, the one in the middle. "I was fourteen or so in this one." Susanne peered over Nicole's arm at the fading image, noticing a teenager who looked a lot like herself at the same age, sitting on the edge of a large stuffed chair and posed with her legs crossed and her hands folded over one exposed knee.

Henri picked up the third one, on the right side. "How about this one?" he asked.

"It was taken when I was pregnant with Edmond," she explained. Nicole was seated on a park bench this time, another prop in some photographer's studio. Her radiant face had filled in with the extra weight of a woman eating for two, her breasts large and full, and her belly protruding and round, almost but not quite as large around as the hoop supporting the creased fabric skirt she was wearing. Susanne didn't recognize herself at all in this last one, most likely because she had never been pregnant. She would probably *never* look like that, she suddenly realized. Did this trouble her? Yes, it did—more than just a little bit; but no matter. There were more important things to accomplish in life, after all. She was much better off without children.

"Well, Susanne?" Henri asked. "What do you think?"

What did she think? Nicole actually seemed to know the people in these photographs and could even explain when and where they were all taken. Was there some way she could have seen them before, maybe with *Grand-maman* in secret, a few years ago before she died last year? Somewhat unlikely; but then again, this theory was hardly as preposterous as the alternative. "Maybe she's seen these photos somewhere before," Susanne offered.

"I have," Nicole countered, clearly indignant. She obviously knew where Susanne was going with this. "I saw them when they were taken."

Susanne ignored Nicole and addressed Henri. "Do you think *Grand-maman* could have been in contact with, let's say, a distant cousin or a niece— one neither of us had known about, who just happened to be named Nicole, perhaps?" Now this was a hypothesis that deserved further consideration.

"Wait!" Nicole said, her face turning red. "I tell you that I *am* the person in these photos; I posed for *all* of them! I already told you how I got here!"

"I know, I know." Even with all of this evidence, the cynical side of Susanne still remained stubbornly unconvinced. "You claim that you were pulled into some kind of 'time-tunnel' when you were drunk and high." She rolled her eyes. "That's a good one!"

Nicole took a step toward Susanne, incited by her comment, but Henri stepped between them before the argument could escalate any further. "Stop," he ordered. "Calm down, both of you. I have more to show you, so Susanne…sit!"

"But…"

"Sit…*now!*" he repeated, his facial muscles tensing. It looked like he meant business. "Please," he added, the polite entreaty, an afterthought, doing very little to take the bite out of his command.

Susanne reluctantly took a seat in the chair that Henri had pulled out for her. "You too, Nicole—but over there." Nicole walked around to the opposite side of the table and sat down. Her face was still flushed, but pink not red.

Henri went to an easel and pulled off the sheet that he had used to cover a painting. "Do you recognize this painting, Nicole?"

"Of course! It's called *Waking Nude Preparing to Rise,*" she answered without a moment's hesitation.

Henri was visibly impressed by her quick response. "Who is the model?"

"Well it's me, of course!" Nicole declared looking proud to recognize and to be recognized.

"Correction," Susanne stated. "The model *looks* like you. She looks like me, too, but you don't hear me claiming that I actually posed for it." Although Susanne protested, she had growing cause to wonder, and she felt herself losing ground in the two-against-one debate…and for good reason. How in the world did Nicole know the name of an obscure, unsigned painting held in private for 130-odd years? And, if she was the model as she claimed, then did she *also* write the note that Henri had found concealed in the back of the painting? If so, the repercussions to Susanne's family identity and career would be life-changing.

"Where did you find this painting?" Nicole asked Henri excitedly, totally ignoring Susanne's outwardly persistent but inwardly wavering cynicism.

"It's a family heirloom that our distant relatives passed along to my late-sister. She totally ignored the rapidly deteriorating condition of the painting for years; and since I am an art restorer, I am in the process of 'restoring' it." He glanced sidelong at Susanne. "Do you want to tell Nicole what we found hidden underneath the paper backing, and what the 'experts' have concluded about it…or should I?"

Susanne breathed in and out to calm her growing excitement and to induce a more 'believing-the-unbelievable' state of mind; but before she could respond, Nicole blurted out: "Did you find my note? I had hoped my Edmond would find it; but I suppose he did not?"

Henri and Susanne looked meaningfully at each other. "He did not," Henri answered. "I discovered it when I removed the backing. Your note was examined by experts at the National Archives, and they dated the paper and the ink to sometime in the mid-to-late 1800's." He retrieved a folder from an adjacent counter, put it on the table in front of him, opened it and delicately pulled out a piece of paper: aged to dirty yellow and with deep creases marking more than a century of being folded. "Does this look familiar?"

"It was not so brown when I wrote it just a few weeks ago, before I…*left*. You see, my identity as a nude model *has* to be hidden from my little boy…" (Susanne couldn't help but notice the present tense)

"…at least until he is old enough to understand. And about his exiled father; well, my mother and I agreed that his *Papa's* identity should be kept a secret too because God forbid Edmond slips up and tells someone—*everyone* would shun him just from the association. I had hoped he would find the note when he's older, and less…talkative."

Susanne decided it was time to say out loud what she had quietly realized a moment before. "So if you're the model in this painting and also the person who wrote the hidden letter, then…"

Henri finished her sentence. "…then Gustave Courbet is the 'father' of our Bruante line."

"Yes, of course; Jean is his father." With the second 'name-drop', Susanne suddenly comprehended. Courbet had three given names: Jean, Désiré and Gustave; and Nicole referred to him using the very *first* one. So 'Jean' was actually 'Gustave' Courbet; and the famous artist was, unbelievably, Susanne's great-great-great grandfather. This meant not only that the woman standing next to her was her great-great-great grandmother but also that there were now *two* rather than *one* notable artist-family members populating the top of their family tree.

"Nicole," Henri said softly, "can you explain this?" He walked over to a drawer in one of his workbenches against the wall, opened it, and pulled out a small sample bottle. "I found this strange material embedded in the paint, but only in certain locations. The substance analysis result surprised me."

"It's hair," Nicole declared. "*My* hair, to be exact."

"Henri?" Susanne queried.

"That's right," Henri confirmed. "The report states that it *is* indeed human hair."

"And you found it painted into the picture only in places depicting hair—is that not correct, Henri?" Nicole crossed her arms and gazed across the table at Susanne with an expression that seemed to say: "I told you so."

"Yes, Nicole, that's precisely correct."

"That was his... ritual. In every one of his nude paintings of me—or any *other* model—my Edmond's father took some strands of plucked hair and mixed them into the paint. He thought that if he put a real part of his subject into the picture, in just the right place, it would breathe some life into his painting."

This was incredible. Susanne's wheels began to turn at a hundred miles per hour because Courbet's practice of imbedding his subject's hair into the paint in his erotic paintings could very well be a way to prove not only that Nicole was actually who she claimed to be, but also Susanne's model singularity theory—an extra, and *much* more important, bonus. "How many of Courbet's nude paintings did you pose for?"

Nicole shrugged. "*All* of them."

Susanne's heart skipped a beat. "Did you model nude for other artists as well?"

"Of course. It is my calling, and *everyone* likes to paint me."

This is when Susanne realized that Nicole's unexpected arrival was fortune's blessing rather than destiny's curse.

CHAPTER TWENTY

It was already getting dark at the end of a very long day—the *same* day: June first, it was hard to believe, of her strange arrival in this even stranger place. Nicole rode in the passenger seat, while Susanne drove.

This was her second experience traveling in what Susanne and Henri had called a "car," so this time around, it seemed almost natural. On the drive to Henri's, though, Nicole had been seated in the back. In the front now, she had a better view of all the dials, buttons, and flashing lights: a truly amazing sight. She had found out that she had a knack for assimilating new information quickly, a talent that she hadn't been aware of until now. Who knows, she might even try her hand someday behind the so-called "wheel," as Susanne called it—maybe for their third trip, whenever that might be. It did not look so difficult.

Susanne had changed her tune—mostly, it seems, because of the hair that Henri had found in the painting of her, as well as Nicole's innocent reference to the artist, her lover and father of her dear Edmond: Jean Gustave Courbet. Susanne and Henri had exchanged some excited words in low tones, trying to digest this newest revelation. Nicole had decided to give them a few minutes. It wasn't every day that you found yourself face-to-face with a time traveler who just happened to be a relative who carried with her the long-awaited answer to a family secret; and although this whole thing wasn't as stressful for them as it was for her, she understood that her presence here—one hundred and thirty-four years out of place and featuring an arrival that could only be described as life-changing for more than one of them—would take some getting used to.

The Courbet connection had created the most 'buzz'. From the back-and-forth exchange between uncle and niece, Nicole surmised that her Jean was nothing short of famous here—known by the second of his two *middle* names, Gustave, rather than his first; and respected as it turns out (*go figure*) rather than reviled. If this fact was a surprise to Nicole, both Henri and Susanne seemed to be doubly stunned (*stupefied* was more like it) to discover the identity of Nicole's unknown partner—until now an empty box on Henri's Bruante family tree.

Now a name could actually be scribbled in that blank space in their pedigree—but not just any name. Henri had told her that Gustave Courbet: *her* Jean, had after his death earned the reputation as the father of a group of painters in France known as the Realists. Nicole had been unaware that Jean was the father of *anything*, except for her now nine-year-old Edmond. Back *there*, in the time she had come from, he had been scorned by other artists; but *here*, he was loved and admired—a turn of events that she had sort of predicted, when she wrote the note revealing Edmond's parentage and her dubious profession, hiding it behind the unsigned painting that would be passed on through the generations, finally ending up *here*. What a shame Jean would never know about his posthumous change in fortune. He would be so proud.

"I was his mistress," Nicole had explained to

239

them after the dust had started to settle. "I was the closest thing to a wife that he ever had. I even lived with him…but he would go no further with the relationship."

"That sounds familiar," Susanne quipped.

"So, you have had men like that?" Nicole asked.

"That's not what she means," Henri had said quickly. "You were on the receiving end, Nicole. Susanne has always been on the delivery end. She's had some very nice boyfriends, too. What a shame they never seem to last."

"Men never do," Susanne responded elusively, after shooting Henri a look that seemed to say, 'Stay out of my business; and while you're at it, keep *her* out of it, too.'

"Oh, I see," Nicole said, taking the cue and backing out of Susanne's personal space with a quiet nod. She did see, though. Susanne was independent, stubborn, and driven. Also, she did not seem like the trusting sort. These character traits, in combination with a self-centered outlook on life, did not constitute a winning recipe for a long-lasting relationship like marriage. No wonder Susanne had never settled down with anyone.

"If Nicole is really who she says (and we think) she is," Susanne continued, steering the conversation back on track, "I have a way now to prove my 'model singularity' theory."

"What's that?" Nicole had asked.

"*You*," Susanne said, simply.

"I don't understand."

"You see, the exhibit you 'toured' on arrival is a display of nude paintings—most but not all by

Courbet. My hypothesis, impossible to prove until now, is that *all* of these paintings feature the very *same* model—hence the designation 'singularity' which, using your hair as proof, will soon be synonymous with the 'first person singular': *you*.

"Slow down, Susanne," Henri interrupted. "First, we need to have Nicole's hair analyzed and compared to these samples from *Waking Nude Preparing to Rise*."

"Of course, of course; that's exactly what I mean." Susanne was literally bubbling with excitement now, and talking a mile a minute— mostly to herself, partly to Henri, and most definitely not to Nicole. "If Nicole's hair, and the hair from this painting, match, there can be no question that she came from the past. How else could her hair end up in a painting from the 1870s, unless she was actually the model? And she *does* look like the nude woman in all of the exhibit's paintings…*and* the photography display!"

Nicole had frowned to herself. Was Susanne referring to the nude photos in the last room, where she had exited the exhibit and escaped into the back hallway? That model was *definitely* not her, given the absence of the nefariously-placed birthmark. "Do you mean…" Nicole began, intending to finish her sentence with 'the nude 'body-scapes' in the museum?' if Susanne had only let her.

"How could I *possibly* continue to argue, if the hair is a match," Susanne raced ahead. "She travelled here for a reason; and *that* reason…"

"…is *not* all about you," Henri finished.

Now it seemed that Susanne was more than eager to believe Nicole's story, for blatantly selfish reasons revolving around her precious theory. Before, she would have argued black in the face of white; but now, she would have taken it at face value if Nicole had claimed she was from the moon. Susanne was out for Susanne; and suddenly, now that she had something to gain, she had turned her colors as if she were a chameleon.

"It won't be sufficient to just match Nicole's hair with the hair from *Waking Nude Preparing to Rise*. We'll have to find a way to collect some samples from the *other* Courbet paintings in the museum, too," Susanne was saying. "I'll think of some excuse to get us in there, at night." She turned to Nicole. "If I showed you some paintings, do you think you'd remember where 'Jean' painted in your hair?"

"*Mais oui.* I remember *all* of Jean's paintings of me. I can show you where to look, but more often than not, his choice was obvious."

She thought back to the time she had posed, barely eighteen, for the explicit one: the painting that he called *The Origin of the World*, in 1866. Jean had teased her, asking where he should place the strands of her hair. She had playfully taunted him back by lifting her head, looking through her open legs to smile suggestively at him—guiding his focus to 'elsewhere': down *there*, as he painted-in the dark and curly details of his banned masterpiece. He had finished it that day and they had celebrated its completion right then and there—Nicole still maintaining the very same position of the past many-months of posing while Jean abandoned the image on his easel to lay on-top and inside of the real thing, conceiving their son together in stroke-

242

after-fertile-stroke of nature's passionate brush. Rejected, of course, by *Le Salon*, the sensational painting never did get a proper showing. Nicole had hung it at the foot of her bed after he left, in her rooftop apartment, right next to her crucifix, as a way to keep it close. It was always one of her favorites, second only to *Waking Nude Preparing to Rise*—and Jean's too, he had always claimed.

"Obvious, you say? That's good," Susanne had said, nearly salivating with eagerness. "If we get some samples from three or four of Courbet's paintings, that should clinch it."

"You can't use evidence that you allege was obtained from a time traveler, Susanne," Henri pointed out patiently. "Everyone will think you're crazy."

"I won't have to say a word about a time traveler, or any specifically-named person at all. All we have to share is the data showing equivalency between the hair from the museum paintings, and *Waking Nude Preparing to Rise*. If the DNA report happens to confirm that Nicole's hair matches too, that's private business and we'll have to figure out what we should do with her, of course; but that's a problem for *later*, and not something that we should publicize."

Nicole didn't like the sound of 'we'll have to figure out what we should do with her', spoken like she was an insignificant afterthought—not one bit; and her guess was that Henri hadn't either, judging from the scowl on his face. Nicole was obviously a secondary concern, now that Susanne's cherished theory had come to the forefront. Henri sat down next to Nicole at the table in what seemed to be a

243

protective maneuver.

In the meantime, Susanne was moving ahead with her manic-sounding diatribe, seemingly oblivious to her listeners. "The important evidence will be provided by comparing the hair extracted from our family painting and the *d'Orsay* pieces. It's beautiful—I won't have to identify Nicole as the model at all! If the DNA results show that the same anonymous model posed for *all* of the nudes on display, then my 'model singularity theory' is validated—*slam-dunk*. It couldn't be more perfect. I'm going to be famous."

Henri rolled his eyes. "Famous or not, we need to take 'first-things-first.'" He retrieved some scissors from a kitchen drawer, but Nicole saved him the trouble by plucking out some strands of her hair.

"This is how Jean always did it," she had explained; and if her true identity was on the line, she wanted to make sure they got it right.

"Thank you," Henri had replied. "My contact in the *Materials Laboratory* can send these off for rapid DNA testing. It shouldn't take very long at all to find out if the hair fragments are identical or different. I expect to have an answer in less than twenty-four hours."

He had kissed Nicole warmly on both cheeks, taking her hands in his. "I never thought I'd meet my great grandmother. You died long before I was born, *chérie!*"

Nicole's heart swelled, looking at this man who so closely resembled her dear late Papa. "And who would have thought that my great grandson would look just like my father! I wish I could tell *Maman*;

244

she would be so curious and intrigued."

"Well, maybe you'll have that chance. You got here somehow, so maybe we can get you back the same way, *n'est-ce pas*?"

Nicole couldn't imagine how in the world they would ever be able to manage that. Her journey from the past had been triggered by who knows what—an accidental fluke, an unexplainable process that no one could possibly understand or reproduce. Or could they? Susanne apparently knew someone who might.

And that was exactly who Susanne was talking about right now, as they drove together back to the apartment on *Avenue Georges V*. Nicole was shaken from her reverie by Susanne's laugh. "It's funny, I just saw a clip of a press conference, from *today* no less, on *France 24*…and there he was—larger than life: Dr. John Noland. We were… *involved* for a while in college, when I was an exchange student in the United States."

"And you think he can help me?"

"If he can't, then no one can. He's made quite a name for himself in a scientific field they call 'time-space quantum mechanics'. From what I've read in the newspapers over the past few months, your problem is right up his alley."

"Truly? In what way?"

"In exactly the way we need. In the press conference, he explained that he's actually sent mice backward and forward in time."

They were approaching an intersection just around the corner from Susanne's apartment, where the dangling light up above them had just turned from green to red. 'Red', Nicole had surmised by

245

now, meant to stop, and Susanne was doing just that. She slowed the car, easing it to a halt well into the white-lined crosswalk. From this position, they could easily see Susanne's apartment, off to the left and across the street; and glancing over, Nicole noticed the same thing that Susanne obviously had.

"Police," Susanne murmured. A white Citroen, marked with an emblem on the door and what appeared to be a colorful lantern on its roof, had pulled alongside an unmarked vehicle that was parked almost directly in front of Susanne's apartment. The drivers were talking to each other with serious expressions on their faces through open windows, the professional interaction leaving no room for doubt that the individuals inside the ordinary-looking dark-blue Renault were gendarmes as well, only dressed in 'plain clothes'. A moment later, the marked car pulled away and drove in the opposite direction down a side street, well before their light turned green.

"What should we do?" Nicole asked.

Susanne didn't answer; but when the light changed, she drove her light-blue BMW straight ahead rather than turning left, pulling over alongside the curb on the quiet street, three blocks down. She turned the key and shut off the engine.

"I think they've put me under surveillance," she commented. "We can't let them see you because after all, you're still 'wanted'."

"So, *now* what shall we do?"

Susanne rummaged through her purse and pulled out a long iron key. "There's a courtyard behind my building that you can access from a walkway, located two and a half blocks behind us,

246

on this street. You can't miss it. A street sign marks the alley—it's called *La Rue Étriqué*." She handed Nicole the key. "When you get to the end, use this to open the gate. Once you're in, keep out of sight. You should hide behind some bushes, over by the wall toward the back of the garden. I'll come down and get you later, once the police in the Renault outside think I'm sleeping. There's a back stairway. I'll let you in, maybe in an hour or so."

"Do not forget me, please." Nicole was only half joking.

"No need to worry about that. After all, we're related!"

Yes, that was true; but nevertheless, Nicole had a feeling that Susanne would turn in her own mother if there were something in it for her. Make no mistake about it, Susanne was keeping Nicole around now because it suited Susanne. Nicole's identity was now a means to an end: one that involved recognition and advancement in her career once she proved her 'model singularity theory' using some real-time and 'past'-time strands of Nicole's hair as evidence.

Well, if her professional aspirations prevented her from turning Nicole in, so much the better; and now there might actually be someone out there who could help Nicole return to where she truly belonged. Susanne seemed optimistic that this John Noland would know what to do. Nicole prayed that she was right. She also hoped that the nature of Susanne's past relationship with the man would not dampen his willingness to help; because if what Henri had said about Susanne was true, Nicole could well imagine that a jilted ex-lover might not

247

be very eager to drop everything and come to Susanne's aid.

Nicole stepped out of the car, watching as Susanne pulled out and drove back the other way. She waited a few minutes, to give Susanne enough time to distract the watching gendarmes with her arrival. Would they stop her after she had parked, while she was climbing the front stairs to her apartment's entrance, perhaps to ask her some more questions about the incident at the museum? In all likelihood 'no', Susanne had said. She felt fairly certain that they had been dispatched to watch her comings and goings, and maybe to follow her when she decided to leave her flat again.

The street was dark and quiet, with no sign of commotion three blocks down, so Nicole clutched the key in her hand and made her own way back, the way they had come. She finally reached the cobblestoned alley which Susanne had correctly ascertained had been impossible to miss. At the end of the walkway, she turned the key in the lock and opened the gate as quietly as she could. The bushes would provide good cover and now it was time to wait. An hour would pass quickly, especially with her eyes closed, she thought; and with that, she settled in with her back to the wall, exhausted— drifting a few moments later into a dead sleep.

CHAPTER TWENTY-ONE

John Noland stepped away from the tour group at the famous Tower of London when his cell phone rang. He didn't want to disrupt the guide, who was gearing up to begin an explanation of the Jewel Room's history. This was John's first trip to London—nearly all business with some pleasure thrown in here and there, like today; and the tour of the historic medieval castle, taking place during some much-needed 'down time', had been fascinating so far. He had somehow survived his well-meaning press conference yesterday, soured slightly by hungry paparazzi and more-than-slightly by a full row of animal rights protestors; but now he could concentrate on the more-sober task of scientific presentations and collegial consultations, scheduled to take place during the next ten days of his U.K. tour.

He could see from the caller ID that his administrative assistant was calling, so he would probably be able to take the call quickly without missing too much of the guide's dissertation.

"Hi Janet. What's up?"

"Sorry to interrupt, but a woman by the name of Susanne Bruante with a lovely French accent just called, asking for your cell phone number. Is it okay for me to give it to her?"

He almost dropped the phone. "Did you say Susanne Bruante?"

"Yes. That's the name she gave."

'Stunned' was the only way to describe his emotions. Susanne? Why in the world would

Susanne be calling him after almost twenty years—and why now?

She had completely ignored all of his attempts to contact her by letter or by phone after she left Chicago that spring so long ago, without a single word of explanation. After a year of silence and many unanswered phone calls and letters, John had finally given up. He had eventually come to the realization that he had grossly misinterpreted their college affair as something serious while she had clearly viewed their relationship as a trivial source of entertainment—a fly-by-night affair that served mostly to pass the time but was never destined, from her perspective, to amount to anything but a fling. It was so very painful to remember how naïve he had been back then, and how easily he had fallen hopelessly in love with her, from the very first moment he had seen her.

Was she calling to apologize? He tried to tell himself that it hardly mattered anymore; but still, a word of explanation would go a long way toward closing the door that she had left wide open when she disappeared. He had long since ceased to care—or so he had thought, until he had heard her name spoken again just a moment ago by Janet on the other end of the phone-line.

"Dr. Noland? Are you still there?"

"Uh… yes, I'm here."

"Well?"

"Well, what?" His mind was elsewhere—at the University of Chicago in 1993, to be exact; and he had honestly forgotten what Janet had just asked him only a few seconds ago.

"I was wondering if it would be okay for me to

250

give Ms. Bruante your cell phone number."

Should he? "I'm not sure. Did she say what she wanted?"

"All right, out with it. Who is she?" Janet was a matronly woman in her early sixties who had been John's secretary for ten years now; and more often than not, she functioned more as a mother than as an administrative assistant. "If I had to guess from your reaction, I'd say that she's probably one of your most recent romantic conquests."

He sighed. She was actually just the opposite. "Hardly. She's an old love interest, and one that I haven't heard from in years." She was the one that 'got away', but he wasn't about to tell Janet that.

"Hmm. Is it a good thing or a bad thing that you're hearing from her now?"

"That's hard to say. I guess it depends on why she decided to contact me, after almost two decades."

"Well, there's only one way to find out," Janet said. "You haven't answered me yet. Should I give her your number, or not?"

He sighed again. Now that Susanne had made the first volley, he couldn't very well refuse to return the ball. Her unexpected phone call had definitely piqued his interest. "Okay, Janet, give her my mobile number, but tell her to wait until tonight to call me, no earlier than eight o'clock London time. I still have some sightseeing to do, and we're just getting to the most interesting part of the tour." He had to admit that it felt good to put her off. Now it was *his* turn to make her wait, although a measly three or four hours was nothing compared to eighteen years.

"I'll tell her. And good luck."

John finished his tour, but while the guide spoke of Edward Longshanks, Henry VIII, and Anne Boleyn, all John could think about was Susanne.

'Susanne Bruante'. Just hearing her name for the first time in almost twenty years brought back all the memories in a nostalgic flash. He saw himself sitting at a long, oak table cluttered with books, in the hushed silence of the library reading room in late October, so long ago. He had looked up from his quantum mechanics textbook, and that's when he saw her for the first time: the gorgeous epitome of what he felt certain was an unapproachable and impossible fantasy. John Noland, shy and overly studious, had never dreamed that such a beautiful woman would ever have an interest in him so he had resigned himself to admiring her from a distance, finding himself spending more and more time at the library, sitting in his usual seat and hoping that she would come to the reading room again—which she did, on one or two occasions. Once he thought she might even have looked his way, if only for a fleeting moment.

And so the months had passed. The fall semester ended and the winter term began; and then one day, he found himself sitting behind an easel on a cold, snowy day in early January, while he waited with the rest of his painting class for the model of the day to emerge from the back room and remove her robe. This was an evening elective for the biophysics major, who had inherited a knack for science from his father and a talented artistic eye from his mother. It was 7 p.m., and the clear winter sky, already speckled with stars, was visible through the domed skylight of the studio. This sitting would be one of three using the same nude subject: female this time; and he would have three short hours tonight: Monday, then again on Wednesday, and finally one week from today, on Monday next, to produce a unique interpretation of her posing using oil on canvas.

The art studio, a vast room occupying the entire second floor of the art building's annex, was a chilly warehouse of creative clutter. One glance at the disorganized collection of metal stools, wooden easels, partly finished projects, and paraphernalia arranged in haphazard displays for various still-life drawing classes drew his attention, tonight as always, to the drastic contrast between the artistic and the scientific. The clean sterility of autoclaved test tubes arranged neatly in dust-free laboratory cabinets appealed to his analytical side, but the limitless reaches of disorder that he always discovered in his imagination whenever he picked up a paintbrush seemed to represent an essential antidote to his all-too predictable mathematical equations.

The instructor set up two portable heaters on either side of the raised platform that he had pushed against the wall in the front of the classroom. Next, he adjusted the lighting by moving a floor lamp closer; then, satisfied, he covered the rough wooden pedestal—an eight-by-four-foot rectangle standing two feet high or so—with a burgundy sheet. He completed his preparations by placing two worn couch pillows against the wall—intended, of course, to make the model more comfortable after the

253

details of her posturing were decided. Accustomed to this routine, John and his classmates had arranged their easels in a semi-circle in front of the set-up so they would all enjoy the same view, more-or-less, of the model's pose.

It felt so primal—it always did. He was surrounded by the organic smells of pine resin distilled into turpentine, musky earth transformed into sculpting clay, flax seed pressed into oil paints, and rock and mineral pulverized into plaster and charcoal. Soon, the aroma of primordial nature would be visually enhanced by a live model, her skin and flesh exposed, her naked body harking back to some ancient sexuality. In a moment, she would be lying there, reclining on a bed of burgundy, the feminine symbol of mankind's creation and the origin, really, of the world's first beginnings; and he, of all people, would have the opportunity to brush her image—and everything it represented—onto his canvas. He looked at his watch. The sitting would begin in two or three minutes, and he was ready.

"Another nude." Paul, the student to his left, gave a short laugh. "I always have a problem with the hands—and the arms, legs, and feet," he joked.

"Your nudes are always perfect, and you know it." John and Paul had been friends since freshman orientation week, and during sophomore year they had roomed together in the dorm. They saw each other less frequently now since their majors: Astrophysics for John and Visual-Arts for Paul, *and* their circle of friends owing to disparate academic concentrations, were so different. They shared this final oil-painting class together, knowing that soon,

254

after graduation, they would be going their separate ways.

"I'm more of a landscape artist," Paul answered. "You're the expert in nudes, my friend—which reminds me, did anything happen between you and that cute freshman at the student center last night? She seemed to like you quite a bit."

"You mean Leslie? I'm her TA in bio, Paul. There's an exam next week, and she had some questions, that's all."

Paul shook his head. "You're a blind man. She likes you, and she's a knock-out."

John waved away the comment. "My interests lie elsewhere."

"Do you mean the brunette from the library you keep talking about?" He laughed. "I'm skeptical, John. I think you've made her up just to get me off your back. I don't think she even exists."

John shrugged. "Oh, she *exists* all right. She's the most beautiful woman I've ever seen and I think I'm in love with her."

"That's ridiculous. You won't even talk to her!"

"I'll talk to her; it's just taking me a while to get up the nerve."

"Three months?"

"I just don't want to rush in too quickly and ruin everything." What he didn't want to ruin, he kept telling himself, was the image of the perfect woman he had constructed of her in his mind…but this was really just an excuse. It was better to live miserably with false hope than to live even more miserably with the disappointment of rejection.

Paul was just about to give John another earful

of well-intentioned but useless advice when the instructor started talking. "You will have three sittings to complete your painting. Ms. Bruante, we're ready for you now."

The model emerged from the side room, and his heart stopped—*not* because she strode confidently to the front without even bothering to tie her bathrobe, her unabashed exhibition of frontal nudity a heart-pounding declaration of female magnificence; *not* because her naked body, fully revealed when she nonchalantly let the cotton garment slide off her shoulders to land at her feet like waves encircling a statue of Venus, was more stunning than even his dreams had ever imagined; and *not* because she was, to him, Aphrodite: incarnate—the epitome of female beauty and the symbol of his deepest and purest sexual longing; but because he actually *knew* her.

When John's jaw dropped, Paul noticed. "What's wrong, John?"

"It's *her*. I can't believe this." John kept his voice low, not wanting their nude 'subject' to hear.

"What do you mean: 'It's her'?"

"It's *her*—the model…she's the girl from the library!"

Paul laughed.

"What's so funny?"

"Well, you certainly have good taste. She's a beauty, all right. If I knew Susanne was your love interest, I would have introduced you to her months ago."

'Susanne'—Susanne Bruante; so *that* was her name. It was beautiful…*she* was beautiful. "What— you mean you actually *know* her?"

256

"Sure I do. She's an exchange student in the Art Department, from Paris. A sophomore, I think."

"You will give us my posing now, for you, Professor?" Susanne asked, her accent exotic and her grammar endearingly stilted.

"I think we'll paint you reclining tonight, Ms. Bruante." The professor offered his outstretched hand to indicate that she should lie on the platform he had so meticulously prepared for her a moment earlier.

With a nod, she gracefully stepped out and away from her discarded bathrobe and strolled, completely and gloriously exposed, onto the slightly raised pallet—the most compelling '*Nude Reclining*' that John could ever imagine and the embodiment of what, to him, represented the definition of sensual perfection. How his hand shook when he held the charcoal pencil in his trembling fingers to trace and shadow her oval face, those elegant cheekbones, the rounded fullness of her breasts, and the smooth curve of her waist and hips. The moment was exquisite—*she* was exquisite: a goddess for his drawing-hand to worship as it filled in what his eyes could hardly believe he was seeing. She was his unreachable and unapproachable ideal—yet here she was, not even ten feet away from him. It was nothing less than a miracle. Fate had smiled on him, and now was his opportunity to smile back—but he had only three nights to do it.

He was painting now, and she was his world. He wondered what it would feel like to touch the strands of soft auburn hair that fell on her delicate shoulders or to explore the greens and browns of her

257

warm and complicated eyes; or, to kiss her smoldering red lips and feel the universe spin out of control around him. One hour, two hours, then three—their time was up, but she promised to return.

The second night, on Wednesday, he worked on her limbs—arms, hands, and fingers positioned just so, thighs and calves smooth and pale, leading to the high arch of two delicate feet and ten perfect toes. How many lovers had those arms and legs embraced with passion and tenderness? How many hearts had been hers, and how many hearts had she broken? Would she, or could she, ever give herself to a man like him? *Never*, he thought sadly as he had left the studio with an aching heart, his work completed for the night. Now he would have to wait until Monday to see her again—five long days and five sleepless nights. How would he survive until the next sitting; but more important yet, what would he do when the posing was finished and she slipped on her bathrobe, walking out of the studio and his life permanently?

Monday, the night of her final nude session, came at last; and with it, he vowed to change his future and his life forever by approaching her, promising himself that with just a few words and a little self-confidence he would make the impossible become possible. Some shadowing here, a lighter tone there—a perfect body nearing complete; and now the burgundy background, the final touches under and all around. How he wished that he could be that very same backdrop, given permission by mere inanimate proximity to touch her, awed and reverent, in those places that heaven had made so

258

perfectly and that only the lucky chosen could adore and caress.

Then, suddenly, their eyes locked—her hazel spark connecting, for more than a moment, with his imploring blue. She kept his gaze captive while her lips parted in what he felt sure was a silent offer, accentuated by a subtle smile that whispered 'come to bed with me' in his disbelieving ear. His heart stopped—it couldn't *possibly* be true! But it was…*wasn't it?*

"Amazing, Mr. Noland." Yes, she truly *was*; but that's not what the instructor, who was standing behind John's left shoulder, was referring to when he had disrupted the visual contact. "Your nudes are simply incredible, and this one is no exception. She's turned out quite well. You realize, of course, that this hobby of yours could easily become a career." The professor was already on to his next critique, but his interruption, to John's dismay, had broken the spell. John tried desperately to make eye contact again, but Susanne's gaze seemed to be occupied elsewhere. Was she flirting with Chad now, who was sitting two chairs over from John? His heart dropped. He should have known—this was *Chad's* dream, not his. It all made sense, really; this girl was way out of his league—a much better match for Mr. GQ, of course. He should have known…

The clock on the wall said ten p.m.; their time was up. A moment later Susanne was excused with a grateful 'thank you' from the professor. She stood in no rush to leave, leisurely exercising her cramped, naked muscles this way and that, with both arms in the air—intentionally provocative it

259

seemed since she remained in full view of the still-gawking audience of artists who were only half-heartedly gathering up their supplies, one eye preoccupied with her post-posing stretches. John couldn't help notice that her nipples were tense like blushing pearls rimmed with salmon-pink, tightened to full attention either by the stimulating chill in the air or by something else entirely. He longed to touch them…touch *her*, in the way that only lovers are allowed.

She no longer bothered to cover up with the bathrobe, which she had left behind in the dressing room for sittings two and three, so she had nothing to don or gather. As she had for the past two nights but even more so now it seemed, she took her time getting off the platform gaining the full attention of the more eager male students who waited keenly for her to wander, as per her usual nightly routine, between the easels on her way back to her dressing room: over there and to the right.

But she didn't follow her usual path. What was she doing? She was actually coming this way, to the left—toward Chad, maybe, who sat in back and over further against the wall: *à gauche*? John's muscled classmate with the chiseled jaw was blatantly eyeing her up and down as he gathered his art supplies, and it certainly looked at first as if she would accept the implied invitation of his lurid stare—but no! For some reason she changed her mind *and* her trajectory. She was walking this way—*definitely* walking this way, there was no doubt about it…directly towards John!

Now, sleek and naked, she veered dangerously closer—so close he could smell her skin, her

260

perfume, and even her sex: elemental, alluring and intoxicating. She slowed down, stepping around his supplies, but facing *towards* him, not away—the front of her body turning to full-view as she sidestepped between his paint box and his easel. And then she stopped for the briefest of moments as if she was studying him and expected him to study *her* in return (how could he not?), standing to face him full-frontal not even two feet away.

She smiled, deliciously and seductively close, lingering for just a moment. She leaned her head forward a few inches and whispered: "*Excusez-moi*," her breath lingering in the air like an invitation; meeting his eye as she had during the sitting for the most meaningful of seconds, but then looking down again. And then before he knew it she was gone.

There was no denying the message in her look; and now, as she disappeared into the changing room, she actually looked back for a moment over her shoulder...at *him*! Maybe it was his dream instead of Chad's, after all; and so, in a split second, it was settled. He would try to approach her because fate, after all, demanded it now—but if he didn't hurry, he would miss the opportunity.

He finished gathering his supplies quickly—no, *frantically*. When she emerged, dressed in jeans and a low-cut V-neck sweater, he timed his exit perfectly to ensure that he would be a step or two behind her on the stairway leading down to the lobby. He rushed to catch up with her, and was just about to offer her an awkward compliment when she abruptly stopped and turned. He barely had time to stop, almost losing his balance as he grabbed the stairway railing. Now, he found himself standing only *inches* away from her, on the same stair no less, face-to-face and eye-to-eye.

Her eyes: what color were her eyes? Hazel, amber, ochre, russet—all of these combined and blended into some kind of magical kaleidoscope of browns. And now, up close, he suddenly noticed the greens, too—delicate slivers of olive, emerald, clover, and teal that shimmered in the flickering fluorescence of the annex stairwell.

"I am a very beautiful statue with no clothes on—*non*?" she asked, unashamed—no, *proud*—of her willingness to expose herself to a roomful of students, most of whom she interacted with on a regular basis in her art major and would have to face in other classes the next day. Actually, she seemed to delight in the shock factor, smiling mischievously as she waited for his response to her self-commentary. He was taken aback that she would draw attention to her unselfconscious nudity with such nonchalance in their first interaction.

Although he wanted to, he wasn't sure if complimenting her stunning body was the most appropriate response, so he decided to choose the middle ground. "Yes, you are a perfect…*statue*. I'm not sure how you can hold a pose for that long without moving. It's very… impressive."

She was so close he could have kissed her; but she beat him to it. Her lips were wet and soft on his, and the brief touch of her tongue shot a fire-bolt of longing through his very core. She withdrew with one hand on his cheek, and the other touching his palm as she handed him a scrap of paper. "*Telephoné mois*, tomorrow…and I be statue for you again, but in private. *D'accord*?"

He spoke French fluently since his mother's family came from Paris; but all he could do was stammer a feeble: *oui* as he watched her walk away, his jaw slack and his eyes wide with disbelief. He couldn't believe it. She was the sexiest woman he had ever seen, and for some unclear reason she had picked him.

Alone then, he had sat on the stair as the last few stragglers from the dismissed art class passed by, unfolding the slip of paper on which she had written her phone number. Now, nearly twenty years later and alone again, he sat in the corner of the Dickens-style English pub, in the heart of London, and ordered a Guinness to accompany his shepherd's pie. He looked at his watch—8:00.

He laid his cell phone on the table, pretending not to care that the screen remained dark and quiet. She might not call until 9:00, or 10:00; or, she might not call at all. It didn't really matter, he told himself; but deep down, he knew it did. The stout tasted bitter, just like his memories; but he had resolved to do his best and let bygones be bygones. It was healthier that way.

What would she say, and how would he react to hearing her voice? Every scenario made him feel nervous. It made no logical sense. He was over her—wasn't he? Maybe so; but why, then, did the thought of talking to her make him break out in a cold sweat? He made a concerted effort to relax. When, and if, the screen turned bright, he would be ready. After all, he had the upper hand, now, not her. She was reaching out to *him*, not the other way around; so if he played it cool, it would all work out. Wouldn't it?

It would. Maybe if he kept repeating it in his mind, it would.

CHAPTER TWENTY-TWO

It was just past eight p.m. 'London' time: 2 June, 2011. It had only been two short days since Nicole had arrived, but it seemed much longer given all they had learned—about paintings, nude models, and family secrets: Bruante, Courbet, and Caillebotte alike; and now it was time to get down to business.

As Susanne sat in her office getting ready to call him, she reviewed in her mind how she would best persuade John Noland to drop whatever he was doing in the U.K. and come to Paris ASAP to help her. She could claim that she had never forgotten him and that she regretted the way she had dropped him years ago, but that would be a lie. The physical aspect of their campus romance had been mutually satisfying, but the emotional investment in their affair had been truly one-sided. She had been perfectly satisfied with the concept of their involvement as being nothing but a superficial fling focused on physical pleasure only, and had had no desire whatsoever to move their relationship into the realm of serious emotional commitment.

Had she led him on? Not intentionally; but after the fact, she later recognized that her failure to openly define her casual intentions had led him to think otherwise. She wanted sex without the endless discussions of love and obligation, and he had seemed to be the perfect solution, at least on the surface. He was attractive, quiet, and reserved; insecure and inexperienced; and so easy to distract with a kiss and a promise that they would 'talk about it later'. How could she have predicted that he would fall so terribly hard for her?

Well, that was his problem in the end, not hers; so she had left without even leaving a note, never feeling a single twinge of guilt as she tossed his unopened letters into the trash and deleted his piteous voicemails without even a second thought for his feelings. He'd get over her; he'd have to.

She couldn't offer him her heart, then or now, but what about her body? He had taken it once— correction, over and over again—for a full semester, but admittedly under false pretenses. The concept of '*l'affaire*' was foreign to him, and instead their intimacy (to him) was a sacred promise: clear and final. He was so naïve, assuming that physical closeness automatically translated into something more. Admittedly, she had never told him otherwise; and he had unfortunately misinterpreted her reticence as some kind of silent affirmation. In the few messages she'd read from his initial mailings, he had moved from puzzlement to betrayal, and she wouldn't be at all surprised if now, after almost two decades, he still felt used.

No, she firmly decided; unless he was still the same green and trusting John Noland from 1993, she would never be able to lure him to Paris with the promise of sex or as an old love newly discovered. There was only one way to get him here, and that was by appealing to his mind rather than to his body. Could he resist the opportunity to see the embodiment of his life's work in a real live person instead of a lab rat? Susanne had watched yesterday's press conference taped on *YouTube* and had *Googled* his experiments and theories, so she

266

knew he couldn't pass up this once-in-a-lifetime chance to see his sci-fi brand of biological-physics at work.

And Nicole was the real thing—Susanne was certain about that now, thanks to the positive match between the hair extracted from *Waking Nude Preparing to Rise* and the plucked strand of Nicole's auburn locks. Henri's contact had been true to his word, turning around the DNA analysis, as promised, in less than a day. It was fascinating, really; but more than just a little bit bizarre. Her great-great-great grandmother, translocated from the nineteenth-century to the twenty-first, was actually her real-time houseguest, hiding like a fugitive at this very moment in Susanne's apartment.

John would come—she felt certain he would—because her strange guest was living proof of his theory. After all, hosting a time traveler was certainly not an everyday occurrence.

Nicole's fortuitous arrival would be a career-maker for Susanne, as well. Once they obtained the samples from the Courbet nudes, Susanne Bruante's name would be on everyone's lips when her 'model singularity' hypothesis became reality rather than conjecture. Who could *not* appreciate this 'first step' in the direction of giving credit-where-credit-was-due; because after all, what did people remember most when they looked at a nude painting? The model, of course—*much* more than the painting's artist. It was high time the 'subjects' of countless nude masterpieces be acknowledged for their boldness in rejecting societal norms—all in the name of art.

But the professional piece was only the start.

267

She had already figured out a way to eventually introduce her family name: proof-positive, into the art history books, whether or not Nicole or Henri agreed to this professionally-necessary disclosure. She would tell a little white lie and claim that Nicole's matching hair, used in the comparison DNA evaluation, had actually come from a brush or a comb stored away in her late-grandmother's attic, engraved perhaps with her great-great-great grandmother's name, Nicole Thérèse Bruante: the very same woman who had hidden the confessional-style letter—signed, sealed and delivered—behind the painting identifying herself as Gustave Courbet's lover, Edmond Bruante's mother, and the matriarch of the Bruante bloodline. In this way, fame and fortune would come calling on Susanne's doorstep twice: first as a brilliant and insightful art historian, and second as the beautiful and talented direct-descendant of the father of Realism.

There's no question that it would be very tricky collecting the hair samples from the museum pieces without obtaining the proper authorization, but there was no other choice. Why? Because she just couldn't risk bringing the Executive Director (his signature a necessary 'sign off' on such an unorthodox kind of retrieval) into her confidence before all the evidence was gathered and *she*, rather than *he*, could take full credit for the startling discoveries. Marcel was a man cut from the same cloth as she was: out for himself and likely to take all the accolades once he learned not only that her thesis was in fact true but also that she had secured a positive ID on the model's true identity.

They would collect the samples, she had

decided, late at night on Monday June sixth, in order to correspond with her rescheduled presentation at *d'Orsay.* Since she would be on-site anyway, she would have a ready excuse to stay in the museum, pretending to work well into the morning hours, as she often did; perhaps going so far as to actually spend the night on her office couch—her occasional practice anyway, especially when the backlog of paperwork had started to pile up. She would let Henri and Nicole in the back way, and then the bizarre vandalism would begin.

The guards assigned to night duty, for the most part, were young and gullible, so chances were good that a particularly suggestible security officer would be on duty that night next week. Why would he question the Assistant Director of Acquisitions and Special Exhibits? She would tell him: "Dr. Leclercq and his associate have just arrived from Belgium. They will be collecting samples from some of our paintings for an international project, so could you please turn off the motion detectors in the special exhibit gallery?" This much should be easy, but the video cameras were another story entirely. They were controlled with a different switch right next to the motion detector shut-off, flush on the surface of the semi-circular table that housed the display monitors. How could she explain the need for video-silence if the collection order was legitimate? She couldn't, which meant that she would have to maneuver her back towards the controls so she could reach behind to disarm the system herself, by distracting the guard physically. She might even have to take the ploy a step further and actually have sex with him (she shuddered, but only mildly

269

since not all of them were entirely unappealing) since her motto was 'absolutely anything that's needed' when it came to achieving her two-fold goal.

Once the motion sensors and the video monitors were disabled, Henri and Nicole would be able to get what they needed without being watched, and without having to worry about the painting alarms being triggered—no muss, no fuss. Then they would leave the same way they came in while Susanne finished up with her patsy in the back office—and that would be that, their caper executed. If the results came back as expected, her well-deserved publicity would quickly follow.

It was a shame, of course, that she wouldn't have the clinching, full results in time for the opening of the 'model singularity' exhibit next week, but it didn't really matter. Her presentation on Monday would be strategically short-and-sweet, including only the analyzed letter that she would present simply for what it was: namely, that Nicole Thérèse Bruante had been Courbet's model for the unsigned piece titled *Waking Nude Preparing to Rise*, and that Courbet was actually Susanne's great-great-great grandfather. She would later supplement this preliminary announcement with the stunning *additional* evidence (gleaned from the sundry collected hairs retrieved from the family painting, the nonexistent hairbrush, and the *d'Orsay* pieces) that this very same nineteenth-century woman had modelled for *all* of the Impressionist and Realist paintings *and* for the erotic photographs that were currently displayed in her exhibit…and in so doing seal Susanne's fate as the premier art historian of the century.

How serendipitous that *Waking Nude Preparing to Rise* had caught Henri's eye and imagination, even as a child; and how fortuitous that he had decided to restore it after inheriting it after her grandmother's death. His interest in the painting had stemmed in part, she knew, from the uncanny resemblance of the model to Susanne; but now a human 'mirror-image' had materialized in-the-flesh by some paranormal coincidence, at the very moment when destiny had determined that she was needed most. But life, as it turned out, was full of even *more* unlikely happenstances with one of them having a scientist as an ex-boyfriend; and one who, by pure coincidence, happened to have a special expertise in time travel.

She must, in just a moment or two, call this ex-boyfriend and time travel expert of hers. How would he react to hearing her voice? He had loved her so, and she couldn't help but wonder if he still did. She thought back to that day in early January, when she had posed nude for a figure painting class as an exchange student in America, surrounded by a semi-circle of admirers, including John, who had sat busily recreating her sensuous curves with oil on canvas behind their easels.

She had undressed for each of the three sessions in the side room, stripping off her sweater and slipping out of her jeans to complete nudity since she never wore a bra or panties, folding the two items neatly on the metal chair in the changing room and placing her shoes underneath. That first night, she had used the bathrobe…kind of—untied, falling open in front, her breasts and the rest of her full-frontal splendor exposed and out there: the enticing appetizer to the whole thing. She had intentionally bared it all long before the professor's signal to start by letting the covering slide off her shoulders, the soft material caressing the small of her back and slipping noiselessly over the creamy-white hush of her *derriere* and the alabaster whisper of her thighs and calves, to land in a silent swirling gasp around her feet like the pedestal supporting a breathing, flesh-and-blood statue of the erotic goddess Venus.

After that first night, she always left the bathrobe behind, hanging untouched on the hook behind the door. Why in the world would she cover up after showing her stuff for a full three hours for the roomful of artsy and (facts-were-facts) desire-filled voyeurs? Truth be told, she was proud of her body: as seductive and tantalizing as Aphrodite's; and actually savored every single second that she could show it off naked. Honestly though, it wasn't just the liberating exposure that thrilled her so much; but instead, it was the way they all looked at her with lust in their eyes and sex on their minds that truly excited her. It was the ultimate tease, really; because she alone was in the driver's seat. Who would she pick out of the crowd this time?

You see, she always selected someone to sleep with after a nude modelling session; and on that day, after the final sitting for this particular three-night pose, she had narrowed it down to two candidates: a quiet, intellectual type (who turned out to be John); and a muscular guy with a chiseled jaw who had a lot going for him in the looks department and wore an expression that told the world he knew it. She was intrigued by John, who sat there so quietly handsome: a man who seemed completely oblivious to his own sex appeal. When he had locked eyes with her toward the end of the session, it was decided, then and there—it would definitely be him.

She remembered timing her exit perfectly, allowing him to follow her closely down the stairs. Then, at just the right moment, she had turned to 'confront' him with a warm smile and a blatant invitation in 'Franglais' accompanied by a brief but provocative 'French-kiss' and followed by a not-so-subtle hand-off of her phone number scribbled on a piece of paper. It hadn't taken him long. He had called her the next night on the dormitory pay phone, and they had agreed to meet at eight p.m. on Thursday, at the café across from the Fine Arts Center.

She had found him sitting quietly at the table by the fire, sketching, of all things—a way to calm his nerves, perhaps, since she could see from across the room that he was very nervous. She shook the cold and a few flakes of snow from her hair, pulling the gloves from her hands and easing herself into the chair to sit across from him at the table. The conversation was stiff, at first, but after a while, he started to relax. As they talked, she took off her sweater which she didn't need due to the heat from the fire, slipping it over her head, feeling much more comfortable now in a scant turquoise t-shirt that hugged her bra-less chest tightly, with just a few millimeters of fabric covering what was easily visible beneath. In her book at least, less was always better than more, when it came to clothing; and that

273

night, she fully expected to undress later with her new conquest, under the sheets.

He had picked up the sketchpad and his charcoal pencil again, looking across the table at her and then down at the paper, back and forth and back and forth, as they continued to talk.

"What are you drawing?" she had finally asked, knowing full well that he was sketching her. She was delighted to learn that they could actually speak French, since he was fluent.

"You, of course," he had replied with a smile.

Of *course* it was. "Can I see it?"

"Not now."

"Later?"

"Maybe someday."

Later, when she had put on her sweater and gloves again, he had politely offered her an escort. She had accepted of course, since it was all in the plan. A few blocks later he had stood with her outside the dormitory doors. He had hesitated just as he had in the classroom stairway; but not her—not even for a second. The air was cold and dry, but her kiss was warm and wet; and as the snowflakes fell urgently down around them, she actually felt him fall, instantly and abruptly, in love with her. She could have stopped it then, knowing full well that she would eventually dump him…but she didn't.

She had asked him up to her room, undressing when they got there with natural ease, just as she had for the art class. She coaxed him out of his jeans and t-shirt, pulling him under the warmth of double blankets, where her body, for that night and many thereafter, was a canvas that he traced with the brush of his fingertips and painted with the

274

touch of his lips. He had wept that night, when their lovemaking was finished—yet another signal that she was playing with fire. How could she have known that she was his first real relationship? Oh well. What was done was done.

She picked up her phone. Her watch read 8:25; she had waited long enough. It was time to call.

It rang once, then twice…and then he answered.

"Hello, John," she said, as though eighteen years had only been eighteen hours. "This is Susanne."

CHAPTER TWENTY-THREE

When their conversation came to an end, John put his cell phone back in his jacket pocket. He had already paid the restaurant bill including tip with his credit card during the phone call, but he dug out a few extra pound notes and set them on the table as he got up to go. The pub wasn't that busy, but he had tied up his table in the corner for an extra thirty minutes while he had talked with Susanne. He nodded to the bartender as he walked out the door.

In the end, he had agreed to go to Paris...but on *his* terms rather than hers, next week rather than immediately—mostly to accommodate his professional schedule but also to make a personal point. She had left him hanging for almost twenty years, so he would do the same but on a much smaller scale amounting to less than a week. Was this trip a wise decision? Probably not, but the lure of a potential scientific anomaly, allegedly materializing for some reason right on Susanne's doorstep, was too much for him to resist. Did he actually believe Susanne's wild contention that she was hosting her great-great-great grandmother at this very minute in her apartment in central Paris? Not completely; but then again, the evidence that she had just presented to him did sound convincing.

Did he question Susanne's sincerity when she offered a cursory apology for what had happened between them eighteen years ago in college? Absolutely. Susanne was out for herself and no one else. Their half-hour discussion had focused almost exclusively on her family problem, with hardly a mention of their heated but embarrassingly one-sided affair at the University of Chicago. If she had felt even a smidgeon of remorse, he would have heard more than one attempt to apologize. Instead, she had sounded more like an attorney trying to convince a jury to give her a favorable ruling. The call was all business, make no mistake; but maybe it was better that way.

Had she even been fleetingly faithful to him, during the three-and-a-half months they had dated? After she disappeared from his life—an unexpected turn of events that had taken him completely off-guard—he had realized, in retrospect that he had merely been a diversion the entire time. He had devoted himself, heart and soul, to her, and she had repaid him by sidestepping the issue of commitment and ignoring his repeated attempts to have her clarify how she really felt about him. Her avoidance of a frank discussion, in his mind, was indirectly deceitful, and there was no question that she had led him on, perhaps even from the very beginning.

How many times had he called her up, wanting to get together on this night or that night, only to have her pretend that she had work to do in the photography studio, or plans with her endless list of female and male friends? She would usually offer him another day as a consolation, and when they finally got together, she was sweeter than ever, and even more passionate in their intimacy than the time before. To him, the sex was more than just entertainment—it really *meant* something. The problem, he later decided, was that he had assumed that she viewed their periodic overnight encounters in the same way. Would it have been that difficult for her to be honest with him from the beginning? If he had known that a nonchalant and casual relationship was all she cared to pursue from the very start, he might have been able to adjust to a non-exclusive type of arrangement; but then again, maybe not. He simply wasn't made that way, and knowing that the sex meant nothing to her would have been difficult for him to come to terms with.

It was just a week before his graduation when he discovered that she had gone. He hadn't seen her for a few days, so he had decided to pay her a visit that night, unannounced, to see if she might be interested in grabbing a bite to eat. To his surprise, he had found the door of her dorm room standing wide open. All of Susanne's personal belongings had been removed.

"Where's Susanne?" he had asked the neighbor from two doors down, an attractive redhead named Claire who was wrapped in a towel, heading back to her room from the bathroom at the end of the hallway.

She had given John a look of pity. "Didn't she tell you?"

"Tell me what?"

"That's so typical of her."

"But where is she?" he had asked, already knowing the answer and feeling as if his world had just collapsed.

"Back in Paris." Claire had touched John lightly on the arm. "You're much too good for her, John. You're better off without her, in my opinion."

Claire was right, of course, but it still hurt—not for just a day, a week, or even a month. He had pined over her for more than a year (and still was,

278

truth-be-told), finally giving up all hope of resolution when all of his letters and phone calls were answered with stony silence from across the Atlantic.

He had been such a different person then, insecure to the point of being self-demeaning, and overly reliant on his impression of what other people thought of him. Her rejection of him had only worsened his low self-esteem, for a time. It had taken years to dig himself out of that hole, and it was only his successful scientific career that managed to rebuild his self-confidence. He could hardly recognize the man he had been in 1993. Today's John Noland could easily handle Susanne Bruante, he told himself, and maybe this trip to Paris was exactly what he needed to finally clear her lingering skeleton out of his psychological closet. Closure was what he needed, and closure was what he would get...*plus* the opportunity, perhaps, to study a human time travel subject.

Susanne's explanation, at first, had been very hard to follow. It didn't help that her manic accounting of the sequence of events, just a little while ago over the phone, had jumped from one day and topic to another, completely out of chronological order. Finally, after some pointed questioning, he thought he had her story (which he couldn't rule out as mentally unstable ramblings) straight.

As he walked back to his hotel from the pub, he thought with analytical excitement about the woman named Nicole: the one Susanne claimed was her great-great-great grandmother, if her narrative could be believed. If Nicole had truly been transported

279

through a *Virtual-Hole* from one *Time-Shell* to another, she would represent living human proof that his concepts related to the time-space continuum were not just the wild imaginings of a mad scientist. He suspected the connection between Nicole's time and his own had been flanked on both ends by a *Common-Object*, present in both 2011 and 1876.

When he had asked Susanne about this, she had felt certain that the *Common-Object* in question simply had to be the painting: Courbet's erotic masterpiece titled *The Origin of the World*. The painting had hung on the wall at the foot of Nicole's bed, in the past; and it was hanging right now, in the present, in the exhibit room at *Musée d'Orsay*, in close proximity to where Nicole had magically appeared, along with two very dead bodies—one apparently a present-day victim who died, perhaps, because he was in the wrong place at the wrong time; and the second Nicole's lover who had been transported with her but did not survive the journey—not even two days ago.

How had the *Virtual-Hole* opened? Why had Nicole weathered the trip, whereas her nighttime companion had not? Was there a way to get her back? These were all questions that would need to be answered, but in person...*not* from far away.

'In person'. Those words gave him reason to pause, just as Susanne's comment had. They weren't talking about a lab rat here, but a *person*. "She'll be your crowning achievement," Susanne had said, in her most persuasive tone of voice. "The ultimate human experiment. You'll be incredibly famous."

280

He had felt uncomfortable when she had said that, and now he knew why. It was one thing sending a mouse back and forth through a *Virtual-Hole*, but quite another to contemplate doing the same thing to a person. Ethically speaking, he was treading on shaky ground here, but it went far beyond that. Susanne, with her usual flair and with one offhand remark, had reduced Nicole from someone meaningful to a simple object. He was better than that; or at least he hoped he was. He didn't need fame because he already had it. Whatever happened when he got to Paris, he pledged to himself that he would do the right thing, and do it with kindness and compassion.

He hadn't even met this Nicole, but already he felt a certain protective affinity toward her. One thing was certain: Susanne was anything but an advocate for the poor young woman. Would Nicole be timid, or intrepid; confused, or assured; frightened, or calm? Would she be the vulnerable damsel in distress? If so, would he be her white knight, or her black? If he could somehow return her to the past, would she welcome that return, or oppose it? How did she feel, what would she say, and what would she want?

And how would *he* feel? Would his compassion rule him, or his science? What would she 'be' like, and would he feel drawn to her? She *looked* like Susanne, according to Susanne herself, but did the resemblance go beyond simple outward physical appearance? It would be best for everyone involved if emotions didn't muddy the waters; if the objective didn't become confused with the subjective; and if what was meant to be, and should be, didn't evolve into what he, or Susanne, or even Nicole, wanted.

His mind was racing; he had to slow it down. *First things first*, he thought. You need to get there before you start worrying about the 'ifs' and the 'maybes'.

He turned the corner and walked the final half block to his hotel, pushing through the revolving doors and making his way across the polished floor of the lobby to the reception counter.

"Good Evening, Dr. Noland." The attractive hotel clerk's accent was easy enough for him to identify by now, after being in the UK for almost a week, as Northern English—maybe even Welsh. Everyone at the hotel knew him, even if he didn't know them, since he was a celebrity of sorts. "How may I assist you this evening, sir?"

He could think of a few things, but he wasn't the type of man to put himself out there like that. He would spend the rest of the night alone—unless, of course, she made the first move. "I'll be checking out in next week: on Tuesday, June seventh," he announced. That was, in truth, the very soonest he could get away, as his lectures at Cambridge first and then Oxford had taken months to plan and could not be rescheduled; but an added bonus to the professionally-driven five-day delay was the surprising amount of personal satisfaction that he felt in delaying his response to Susanne's 'beck-and-call'.

She looked up his reservation in the computer. "That's five days early, Professor. Hasn't everything here been quite to your liking?" she asked with a pretty pout. "Perhaps we just didn't

282

show you the right kind of hospitality?" There might have been a twinkle in her eye, revealed when she brushed away some strands of strawberry hair with fingernails painted a noticeably similar shade, but he couldn't be quite sure.

"Everything has been just fine, Carrie," he replied, not having to read her nametag since she had been on duty every night since his arrival. "I need to leave just a tad early on a business matter. Could someone get me a schedule for the Chunnel train to Paris?"

"I can do that for you, Dr. Noland—straight away." She looked across the counter at him and bit her lower lip, as if considering her next move. "I'm afraid the internet seems to be down at the moment. When it's up again I can print it, and slip it under your door? You see, I'll be off my shift soon so it would be no bother at all, really, for me to deliver it to you personally."

Message received, loud-and-clear. "That would truly be lovely, Carrie. Just knock on the door rather than slipping it under. How wonderfully accommodating of you, really." It seemed that he would be doing "casual" again tonight—the usual routine. How apropos, he thought, a little sadly. Susanne had taught him well, and tonight's little adventure would serve as a bittersweet reminder that the lessons she had taught him had lasted a lifetime.

"The pleasure, I think, will be all mine." And *his* as well, she implied, as she gazed directly in his eyes while flashing him a mischievous smile. "We can't have you leaving London, after all, with anything but the fondest of memories."

283

John had no trouble whatsoever imagining the 'fond memories' she was referring to. His life was full of this kind of memory. What a shame, really, that thanks to Susanne he could not really think back on any more meaningful others.

PART III

A FEW DAYS LATER
JUNE 6 - JUNE 8, 2011

CHAPTER TWENTY-FOUR

Michèle Crossier stood in back of the gallery waiting for Susanne Bruante's presentation to start. She had gained access with her badge, presenting it in lieu of the ticket everyone else seemed to have for 'Monday 6 June, 2011: *Courbet and Contemporaries: Model Singularity* Pre-Opening Night' and hoping that in plain clothes she would blend in with the crowd, just as if she were another inconspicuous art critic or journalist.

To Michèle's surprise, there was hardly a crowd to blend in with. The turnout was meager at best, and Michèle thought she knew why. Anyone who was anyone in the art world did not really care if the same or different models bared it all for Courbet, Manet, Caillebotte and the like. Personally, Michèle was intrigued primarily because Caillebotte blood ran strong in her veins, passed down through the generations by her great-grandfather, Jean Caillebotte, who was Martial Caillebotte's wayward-son. Martial had been a well-known photographer, and had purportedly created the 'body-scape' series that Susanne had included in her 'model singularity' exhibit.

Michèle had been here just five nights before, in the early morning hours of the first day of June,

285

surveying the adjacent crime scene in the 30 by 30-foot alcove-room located off to the left of the first special exhibit hall—pondering the 'how-what-where-and-when' of two dead bodies with Pascal Bernier, the medical examiner. It seemed strange that they would still hold the program in this third special exhibit room, so close to the location of a double-murder that had just been committed not even a week ago; but then again, this room was the largest of the four and business must go on. *D'Orsay* was not about to cancel an exhibit that promised to keep the cash registers ringing.

Deciding that she might as well make herself comfortable, Michèle decided to take a seat in the back row, against the far wall and underneath a painting by Courbet titled *Le Sommeil* (translation: '*Sleep*'). As audiovisual personnel busied themselves with the set-up of a laptop, screen, and projector at the front, Michèle took a moment to study the notorious nude couple hanging behind her. The brunette, peacefully asleep, lay with her right leg draped over her female partner, while her left leg was gently wedged in between the blonde woman's legs. The 'latter's' left hand rested intimately on the 'former's' right leg, while her head was pillowed cozily on her lover's near-breast. Both of the women's faces drew in the viewer, their peacefully content expressions intimating a physical encounter that, now ended, had resulted in this satisfied post-coital slumber.

But was it really the look of universal contentment that seemed so familiar to Michèle? No, it was something more. The brunette's face itself distinctly reminded Michèle of someone; and she didn't realize exactly who, until that someone walked in through the main archway accompanied by a tall man with combed-over hair who just had to be the museum's Executive Director.

Michèle looked back and forth, from the model in the painting to Susanne Bruante, and back again. Odd that the brunette pictured in the Courbet nude really *did* seem to resemble Susanne. Was Michèle's mind just playing tricks on her? Susanne and Courbet's model shared the same shoulder-length auburn hair; identical full and perfect lips; indistinguishable twin noses, both of them slightly upturned; and matching cheekbones, high and prominent. In fact, the woman who was about to take her place behind the podium could have easily passed for a replica of Courbet's model.

Ridiculous. The case was definitely getting to her. It was Susanne Bruante in the videotape, Susanne Bruante at the podium, and now Susanne Bruante in the painting? Michèle would need a long vacation, after this case was solved, or a good psychiatrist…or *both*.

Michèle watched as Susanne glanced out into the nearly nonexistent audience, surveying the attendants; and then after two or three seconds, Susanne's gaze rested on Michèle. The look in her eyes said that she recognized the policewoman immediately, but that it didn't matter to her one way or the other that Michèle was stalking her. The woman was cool, verging on arrogant. Anyone else would have felt intimidated to have the police shadowing her, but not this one. Every morning, she waved flirtatiously to the men on the surveillance detail as she left her apartment, and when she

287

reached her destination—getting out of her light-blue BMW one shapely, bare leg at a time—she would wink and smile at them again as she passed their parking spot two or three cars behind, intentionally teasing them with the sway of her hips on five-inch heels. It was unbelievable, but it didn't really matter because Michèle's professional sights were about to be focused elsewhere. She had just a few more questions for Susanne that she'd cover when she cornered the Assistant Director after her opening remarks, and then she'd be prepared to bring Henri Bruante in for questioning in the morning.

She saw Susanne whisper something deferentially to her companion, in a manner almost but not quite obsequious. There was no question about it: he was the Executive Director, Marcel Lauren—Susanne's boss, lover, and alibi all rolled into one: a three-for-one special. He should have been disappointed with the poor attendance, but if he was, he certainly didn't give that impression. He smiled pleasantly in response to whatever Susanne had just told him and then took his seat in the front row.

Now that Michèle thought about it, though, the director's unconcerned reaction to a close-to-empty room made perfect sense. Susanne's contention that all of the nude women pictured in the various pieces of artwork were the same model must have seemed as completely inconsequential to him as it was to the rest of the art world. *So what?* she could almost hear him think. In reality it would be in the museum's best interests to distance itself from its Assistant Director's speculations, which verged on the nonsensical. Having most of the invitees turn out as no-shows was probably a big relief to Lauren, whose museum relied, in part, on donations from mainstream benefactors who would frown on Susanne's preoccupation with 'fringe' conjectures. Having only a handful of journalists in the audience tonight was the perfect way to limit the number of scathing reviews in tomorrow morning's newspapers. In fact, Michèle wouldn't be at all surprised if Lauren had actually engineered tonight's poor turnout.

Susanne stepped up to the podium, testing the microphone with a gentle series of taps with her index finger. Michèle found it interesting that Lauren had not even bothered to introduce her.

"Welcome," she said. "I'm glad those of you who are here tonight were able to make it." She didn't seem to be bothered by the poor turnout either, almost giving the impression that today was just a prelude to something bigger, yet to come. "I'm Susanne Bruante, Assistant Director of Acquisitions and Special Exhibits and the creative architect of *Courbet and Contemporaries: Model Singularity*. Our apologies for canceling the original date for this preview last week, but you're all aware of the unfortunate reason for the last-minute rescheduling." She paused soberly, seemingly out of respect for the recent crime victims; but then resumed almost cheerily just a few seconds later. "The doors to my fascinating exhibit will open to the public tomorrow morning, but tonight, you'll be able to peruse the four-and-a-half galleries devoted to the conceptual theme I'll be discussing with you, without having to fight the crowds."

One thing was certain; there were no crowds here tonight to fight. Michèle settled herself in as Susanne continued. "It has taken quite some time and energy to acquire or borrow the paintings that you see hanging on the walls of these rooms tonight. I contend that each piece of work—whether it be painting, drawing, sculpture or photograph; and whether created by Courbet, Renoir, Degas, Manet, the Caillebotte brothers or various others—features the same daring model who boldly defied societal norms, not simply by posing nude but in many instances, as you will see, by allowing the most shockingly intimate artistic viewpoints of her unconcealed body."

Michèle looked around, quickly counting the heads and comparing the result to the number of chairs in the room, most of them empty. Fourteen attendees occupying room for ninety, and some of the people there, probably four or five, were almost certainly museum officials. Susanne would not be making much of an impact by convincing this gathering that her theory wasn't rubbish.

"Gustave Courbet is best known as a landscape artist," Susanne said, "but his nudes, rather than his pastoral scenes, arguably represent his most enduring legacy. In accordance with historical precedent, an artist's most controversial paintings usually make the most lasting impression; and in Courbet's case, one cannot emphasize enough the accuracy of this observation. A mere handful of his nude paintings—all of them considered scandalous by nineteenth-century standards, and some of them regarded as provocative, still—have become the most memorable works in his vast collection of over five hundred artistic renderings."

She stopped a moment to take a sip of water, and then gestured to a museum official standing in the back, who dimmed the lights. She walked over to a small table to the her right and switched on a slide projector which threw up on the screen behind her an image of a woman's genitalia: larger than life. "Consider, as a case in point, *The Origin of the World*—a piece of artwork that is unique in its conception as well as its historical isolation. This painting, which all of you will be able to view momentarily in the alcove room, was banned from exhibition for over fifty years due to its explicit portrayal of a woman's genital area.

"Other examples include *Two Nude Women* and *Le Sommeil* (her naming of each piece was accompanied by a slide of the artwork), both exceptionally controversial because they overtly suggested an intimate relationship between the female models; *Woman in White Stockings* (slide number 4 appeared on the screen) criticized by the moral majority when it was initially shown because of the openly lascivious expression on the model's face, as well as the shocking posturing of her legs; and *Le Bacchante* (the fifth example) shunned by the conservative members of the Parisian Salon because Courbet's depiction of the sleeping woman suggested, to many, the recuperative slumber after a drunken sexual encounter that had taken place outdoors. Even his masterpiece—*The Artist's Studio, a Real Allegory*—was rejected when Courbet submitted it for display at the *Exposition Universelle*, on the pretext that the canvas was too large." She pressed a button on her remote, and a picture of this painting appeared on the screen. "In reality, this piece was rebuffed because of the sexual innuendo inferred from the close proximity of the nude model to the painter in the scene. Courbet was forced to exhibit this piece, along with forty of his other paintings, in his own gallery, since no one else would show them.

"Courbet had an obvious interest in the sensual side of the human form, and he had a true talent for depicting the nude subject. We have managed to gather all of his most notable nude paintings in these rooms—plus some others, equally notorious in their subject matter, that were discovered in Gustave Caillebotte's country estate called *Petite Gennevilliers*, hidden in a secret closet under the stairway." Her smile had broadened, as if she knew something that no one else did and could hardly wait to eventually reveal it.

Michele's ears perked up, just a little. She had heard vaguely about the discovery made under the stairs in her great-great-great uncles 'retirement' estate; but being that she was descended directly from Martial's son, Jean, rather than from his daughter, Geneviève, she had no familial rights to the 'find'. This was because Geneviève was 'two-fold' entitled, inheriting the entire Gustave Caillebotte estate (from the house itself to the artist's vast collections of stamps, personally-built yachts and unsold Impressionist paintings) not only due to a specified clause in her marriage contract but also since her brother, Jean, was a 'ne'er do well' and had been legally disowned. Because Michèle (along with her parents, siblings, aunts, uncles and numerous cousins) had been intentionally excluded from family-affairs by the 'legitimate' branch of the family, she could learn nothing more about the goings-on in the Caillebotte world than what she could periodically glean from this gossip column or that one. Not that she cared, really. Michèle, by intention and born from a deep-seated bitterness cultivated by her mother and those disenfranchised relatives that came before, knew precious little about the 'half' of her heritage that descended from Martial Caillebotte's bloodline. With their 'me-not-you' attitude that went back for generations, who could blame her for deciding to ignore them. '*Good riddance*' was her motto, and it had served her well all these years.

So, how had Susanne gained access to the 'lost collection'? Did she have some personal ties to the Caillebotte family? It was not impossible to imagine that Susanne might be sleeping with a well-positioned cousin or nephew of the moneyed family line but she pushed the sordid thought aside because there were other, more plausible, reasons for the museum acquisition. After all, Susanne was a prominent *d'Orsay* executive and art historian, so of *course* she would be given access usually reserved for those individuals moving in the right 'circles'. As these thoughts raced through Michel's ever-active mind, she tuned back in to the Assistant Director who was continuing her presentation.

"We know from reliable…*sources* that after Courbet was self-exiled in Switzerland to avoid paying a fine for his role in destroying the Vendome Column, he left his erotic pieces with 'someone' and eventually gave her permission to sell them—to Gustave Caillebotte, believe it or not, who was not only a prolific artist but also an avid art collector." *What a strange coincidence*, Michèle thought. *How in the world were the Courbet's and the Caillebotte's associated with each other? Certainly not by blood!*

The projector, on Susanne's finger-command, sequenced rapidly through a series of paintings, photographs, and a sculpture while the Assistant Director continued talking. "These pieces from the 'lost collection' feature, for the most part, nude 'sensual' paintings created not only by Courbet but also by a wide variety of other artists including Manet, Renoir, Degas, Lefebvre, and Caillebotte (only one). Also discovered along with these pieces were an assembly of erotic photographs attributed to Martial Caillebotte, and an unfinished sculpture..." (the slides stopped on a photo of the marble carving depicting a woman's naked torso) "...that we believe René Caillebotte, the middle brother, had been working on immediately before he died suddenly in 1876. Unfortunately, the sculpture, which we had on site, was damaged during the 'incident' and has been removed for repairs, so you will not be able to view it tonight. Regardless, *all* of these pieces uncovered from Caillebotte's century-old hiding place have one thing in common: the model."

Susanne looked out at the audience triumphantly, as if expecting applause. The reaction was a few acknowledging nods and some nondescript murmurs. "You see, it seems that Caillebotte had become obsessed with collecting this particular model's 'body' of work; and my fastidious research has nearly identified, after almost one-hundred-and-fifty years of mystery, her identity."

'Nearly'? This did not sound very scientific to Michèle, and apparently one of the reporters had come to the same conclusion. "This is pure conjecture, Ms. Bruante. Do you have any proof?"

"In fact, I do." She hit the switch on the projector remote to move the slide which caused Michèle to sit up a little bit in her seat. *Now this might be interesting*, she thought as she peered at a magnification-photo of a letter that had appeared on the screen.

"This letter was discovered accidentally by a local art restorer, papered into the back of an unsigned and unfinished nineteenth-century painting called *Waking Nude Preparing to Rise*." Susanne glanced over at the Executive Director, who had taken a seat directly in front of her in the first row of the audience after retreating from the podium at the start of the presentation, with a look that seemed nothing less than smug. Had Susanne hidden the existence of the letter from Lauren, even going so far as to have it analyzed and authenticated without his approval? It seemed so, and honestly Michèle was not at all surprised. This woman had nerve. "I had this letter analyzed by materials experts at the National Archives," she said, confirming Michèle's suspicion. "They have confirmed that the paper and ink can be dated to the late nineteenth century, which corresponds to the date on the letter: *10 May, 1876*. Shall I read it to you?"

This time, the audience reacted with universally enthusiastic nods. "I thought this would interest you." She cleared her through and took a sip of water, before reading.

My dear Edmond. As I write this, you are still of a tender age and cannot be expected to understand my profession, and passion. But when you are older, you will learn that the human body, beautiful and sacred, is truly worthy of bold and honest depiction in life as well as art—a contention that eventually led to my calling.

I confess to you that I am the nude model you see in this painting as well as in countless others, created as a celebration of the female body by your father. I will tell you (in confidence now but when I am dead there will be no reason to hide it) that I posed in the most revealing positions imaginable as an attestation of nature's beauty created by God— not only for this piece, but also for many others created by your Papa, and by many other famous Parisian artists as well. I am proud of them all, and have no regrets except that I had to keep my vocation concealed from you because of the stigma that being the son of a nude figure-model would cast upon you.

Which comes to the next revelation that may very well surprise you even more than learning that your mother was an erotic artist's subject. Your father was the infamous painter Jean Gustave Désiré Courbet. He and I both decided to hide the truth of your paternity for your own protection. By the time you (or your children, or your children's children) read this, your Papa's controversial artistic and political reputation will be well documented in the history books, so you will no doubt understand our efforts to separate you from

296

the Courbet name. Even more than being the son of a nude artists' model, your status in society would have been relegated to the dregs, if anyone found out about your paternal blood-line. So it is that you have been and will continue to be raised by your grandmother: Elle Bruante, so as to shield you from your mother and your father's cursed and ill-wanted 'fame'.

I love you dearly, my Edmond...as did your father. I pray to the highest power that you will remember the both of us with fondness, and an understanding of why we did what we did.

Your mother always,

Nicole Thérèse Bruante.

At the mention of the family name 'Bruante' an audible intake of a dozen-odd breaths and a palpable buzz of surprise could be heard traveling through the room. "Are you related to her?" a reporter sitting in the back called out.

"Indeed I am," Susanne replied without hesitation. "She was my great-great-great grandmother." Which meant, Michèle realized probably at the same time that everyone else did, that Susanne Bruante was a direct descendant of Gustave Courbet: her great-great-great grandfather. "Which leads us to *this*..." Susanne advanced the slide again to a photo of a nude painting of a woman sitting with her legs underneath her, leaning on one arm with her head turned seductively to one side. "This is our family painting called *Waking Nude Preparing to Rise*, passed on directly from Nicole Bruante to her son Edmond, and then through the generations to end up with my uncle: Henri Bruante. He is the art restorer who discovered the hidden letter. Does this model look familiar?"

She most certainly did. The woman posing in the painting looked just like Susanne Bruante, and was also a perfect match to all of the models depicted in the paintings surrounding them in the Special Exhibit galleries. "It goes without saying that this model—one and the same with the woman who stashed her letter of confession to her son, Edmond, between the canvas and backing paper of this very painting—is Nicole Thérèse Bruante: Gustave Courbet's lover, and the nude model for *all* of these erotic paintings and photographs." She moved her arm in a circular, sweeping arc to indicate their surroundings. "And she is our 'singular' model: the 'star' of my 'model singularity' exhibit."

This was more impressive than Michèle had expected; but some members of the audience still seemed skeptical. "Do you have any *physical* proof, Ms. Bruante? Your story would be much easier to swallow if you provided something uncontestable," a reporter sitting in the row ahead of her commented.

"You mean something like...*DNA*?" She said it as though she did, indeed, have it. DNA would be the game-changing clincher, but there was no way in hell that Susanne would be able to produce this type of incontrovertible biologic proof that a painted image on a canvas belonged to a specific individual who had been dead these past 140-odd years—and no one in their right mind would expect her to. "No, I do *not* have DNA...right now," Susanne admitted, answering her own question but accenting her response with a devious smile accentuating the meaningful pause; "but don't you think that might be asking too much?" The self-satisfied expression on Susanne's face as she countered the reporter's unreasonable 'request' for evidence-based confirmation seemed, to Michèle at least, to lack the exasperation or frustration that one would normally expect when interrogated in this fashion.

"Not at all," another reporter chimed in, just like another wolf joining in with the pack. "How do we know your great-great-great grandmother didn't 'plant' the letter in the painting with the intention of taking credit for someone else's work. That kind of thing happens all the time."

"We'll see," she responded cheerily. "I think that's enough for now, don't you?" Did the abrupt ending of her presentation (which had taken everyone off-guard judging by the looks Michèle saw on most people's faces) indicate that she was not willing to engage in a back-and-forth argument that she couldn't possibly win; or had she simply thrown in the towel? It hardly seemed so. Michèle had a strong suspicion that they hadn't heard everything, and that Susanne was saving some additional evidence for another day. "Please enjoy some light *hors d'oeuvres* in the lobby," she added, "after you've taken a few minutes to view the exhibit."

And that was that. Susanne quickly packed up her laptop and started toward the doorway that led out onto the marble catwalk overlooking the sunken ground level of *d'Orsay*. Michèle was on her, though. The slippery Assistant Director wouldn't be able to escape that easily.

"Mademoiselle Bruante," Michèle called after

her. "Could I have just a few moments of your time?"

Susanne pivoted on her heel. "Why certainly, inspector. Walk with me?" she suggested, her tone actually amiable.

Of course Michèle would walk with her. She could be as pleasant as the next person and would even match Susanne's fabricated sweetness. Walking, running, or sitting, Michèle was determined to get her woman.

Or man, as the case may be. Michèle had a theory of her own; and if her evolving hypothesis panned out, the man in question went by the name of Henri Bruante.

CHAPTER TWENTY-FIVE

Susanne led Inspector Crossier down the catwalk, around the corner, and through the set of double doors off to the right side of the lobby, behind the ticket-counter, that led to the back hallway of administrative offices. "What can I help you with?" she asked the detective, as they stopped outside her office door about half-way down the corridor.

"I need some information about your uncle, Henri Bruante. Before that, though, I wanted to tell you that the DNA evidence has essentially eliminated you as a suspect."

"Of course it has," Susanne replied, with just a hint of condescension. "I wasn't there, remember?"

"Yes, I remember," Crossier said. "I just thought you'd be curious about the results."

"As long as they exonerate me, that's all I really need to know."

"I suppose; but then again, the DNA analysis uncovered something very interesting that involves you, indirectly."

Curiosity killed the cat, Susanne thought; *but this feline has eight lives left to go.* "You've got me wondering now, inspector. Do you want me to guess, or are you going to tell me?"

"I'll tell you. The DNA results absolve you, but they implicate another Bruante."

Another Bruante? Crossier had just mentioned Henri a moment ago, but he hadn't been at the crime scene either. Nicole had, though; so in all likelihood, then, this 'other' Bruante to whom

Crossier was alluding would be Nicole. "Who, exactly?" Susanne asked, feigning ignorance as she opened her office door part way, turning around and blocking the detective's entrance with her body.

"Why don't you let me into your office? We can talk about it inside."

Should she let her in? There was really no reason to be obstinate, except for the pure thrill of it, so with a shrug she stepped aside. "I'll give you five minutes," she answered, pleasant as could be. "Fair?"

"Fair." Crossier nodded and stepped past Susanne. "May I sit?"

"Don't make yourself too comfortable. I have quite a bit of work to do, on our next special exhibit." Susanne might as well feed the 'queen-bee', and the information would trickle down to the workers. "The papers have been piling up, literally." She pointed to her desk, in order to prove it. "You should tell the guys parked outside that they might as well settle in. I'll be sleeping here tonight."

Crossier didn't react—not even a hint of surprise. *Perfect.* Once the surveillance detail got the word, they would let their guard down, maybe even catch a few winks out there themselves. With the diversion of Susanne's flawlessly placed misinformation, the last thing they would be focused on would be her activities inside the museum.

Inspector Crossier sat on the couch, crossing one bare leg over the other. She was dressed in a knee-length skirt that actually showed some skin—right up Susanne's alley. This policewoman was certainly attractive, with shoulder-length hair:

unbleached and naturally blonde, startling green eyes, and measurements that even Susanne might envy. Well, almost. Susanne definitely had her beat in the chest department.

She and Michèle Crossier probably had a lot more than good looks in common. Susanne didn't need to be a psychic to know that Michèle was career driven, just as she was; and, given the ring-less finger, she had probably sacrificed her personal life, just as Susanne had, in order to succeed at her job. Had Michèle ever been married? Unlikely, was Susanne's guess. A husband would just get in the way, and so would children, for that matter. This had always been Susanne's viewpoint, and Michèle seemed the type of person who would share in that philosophy, one hundred percent.

"You were about to fill me in on family matters, weren't you?" Susanne reminded her.

"Yes, I was. We found a pubic hair on our victim's genitals, and it doesn't belong to the dead man. Our theory is that he had sexual relations with someone right before he died, and that person left something behind."

A hair, again? It seemed that the best theories these days involved hair, in one form or another. "It wasn't *my* hair—we both know that. So, whose hair was it?" Susanne knew exactly whose hair it was, of course. The time tunnel had pulled Nicole and her bedmate in, killing the man and sparing Nicole, for some reason. The hair, 'extracted' by traction, was Nicole's, because she was the person who had had sex with the victim right before he died.

"Luckily, the hair had been pulled out by its roots," Crossier explained, "consistent with the type

303

of mechanical influence one would expect during intercourse. This means that we had the follicle with attached skin, freshly torn from our victim's partner from the friction of their lovemaking, to work with. A hair fiber alone can only provide mitochondrial DNA for testing; but a hair follicle affixed to its plucked-out root is quite a different story. Our CSI lab ran a complete chromosome analysis on the hair follicle, and on your DNA. Guess what we found."

"I'm not in the mood for guessing games, inspector. I give up. What did you find?"

Crossier ignored the edgy comment. "We found high DNA concordance between your sample and the hair sample, but not a complete match. Someone related to you slept with the victim right before he died. Do you have any idea who that might be?"

Susanne would continue to play dumb. "You mentioned my Uncle Henri a few minutes ago. I honestly didn't think he was gay, but these days you never can tell." She tried to put on her best contemplative face. "It's true he never married…"

"We'll get to Henri in a moment," Crossier stated. "Our victim's lover was a woman, not a man. Chromosomes don't lie."

Susanne shrugged. "I'm afraid I can't help you. I don't know the victim, and I have no idea who might have slept with him before he had his unfortunate accident."

"I realize we're talking about your family, Mademoiselle Bruante, and blood is thicker than water. I also know that your instinct is to protect your own; but your relative, whoever she is, might be in danger. If you want to protect her, then give me her name. I don't think she's the perpetrator, but another victim. All I want to do is try to help her."

Maybe so, but the chances were slim that a twenty-first-century homicide detective would be able to help a nineteenth-century time traveler. That's what ex-boyfriend scientists were for, and that's exactly who would be arriving tomorrow afternoon on the Chunnel train from London. The only way Michèle Crossier could possibly help would be to get her nose out of Susanne's business, but Susanne couldn't see that happening anytime soon.

Or could she? It dawned on her that there just might be a way to put Crossier's nose onto a completely different scent. Susanne couldn't give up Nicole, but she could suggest some alternatives that would steer the inspector out of Susanne and Nicole Bruante territory and right down a blind alley.

Susanne sat next to Michèle on the couch, playing the unwilling conspirator. "Look, I honestly don't know anything about this horrible business, but I have some ideas. My father's half-brother, Uncle Jacques, had a drug and alcohol problem. He got into some trouble with the law, and my grandmother disowned him. I'm not in contact with my cousins, but none of them ever amounted to much. You could start there, perhaps."

Michèle had her cell phone in her hand and touched the 'Notes' icon. "Can you give me some names and addresses?"

"Names, yes; addresses, no. My grandmother, the family matriarch, was hard and unyielding; when she was done with someone, she was done. When she disinherited my uncle, my cousins: three boys and a girl, were black listed too."

"I'd like to speak to the girl."

Susanne nodded knowingly. "I think that's a very good place to start. Her name is Claudine Bignon." She spelled it. "The last I heard, she was working in Pigalle, I think as a dancer…or something more, actually." She shook her head. "It's a shame, really. My Uncle Henri is in touch with her every so often, now that my grandmother has passed away. He says she's very pretty. She could legitimately do much more with her good looks than what she's doing now."

Crossier typed the name in her phone, the look on her face unmistakably satisfied. Susanne felt satisfied too. What a stroke of genius, planting the 'Claudine Bignon' prostitution lead! This was Susanne's best idea yet, resulting she hoped in a protracted wild goose chase that would waste days and days of police time, ultimately leaving Crossier empty-handed in a case that had nothing whatsoever to do with the world's oldest profession, and could never be solved.

The inspector put her phone down on the couch between them. "Thank you, I'll find her. Now, speaking of your uncle Henri—"

"Yes, what about him?"

"He's an art restorer, isn't he?"

"Yes."

"With a home workshop?"

"Yes."

"But he works as a private contractor at various museums in greater Paris, isn't that true?"

"Of course." Susanne was fully aware that Crossier knew all of this already; she was just playing the role of hard-nosed investigator. "Let's just get straight to the point. My uncle is employed often by *d'Orsay* as an on-site art conserver. He just finished a job there, in fact—a day before the murders."

"I know that," Crossier said; "and also that his latest project was the Caillebotte sculpture that was unfortunately damaged during the incident. Do you know if he used a certain heavy-duty, yet *portable*, piece of machinery to clean the surface?"

Susanne thought she knew where Crossier was going with this. The detective seemed to think that Henri had used the high-pressure sculpture-cleaning submersion-apparatus to perpetrate the crime. Now that *was* an ingenious hypothesis, she had to admit; but quite a stretch. "He uses that equipment quite regularly since lately, most of his jobs at *d'Orsay* have involved sculptures for some reason." She might as well lead Crossier down *this* path, just as she had led her down the 'streetwalker' road just a moment before.

Crossier scratched a notation or two on her pad, indicating that she had registered Susanne's 'lead'. "Do you know if Henri is romantically involved with anyone?" she asked, leaving art restoring gadgetry behind and moving on to a totally different Henri-centric topic.

"You'll have to ask him."

"I intend to. I just thought that if his sexual leanings were slightly off-center, if you know what I mean, he might not be as open to discussing it as you might be."

"If you're asking if he's straight or gay, I would have to say straight. He's had too many lady friends to count over the years."

"But he never married?"

"No; but maybe he just never found the right woman to settle down with."

"Or maybe he has a secret life, and all the female companions are just a cover?"

Susanne shrugged, putting on a face that she hoped would be interpreted as noncommittal. Henri was straight as an arrow, but if Inspector Crossier left tonight with more questions than answers, all the better.

Susanne quickly tried to envision Michèle's thought process, which would need to integrate deviant sexual behavior, prostitution, a perverted night-shift museum worker, homosexuality, a couple of Bruante 'black-sheep' family members, and an industrial-grade murder weapon—all representing essential components of the 'criminal plot'. She tried to think like Crossier and came up with the following scenario, with Claudine 'the prostitute' playing Nicole's role.

Henri was gay and was in love with the naked mystery man aka René, who actually swung both ways and probably wasn't as enamored with Henri as Henri was with him. René, either for money or fun, had become the central 'actor' in a sexual encounter involving Claudine and the museum guard: Charpentier, who was either involved as a participant or as an observer. A jealous Henri found out about their plans and caught them in the act, precipitating a fit of rage whereby Henri, the jilted lover, would have pulled his cheating 'partner' out of the fray and incapacitated him somehow—but not with a blunt instrument, since (as Nicole

308

described it) the outward appearance of René's body was 'pristine'; so maybe an injectable sedative? That would do the trick, and for that matter may have been used on Claudine, in order to spare her the horror of witnessing a double murder; *and* on the night guard as well—unless Charpentier had been 'taken out' by a blow to the head, carefully placed so that it would correspond to the eventual location of his life-terminating skull fractured sustained on the sculpture, early on in the soap-opera.

The timing of the murders would be problematic to explain, mainly because Charpentier's ultimate cause of death via 'head meets stone' would have sent the pedestal and its sculpture toppling to the floor, triggering the alarms and re-activated the video-feed—unless Claudine was actually an accomplice rather than a victim, staying behind with instructions to topple over the pedestal and sculpture *after* the fact, activating the alarm system and cameras as a way to inexplicably call attention to the murder scene and summon the authorities. Another possibility, perhaps, was that a drugged Claudine after regaining consciousness had inadvertently stumbled into the pedestal, knocking it to the floor along with the sculpture while the cameras took their time re-starting. Maybe she passed out again immediately after her collision, which would explain her motionless positioning on the floor when the video-feed rebooted.

She would love to be a fly on the wall, ease-dropping on Crossier's forced and (honestly) ludicrous explanation of everything that may have happened before those cameras started rolling again.

309

She most likely thought that the time-portal 'crush' injury had been caused by stuffing René's body into the sculpture-cleaning machine and turning on the positive-pressure; but why in the world would Henri have gone to this kind of trouble when he could have very easily injected double or triple the amount of narcotic thereby committing a significantly 'cleaner' and much less cumbersome murder-by-overdose? Did she think that he was sending some kind of 'message' in the undertaking, leaving his 'calling card' by using a piece of art-restoration machinery? Or perhaps she thought that René and Henri shared the same profession making the selected mode of death personally symbolic, somehow? None of this made any sense at all; but the absurd hypothesizing didn't stop there.

Crossier would then need to postulate that a slightly frail sixty-something year-old man (with or without the help of a slim, 120 pound Claudine) would be capable of man-handling the much younger and heavier 'René', not only in an out of the cleaning machine but also dragging him across the floor to position him near the already-unconscious Charpentier. Then he would need to lift Charpentier's dead weight and push him so forcefully against the sculpture that his skull would fracture and the pedestal would tumble simultaneously. Then, working faster than the speed of light in order to avoid being seen by the now-rolling cameras, he would have had to intentionally position the two naked bodies entangled together as if in a male-male sex scene gone terribly wrong; and last but not least, he would have to exit the special exhibit galleries taking his rolling murder weapon

310

with him, all in the span of a few seconds in order to avoid being caught red-handed on video-tape when the cameras re-started.

There's no way Henri could have done all this without accomplices, Crossier would likely surmise; but even with an assembled band of criminals, the story was nothing short of ridiculous which is what you get when you try to solve the complexities of a supernaturally-conceived jigsaw puzzle by forcing real-time pieces into the enigma. The police were trying to solve a crime that had never occurred; because after all this was no murder, but rather an unfortunate accident that resulted from a fatal journey through a 'time-tunnel', of all things! *Good*, Susanne thought; *let them spin their wheels*; because the longer they tried to fit a square peg into a round whole, the more time she would have to figure out what to do with Nicole; and the more time John Noland would have to determine whether he would actually be able to send her back to where she belonged.

"As far as a secret life goes, anything is possible," Susanne finally replied. "You'll have to ask Henri, though. I can only give you educated guesses; he'll be able to give you the facts." She looked at her watch. "It's getting late, and I have some work to do. Are we finished now?"

Crossier picked up her phone, smiling pleasantly as she stood up. "Thank you for the information, Mademoiselle Bruante. You've been quite helpful."

Susanne couldn't be fooled that easily. The police might be following some other leads, but Susanne wasn't completely off their radar screen.

She had to be careful where she stepped because there were still plenty of landmines out there.

"Anytime, inspector," Susanne replied, smiling back at the detective just as pleasantly. "Have a good night."

***

It had gone very well, all things considered—both the presentation and the unexpected visit from Inspector Crossier. Granted, her opening remarks tonight had been made to only a handful of listeners, but that really didn't matter. Soon Henri and Nicole would arrive—stealthily by taxi with a designated drop off behind the museum at the service access entryway; and then the sample-collection would begin while Susanne distracted the night guard with her womanly charms.

Earlier that afternoon, she had paid the mail-boy a small fortune to move her car out of the basement parking garage to a spot on the street, two blocks behind the museum. She would need her vehicle later, but somewhere off-site— far away from the four nosey video cameras located one at each corner of the employee car-lot; and far away from the four equally-nosey eyes stationed right in front of *d'Orsay*. At the designated time, she came out in front to smoke a cigarette, sitting on a bench not even five yards away from her intended audience in the white Citroen; crossing her bare legs, naked to the upper thighs, seductively; flirting with impossible-to-ignore purpose to the far left, while the mail-boy pulled out the light blue BMW at the precise moment they had agreed upon, way

312

over to the right. She had even thrown the gendarmes a kiss once she saw the car turn the corner at the street-light a block away—her usual playfully-sarcastic routine anyway, making sure they had no reason to suspect that at the same moment she was flirting with them, her vehicle was being relocated on a residential block, ready and waiting for a late night (or rather, early morning) 'getaway'.

The results from this evening's collection, combined with the hair analysis from both *Waking Nude Preparing to Rise* and her past-meets-present relative (whose hair, she would say, was retrieved from an engraved nineteenth century brush or comb belonging to the artists' model in question) would be the *coup de grâce*, trumping all of the circumstantial evidence that had been the crux of her argument until now. It would be *those* results that would make her famous. The second press conference would be a memorable once-in-a-lifetime, standing-room-only event, in contrast to tonight's meagerly attended prelude to the real thing.

Sitting down at her desk, she glanced at her watch. It was 9:30 p.m. She had two hours to kill until Henri and Nicole's pre-arranged arrival time, right before midnight. Henri would text her, and she would let them in through the service entrance. Then the fun would begin.

Well, she might as well make use of her time. She *did* have another exhibit to plan—that much was true; so she pulled a pile of paperwork from the other side of the desktop toward her, and got started.

Soon, very soon, her theory would be

confirmed with the irrefutable certainty of DNA analysis. She could taste the victory again, and it was truly delicious.

CHAPTER TWENTY-SIX

Henri waited with Nicole for Susanne to answer his text message by letting them in. The taxi had dropped them off in the back, no questions asked; and just as Susanne had instructed, they had followed the down-sloping concrete driveway all the way to the bottom. They had found themselves in front of an industrial-sized garage door, locked and secured of course, which Susanne had explained led into the museum's basement acquisition warehouse. On the far right, a steel door without an outdoor handle would open momentarily from the inside, as soon as Susanne made her way from upstairs via the service elevator in response to his text.

Henri had his bag, which contained all of the equipment he would need to collect the hair samples from the paintings. It wouldn't take more than an hour or so, as long as Nicole pointed out exactly where in each picture he should concentrate on carefully teasing out one single fiber from paint that had aged for a century and a half. It would be meticulous work, requiring caution and patience to extract a single hair, or portion of one, without damaging the surface of the painting. Henri had the experience and the know-how to do the job right—as long as he knew precisely where to look.

"I will show you," Nicole had promised. "I remember, do not worry."

It was funny to hear the formality of her language—the old-fashioned grammar and the antiquated syntax, all of it sounding so out of place coming from someone so young, but born so long ago. Henri had to keep reminding himself that Nicole had lived in another time, where the conventions of the nineteenth century had left its indelible mark on her speech and mannerisms. Otherwise, in Susanne's clothes (including the designer jeans and the trendy Express t-shirt with "*Oo la la!*" written across the front) Nicole seemed completely modern in her appearance. The clothing fit her perfectly, in a way that went well beyond the matching size. They suited her somehow, much more than the long dresses and the buttoned boots that she had worn in the fading family portraits they had looked at together just the other day. Henri almost had the feeling that she belonged here, rather than there. Perhaps she did.

Nicole's way of thinking, too, was anything but antiquated. You might say that she had left everything pre- '*Belle-Époch*' behind her, except that she had probably never held to those conservative beliefs to begin with. Was she a woman ahead of her time, independent and self-assured, uninhibited and unconcerned with other people's opinions of her? Undoubtedly—and now she had become the literal materialization of this aphorism. Somehow she had ended up here, exactly 135 years after her time, and she seemed anything but out of place.

"Posing was my life," she had told him on the ride from Susanne's condo to *d'Orsay*. Henri had hired a taxi, picking her up right in front of the little alley that led to the courtyard behind Susanne's apartment building. Although the surveillance car had followed Susanne to work and had not returned, they had all thought it best for Nicole to use the back way for all of her comings and goings, just to be certain that no one saw her. Henri had watched her put the small ring of extra keys that she was holding into a shoulder purse that Susanne had given her, as she pulled the taxi door closed behind her and slid in beside Henri in the back seat.

"How was it viewed, in those days?" he had asked, referring of course to the nude modeling.

She had shrugged. "It was not something usual for a woman to do. People were shocked by it, including my mother, but I did not care. I love posing naked—it is so very natural." She had paused for a moment to think. "The feeling it gives me is hard to explain. It is freedom and rebellion; it is daring and boldness; it is me standing up to everything that is timid and little-minded, and saying to them that I am beautiful and proud, and that I am not going to hide it. I am not afraid to show people who I truly am, Henri, and posing nude is my way of doing just that. It is beautiful, I think."

It was beautiful—and she was beautiful, there was no argument there. The paintings of her had captured both her sublime image and her spirit with a permanence that would represent her legacy. Courbet had brushed some oil onto canvas-after-canvas-after-canvas, transforming something inanimate into something that pulsed with life. His renderings of Nicole's peerless body had essentially made her immortal—her essence captured in time forever. It was, and she was, a thing of beauty.

"Which other artists did you pose for?" Henri had asked, curious.

"I posed for Édouard Manet a few times; Pierre

317

Renoir; Edgar Degas; Henri Latour; and Mary Cassatt, right before she returned to America." She paused, and then laughed. "I think this is turning out to be a very long list! We cannot forget Jules Lefebvre, who painted me many times, *always* in secret because he and Jean were not on friendly terms at all—in 1868 for a beautiful painting of me that he called *A Reclining Nude*, and again in 1870 for one of my favorites: *La Vérité*. And of course the Caillebotte brothers: Gustave, and poor René. He will never finish his sculpture of me now." She was no longer laughing as her expression turned visibly somber with the mention of her dead lover.

"And don't forget Martial, too," Henri added, moving the subject somewhat away from René but not entirely, out of deference for her loss but hoping to brighten her mood a little bit with the deflection.

"Oh no; *never* Martial."

"But what about the 'body-scape' photographs that Susanne is constantly referencing? She has included those in her 'model singularity' exhibit because of the model's...*appearance*."

She shook her head. "*Non.* He wanted me to pose that way for him, but I refused. He is disgusting."

"So who is the model for those photographs?"

"I saw them, when I was running away last week. I admit the model looks like me, but there is no birthmark."

"Birthmark?"

"Yes. It's in a very intimate place that is shown very clearly in a few of those pictures. Without the birthmark it *cannot* be me. Plus, there is something else."

318

"What?"

"This is very embarrassing but I will say it quickly. That model is *bare* down there where my birthmark should be, and I am not."

He nodded thoughtfully, catching her meaning immediately. He was not at all bothered by the 'focal point' of their discussion since he had always contended that the human body was beautiful and that just because certain body parts were used for the act of procreation didn't mean that they should be considered 'taboo'; but he *was* a little bit uncomfortable having this type of conversation with an attractive young woman—a relative, to boot—in her sexual prime. He had to remind himself that this wasn't just *any* gorgeous thirty-something woman who modelled explicitly nude for a living, but actually his great-grandmother who had 'come down' in time, which definitely threw a less titillating light on the sensitive nature of their dialogue. "Is it possible, Nicole, that you agreed to model for him *after* your return to the 1800's, and that you agreed to alter your 'appearance' down there? This could be a sign, perhaps, that Susanne's ex-boyfriend will be able to send you back, allowing you to pose for them."

Her face brightened slightly but clouded by a frown. "Do you really think so? I pray that this is true; but still…what about my birthmark?"

"They use fancy techniques, these days, to remove blemishes from photographs. Maybe Martial did something similar to the negatives back then and 'erased' it?"

"But why would he do so?" Henri thought he saw her blush, slightly. "It's very pretty!"

319

"I'm sure it is; but perhaps he wanted a 'cleaner', more pristine appearing photo-set? You never know with these artists!" Now *he* was blushing; but it was certainly true. Martial, in trying to be an 'artistic' photographer, may have taken certain liberties with the photo-set to enhance his intended effect.

The prospect of actually returning to the past had lifted Nicole's mood significantly, but it had an entirely different effect on Henri. What would happen when John Noland entered into the picture? Henri didn't know much about Susanne's scientist friend, but he hoped that he would be able to help them without publicizing Nicole's time-travelling experience and using it to his advantage. One thing seemed clear, though; and that was that he would *not* let this perfect stranger turn Nicole into the equivalent of a circus freak. Henri could see the media frenzy now, led by the paparazzi, with accompanying headlines such as, "*Nude Time Traveler Exposed*," and "*Sexy Artists' Model Poses Naked—Any Day, Any 'Time'.*" If his great-grandmother needed protection, Henri would be the one to provide it, and he would *not* let her down.

Aside from a sense of family obligation, he truly liked her. She was levelheaded, thoughtful, intelligent, and kind—a strong woman, but totally selfless, unlike someone else he knew. Funny, how the genes for physical appearance had been passed down through the generations, from Nicole to Susanne, without even a hint of dilution, yet Nicole's personality traits had ended up elsewhere, entirely—except for the exhibitionist ones, of course. Susanne had loved the nude pose as much,

320

or maybe even more, than Nicole had. They both had it in their blood.

Finally, the door opened and Susanne motioned them in. It was dark inside, but Susanne held a flashlight in her hand. "This way," she instructed them, and in a moment they stepped into a triple-sized elevator with padded walls, designed for moving equipment and heavy pieces of artwork such as sculptures from the warehouse and art restoration workshop downstairs, into the museum exhibit areas upstairs. Susanne pressed the button that would take them to the ground-floor level, and the elevator lurched upward. A moment later, it opened onto a granite balcony that connected two catwalks on either side, used by the museum to display a number of Rodin sculptures, stone and bronze alike. Directly below them, they could look over the sunken expanse of the museum's belowground exhibit space that eventually ended in a wide stairway leading to the front lobby on the opposite end, flanked by two similar stairways leading up to the left and right end of the catwalks respectively. At this location, they were well out of the night guard's earshot and video-monitor view.

They had worked it all out beforehand. Nicole stepped off the elevator, leaning against the wall off to one side, patiently prepared to wait. After all, it simply wouldn't do to have her seen side-by-side with her double. Henri followed Susanne, zigzagging through the Rodin display and onto the walkway on the left side, walking behind her as she led him into the front lobby for the fictitious introduction. "This one will be easy to convince," Susanne explained to Henri in a low voice over her shoulder. "He has the hots for me."

Didn't they all? he thought with a smile.

CHAPTER TWENTY-SEVEN

Susanne walked with an inviting feminine sway on five-inch heels, meant to draw attention to her shapely *derriere*—enticingly accessible under a light skirt where groping hands would soon discover the absence of panties. She wore a V-neck blouse that accented her voluptuous, underwire-absent assets underneath that screamed 'carnal reward': an outcry that she was fairly certain this particular night-guard would hear, loud and clear, when he saw her.

"Are you sure you want to do this?" Henri had asked, overly concerned about her integrity and the 'immorality' that the staged encounter represented. "It's only sex," she had responded; and she truly believed it. Why did everyone place the animalistic act of reproduction on such a high pedestal, when it was really something quite ordinary…and so much fun, to boot? Tonight's escapade would be a delicious 'win-win' from both a physical and a psychological standpoint, since 'taking advantage' was right up her alley.

Pierre was well-built in his early forties with a three-day hint of beard, sitting with his feet up watching the video monitors when they approached. He was not at all surprised to see Susanne since she had personally signed the late-stay register earlier while she had still been dressed professionally, having only just finished her opening night presentation; but he *was* surprised, to say the least—his eyes literally bugging out—to see her dressed in this particular change of clothes…*plus*, he hadn't

323

expected her to be accompanied by a companion.

He took his feet off the desk and eyed them both—her with unconcealed lust and Henri with blatant suspicion. "Who is this?" he asked, none too friendly.

Henri, as instructed in advance, had hung back a little, obscured just enough in the shadows between the junction of the lobby and the catwalk that it would be easy enough for Pierre to see him, but very difficult for the surveillance team watching from a decent distance outside to identify him as anyone in particular let alone Henri Bruante: a man 'of interest' to 'the 36'. The last thing they needed was for Susanne's uncle, already under suspicion and on Crossier's radar, to be recognized.

"Good evening to you too, Pierre," Susanne responded pleasantly. "This is François Leclercq, one of our conservators. He's an art historian from Brussels, who has been engaged by the EU Endowment for the Arts to collect materials samples from various paintings."

Pierre looked Henri up and down, as if he were trying to confirm the name by matching it with his appearance. He didn't look convinced. "François Leclercq?"

"Yes," Susanne said. "His team will be studying the composition of various oil paints used by the great Masters from different eras. He needs samples from some of our Courbet pieces."

"And why, exactly, does he have to collect these samples in the middle of the night?" It didn't seem like he was buying it.

"Monsieur Leclercq has a long day scheduled tomorrow at the Louvre," Susanne explained. "If he

324

can squeeze us in tonight, then he'll be able to catch tomorrow evening's flight to Madrid. He's on a very tight schedule, you see."

"No one told me about this, Mademoiselle Bruante. I'm not sure I can let him in without the proper authorization."

"*I* am authorizing it," she declared firmly, while at the same time adjusting her low-cut blouse in order to draw Pierre's attention elsewhere. Interesting, how she was able to combine the insinuation of seduction with the unquestionable assertion of professional authority. Leave it to Susanne to invent a whole new blend of persuasion.

Pierre's eyes flicked downward at her cleavage and then up again. Susanne's strategy was having the desired effect. "This was all arranged at the last minute," she added offhandedly. "Monsieur *Le Director* has approved it, take my word; and I'll be personally supervising Monsieur Leclercq's interaction with our paintings..." (she paused and looked meaningfully at Henri, just as the 'script' had detailed) "...in just a few moments. If he would like to head over *alone* to the special exhibit galleries and get started, I'll stay here to help you, uh...file the documents."

Pierre hesitated for a few more seconds, obviously confused about nonexistent documents and where he might be expected to file them; but when Susanne caught his eye again by tracing the bulging seam of the front of her blouse suggestively with a blatantly seductive fingertip, he suddenly understood. He was none-too-bright, this Pierre; but definitely worthy of a roll in the hay. "I suppose it makes more sense to collect the specimens at night, anyway," he said, as if trying to convince himself. "That way, Monsieur Leclercq won't interfere with our patrons during daytime business hours."

"Exactly!" Susanne moved over to the other side of the video-monitor desk and leaned over on outstretched arms, giving Pierre, who was now standing awe-struck right next to her, an even better view of her partly exposed bust. "You'll have to turn off the motion sensors in all of the special exhibit galleries, since Monsieur Leclercq will be collecting his specimens from paintings located in those rooms. Isn't this the control switch?" Susanne had intentionally positioned herself right next to the side-by-side circuit-breakers for the artwork-connected motion sensors, *and* the museum cameras. All she would have to do is seduce Pierre with her back facing this two-button panel, within reach of a backward-searching hand to inactivate the video feed.

"Yes," Pierre responded vaguely, pressing the motion sensor shut-off button as if in a trance—his gaze still fixed on Susanne, mesmerized by her proximity. She turned 180 degrees, positioning herself perfectly for her next move. "You can go about your business now, Monsieur Leclercq," she called over her shoulder to Henri. "I will join you there shortly."

Henri would work quickly—expertly extracting the hair using carefully-prepared solvents that would soften the paint without removing it, after being instructed on exact location by Nicole. He would need a good twenty minutes per painting, and they were planning on selecting three: so an hour of play-time would suffice, during which the delicate project would be executed in complete video-silence and as a result, untraceable circumstances. If Pierre came back down to earth later after recovering from 'nirvana' provided by the woman of his dreams, deciding to contact Marcel or someone else in museum administration to double-check her story, she would just deny, deny, and deny. It would be her word against his with a little blackmail added—because Pierre had a wife at home: the mother of his two young children, who would be none too pleased if she found out about his infidelity by way of a phone-call from a certain home-wrecker.

She pulled him close as she heard Henri's footsteps fade, kissing him with feigned passion while unzipping him ever-so slowly with her right hand—the simmering tease meant to distract him from noticing her left, which had reached behind and settled on the camera switch. She reached into his pants at the very same moment of single-finger shut-off, concealing the 'click' with a heavy moan, which Pierre mimicked. He reached feverishly under her skirt, gasping slightly when he discovered her nudity beneath.

"Not here," she murmured, trying to conceal her anxiety because in a second or two she was certain that he would notice the now-blackened video monitors. "Anyone looking in from outside can see us through the front windows," she added practically…which was true and also in-part completely intended, because *this* way the goggle-eyed surveillance team could see that she was still 'on-site'; so he grudgingly allowed her to remove his hands from her naked backside and take them in hers. Before he could resist she spun him around so that his back now faced the screens and led him into the control room, gazing over towards the glass museum-front and in the general vicinity of her law enforcement 'audience' as a final tease, before closing the door behind her with a quiet sigh of relief.

Now the trick would be slowing him down because he was already so eager that once they started, she was fairly certain that the entire interaction would only take a few minutes. "Should I dance for you?" she asked.

The answer was of course 'yes' because there is no full-blooded man on the continent or elsewhere who would *ever* think of turning down a sexy striptease from a woman like Susanne as a prelude to ecstasy.

CHAPTER TWENTY-EIGHT

Susanne dressed quickly after they had finished, concerned that she hadn't given Henri and Nicole enough time to collect the samples and determined to scope things out well before Pierre could recover from his little erotic adventure. It had taken her about thirty-five minutes for voyeuristic foreplay: top and bottom peeled off in the slowest performance of her 'career', and then another twenty to execute the drawn-out act itself, totaling fifty-five: just a little short of the required hour that she had calculated they would need. Pierre would fortunately be slowed by the post-coital lethargy universal to all men after exerting themselves as he had, and in addition he had more clothes and paraphernalia to put on than she did; so she had maybe five minutes but no more to run back into the museum and make sure that her relatives had vacated the area, then double back and turn the video cameras back on. The plan was for them to meet her next to the service area, at the same spot they had left Nicole when initiating the ruse at the front desk. She hoped they were there already.

"I'm going to the restroom to clean up and then to check on Monsieur Leclercq," she explained even though he hadn't asked. "If he's finished I'll be escorting him directly back to the hotel." She winked at him. "Thanks, big guy! Let's do this again soon, okay?"

"Definitely," he mumbled sleepily from the break-room table in the corner, still lying naked, flat on his back and limp as a ragdoll. She had drained

329

him, for sure. "See you around."

This was perfect. Judging from his tortoise-like appearance she hoped he would move just as slow. Holding her heels dangling on two fingers (since if she wore them they would just slow her down) she dashed barefoot passed the still-blackened video screens which she didn't dare risk reactivating now, just in case Henri and Nicole weren't finished yet. She ran down the catwalk towards the designated rendezvous spot and within thirty seconds found herself in front of the service elevators…alone.

"*Merde*," she whispered, crossing immediately over to the opposite-side catwalk and rushing into the special exhibit galleries where she found Henri in the alcove room apparently just finishing up—squatting over his utility bag, zipping it up, and combing the hair out of his eyes with his fingers as he stood. Nicole she saw distantly visible through three archways in the fourth room examining the erotic body-scapes. "We need to get out of here quickly," she panted between heavy breaths. "Did you collect them?"

"Oh yes," he beamed. "Nicole knew *exactly* where to guide me. After she made the positive identifications there wasn't much for her to do, though, so she's been wandering around. Those photographs particularly intrigue her because she claims the model isn't her."

"That's ridiculous…of *course* it's her; but we don't have time right now to discuss it. Nicole!" Susanne hissed in a whispered call, immediately getting her attention. "Come on, let's go!"

A minute or so later they were all assembled back at the elevator. "You stay here," Nicole instructed, handing Henri her heels for safe-keeping, "while I go back to the front and turn the video cameras back on." Praying that Pierre hadn't emerged yet from his stupor, she hurried back down the catwalk, but stopped short as she turned the corner going into the lobby. She was a moment too late because there was Pierre, his hair disheveled and his shirt only partly buttoned with a combined look of anger and disappointment clouding his face, standing dumbfounded at the semicircular video-display desk...phone in hand.

"Pierre," she said, unable to control the alarm in her voice. "What are you doing?"

"The cameras were off," he replied, looking over at her accusingly, "so I turned them on; and can you guess what I saw?" He didn't wait for her to answer. "A woman wandering through the galleries." At least he didn't mention the 'family resemblance', which only meant that he hadn't had sufficient time to analyze the footage but at least she needn't worry about this complicating detail...for the moment. "Was she 'authorized'," he continued sarcastically, "just like your so-called 'Monsieur Leclercq'?"

She approached him cautiously, like a skittish animal ready to bolt. "Calm down, Pierre. I can explain."

"You can save your explanations for someone else. This is out of my hands now. You see, I called the 'Chief'..." (he was referring, of course, to Guillaume Laroche: the head of security) "...and he didn't know anything about an international team coming to collect 'samples' tonight. He's getting in touch with the Executive Director, right now, to double-check."

This was bad…*very* bad; but she immediately saw a way out—at least regarding the 'authorization' dilemma. She pretended to be unconcerned. "The woman is Monsieur Leclercq's assistant…" (she didn't bother to explain why an 'assistant' would stay back rather than accompanying them to the lobby earlier, because of course this didn't make logical sense) "…and we *do* have authorization." She pulled her cell phone, already pre-programmed to reach Marcel on his pre-paid device, out of her purse as nonchalantly as possible—even though she knew that time was of the essence. "I'll call Marcel right now to prove it!" She walked across to the other side of the lobby turning her back towards Pierre, hoping that he wouldn't be suspicious of her initial 'privacy requirement'. If things went her way she would actually hand the phone over to him later for verbal confirmation of the after-the-fact authorization that she hoped to secure, straight from the horse's mouth.

She waited impatiently for the director to pick up, tapping the ball of her bare foot on the cool veneered wood. The line rang once, twice, three times, four times. "Pick it up, Marcel," she pleaded under her breath. Getting his voicemail was simply not an option.

"Hello," he finally answered, his voice hushed. She imagined him, once again, sleeping next to his average-looking wife when his cell phone startled him awake. Seeing Susanne's name on the caller ID, he would have rushed out into the hallway, taking the call secretly, as he always did on the rare occasions when she called him after hours. "What is it, Susanne?" His voice sounded edgy and irritated, but unquestionably clueless. Thank God she had reached him before Laroche! "Jeanine will find out about us for sure, if these late-night phone calls don't stop."

Last week, it had been the police calling him at one o'clock in the morning, but now it was her, waking him at an ungodly hour with a phone call that, he would shortly discover, had nothing whatsoever to do with their relationship. This time, it was all business as she rapidly explained. "You'll be getting a call in a moment from Guillaume Laroche," she disclosed in a low voice, deciding to launch right into it since her timing was undoubtedly right down to the wire; and sure enough, as soon as she said it, she heard the shrill ring of Marcel's house phone in the background. "That's him now, Marcel. Hear him out if you'd like but don't respond at all; just tell him that you'll call him right back."

"Why?"

"I'll explain it to you as soon as you get rid of Laroche. *Do* it, Marcel. I promise, you won't regret it."

"Okay, okay; hold on a second." He sounded annoyed, but she would be able to appease him in a moment with her offer of partnership.

She waited, while he walked down his house stairs to the ground floor to answer the phone. "Lauren, here," she heard him answer a few seconds later, his voice muffled by distance but still audible. "Yes, yes; I have her on the other line right now." Then, after a momentary delay, during which time he was undoubtedly listening to Laroche hanging her out to dry, she heard him say: "I'll call you back shortly."

He was back on his prepaid mobile with her. "What in the world are you up to? Guillaume says you're in the museum with some kind of international art historian who wants to collect samples from some of our paintings. I didn't authorize this, Susanne."

She could hear him seething through the phone line. Had she gone too far this time, not only by undermining Marcel's authority, but also by placing three valuable pieces of artwork at serious risk of being damaged? Admittedly, her judgment had been colored by the promise of professional accomplishment and validation, but that hardly meant that she had made the wrong call by deciding to go behind Marcel's back for the sample collection. 'Wrong' was a word that simply was not in her vocabulary. The problem here, to put it simply, was that she had been caught. That was her mistake—nothing more, nothing less.

But there was no point in lingering in the past. Now was the time to fix things, and she intended to do just that. "Remember my uncle, the art restorer?"

"Of course I remember him. Thanks to him, you had some additional circumstantial evidence to present tonight, in support of your 'model singularity' theory. That letter was a historic 'find', I'll admit; but it adds nothing incontrovertible to back your thesis."

"I know that. But he found something else in *Waking Nude Preparing to Rise*, Marcel—something that I think will interest you greatly."

"What?" She could hear his skepticism; but in a minute, he would change his tune.

"During my uncle's analysis of the painting, he noticed some organic material embedded in the paint."

"What kind of organic material?"

"Hair."

"Did I hear you correctly? I thought you just said 'hair'."

"I did. He found human hair, integrated with the paint. It was blended into the image, in a location corresponding to the model's hair in the picture."

"That's very interesting, but I fail to see the relevance. Unless you enlighten me, you and your 'international expert' (who I assume is your uncle) will find yourselves serving time for destruction of national property."

That was cold, especially considering that she was his mistress; but then again, they were long overdue for another hotel room marathon. With all the commotion, she had been shirking her duties. She'd have to remedy that, and fast. "I'd miss our little get-togethers if I ended up in prison, Marcel—which reminds me that we haven't had a conjugal visit in *way* too long. How about this morning (it was well past midnight)—early…as per our 'usual'?" Today was Tuesday, which often started with an 'executive board meeting' requiring advance preparation at five a.m. or so, taking place (unbeknownst to his naïve and unsuspecting wife) in a hotel room instead of the office. A few hours of 'hard' encouragement would go a long way toward softening him up.

There was a pause, and she knew she had him. "Yes, that would work. But back to this business with the hair—"

"All right, listen carefully. When I found out that my great-great-great grandmother was the model for *Waking Nude Preparing to Rise*, and when we found the piece of hair imbedded in the painting, it occurred to me that maybe the hair was placed there intentionally, by Courbet."

"Why would he do something like that?"

"As a way to 'breathe life' into an inanimate representation of a real person by putting a living 'piece' of her into the picture. It makes perfect sense, Marcel; and could have very well been a Courbet 'trademark' which I'm determined to prove."

"I get it," he responded. "So is this why you're in the museum collecting 'samples'?"

"Of *course* it is…from three of Courbet's most erotic paintings on display in my special exhibit, in the hope that we will discover some embedded strands of hair, just as we did in *Waking Nude Preparing to Rise*. But there's more, Marcel."

"Go on."

"My grandmother recently died and my uncle 'inherited' a number of boxes containing family possessions, that she had stored in her attic. I just so happened to find a hair brush engraved with the name: 'Nicole Thérèse Bruante'; and believe it or not, there were still strands of *hair* interwoven in the bristles so I sent them for DNA analysis requesting a comparison to the fragments we retrieved from the family painting." The story sounded so plausible that even *she* was beginning to believe it; so why wouldn't he?"

"And?" It seemed from his tone of voice that he had taken the bait—hook, line and sinker.

"The two hair samples are perfect matches."

"Do you know what this means, Susanne?"

Of *course* she knew. It meant that she had now shared her great art history breakthrough with the man with whom she least wanted to share it; the man who could very well double-cross her and take the credit for all her years of hard work, if she didn't handle him delicately, to say the least. She had had no choice, though—because without Marcel's authorization, she and her uncle were screwed. "Yes, Marcel." She would have to spell it out for him, it seemed, even though he knew very well the implications of her fortuitous discoveries. "This means that my model singularity theory is no longer hypothetical, but *fact*. Not only that, but if the hair samples my uncle successfully extracted from the Courbet paintings tonight match the other two DNA samples, then we have positively identified an actual person that we can identify as our 'singular' model."

"This is amazing, Susanne; but you should have run this by me first," he said, his tone becoming increasingly indulgent by the minute.

"Yes, I know I should have, and I regret that now. I just didn't want to risk another moment's delay, so I thought I'd just get the samples, quick and dirty, and we'd be done with it."

"A team of restorers working in a closely controlled setting should have handled a job of this magnitude. This was incredibly irresponsible of you, Susanne. You've placed these paintings at risk

337

of sustaining surface damage from an inappropriately executed collection procedure."

"Look," she countered, "all three specimens have been successfully retrieved and none of the paintings have been damaged. Henri is the most experienced restorer in the business. He knows what he's doing better than anyone else we could have hired, so that's why I pulled him in on this emergency job."

"But still…" It seemed that there was something more that she needed her to 'spell out' in exchange for his retroactive authorization: namely, a gold-plated carrot. "Look Marcel; once we have the DNA analyzed from the samples, we can share the recognition. We'll be equal partners in this. Deal?" If she knew Marcel like she thought she knew him, he would willingly turn a blind eye to, or even *condone*, her unconventional collection methods if she offered him an alliance. A discovery like this was a once-in-a-lifetime opportunity to advance his career as a co-contributor, and make a name for himself. He wouldn't turn her down.

She didn't have to wait long for his answer. "Deal."

"Great," she said, while turning to walk back across the lobby. "I'm in a bit of a pickle here though, with the night guard. Would you mind very much talking to him? He needs to hear it from you that I had your official, personal authorization to bring in 'Monsieur Leclercq'." She was only a few feet from Pierre now, and she said Henri's alias loudly enough for him to hear. "It's the Executive Director," she explained, handing Pierre the phone. "He has something to tell you."

Pierre listened attentively, nodding his head a couple time and repeating "I understand, sir," more than once. Finally, he handed Susanne her phone back with a sheepish look on his face. "You win," he said.

She smiled as she took her phone from Pierre and placed it on her ear. "All good?" she asked.

"Yep. How long will it take for the DNA testing to be completed?"

"Aren't we anxious. Forty-eight hours, at the most. My uncle has a contact."

"Good." What would come next? The after-the-fact authorization, perhaps, signed and sealed, but with the date falsified. Knowing how he though, she felt certain he would store it away, waiting until later to file it through the proper channels *after* he made certain that the paintings weren't damaged and that the DNA testing had hit it big. "I'll swing by the office in a few hours and get all the paperwork together for you to sign," he said, confirming her suspicion. "We can take care of it in the hotel room."

She ended her call and stared Pierre down. "I *told* you I had authorization."

"Whatever." He waived away her 'win' dismissively. "We still have the little mystery of the silenced video cameras to deal with, though."

She shrugged. "I must have accidentally leaned on the button when you were 'attacking' me.

"It was mutual, and you know it."

"Maybe; but a well-placed call to either your wife, or to one of my buddies in law enforcement, could make things very messy for you."

"Alright, alright…what do you want from me?"

"Erase the footage taken when you re-booted the video cameras just a few minutes ago."

"If you had the proper authorization and everyone who was here was *supposed* to be here, then why do you want the evidence destroyed?"

Susanne shrugged. "I'm just being overly cautious. First of all, this night-time outing is 'top secret' and the Executive Director and I don't want any of our competitors 'scooping' us; and second, my arrangement with Monsieur Lauren as it relates to this particular project is a bit...*unorthodox*, as you could probably tell just based on the lengthy duration of our phone call. Marcel and I don't want anyone who might be nosing around to get wind of what we're up to. So...erase that segment and tell anyone who asks that you fell asleep with your elbow on the shut-off switch, which will explain away the hour-plus of absent video-feed."

Now he was just like putty in her hands—go figure. She followed him into the control room where she 'supervised' the destruction of evidence; then she kissed him condescendingly on the cheek, turned away, and showed him her stuff from behind as she sauntered away. It felt good to always end up on top—her favorite, and usual, position. It felt very, very good indeed.

CHAPTER TWENTY-NINE

They retraced their steps, down the service area, out the back, and furtively through the well-past-midnight shadows until they reached Susanne's light blue BMW, parked two blocks away behind the museum by a well-paid mail-boy yesterday. What had happened in the lobby during the past twenty minutes, while he and Nicole had waited nervously for Susanne to 'check out' the situation with her sexually-gullible security guard? Henri was curious, but didn't dare to ask since he could tell from Susanne's uncharacteristic silence that she was in no mood for explanations.

They got in, with Henri sitting in the passenger seat, Nicole in back, and Susanne behind the wheel since she was the only one of the three of them who could drive. The plan was to have Susanne 'chauffer' her two relatives home instead of using a taxi, since hailing one this time of night would have been close to impossible. She would drop Nicole in the alleyway in back of her flat first, followed by Henri at his house in the 'Latin' district, and then back to reclaim her parking spot on the street. She would sleep on her couch in the museum, for the sole purpose of keeping up the charade for the 'dynamic-duo' out front; and in the morning she would pay the same mail-boy the very-same small fortune to retrieve her car for her, replacing it in the garage while she enjoyed another flirtatiously-distracting cigarette break out front.

They suffered a semi-tense mutual silence imposed by Susanne's foul and pensive mood, giving Henri plenty of time to re-enact the last hour-and-a-half in his mind. Nicole had initially made a bee-line to *The Origin of the World*, but stopped short a good three yards away. "That's the painting I have hanging at the foot of my bed. It was always my favorite...but now, not so much." Tears welled in her eyes. "It killed my poor René, and left me stranded in this strange time and place."

"I know this is difficult, Nicole; but this painting, I think, will be the best place to start."

"I am afraid to stand too close, Henri. This might sound silly, but what if it sucks me in again, just like it did before?"

True...she *did* have a point; except that something (maybe wine, maybe drugs, maybe sex, or maybe a combination of all three) had precipitated the last 'journey'; and none of these preconditions were in play now. Given the unlikelihood of a repeat performance, he decided to use some humor to lighten the moment. "Well, if it does, you might end up back home."

"Or somewhere else entirely."

True again. "You're right, Nicole," he admitted, somberly this time; "so how about you stay put, right where you are; and tell me from a safe distance—where in this painting did Courbet insert your hair?"

Nicole pointed without hesitation in the general vicinity of the intimate triangle forming the central focus of the painting; but with her standing so far away, Henri could not tell exactly where she meant. "I'm afraid you'll have to describe the location, since we can't risk having you move any closer," he told her quietly.

"On my inner right thigh, right at the crease near my fold where the regular skin begins…covered by my 'private' hair."

"Here?" Henri asked, his finger nearly touching the awkward anatomy depicted in the painting as he pointed. He felt distinctly impolite, inquiring so bluntly; but it couldn't be helped.

"Yes, Henri," she confirmed without even the hint of a blush. "Jean brushed in my hair right there."

Henri had reached into his bag to withdraw a small notebook that he had packed for this express purpose. He quickly sketched the landmarks between Nicole's legs and made a careful notation with a couple of X's to guide him in the upcoming collection process. "Okay, I've got it."

He breathed a quiet sigh of relief now that they had located the spot where he would very soon concentrate his efforts, because naturally he felt a little uncomfortable examining a representation of Nicole's genital area while she stood by watching. They would move on now to the next painting, located in another room entirely where Nicole would be completely safe from whatever 'influence' *The Origin of the World* might still have on her. "Which other two of Jean's paintings of you should we sample?" He thought to give her some modicum of control, by choosing.

"How about *Woman with a Parrot*?" She pointed at the painting, which was visible hanging in the adjacent room, just beyond the archway that separated the alcove from the first exhibit gallery.

Nicole had led Henri over to the painting, crossing her arms and analyzing it with a mixed expression of pride and nostalgia. "Jean painted me in this one right after we did *Le Sommeil*," she said. "It was a very difficult pose to hold."

It must have been, Henri thought as he studied the image. Nicole's left arm was positioned straight up in the air, holding a stuffed bird. After only ten or fifteen minutes like that, her limb would have most certainly fallen asleep.

"Lying with Céleste in the other painting was so much easier." Nicole was referring, of course, to *Le Sommeil*: the piece that she had referenced only a few seconds ago picturing her entwined with a female lover, happily asleep with an after-the-fact look of satisfied contentment. "*So* much easier," she repeated, "and so much more fun!" She wore a coquettish grin that was so devoid of pretense that he couldn't help but smile. Nicole's open-mindedness undeniably belonged *here*, in 2011, rather than in 1876.

"I realize he put your hair in the...*hair*," Henri commented, "but where, exactly? There's so much of it in this painting." He made another rough sketch in his book, while Nicole pointed to a wave of locks that flowed along the nearest edge of the white-sheeted covering on her cot.

"So, what about the third one?" he had asked, knowing before she told him that it would probably be *Le Sommeil*. "The one with Céleste," she confirmed without hesitation. "It's in the third room. I know because I saw it when I was being chased."

They moved to the third room where she showed him the location of the embedded hair; and then wandered off to look at the other paintings,

344

almost like a regular contemporary museum-visitor leisurely appreciating all the artwork on a Sunday afternoon. He had worked in reverse, starting with *Le Sommeil*, moving on to *Woman with a Parrot*, and ending with *The Origin of the World*. It was while he was collecting the samples from the depiction of Nicole's genitals that she came back in, hanging back in the archway between the first room and the alcove to ensure her own safety, commenting to Henri on her thoughts about the self-guided exhibit tour that she had just completed.

"There are so many paintings that seem to picture me as the model, but I do not recall posing for them. I know why, though; the years printed on the descriptive plaques explain the reason."

"Those paintings are all dated *after* 1876—correct?"

"Yes. I must say that this gives me reason to hope that I will eventually go back. I like it here, but this is not where I belong." Henri wasn't so sure about that. Nicole seemed right at home and had adjusted remarkably quickly to a very strange world that, for most, would still be profoundly overwhelming. "But those erotic photographs," she continued, shaking her head. "It's very hard to believe they are of me. I cannot stand Martial and even now, I cannot imagine agreeing to those pictures."

Henri shrugged. "One can never predict the future. Perhaps the circumstances changed...or *you* did."

"I suppose."

"Or *Martial* changed. This kind of thing happens, you know. A person can be completely different at age forty compared to age twenty, for instance."

"But no hair? And no birthmark?" She had left these questions and her doubts dangling in the air, returning to the last gallery to view the photographs again with either a more accepting or a more critical eye (Henri wasn't sure which) as he finished up with *The Origin of the World.*

Now Nicole, breaking the awkward silence and speaking from the back seat of Susanne's car, brought up the topic of the 'body-scapes' again. "Henri, I think you are right about those photographs. I must have posed for them sometime in the future..." (she paused to clarify) "...of my past, that is."

It sounded so strange to put it that way, but of course that was the most accurate description of the 'timetable'. "Why are you worrying so much about those photos?" Susan asked with annoyance. "The materials experts dated them to circa 1888, so there's no question you posed for them after we sent you back..." (Henri couldn't help notice the past tense, indicating that Susanne likely viewed Nicole's return to the nineteenth century a 'done deal') "...but beyond the time-travelling 'logistics', it's obvious to me and everyone else that they're pictures of you. Who *else* looks like that?"

Since Susanne's question was rhetorical, nobody answered; but Henri thought: "*You, for one,*" with a quiet laugh to himself. He felt sure that Susanne would have agreed to an explicit photoset like that in a heartbeat, had she been in the right place at the right time; which led him to fleetingly wonder if Susanne had an unmentionably-placed birthmark, too—born from the very same 'genetics' that had created a perfectly identical facial and bodily appearance in two women from disparate generations spaced almost a century and a half apart (or in two *men* for that matter: himself and Nicole's father). Had every freckle and blemish been perfectly duplicated, just as two noses had been positioned just-so and the browns and greens of twin-like eyes produced in exact swirling symmetry between the two? If not the auburn hair: a flawless match, then why not a birthmark? It was a fascinating idea to ponder, for sure.

Susanne went on, addressing Henri rather than Nicole as though her great-great-great grandmother wasn't even present. "Why is she even questioning it?"

"Because of the 'landscaping' between her legs…or rather the lack there-of, along with an absent birthmark." It was probably best that Henri responded anyway, saving Nicole some embarrassment when it came to word choice.

"That means nothing. It's easy enough to shave 'down there', and *far* preferable from my standpoint than going 'natural'; and the lack of a birthmark just means that the photos have been doctored. Even in the early days of photography, I'm certain they could touch things up if necessary. Is it a mole?" Susanne asked.

"Yes." Nicole responded for herself this time. "I like it very much."

"I don't know *why* you would. Something like that might be viewed as a defect so no wonder Martial erased it in the photographs. If I had one, I'd make it disappear *pronto* with plastic surgery since I *always* strive for perfection, especially in that particular anatomic region."

So the answer to the 'does Susanne have the same birthmark' question was a definite 'no'—revealed in the most egotistical way imaginable. Since no further commentary was forthcoming, Susanne changed the subject. "Since we're on the topic of 'disappearing', we need to be more careful keeping Nicole out of the spotlight. She was caught on videotape towards the end of our retrieval adventure just now, and it took some doing for me to strong-arm Pierre into erasing it."

This was the first mention of a job almost-gone wrong, which startled Henri. "How's that?" he asked.

"I really don't want to talk about it. Let's just say that I put a lot more on the line than my nonexistent virginity tonight."

'Disappear' seemed an ominously appropriate term for Susanne to use. Henri looked sadly at Nicole in his sun-visor mirror. The poor girl had disappeared, not by choice, from a distant time and place. If Susanne eventually had her way, Nicole would disappear again, leaving *this* time and place to go—where? It seemed doubtful that Susanne's scientist friend would be able to guarantee a round-trip ticket back to Nicole's old life. Even if he could, was that really the right place for her? Where did Nicole truly belong? And now that she was here, what did fate intend for her? Henri sighed. Philosophy had never been his strong point, so he would just have to leave that to the experts.

But was John Noland the right kind of expert? Perhaps he was; but then again, perhaps he wasn't.

Time would tell, very shortly—tomorrow, in fact. When the expert arrived tomorrow, they would know.

CHAPTER THIRTY

Susanne dropped Nicole off right where she had started just three hours before, back in the little alley that led to the courtyard directly behind Susanne's apartment building; barely slowing down it seemed, declaring that she was "in a rush" to deposit Henri and get back to the museum, where she would "catch some shut-eye" as she put it, on her office couch, before heading out again almost immediately to meet Marcel: her current sexual 'affair' and boss rolled into one, in a hotel room.

Nicole had learned, while sitting in the backseat of Susanne's car, that her image had been captured tonight on something called a 'video camera', which seemed to greatly concern Susanne; but just like her birthmark, it seems they had the capability of erasing it—which they did, just like that. Susanne was happy again; and when Susanne was happy, *everyone* was happy.

As Nicole walked toward the alley with the large metal key in her hand, she thought to herself that she really liked it here—correction, *loved* it. Everything was so convenient and so incredibly comfortable. These vehicles they called autos, for instance, transported people to distant places in no time, and luxuriously. Carriage rides were always so bumpy and slow, and the odors were often overwhelming.

Susanne and Henri had no idea how lucky they were. It wasn't just the modern transportation that made it so wonderful to live here; it was all the devices that made it so easy to do much, much more than simply exist. Her life had been very difficult in 1876, although she hadn't known that when she was there. It always took a comparison to point out how perfect or deficient something was, and the contrast between 'then-versus-now' was as extreme as 'night-versus-day'. How strange that now she had been given the rare opportunity to compare them yet here she was. Who would have thought that she would be able to take a peek into the future?

It was more than a peek, of course. Now that she had experienced life here, it would be very difficult to leave—assuming that leaving was even possible. But did she have any choice in the matter, really? Even the most simple-minded individual could understand that transporting someone from the past into the future might drastically change what was meant to be. Nicole's absence from where she was supposed to live her life: there in the past; as well as her presence in a place where she shouldn't be: here in the future, could both alter events in a way that would unquestionably have important repercussions for other people around her, or even for society as a whole.

Granted, she wasn't someone important like 'her' Jean (known to everyone here as Gustave) Courbet; but being common instead of famous did not necessarily make her a less valuable individual, at least to the people whose lives she had touched. Or *would* touch.

Take Edmond, for instance. She had already been absent from her son's life for exactly one week, and she was starting to imagine, in nightmare-like vividness, more than just a few time-altering scenarios that might have already resulted from this deprivation. Granted, she only saw him every so often anyway, but what if he was ill? Or what if missing their Sunday rendezvous two Sundays from now, or *another* afternoon get-together next month or next year, placed him in harm's way? She was his mother, and he was her baby (even though at age nine he was getting so big); so she was expected to be there, right by his side to protect him. But she wasn't. She would go back there, if she could, for Edmond's sake; she had to, didn't she? Of *course* she did. That's what mothers did, after all.

It had been a long day, and she was tired. The entire city was asleep, it seemed, and that's where she would be in a little while, too. She slid the old-fashioned brass key into the garden gate, turned it halfway to the right, and swung the grated iron door inward. She stepped carefully onto tightly fitted stone pavers, the path somewhat difficult to see in the darkness, taking a diagonal route across the courtyard directly to the back door, over to the right. She had a key for that, too: a small, flat one that fit into both the dead bolt and the doorknob locks. When she was inside, she took the side stairs up two flights, using the last key on the ring to let herself into Susanne's apartment: *3B*.

She felt at home here, even though she could clearly see through Susanne's ulterior motives for letting her stay. Nicole liked the little guestroom: her home away from home, with the walk-in closet stocked by Susanne with a variety of clothes that fit Nicole perfectly and were right in line with her newly discovered sense of style.

She also liked the bed, large enough for two but

intended for one, with an enormous, thick mattress that was so much better than the feather matting she was used to—that thin rectangle of stingily-stuffed fabric that did little to soften the wooden slats of her cot underneath her. She couldn't wait to climb into that bed right now, naked and exhausted, pulling the sheets and blankets around her for the sound and dreamless sleep she sorely needed in preparation for the next day, which would begin only a few hours from now. She would meet John Noland when he arrived tomorrow, sometime after lunch-time—an experience that she predicted would be lengthy as well as stressful.

She made her way down the hallway, her first stop the bathroom, to the left, where she pulled off her t-shirt, arms crossed at the bottom lifting it smoothly up and off. Her breasts were naked under the thin cotton fabric with nipples hardened by cold—her shivering body more than ready for the warm, steamy wetness of a hot shower. She pulled off her jeans and stepped into the extravagant cascade of clean water, yet another modern convenience, closing her eyes and soaking her hair with the dripping caress of the pulsing stream. Her nudity, soaped and slick, trickled in slippery rivulets until it was rinsed a sensuous clean.

A white terry-cloth bathrobe doubled as a towel, and by the time she moved into the bedroom, her body was dry. Bathrobe off, she lay it on the foot of the bed, and in she crept, between cool sheets and into the warm and inviting summons of double blankets. She settled in, her head on the pillow; and in a matter of seconds, she fell fast asleep.

Her hope for a dreamless sleep did not come true, though.

***

Nicole followed the winding street, in her dream, as it led from the top of *Butte Montmartre*, down and down toward the bottom of a hill. It was June eighteenth: the third Sunday of the month; and in just a little while, she would see her Edmond. Her mother had marked the calendar and was sure to send him on his way to their meeting place: *Place Pigalle*, with plenty of time to spare for their mother-son rendezvous at twelve noon.

It was a very hot day—unseasonably so; and it would be so refreshing to sit on the edge of the fountain while Edmond played with the gift Nicole had bought him. She imagined how his eyes would grow wide when he unwrapped the replica of a steamship that he would eagerly add to his growing collection, after he tried it out on the rippling surface of the fountain-pond. She could almost see his innocent face focused intently on his boat, but occasionally taking a break from his game of 'pretend' to splash his mother happily with a handful of cool water.

It would be so very nice to see her little boy. She missed him, but the arrangement she had worked out with her mother for Edmond to stay full-time with his grandmother was really for the best, at least for now. Although her widowed-mother didn't have much, she had more—*much* more, by far—than Nicole had. Thank God for her mother's generosity and love. Without her, Nicole

354

would probably be out on the street. And Edmond? She didn't even want to think about it.

It was ten minute to noon, a few hours prior to the peak of the day's heat but already stifling. She wore her summer dress with the bare minimum of undergarments, but it was still too much for such a warm day. How she wanted to strip it all off and toss the clothes aside, as she had been doing for René daily as he chiseled away at the marble block, transforming it magically from nondescript stone to a strikingly life-like replica of her nudity—inch-by-inch, moving downward from her naked breasts and finally, just the other day, to unmentionable below-hip realism.

She tugged at her collar, moist with perspiration already, though she was only halfway down the hill. What a shame that the convention of clothing, intended to warm the body in cold weather, had somehow been carried over into the summer months. Nudity would be so much better, in the face of such heat; but, oh well—who was she to question the rules that people had imposed upon themselves?

Down and down she walked, until finally the street opened into the bustling expanse of *Pigalle*. She turned right and passed by a nightclub that featured the latest Parisian rage: the gaudy burlesque. A dancer rushed in front of her, late perhaps for her upcoming shift, dressed in a red skirt that showed a shocking amount of leg. Nicole laughed to herself. She herself routinely showed that much leg, and much more, whenever she went to her 'job'. She imagined, with a smile, how she would shake up the place, if ever they hired her as one of their cabaret girls. She was no dancer, though; that was the problem. Her talent lay in showing excess skin, not in moving it.

She saw the fountain now, across the way and on the other side of *La Place*; and between Nicole and this destination, she had horses, and carriages, and pedestrians to contend with—too many to count. Edmond loved the bustle of activity down here, and that was yet another reason why she had chosen *Place Pigalle* rather than the *La Butte Montmartre* for today's visit. Nicole shaded the sun from her eyes with her hand, searching for them across the busy courtyard; and then she saw him. Nicole would just wait for this carriage to pass, and then she would cross.

Edmond saw her too—he was waving his arms, and probably calling her name. She couldn't hear him, of course, but she imagined his voice, screaming "*Maman, Maman*," in his excitement to see her. The busy traffic of horse-led carriages separated mother from son, producing a chaotic barrier to their reunion; so Nicole would have to hurry if she wanted to make it across before this next one—black, large, and ornate, trimmed with silver, being pulled at a fast clip by not one but two horses. The driver sat on top, dressed in a tailcoat and hat. This one belonged to someone wealthy.

She waved back to Edmond and then rushed ahead. Edmond matched her pace, accelerating his walk into a run; and then abruptly taking off as fast as his nine-year old legs could carry him—unaware it seemed of the oncoming carriage. Now Nicole could *really* hear his voice, shrill and delighted, as he raced toward her—right into the path of the approaching hansom cab.

Nicole realized with horror that in a moment, the two horses pulling the shining carriage behind them would trample her little boy. They barreled forward—eight battering, hammering hooves trotting at full speed. The driver saw the danger at the same time Nicole did, and although he pulled back on the reins frantically, he would be unable to stop the horses in time to save her child.

Nicole sprinted forward, reaching Edmond at the same moment the horses did—reaching for him, touching the cloth of his shirt, grabbing his arm, pulling him away with her eyes closed tightly against the dust that swirled in a choking cloud around her. She had him…or did she? She felt him next to her, against her, behind her—thrown by her last effort out of harm's way; unless, of course, she had failed. She would never know because even as it was happening she realized that she would pay a deadly, deathly price for her mother's love and duty.

The horses were on her—heavy hooves and whinnying screams and blood-soaked iron. Where was Edmond? Was he under her, or beside her—or behind her? *Oh God, make him be behind me!* Her face was on the ground, her body was in the dirt, and her soul seemed to be floating upward. Her body felt like someone else's, and at that split second—during that fateful moment of impact, right before it all went black—she felt as if her eyes were looking forward and backward, up and down, out and in, all at the same time. She was reversed and inversed—her location in the here and now, and the 'there' and now, a reflection of a bizarre rearrangement caused by her journey through the time-tunnel that had landed her far, far ahead of herself, so that her near future in 1876, as seen from 2011, had now become her distant past.

Nicole awoke with a start. This was nothing imagined, no bedtime reverie—no dream, no fantasy, no invented illusion. She had just seen her own death.

This was a memory...and it was *real*.

CHAPTER THIRTY-ONE

Susanne told Henri immediately after dropping Nicole off to expect a visit from the police shortly, to bring him in for questioning. "Inspector Michèle Crossier paid me a visit this evening, right after my exhibit lecture," Susanne informed him. "You came up more than once in our conversation, so my prediction is that they will come for you in the morning."

She waited for the light to change, and then kept driving. "Are you still a suspect?" Henri asked.

"Apparently not," she replied, "but *you* are." She went on to describe her chat with the inspector, including the detective's interest in Henri's restoration work on the Caillebotte sculpture using the portable high-pressure submersion tank, on site at *d'Orsay*; as well as her inquiries regarding his sexual preferences. "She wanted to know if you were involved with anyone."

The detective's curiosity about Henri's romantic leanings made him laugh, but her queries about his work at d'Orsay didn't. Because he had never married, many people made assumptions, and that didn't bother him one bit. He had never concerned himself with what people thought of him; in fact, it was kind of fun to be the source of speculation. He was happily heterosexual, enjoying an occasional interlude here and there in private, while the rumors circulated in public. Maybe he should have settled down—but why? He just couldn't be bothered with the work and time involved in maintaining a committed relationship.

In that respect, he and Susanne were on the same page.

"Does she think one of the victims was my lover?"

"She didn't spell out her theory, but my best guess is 'yes'. Thinking like her, I believe the working hypothesis is that you were René's partner, but that he was bisexual. When you crashed his three-way 'party' in the museum, you took out the voyeuristic security guard with a blunt object to the head before he could join in on the fun, then moved on to kill your cheating lover with an industrial-grade sculpture-cleaning machine."

"Hmm. That's an inspired theory, really. You've got to give her credit for some very creative thinking. What about Nicole, then? I guess I decided to 'spare' her?"

"Probably, but only after sedating her with a syringe-full of fentanyl or phenobarbital, injected just like you see in those spy movies right into the jugular vein. Alternatively, you may have enlisted her as an accomplice not only to help perpetrate the crime but also to stay behind and topple the pedestal and sculpture."

This actually made him laugh. "Why would I want to alert the authorities by activating the alarm system, or turn on the cameras so they could capture everything 'after-the-fact' on video feed?"

"You've got me."

"Well you've certainly made me wonder if Inspector Crossier's imagination is as fertile as yours."

"I'm willing to bet you'll find out first thing in the morning."

No doubt he would. "So how is it you're 'off the hook' so quickly?"

"The pubic hair they found on the man's genitals (*and* some blood on the floor under the archway) belongs to a woman whose DNA showed genetic concordance with mine...but not a match. They also found some drops of René's semen on the floor where his 'love interest' was lying, leading them to conclude that a female Bruante who was not me had sex with René immediately before he died."

"Nicole, of course; so *that* much is true."

"Right; but the police don't know about her, and obviously we don't *want* them to—so I decided to feed Crossier a false lead."

"What would that be?" Henri had no idea what to expect. With Susanne, it could be anything.

"She asked me if I had any questionable relatives. Well, it turns out I do. I gave her Claudine's name."

His mouth fell open. "Claudine? Why would you involve that poor girl? She's had a tough enough life already, as things stand."

Sometimes, the extent of Susanne's insensitivity was mind-boggling. Claudine was his nephew Jacque's only daughter: an attractive young woman who had paid the price for her father's disinheritance. Forced to strike out on her own long before she turned twenty, she had found a dingy apartment in *Pigalle* and decided to use the only asset she had to survive—namely, her body. Now, she made a close-to-decent living doing some very indecent things, but she didn't seem to mind.

"I like stripping," she had told Henri once. "The exposure is so thrilling." When it really came

361

down to it, though, how much different was *that* kind of nudity, *or* taking money for a service, compared to Nicole's kind…or Susanne's, for that matter? The exhibitionist gene definitely ran strong in the Bruante line, passed down through the generations to express itself in more than just one of Nicole's female descendants.

Susanne waved away Henri's concern. "Look, *Ton-Ton*, this case the police think they're investigating isn't a case at all. There's no foul play involved, and no one is guilty of any crime. The 'time-tunnel', or whatever you choose to call it, killed Nicole's little playmate—*not* Claudine, or me, or you. *None* of us will be arrested, because the police won't be able to find one shred of evidence to convict us, because *all* of us are innocent."

"But—"

"Relax, Henri. All that will happen to Claudine is the exact same thing that has already happened to me, and is more than likely to happen to you in the morning. She'll be questioned, then they'll take her DNA sample, and then…that will be that. When the results come back again showing genetic concordance but no match, the police will be left scratching their heads, and Claudine will be allowed to continue dancing around her pole, every night if she wants, to her heart's content."

It wouldn't pay to argue with her. Yes, nothing would come out of all this, but there was considerable stress involved in being the focus of a police investigation. Henri could certainly handle it; but he wasn't so sure about Claudine. He resolved that he would try to reach her by phone, to warn her—as soon as he closed his front door behind him; or, if unsuccessful, in the morning…that is if he wasn't otherwise disposed himself, answering questions at the crack of dawn at '*the 36*'.

As soon as he got inside, he retrieved her number from his address book and tried to reach her from his land-line—not surprisingly getting voicemail, assuming that Claudine was probably otherwise engaged with a dancing set or perhaps with a private client. He slept a fitful five hours and then tried her again after rising, with no luck; so he headed out, exiting from the side door leading into and out of his upstairs living space at about seven a.m. with the rising sun in his eyes, down the wooden stairs and into the well-manicured strip of greenery at the side of the building, and finally into the street.

His intention was to drop off the extraction-specimens first thing to his 'contact' at the DNA lab, who had agreed to run the samples herself in exchange for a dinner date, next week. That wouldn't be a problem. They had been 'off and on' for as long as he could remember, and a little bit of "on" was probably long overdue in any case. It had taken less than an hour to finish this errand when a phone call from his turmoil-attracting niece added an extra item to his morning 'to-do' list.

"I just spoke with Nicole on the phone," Susanne said. "*She* actually called *me*! It's a funny thing, how she has adjusted so quickly to modern-day technology." Yes, it was—a fact that only furthered Henri's growing sense that Nicole really belonged 'here' rather than 'there'. "Anyway, she just told me something very interesting, that got me thinking. Are you up for another research project?"

363

It had taken him several hours to find the information Susanne had requested him to search out but now he had it—folded neatly in his jacket pocket, copied from digital media files at the comprehensive newspaper archives of Le Bibliothèque Nationale de France. He called Nicole on his mobile while walking back to his apartment at around noon, to report his success.

"Great," she exclaimed. "We can talk about it tonight, over cocktails."

"That's fine, unless I'm in prison."

"Don't be ridiculous. If you're questioned today it won't take long and then they'll release you pending your DNA analysis. I'm off right now to the Chunnel station to pick up our travel consultant."

Would John Noland really have a way to send Nicole back? To Henri it seemed doubtful; but maybe that was just wishful thinking on his part—wishful because he actually wanted her to stay. To him, Nicole seemed happy here, so why risk her life by attempting the unthinkable? If she stayed, though, where would she live, and what would she do? That was easy! Since Nicole couldn't possibly stay with Susanne on a permanent basis (an option that was simply out of the question, the reasons far too many to count), she would just have to stay with him—and he had already made some of the residential plans.

Henri worked on the ground level of his house, refurbished to fit his art-restoring needs; did his living on the *premier étage*; and slept under the rafters, on the *deuxième étage*. He could move his bedroom down to one of his guestrooms on the first level, giving the attic space to Nicole and creating a temporary garret apartment for her that would probably remind her of her previous living quarters in Montmartre—but a much more comfortable version of it, he was sure. He could take her under his wing, find her a job, screen her dates—his great-grandmother, transformed no less by a fluke of time into the daughter he had never had. It was nice to think about that, but very troubling to think about sending her away. One thing for sure, there was no such thing as a time machine, which meant that this visit from Susanne's ex-boyfriend would probably (*hopefully*) be a bust.

As he approached his house from around the corner, he wondered if Crossier would be there now, waiting to take him in for questioning; and sure enough, as he started down *Rue du Bac*, there she was: the steadfast Detective Crossier, standing impatiently in front of the business entrance to his home workshop, just as Susanne had predicted.

CHAPTER THIRTY-TWO

Henri Bruante hadn't even looked surprised to see her. Michèle Crossier had gotten there just a few minutes earlier, standing with her arms crossed in front of his house a few minutes past noon, trying to decide if she should linger there or return later, when she saw him approaching down *Rue du Bac* from around the corner of the street's intersection with *Saint Germain Boulevard*. Now, she waited patiently as he unlocked his door, a tedious process that involved three keys and the de-activation of a security alarm that was operated by a touch-pad located just to the right of the doorjamb. Henri often had costly artwork inside, perhaps even now, Michèle assumed, which explained the semi-paranoid behavior.

She knew exactly why she hadn't taken him off guard with her visit. His niece, Susanne Bruante, had undoubtedly warned him that the police would most likely come to call; but that was all right. The questions she had to ask him did not require the element of surprise, so it didn't really matter that he had been expecting her. The Bruante relative, Claudine Bignon, on the other hand, had been taken completely off-guard by Michèle's visit earlier this morning—and that had been a beautiful thing, indeed.

A thoroughly surprised, naked Claudine clutching a bath-towel to her chest had answered the door to her studio apartment at 7 a.m., revealing over her shoulder a man in her bed that she claimed was her boyfriend. Michèle knew better than that

366

after seeing the panicked look on his face when she had flashed her badge, *plus* the way he had scrambled to get dressed and excuse himself in a nervous rush—brushing past Michèle who was still standing in the hallway just as though he had been caught red-handed doing something thoroughly immoral if not illegal.

Michèle had suspected that the attractive young stripper solicited clients on the side, and that she might also peddle in small-time drug trafficking as a sideline; and although prostitution was not against the law in Paris, 'dealing' was. Perhaps the guy in her bed was one of Claudine's suppliers, getting a little 'extra' on the side (whether paid for or not) just to sweeten their deal. Sure enough and as if in response to Michèle's musings, Claudine looked uneasily over her shoulder at a plastic bag poking out from under the mattress, probably thinking that if she had only looked in the peephole before opening the door, she could have flushed the entire stash down the toilet.

Michèle stepped into the apartment on Claudine's 'invitation'. It was a tiny, well-kept efficiency with a pull-out bed on one wall (the sheets a tangle of sweaty passion) and a stove and sink on the other. The place was bare bones when it came to furnishings, but spotless and neat. Claudine motioned toward one of two metal kitchen chairs so Michèle sat, studying the girl's appearance while she pulled on an oversized t-shirt to cover her nudity. She resembled her cousin, *d'Orsay's* assistant director, for sure—not identical, but close enough, maybe, to pass for the Susanne Bruante lookalike whose image, diminished by camera-distance and the limitations of digital reproduction, had been captured on the video footage from the museum crime scene. Claudine's dark hair was wild and unkempt—undeniably sexy in a '*you caught me in bed with my legs spread*' kind of way; and her hazel eyes were the typical Bruante shade, except bloodshot. Her nose was Susanne's too, but the shape of her face was more oval, less narrow, while the curves of her body were slightly more pronounced—narrowing inward from a less-generous size C rather than Double-D bust to a very slender waist, and then out again and gently down, her hips tapering into long and shapely legs. She was pretty, even striking.

What a shame Claudine Bruante-Bignon had settled for this kind of life; but that's what happens when a branch of the family is disinherited. She knew all about this from personal experience, since her great grandfather on the Caillebotte side (Martial's son, Jean) had been disowned in much the same way as Claudine's father had—never recovering personally from the blow and sending repercussions down a bitter handful of generational lines. Michèle, independent and successful, had escaped the family curse of pre-ordained failure but many of her cousins had not. She would be 'easy' on Claudine but only as it related to drug possession, because if the stripper was involved in any way, shape or form in the double-murder case, Michèle would be 'on her' like a cat on a mouse.

Michèle had glanced meaningfully at the package poking partly out from under the bed, making sure that Claudine noticed…which she did—her face blanching pale when she realized the

368

police officer was 'onto' her. Good. The girl would talk if she thought that it would save her skin.

Michèle wondered how such a pretty girl, who could have easily used her good looks to secure a legitimate job as a model in advertising or fashion, had ended up like this selling her body for money and probably acting as a go-between for some minor drug dealers in the red-light district. Perhaps the gig as a *'putain'* had started with a large tip from a stage-side admirer, given in exchange for a quick liaison in her apartment after her shift was over. The word would spread quickly in those circles, and before she knew what had happened, Claudine might have had two or three takers a week, showing up for Claudine's strip show in their business suits and ending up naked in her bed exchanging money for sex shortly after closing.

Maybe it had become too much to handle for Claudine, alone; perhaps the man who approached her unannounced as she exited the dressing room one night offering to manage the confusing stream of after-hours customers seemed so sincere, so kind, and so competent. In short order, Claudine had started making much more money working for him than she had ever made on her own—but at a dreadful price.

Michèle had looked closely at Claudine, easily imagining the subservient employee being lured into increasingly dangerous liaisons, undoubtedly with the promise of substantial monetary compensation. Little by little, perhaps, things had gotten out of hand. So many young women in Paris—not only strippers, but also students, and waitresses, and even housewives—had turned to the

369

easy and lucrative sideline of prostitution, so why not Claudine? It made sense—complete and logical sense. Were there drugs involved? Undoubtedly. Often, the two professions went hand in hand.

Now the case was becoming more and more 'colorful' if prostitution cheapened by drugs had been involved in the criminal motive. Michèle was feeling more confident by the minute that the girl's DNA, once collected, would match the Bruante 'biologic material' recovered from the crime scene, which (if true) meant that she could begin to fine-tune her hypothesis, which now involved not only sex-for-hire but drug-related coercion, given the new person-under-consideration.

What if the security guard had been Claudine's client and had hired her for a pricey, contrived sexual fantasy taking place in a public setting transformed to private at the moment of camera de-activation? Charpentier, being employed by the museum in the dead of night, would have been able to provide access for an interaction that, from the start, he may have only planned to watch. So, who was their 'John Doe' if not the highly-paid masculine counterpart to Claudine's feminine—executing their arousing sexual interplay right there on the floor of the special exhibit alcove-room with the naked Charpentier standing over them, enjoying a particularly voyeuristic view of their stimulating performance. John Doe's 'identity' as either a random male prostitute, Claudine's 'pimp', her drug-supplier wanting a piece of his subservient-employee's 'action', Henri's lover, or a fellow art-restorer who had gotten wind of a seedy financial opportunity conveniently tacked on to a museum

370

job didn't much matter. Why? Because Henri would be out for blood regardless, since his favorite great-niece was involved. All of this fitted perfectly for the 'live'-action part of Michèle's theoretical scenario; but how about the 'dead'-ending?

Enter Henri, stage left, either alone or with assembled accomplices. Being a blood-relative of female-prostitute number one, and quite possibly the lover of male-prostitute number two, Henri would be driven by two emotions: the first, jealousy that had most likely escalated to rage long before his arrival on the scene; and the second, a familial urge to protect Claudine, who he would likely view as a victim spiraling morally out of control not by her own choice but because of the whims of her greedy pimps and handlers. Perhaps Henri knew in advance about the tawdry rendezvous, gathering some willing allies and letting himself, and them, into the museum with the access card he used every day to work on the Caillebotte piece in the basement; sneaking quietly up to the exhibit galleries rolling the sculpture 'cleaning-machine' smoothly behind him and with his imagined compatriots trailing after; and waiting patiently, having reached a strategic position just around the corner from the alcove exhibit room where he would bide his time until his three-fold focus—two on the floor and one standing aside, naked and intent—had reached their coordinated coda.

The timing would be tricky because once the pedestal and sculpture were overturned the alarms would sound and the de-activated cameras would turn on again, catching all the action on a now powered-up video-feed. Charpentier could have been easily incapacitated with a blow to the head—carefully placed so that the true terminating injury: the skull fracture sustained against the hard stone of the sculpture, would be located in the same position once executed as the last action before escape. As far as Claudine's 'partner' goes, Henri may have sedated him using an injection straight into the jugular vein just like in a cheesy spy-flick. This would allow for a leisurely perpetration of 'death-by-industrial-machine'; but the question, really, was 'why'?

Why use such a cumbersome murder-weapon to 'do the deed' when something more 'traditional' (for instance using an excess of fentanyl or phenobarbital in the sedative injection to induce an overdose rather than just fleeting unconsciousness) would have surely fit the bill? And then there was the perplexing lack of an evidence trail. Forensics had recovered no biologic material whatsoever on the 'pathway' leading from the crime scene to the service elevator, and down into the basement restoration room; and add to this the absence of any blood, skin, hair or human secretions on the outside of the pressure chamber and she was left with a seemingly unsolvable puzzle. The *inside* of the presumed murder weapon was clean as a whistle, too—a fully anticipated consequence of the chemical wash that Henri and associates had likely instituted when he returned it to the basement; but still, she had expected *something* rather than *nothing* to come from their scrutiny of the perpetrator's journey from point A to point B.

This is where the story broke down, despite all of her convolutions to fit the sensational plot with the facts on hand. Case in point was the question mark, in bold, surrounding Claudine's role in the murder plan. Was she an accessory to the crime and a 'plant' rather than a victim—perhaps even staying behind after Henri and his 'gang' to intentionally topple the pedestal and sculpture in some kind of an illogical, deliberate summoning of the authorities? If so she would have had to have rushed back over to the archway to feign unconsciousness while the alarms blared and the cameras sluggishly awoke, since the video-feed images showed her lying motionless in this location when they re-started. Or, had Claudine been drugged at the same time as her bed- (or rather, 'floor'-) fellow and stumbled into the pedestal when she came-to, turning over the statue in her over-medicated state only to pass out again immediately afterwards right there on the floor between the special exhibit galleries? Try as she might, the details of 'crime drama starring Henri and Claudine: Part Two' simply didn't add up to a credible case-scenario. Until now Michèle's queries outnumbered the explanations many-fold but she hoped to invert that ratio with today's question and answer session.

Claudine had denied it all at first, beginning with the prostitution but then, when her visitor took another deliberate look or two under the bed, Michèle's prime-suspect (or perhaps 'victim' would actually be more appropriate designation for the poor girl) had suddenly become more talkative.

"Who's your pimp?" Michèle had asked pointedly.

"There's more than one."

"Have any of them ever threatened you?"

373

"All the time."

Now they were getting somewhere. "Serious threats?"

She had shrugged and wouldn't look Michèle in the eye. "Sometimes."

If Claudine had been an unwillingly participant in the sex activities at the museum coordinated by one of her pimps or even a drug-boss, she would have then had a motive to 'call in' her great-uncle for 'protection': the deadliest kind. This is why Michèle felt ever more certain now that this young woman was the one they had seen on the museum footage, and that the mystery man who had had sexual relations with her was either directly connected to Henri—personally or professionally; or alternatively he was one of her illicit sex or drug activity-related 'handlers'.

"Where were you on Wednesday, the first of June, between the hours of midnight and one a.m.?"

Claudine had not been working at the strip club and she denied having had a client in her bed that night, which meant that she had no alibi; so now all Michèle needed was the DNA evidence—a sample swab that she had obtained after bringing Claudine in to the evidence lab downtown, tail between her legs. After the genetic confirmation she would collect Claudine a second time and bring her back in to '*the 36*' for a much more comprehensive 'under arrest' interrogation.

And '*the 36*' is where Michèle had just come from as she waited, a bit impatiently, outside Henri's house on *Rue de Bac*. Now it was finally time, long overdue, to concentrate on the 'elder' Bruante, who had just taken the third key out of the

374

third lock, opened the door to his workshop, and invited her in with a gracious smile.

CHAPTER THIRTY-THREE

"Would you like something to drink, inspector?" he asked as he motioned her inside, the picture of composed and unruffled calm.

"That would be nice," she agreed, thinking that accepting the offer would not only give an excuse for dragging out the questioning, but during the time it took for him to prepare a beverage she could snoop around a little bit.

"Café?"

"Yes, if it's not a bother."

"Sit down if you'd like and make yourself comfortable while I go upstairs to the kitchen to brew a couple double-espressos. I'm sure you've been putting in some long nights with the ongoing investigation and can use a 'pick-me-up' even more than I can."

He was certainly hospitable, if nothing else. As Henri disappeared up the staircase, she navigated around to the other side of a long table where her gaze and attention settled on an unfolded chart of some kind, consisting of more than a dozen sheets of industrial-sized paper taped together. Leaning on both palms to get a closer look, she realized when she saw the branching names and dates that it was a Bruante family tree; and one particular side-branch sent a sudden lightning-shock of surprise right through her.

"Caillebotte?" she said out loud. But, that was *her* family—or at least it had been, before her great-grandfather Jean had been disowned. This was an impossible coincidence, to put it mildly. Here she was, the inspector in charge of a sensational murder investigation where just about all of the 'persons of interest' were, unbelievably, related to her.

Stunned, she took a seat and tried to work out the relationships in her head by analyzing the Bruante-intermingled-with-Caillebotte heritage laid out in front of her. Michèle's great-grandfather (Jean Caillebotte) had a sister: Genevieve, who was Michèle's great-great aunt. Genevieve Caillebotte had married Marcel Pierre Bruante, who was Henri's father (*go figure*), and Susanne's (as well as Claudine's) great grandfather. This meant that Henri, Susanne and Claudine were all Michèle's *cousins* removed once, twice or at the most three times by generations. How should she plan on handling this unexpected conflict of interest? Ignoring her discovery at least for the moment seemed the most prudent plan, since she would need time to process the information…although she thought she already knew where her decision would land.

There was certainly no love-lost between her Caillebotte ancestors and her suspects' forebears, so if anything the privileged 'half' of the family was due for their come-uppance. If she was destined to facilitate the down-fall of a malicious and mean-spirited vein of a shared blood-line, then so be it. God knows she was not about to sacrifice her skyrocketing career by bowing out of the most important case of her life, just because she happened to be related to a gaggle of related wrong-doers. No, she was certain of it—she would keep this quiet.

She hastily pushed her chair away, got up, and

relocated to one of two armchairs arranged partly facing each other with a small coffee table separating them in between, in the corner of the room just to the left of the front entry-door (approaching it from the interior of the work-room). This way Henri would never even suspect that she had seen their shared-lineage, displayed so conspicuously on his work-table. Not that he would suspect in a million years that they were related; but why risk it? Given his attention to details as they related to the Bruante line, who's to say he didn't have a similar family tree illustrating the Crossier connection to Jean Caillebotte stashed away in a closet upstairs as well.

Henri came down the stairway momentarily, balancing a serving tray with two cups of espresso on it in his hands. He took a seat in the other chair, handing Michèle the dark black coffee. "Sugar?" he asked.

She nodded and helped herself to two cubes which she stirred into her espresso thoughtfully. "I had a little visit this morning with your great-niece," Michèle informed him after taking a sip, eyeing him carefully for a reaction while trying to suppress her *own* reaction stemming from the remarkable fact that Claudine was actually her first cousin, twice removed…or something like that. *How bizarre*, she thought.

"Which one?" he asked, his expression flat.

"Claudine Bruante Bignon." He nodded, as if he had expected that answer. "When were you last in touch with her?" Michèle continued.

"I tried to call her this morning, but got her voicemail."

He had probably intended to give her a warning, but Claudine had been otherwise engaged. "When did you see her last?"

"About a year ago. We're not that close."

"Are you sure you didn't see her in the early morning hours, on June first?"

He shook his head. "No," he replied calmly, without even a hint of edginess. "I didn't see her then."

"Where were you that morning?"

"Here, at home—asleep."

Henri Bruante had no alibi either. Today was Michèle's lucky day, and she was hitting pay dirt. "Have you been working for *d'Orsay*, restoring a marble sculpture?"

"You know I have, or else you wouldn't be asking," he answered, his tone blasé.

"Have you used the portable, high-pressure restoration tank in the basement lately?"

He raised one eyebrow—the first reaction that had registered on his face so far. "Yes, in fact I have," he answered calmly, "while I was restoring the Caillebotte sculpture."

"On the thirty-first of May?"

"No; a few days before that. I finished cleaning and restoring that piece right before the weekend— on May twenty-seventh to be exact, specifically so it would be ready for installation on its pedestal in the special exhibit gallery on the thirty-first, in time for opening day."

"Have you used it since finishing your job?"

"No. My work on that particular project is complete, and *d'Orsay* doesn't need me for anything else at the moment."

379

"Does anyone *else* know how to operate the pressure tank?"

"Certainly. The museum contracts with other restorers from time to time. They *all* know how to operate that kind of machinery."

"What kind of damage do you think that machine would do to a human body if it was sealed inside and subjected to the positive pressure without surrounding liquid to temper the external force?"

He looked past her, his gaze focused on the wall somewhere but really inward. "If someone were to turn the positive pressure switch on after sealing the chamber; and if the adjustable panels were locked flush on the surface of that person's body, I suppose he or she would be…crushed."

'Crushed' he had said—*her* thought, exactly.

Henri agreed to go down to the station for fingerprinting and for DNA testing, to use for matching fingerprints and DNA on both old, and new, evidence. They would find Henri's fingerprints, of course, on the statue since he had worked on it, *and* his DNA, potentially, on or around the pedestal if he had assisted with the installation; but there would be no way for him to explain away a thumbprint or his biologic material *on* the victims, or on any surface other than the sculpture, its display-stand, or the outside of the high-pressure submersion tank. This is why she had arranged, just this morning, for the forensics team to revisit the scene of the crime, brushing for fingerprints and checking for strands of hair or epithelial tracings that they may have missed the first time around in the alcove room.

So it was that Henri was the second Bruante

(and also her second not-so-distant relative) to visit the processing area of the police station within the span of two-hours. This was *not* a good day for the limb of the Bruante family tree descended directly from Genevieve Caillebotte; but a very good day, indeed, for a certain homicide detective whose heritage harkened back, straight as disenfranchised blue-blood's arrow, to Genevieve's unfairly ostracized brother: Jean.

CHAPTER THIRTY-FOUR

John Noland stood outside *Gare du Nord*, Paris's central rail station. His journey on the *Eurostar Express* from Waterloo station in London had been rapid and comfortable, taking less than three hours, 'door-to-door'. Although he had chosen a partially protected location to wait for his ride, he was still getting wet. The rain, which had been coming down in buckets when he first stepped outside, had slowed down substantially; but still, each gust of wind sprayed him spitefully.

He looked at his digital wristwatch, which read: *1:20 p.m., Tuesday 7 June, 2011.* Susanne would be here any second now, in a light-blue BMW, she had said. As he peered into the drizzle, he thought he saw it now, approaching from the left side of the train station, cutting across *La Place Napoléon III.*

He wondered if the years had changed her physically. She had been so incredibly beautiful then; would she still be as stunning, now? Would he still feel that same uncontrollable attraction that had overwhelmed him on that first day he'd seen her at The University of Chicago's undergraduate library in 1993; or the identical heart-pounding desire that had saturated his entire being when he had watched her flaunt her perfect body in front of a roomful of artistically-idolizing eyes, letting her loosely tied bathrobe slip unashamedly to the floor that first day she had modelled nude for the painting class his senior year? The very thought of her raw sexuality kept him awake nights during their four-month relationship, long after she had left him...and sometimes, even now. To say that he had fallen deeply in love with her would be a gross understatement, which explained why the callous way she had left without a single word of explanation or even a simple goodbye had scarred him for life.

But that was then, and this was now. He was over her—or at least that was what he kept telling himself. He had a worry, more than just subconsciously, that romantically speaking he might 'relapse' when he saw her, groveling at her feet for a second chance nearly two decades later—a reaction that he desperately hoped he had the willpower to resist. He reminded himself that she had called him to enlist his help with a scientific anomaly, *not* to rekindle a relationship that he now knew had been entirely one-sided. It might help if her beauty had faded since it would be so much easier to focus on the problem at hand if he could put the old, desirable Susanne away and replace her with a new, unappealing one.

Although it felt superficial to think that way, he knew it was true. Physical attractiveness had lured him into a painful relationship before, and, like most other men, he could easily be fooled again. He would have to keep his guard up, or else he might easily revert to the way it had been—or, more accurately, the way *he* had been: the young and vulnerable John.

As her car approached, he thought about how he had exalted her in his mind as the ideal woman, physically; and how his unrestrained adoration had caused him to be totally blinded by her wild and raw sex appeal. He flashed back to that night at the café, their first date. He had sketched her where she sat, across from him at the small corner table by the fireplace. She had worn a grey sweater-coat, which she quickly removed because of the heat from the fire. He knew full well what her body looked minus the tight turquoise t-shirt that pushed revealingly against the rounded fullness underneath, giving him more than just a hint of the details that he longed to actually touch, up close and personal, rather than simply admire visually from a distance. He had seen it all before: her splendid nudity, just a few yards away from him on the model's pallet—so near, yet so far…and seemingly so completely unreachable, then.

That night she was anything but unreachable, offering herself—body and (little did he know at the time) *not* her soul—to the shy and insecure intellectual, barely in his twenties, who had somehow found himself sitting a single arms' length away from the woman of his dreams, just on the other side of the table at his favorite campus café. He quietly sketched the wavy fingers of her rich auburn hair falling downward and intermingling with the panting wisps of rising steam from her mug of cocoa—both brushing lightly where they met on her chest and drawing pointed attention to what the cotton barely covered. He drew the slender fingers of aromatic smoke as if they had a life of their own, breathing in and out and up and around the swell of her curving bosom—transformed by charcoal on his drawing paper into lines of curling grey. Her face, her arms, and her breasts became one and the same with the fire, smoke, and steam: images captured crudely on paper that he would spend hours completing later.

He had truly treasured that drawing of her, which had taken on a special nostalgic significance after she had left him. She was the goddess who had inexplicably chosen a mortal, and now all that he had left to prove it was that charcoal sketch, which he still kept in the bottom of his dresser drawer.

He was still engrossed in these past memories when her car pulled up, drawing him reluctantly back into the present. She opened the passenger door for him from the inside and he got in, wet from the weather, and closed the door; delaying the inevitable just a few seconds longer, by focusing his gaze on the windshield and the unrelenting wipers, which mercilessly kept time against the raindrops. "It's really raining out there," he said nervously in fluent French. Strange, how fearful he was to face her, troubled by the delicious fear that she might still be as gorgeous as he remembered. He took in a deep breath to steel his nerves, pulling the seat belt across his chest at the same time, turning partway in his seat to greet her, and actually fumbling with the buckle latch.

Yes, she was still, without a doubt, indescribably beautiful; and to his mixed disappointment and elation he noted that in fact the years had added, rather than detracted, from her physical beauty. "You haven't changed a bit," he managed to say, feeling as though his words were tripping over each other. The current 'iteration' of her attractiveness was enhanced, it seemed, by a palpably egotistic self-awareness that was only partly 'there' in college—a recognition that literally emanated from her, with aura-like conviction, that her desirability was difficult, if not impossible, to match.

"And you haven't exactly lost your good-looks either," she teased, shaking out her hair with a sidelong glance, which he sensed was meant to test the waters between them. Yes, she was flirting; but no, it wasn't sincere. He wouldn't take the bait, because if he did, she'd reel him in and toss him away again, just as she had before.

He drew in a breath, determined not to show her that his weakness might still be 'her'. "So, this is Paris," he said, resorting to small talk, hoping perhaps that diverting her with the trivial would save him.

"Yes, it is." She gazed over at him for a moment, sizing him up it seemed, and quickly inferring from his stony face that he had no interest whatsoever in rekindling their romance. To his great relief, she launched directly into the matter at hand. "Here's the deal, John. I need you close. If you're going to help me, there's no possible way you'll be able to do that from a distance. Cancel your hotel reservation. I have two extra rooms at my place. Nicole's in one, and you can take the other."

He started to object, but she interrupted him with a gesture, unwilling to hear anything that threatened to contradict her agenda. "Look in the rear-view mirror," she commanded. He did, and saw a dark-blue Renault following very close behind them. "I'm being tailed. If you stay in a hotel room, they'll never believe that you're my boyfriend."

What in the world had he gotten himself into? He hadn't expected the police to be right on top of them; and that being the case, the first few seconds of this crazy reunion had already taken on a surreal quality. Boyfriend? This was a serious problem. He had come here on a scientific adventure, but it looked like she intended to draw him into a soap opera instead.

"I'm sure they snapped a photo of you as you got in, and they've already sent it in to headquarters. Their computer techs will be able to ID you with no problem. Your face has been all over the Internet lately."

"Susanne, I'm not sure this is what I signed up for." This was outrageous, actually. He felt his face turning red. "The last thing I need is trouble with the Paris police. Do you understand that this could even become a diplomatic issue?" He could see the headlines now: 'American scientist arrested as an accomplice in the *d'Orsay* murders.'

"Come on, I didn't drag you here against your will." She turned the wheel sharply and took a corner rather too fast as she glanced in the rear-view mirror. "You knew the story, John. I told you everything on the phone last week." She shrugged. "Go back, if you'd like. I'm not holding you captive."

He told himself to calm down. This was a once-in-a-lifetime opportunity, after all. If what Susanne had told him was actually true, a discovery of this magnitude could very likely propel his career down a path leading directly to a Nobel Prize. He pushed his anger down a level, consciously willing himself to relax.

She must have seen from the look on his face that he was weighing the pros and cons, and that the pros were winning. "If you can send Nicole back, it will be a 'win-win' for both of us. I don't need her here anymore—she's served her purpose, and now she has to go. For you, proving that someone can travel from one time to another by actually *doing* it would guarantee you more than just a page in the history books. You'd be the most famous scientist the world has ever known—bigger than Einstein, even."

Then it hit him. Eighteen years had passed, but Susanne's '*modus operandi*' was still the same. Nicole was no longer useful, so Susanne would toss her away—just as she had tossed *him* away, after he had served *his* purpose. She had done this to him without feeling even a tiny bit of remorse; and even now, there were no apologies. Why? In a rare moment of insight, John suddenly understood; and now, it all made sense.

Susanne would never say she was sorry, because she didn't even realize that she had done anything wrong. Susanne was the very epitome of selfishness: a person who was so completely focused on herself that she could see nothing beyond her own wants and needs. Her narcissism had made her oblivious to other people, to the extent that it never even occurred to her that she was being hurtful. He suddenly realized that there was nothing inherently malicious about Susanne— she was just incredibly self-centered, a truth that did not entirely excuse her actions but went a long way toward explaining them. Being out for herself did not necessarily make Susanne a bad person—just an egotistically unmindful one.

Well, one thing was certain—this was not *his* style. Yes, he would try to return this Nicole to her rightful place in time, but not just because it would make his work—his 'science'—famous. If it was possible to send her back, he would, because having her 'here' instead of 'there' could drastically change the course of intended events. Imagine, for instance, if Nicole was supposed to have children that wouldn't be born now, because she was residing in the wrong *Time-Shell*. Or, what if she had been an integral part of some life-and-death event in 1876, but the crucial outcome was altered because she was not there to prevent it—or to *cause* it? If he could return her to the past, he would—but he would do it for science, and for humanity; he would do it to preserve the order of things, and to ensure that what should be, would be. If he became famous in the process, then so be it; and if he didn't, that was all the same to him.

But these thoughts gave him reason to pause. What about Nicole? He realized again, as he had after his phone call with Susanne while he was in London, that they were talking about a human being, not a lab rat. Susanne might view Nicole as an insignificant means to an end, but John refused to subscribe to this philosophy. He hadn't even met Nicole, but that didn't really matter. She was a person, and she deserved to be treated like one.

"All right," he finally answered. "I'll stay. What's your plan?"

"Your agenda here needs to be viewed as anything but professional. Act like we're involved when we get to my place."

He could do that—a little handholding wouldn't kill him. He nodded his assent. "Okay." This charade would probably even help him gain the closure he so sorely needed. If he could touch her without feeling that old thrill, it would spell victory.

They drove on, and he used the opportunity to call the hotel on his cell phone and cancel his reservation. Finally, Susanne stopped at a light; and when it turned green, she turned down a street that was marked at the intersection as *Avenue Georges V*. "I think we should cut them a break. I'll introduce you when we get out."

She pulled in to a parking space on the street, directly in front of a building with three levels that he assumed was her place of residence, and cut the engine. She smiled mischievously. "This will be great fun. You get out first, and then open the door for me. That way you'll look like the perfect *petite ami*."

The rain had stopped. He got out of the car and walked on puddled-pavement over to the driver's side to play his role. He opened the door; put out his hand; felt her skin on his, a distant memory suddenly revived; helped her out, her body brushing dangerously close to his as she stood; and closed the door with his other hand, surprised—no, *shocked*— to feel her pull him toward her. Before he could resist, she was actually pressing her body against his, and then her lips. The kiss was soft, wet, and lingering. He started to feel dizzy.

But wait—was the kiss sincere? Hardly. She disengaged, and warm turned to cold in a heartbeat, the manufactured passion just a show, yet another means to an end—a meaningless ten seconds of feigned intimacy, intended to lend credence to Susanne Bruante's agenda. She hadn't changed—

she would *never* change; and somehow, this realization felt good. She was not the one—had never been the one. Susanne was Susanne, intensely focused on her own wants and needs, then and now—the polar opposite of what John Noland truly desired, *and* required, in a partner. Claire had been right, that day in the hallway when she had broken the news to him that Susanne had left without even bothering to say goodbye. He *did* deserve better; he could see that now. Funny that it had taken him eighteen years and a trip to Paris on a rainy day to finally come to that realization.

"That should do it," she said, just as if the kiss had been some kind of a business transaction. She took his hand in hers, the touch of her skin on his no longer quite so electric, leading him to the trunk where he grabbed his one suitcase, and she the other.

"Yes, that *should* do it," John said with a smile. At that moment he realized that he was over her, once and for all. He was free.

He followed her lead, putting the suitcase on the sidewalk and following her across the street to the blue Renault where two red-faced gendarmes sat inside. She knocked on the glass with a knuckle, and the window came sliding down.

"*Bonjour, messieurs*," she said. "How's your 'Susanne Bruante' duty going?" The police didn't know how to respond to the question, but it didn't seem to matter to her—she just kept on talking. "I want to introduce you to my boyfriend, Dr. John Noland. Just so you don't wonder, he'll be staying with me for a few days. You can mark him down as 'present' on your surveillance log."

She pulled him away, one arm around his waist; and after they crossed over to the other side of the street, she drew him against her again. He was elated to recognize that the second kiss, although superficially more passionate, was actually even more disingenuous than the first; and *this* time he felt absolutely nothing. What a beautiful, beautiful moment. Magically, Susanne (correction: the *memory* of Susanne) no longer held him. It was over and he could finally move on with his life.

He followed her up the stairs: four sets, up and back, and up and back again; the journey leading them from the ground level, on to the first floor landing and then up, finally, to the second. Susanne opened the door to her apartment and stepped through with John and his luggage in tow, into a spacious foyer with a hallway directly ahead leading to several bedrooms and a bathroom. He saw a dining room with a kitchen hiding behind a swinging door to his right, and a living room to his left.

Susanne craned her neck forward, looking into the dining room and then the other way, into the living room. "Nicole must have gone back to sleep," she said. "She had a rough night."

"Why?" he asked.

"A nightmare—one that will probably be of great interest to you."

He gave her a quizzical look. "The interpretation of dreams isn't my specialty. You'll have to find yourself a psychologist to help you with *that* specialized problem."

"No," she countered, "this dream is right up your alley. You'll see. We'll talk about it when

392

Uncle Henri comes. I sent him on an errand to find us some proof."

What in the world was she talking about? "Proof—of what?"

"Nicole thinks the dream was a memory," she answered, in a matter-of-fact tone of voice. "Let's see what Henri comes up with." She looked at her watch, the frown on her face intimating more irritation than it did concern. "I wonder if he got held up, somewhere. He should have called back by now. I'll try to reach him in a few minutes."

She headed down the hall, and John followed with a shrug. He would find out what she was talking about soon enough, he suspected. As they approached the first room on the left, Susanne stopped for a moment and tapped on the closed door. "Nicole," she called. "Our time travel consultant is here."

John heard what sounded like rustling sheets, followed by a voice calling back from inside. "*Mon Dieu*," the voice said, "I did not mean to sleep again, for such a long time."

Susanne continued walking, motioning for John to follow. She opened a door to her right, just a few paces down the hall and across from Nicole's room. "You can stay in here," she said. "I think you'll be comfortable."

He was just about to enter with his two suitcases, when the door behind him opened. He turned, and his mouth fell open.

There she stood: a virtual replica of Susanne but maybe ten years younger; and there *he* stood, speechless. The resemblance was more than astounding, to the extent that he never would have

393

believed it if he hadn't seen it with his own eyes: the rich auburn hair falling across her shoulders and curling slightly to touch her angled jaw and prominent cheekbones; the hazel eyes—competing brown-against-green swirling with equal intensity in a beckoning dual; the petite, slightly upturned nose; and a body, covered loosely by a terrycloth bathrobe, that promised to be a duplicate of Susanne's underneath. In a flash, he recalled that night when Susanne had emerged from the dressing room at the art studio in a similar terrycloth robe boldly left untied—her taunting frontal nudity intentionally visible. Nicole's robe now, unlike Susanne's then, was tied, but in her rush to open the door the loose knot came undone and a sensual 'moment in time' was oddly duplicated. His eyes drifted downward, he couldn't help it. When she saw where his gaze had settled, she realized what had happened and hastily grabbed the front of the bathrobe, pulling the two halves closed, her neck flushing from alabaster to a subtle shade of pink. Nicole's discretion was obviously not a character trait that Susanne shared.

John couldn't help but recognize that Nicole's outward appearance might be all Susanne, above and below the neck—but what was she truly like, below the surface? He wondered to what extent Nicole's personality, attitudes, and viewpoints corresponded with her present-day counterpart. *Genetics is a funny thing indeed*, he thought, as he found himself gawking at a full-fledged case in point, standing right here in front of him.

The moment of mutual silence had become awkward as he tried to find his voice, which had been lost in the ambient force called 'Nicole'. He feared that his 'adolescent' reaction to Nicole's fleeting nudity, ogling her with a stupid schoolboy's face, had made him appear inexperienced and parochial. He was here, after all, to provide his advice and to use his skills to deliver a solution to her problem, so he would try to recover his fumble with projected intelligence and professionalism. "It is truly a pleasure to meet you, Nicole. I'm John," he stated with assurance, holding out his hand in greeting.

"Bonjour, *monsieur*," she responded, with a smile that would have melted an iceberg. "I am happy, too, to gain your acquaintance." She used the old formal French: the prim and proper grammar that old Madame Barrat had taught him in school— her chalkboard-stick in hand as John sat attentively, three days a week, in the front row of French III when he had studied the language in prep school. It was funny to hear the old-fashioned styling coming from someone so young; but Nicole had purportedly come from a different time, after all. John shouldn't have been at all surprised.

Nicole took his hand to shake it. Her touch felt familiar, and for a good reason; because as John looked down he noticed that Nicole had Susanne's fingers, too. He gazed into her eyes for one fleeting second, but had to look away because half a second more and they would have held him captive forever, just as Susanne's had eighteen years earlier. Would her lips feel as soft, her skin as smooth, and her hair as lush as Susanne's? He actually started to sweat. *Oh God, help me*. He feared that if he didn't get control of himself now, it was going to happen all over again. He had to control himself; *had* to stop it from happening again.

He looked into her eyes, just one more time…he couldn't resist. He was a moth lured irresistibly into the light, despite its promise of certain death; a mere mortal, powerless to resist Aphrodite's seductive spell; Romeo, bound by fate to throw himself at Juliette's feet despite the tragic consequences. In an instant measured out timelessly by his desperate, pounding heart…he knew.

It was too late—*much* too late to stop. He couldn't control himself. It had already happened.

CHAPTER THIRTY-FIVE

Nicole stepped out of her bathrobe, standing nude in front of the closet to sift through the clothes hanging there with one hand, trying to pick out what to wear. After a second, she pulled out a white cotton sundress patterned with red flowers along the bottom, the blossoms climbing up ivy-like in a diagonal across the front to connect with a dense bed of colorful petals encircling the chest. She slipped it over her head, settling the straps over her shoulders and adjusting the flowered bosom just so, over her uncovered breasts. Susanne had lent her some bras and panties, but why bother? A dress like this one was meant to touch on nothing, fabric whispering directly on tingling skin, breathing a soft and secret moan of indulgence to barely hide what pushed gently and significantly outward, firm and supple beneath.

He was handsome, this John Noland—but he didn't seem to know it. His sandy hair was cut short, the style in this time for some odd reason, but the barber had left enough on the top for John to push some over to the side, the wavy strands touching on the line of his two intelligent and serious eyebrows. Men where she came from always let their hair grow, and she couldn't help but imagine John's hair that way—long, thick, and lush, pulled behind and tied against the back of his neck, perhaps with a string that she had knotted. She sighed, lost in that vision as she considered some shoes, but then decided against it. She preferred bare feet; anyway, she would not be leaving the apartment today.

Yes, this John Noland had an attractive face and a very appealing body, too. She could see the lines of his stomach, tense and firm, between the widely spaced buttons of his crisply pressed shirt, just as she could see his chest, sloping outward to broad shoulders, not overly muscled but definitely strong. She thought his neck was perfect, not too long or too short, supporting a strong and masculine jaw, full and expressive lips, a thin nose—and those eyes. They were crystal blue; and although they had met her gaze only briefly (twice, to be exact), his azure and her green-tinged-brown had shared an undeniable moment of understanding. He was attracted to her too, she could tell—she could *always* tell.

She felt a little bit guilty, because of René; but having someone else to think about (a fantasy, really—a dream that would never actually become reality) actually helped to quiet the sadness and pain that she still felt from her recent loss. She didn't think it cheapened René's memory to feel physically attracted to another man, especially since she knew that nothing would ever come of it. The fact of the matter was that John had come here to help Susanne get rid of her 'problem', and he seemed like the type of man who always took his job seriously. Anyway, it was unrealistic to think of him as anything more than a doctor, a mechanic, or a technician; and in fact, it would be in her best interest to make sure that she didn't. She wasn't normally the kind to love them and leave them (unlike Susanne), and it would be no fun to fall for someone from another time and place, just as she

398

was getting ready to return home. There could be no relationship in this bizarre situation anyway, where the possibility of being transported back to 1876 loomed over her like a dark reminder of her utter unavailability. She must think with her head and not with her heart, she reminded herself; and that way, everyone would be much better off.

She headed out into the hallway and down to the foyer, following the sounds of activity to the left. Susanne was in the dining room, setting out some food. Walking in quietly, Nicole pulled out a chair, sitting down at the far end, with her back facing the front entryway and the hallway leading to the bedrooms.

"Your old boyfriend seems very nice," Nicole said.

Susanne shrugged. "It doesn't really matter how nice he is, as long as he's able to help us."

"Was he a good lover?" It just came out, before she could stop herself. She was wicked to ask, but she simply couldn't resist—she just *had* to know. One thing about fantasies: the more you colored them in, the better the image turned out.

Susanne nodded, completely emotionless. "*Oui.* Let's just say that he really knew what to do, for someone so inexperienced."

That could mean one thing only. "So, you were his first?"

She nodded again. "He admitted to it, afterward. I would have never known—it came so naturally to him, somehow."

"You ended it, not him, I am sure. You must have really hurt him, when you left."

"*C'est la vie.*" Susanne arranged some fruit on

a plate matter-of-factly, which matched her tone of voice perfectly. "He got over me, so no harm done—*n'est ce pas?*"

Nicole felt certain that *plenty* of harm was done. Poor John. She wished she could console him, but she tried to steer her thoughts away from that particular corridor. "He is very handsome," she said quietly, almost to herself. He was *very* good-looking, there was no denying it, and Nicole was not the sort of person to keep her thoughts to herself.

Susanne shot Nicole an unpleasant glance from across the table. "Don't get any ideas. Remember, you'll be going back soon, if all goes well."

That comment really got Nicole's hackles up. She didn't need that kind of self-serving advice from anyone, especially her egocentric great-great-great granddaughter. Nicole was more than capable of deciding about these things herself. She had half a mind to go right ahead and follow her animal instincts, just to see how Susanne would react. She wouldn't, of course—too many people would get hurt; but it felt very nice to imagine it.

"I called Henri," Susanne said, changing the subject. "He was held up with the police for a while, but he's on his way here now. He found it." She said it almost triumphantly, and Nicole's heart dropped.

She knew that her dream wasn't just a dream, but an actual memory. Now that Henri had uncovered some hard evidence that her suspicion was in fact true, it brought the horrible reality of it all abruptly out of the shadows and into the harsh light of day. What would happen now if she went back to 1876? If she returned, would she die that grim and dreadful death she had foreseen—no, *remembered*—in the early morning hours of a sleep that had been interrupted by the unthinkable? Or would she remember it all, when she got back, and alter the fate that awaited her, somehow, with this gift of foreknowledge? Maybe she would change the meeting place she had arranged in advance with her mother; perhaps she would cancel her visit with Edmond altogether. That way, he wouldn't rush out in front of the carriage in his excitement to greet her; and if he didn't need to be saved, Nicole wouldn't need to die.

There was only one problem with this hopeful scenario—namely, that Nicole might not remember that she was destined to die at *Place Pigalle*. It stood to logic that existing in the future as she was at the moment, she had been able to recall an event in her past; but there was no assurance of the reverse. To put it another way, looking forward from her 're-entry' time-point in the past (should she return, willingly or unwillingly, to the nineteenth century) to a future incident that had not yet transpired (namely, her own death) might not lend itself well to recollection; and if she had no memory of the impending tragedy to warn her, she would of course have no reason to change her plans. She shivered. What a horrible, terrifying thought.

But failing to return could result in something much worse. What if Edmond's actions remained unaltered by Nicole's absence, and he still decided to run straight into the path of the galloping horses because he thought he saw someone who looked like her? What would happen to her precious nine-year-old boy if she wasn't there to save him? Nicole envisioned her only child running right under the crushing hooves of the carriage horses because she had not been there to save him—his face in the dirt instead of hers; his blood on the road and his screams in the air, not Nicole's; his soul rising up to see itself, down there, a trampled and unmoving body, rather than his mother's; and his life taken much too early—the wrong life in fact: his instead of hers.

"We'll need John's input on all this—you know, to tell us what it all means, and what we can do about it," Susanne said.

What it all means? It meant nothing to Susanne, that much was clear. All she cared about was her theory: the one that until now had simply been conjecture; the one that Nicole—in her accidental translocation from 1876 to 2011, from her nineteenth-century apartment to Susanne's twenty-first century work-place—would uncontestably prove. To Susanne, Nicole wasn't even human; she was just a piece of incontrovertible evidence that could be shelved away forever after being registered in history's log-book. Nicole's hair, imbedded in the paint from three Courbet paintings and containing something they called 'DNA', was going to make Susanne rich and famous; and what would Nicole get in return? A one-way ticket back to a grisly death; *that's* what.

"Before I can tell you what even a small part of it means," the voice behind her said, "I'll need a lot more information." She turned and there he was, passing behind her over to the right, changed out of his dress clothes and looking much more casual now in jeans and a deep blue t-shirt a few tones darker than his eyes. He pulled out the chair immediately beside her and sat down, dangerously close to her—*much* too close.

He looked over at her, and their eyes locked again—a brief and momentary joining, yet full of meaning. He was trying to hide it, but she could see right through him. He wanted her, she could tell; but she could also tell that he was fighting the feeling as hard as he could. Why? For more than one reason, she felt sure. First, he was not here for pleasure, far from it; and second, getting involved with his 'assignment' was simply not in line with professional decorum. But there was another reason—she could sense it. He was scared of her— *terrified*, in fact, and she thought she knew why.

It was her appearance that frightened him so. She looked exactly like Susanne, after all, and that would be a source of distress for John if Susanne had broken his heart so long ago. Nicole tried to imagine what it might be like for him—finding out that his time-travel project could easily pass for Susanne's twin. The first thing he might conclude is that Nicole and Susanne were interchangeable, both of them the same person inside, as well as out; and that would be enough, on its own, to give him pause. Just on principle, Nicole would have to dispel that fear—in fact, she felt determined to do so.

Did it really matter what John thought of her? Of course not; but she was *not* Susanne, and it pained her to think that just because they looked alike, John might assume that they were alike in every way. She was her own person, more dissimilar when likened to Susanne than similar, and she would make that clear to John if that were the last thing she did before disappearing back into the past.

The video monitor by the door buzzed. "Speaking of information, that must be Henri," Susanne said lightly. "He'll be quite informative, I predict."

"Your uncle?" John inquired.

"The very same." Susanne went to the electronic remote to push the entry button.

"He's here because he found it," Nicole murmured softly, feeling numb. In a moment she would see it, and it would all come true. It would be real.

John leaned toward her: a show of support; very close now, touching his hand on her bare arm for the briefest of moments, the gesture so concerned, so compassionate, so kind…and so loving. Had his fingers trembled when he placed them, with more than just a hint of intimacy, on her skin? She thought they had; and to her surprise, she was trembling too.

Had she fallen in love, at first site, with this beautiful stranger who seemed to hold her life (and possibly her death) in the palm of his hands? She had arrived here against her will by means of a fatalistic process that had killed her lover, only to throw her into the arms of someone on whom her very existence (happy or sad, with him or without him, living or dying) utterly depended. They were connected, he and she, in ways that only a heavenly force could design or foresee; and she didn't have the strength, or the desire for that matter, to fight it.

She knew, at that very moment, that she would give herself over, body and soul, to John Noland if he asked her. *Forgive me, René...forgive me; but I want him so.*

"Found what?" John asked, his voice quivering slightly. Did he know?

"The obituary," Susanne answered in a 'ho-hum', deadpan tone that made it sound as if she were talking about an invitation to a garden party instead of a death notice.

"Whose obituary?" John countered, unable to hide the look of dread on his face as he waited for her answer.

Nicole's mouth felt dry. She looked into John's eyes again, and this time he didn't look away. Was he giving her permission? His eyes said 'yes', and so she put her hand on his and kept it there. It felt right—to both of them, it seemed.

"Mine" she whispered.

CHAPTER THIRTY-SIX

Susanne buzzed him in almost immediately, but Henri lingered a moment, looking out of the corner of his eye at the surveillance car that had followed him, block by block, as he had made his way on foot from the police station to Susanne's apartment.

The car, a white Citroen, had stopped right next to a dark-blue Renault: Susanne's tail, no doubt, both of them just idling there with the windows down as gendarme spoke to gendarme. Then, just as Henri was about to step into the building, the white car eased into reverse, the driver giving an all-clear nod to his colleague. Henri turned part way as he entered the foyer; and as he did so he saw the blue car, which had pulled out of its parking space, speed past him on its way to who-knows-where. As he climbed the stairs to the second floor landing, Henri glanced out the front window, making a mental note of the white Citroen's new vantage point—directly across the street from Susanne's building, parked in the blue Renault's previous spot.

Was it their change of shift? Maybe, but he seriously doubted that. The fact of the matter was that Henri, rather than Susanne, was now the person of greater interest to the police; and Henri would bet his last *Euro* that later, when he left Susanne's apartment to head home, the white car would discreetly pull out and follow him again, keeping a safe but hard-to-miss distance, as he walked from *Avenue Georges V* to his house in the *Saint-Germain-des-Prés* neighborhood, a good twenty blocks from here.

He wondered what type of man this John Noland would turn out to be. Henri patted his inside jacket pocket, just to ensure that he still had the photocopy of Nicole's obituary that he had carefully folded and slid inside when he had left the library. This changed everything, in Henri's opinion. Susanne seemed to think that her ex-boyfriend: a scientist with (coincidentally to the point of appearing utterly unbelievable) expertise in the field of time travel, would be able to send Nicole back to the past. But how could they possibly consider doing that now, if it would mean certain death for their misplaced ancestor? In Henri's opinion, Nicole should stay; but what would John Noland say?

There would certainly be ramifications, in a scientific sense, from keeping someone from the past living here in the present; but could it be worse than carrying out a ghastly and unjust death sentence by re-establishing the status quo? Henri would make his vocal argument, and they would go from there. He could only pray that their time-travel consultant had a sympathetic heart as well as an astute and analytical mind.

Susanne was waiting for Henri when he reached the top of the stairs, standing in the doorway to let him in. He followed her inside, eager to meet this scientist, whom he found sitting next to his subject, Nicole, at the dining room table. Curiously, he caught a glimpse of Nicole's hand resting on John's before she hastily removed it when she saw Henri and Susanne enter the room. Was this a good sign, or a bad? It was too early to tell.

John Noland: tall and slim, with sandy blonde

hair and piercing azure-blue eyes, stood up, politely extending his hand to greet Henri. It struck Henri that seeing the two of them seated next to each other, especially holding hands, gave the distinct impression that they were a 'couple'; and a well-matched one, to boot. Granted, their romantic 'involvement', if it eventually came to pass, would be an uneasy and artificially arranged one—the two of them thrown together by sheer circumstances; and the eventual outcome of their pre-destined blind-date anyone's guess.

"I'm Dr. John Noland," the bio-astrophysicist said, with a serious look on his face. There was something in his eyes, though, that told Henri that this man had empathy. No, John Noland definitely wasn't just a robot. Henri sensed immediately that this was a man who would take both the 'human' and the 'humane' into consideration and factor them prominently into the equation.

"I am Henri Bruante." He shook John's hand whose grip was firm and confident, matching Henri's. You could tell a lot from someone's handshake; and this man had principles. He wouldn't let them down. "I'm glad you're here, and I sincerely hope you can help us." Henri glanced at Nicole, whose face looked paler than it had looked the night before. The poor girl was scared. "Help *Nicole*, that is," he corrected himself…because, after all, this was about Nicole, wasn't it? In Henri's mind, nothing else really mattered at this point.

"I'm not certain I can help," John said. He was honest, too. "I'll need some background information first, and then we'll see."

John Noland sat back down and gripped

Nicole's hand, briefly but reassuringly. Henri breathed a sigh of relief. *Thank God.* This was a man with a level, intelligent, and compassionate head on his shoulders; a man with a soul. Henri couldn't help but have a good feeling about their American guest; and first impressions were, after all, his specialty.

Susanne took a seat at the head of the table. His great-niece was very quiet, taking it all in, it seemed. What was she thinking? It would be interesting to eventually see where Susanne stood on all of this. One thing was for sure: she wouldn't be in favor of Nicole's staying in this century. Having her twin close by would just be too weird— and, quite frankly, Susanne didn't do well with competition. Not that Nicole would directly vie with Susanne for anything in particular; but just the thought of having a 'double' around to divert attention from the one-and-only Susanne Bruante would be enough to incite more than a little jealousy.

"Should we start with what you found at *Le Bibliothèque Nationale*?" Susanne asked. Apparently, she was planning on functioning as the moderator.

With some trepidation, Henri pulled out the copy of the newspaper clipping, unfolded it, leaned over, and placed it face-up on John's empty plate. "Did you tell him?" Henri asked.

"Not really; but it's spelled out right there for him." Yes, it certainly was. John took a few seconds to read it, his eyes moving back and forth, his eyebrows knit with concern by the time he had reached the end. Good thing this American spoke

409

and read fluent French. It would have been difficult to work through the complexities of what lay ahead if translation had to be thrown into the mix.

"Does this date," John inquired, turning the obituary around so it faced Henri and placing his index finger directly on the line that showed a date of *18 June 1876*, "correspond with Nicole's date of death in your family records?"

Henri nodded. "Yes, unfortunately it does; and not only that, but Nicole's dream seems to match the family story that my great-grandmother died in a carriage accident."

"Nicole's dream?" a confused and still incompletely informed John Noland asked.

"A nightmare," Susanne clarified, her tone of voice characteristically unsympathetic in the face of these troubling discoveries. "Nicole can fill you in."

Nicole, in the hot-seat, swallowed hard—her gaze focused on a plate of fruit right in front of her while the other three focused on her. It was clear to Henri that this would be very difficult, emotionally, for her to recount. "I was back at home," she began, her voice low, "in Montmartre, going to meet my dear Edmond at *Place Pigalle* on the day that we had decided. He stays with my mother, you see, and we agreed that he would meet me in the square at noon, on the third Sunday of June. When I got there he spotted me from across the square, and…" She covered her face with her hands, overwhelmed; while Henri handed her a napkin that she used to dab the welling tears from her eyes.

"Go on, Nicole," John encouraged her, kindly. "It's okay."

"He was jumping up and down and waving at

me in his excitement; then he started running, without paying any attention to the carriage traffic separating us." She paused and glanced downward for a few seconds either trying to recall or, more likely, loathe to bring back the horrifying memory; and then turned towards John and looked up, with renewed resolve, directly into his eyes. "I think I saved him, but I can't be sure. He ran in front of the horses, but I did too. He was in front of me, then next to me—and then maybe behind. I grabbed him by the arm, I pulled him around me…but then they were on us—on *me*. I remember the hooves, the blood, the dirt, the screams. And then it all went black."

"If this is what really happened in 1876," Susanne interjected, "can science explain how a person can actually remember something that hasn't happened to them yet?" She didn't sound skeptical, just curious. It seemed as though she knew John would be able to give them an answer.

John was hardly stumped. "Quite frankly, I think this phenomenon is easy to explain, given the circumstances. Think about it. From Nicole's perspective in the here and now, everything occurring prior to the year 2011 happened in the past, including events in her life that didn't physically transpire before she was sucked into the *Time-Tunnel*. She remembers her death on June eighteenth in 1876 *now* because it's an incident that no longer exists *ahead* of her on the river of time, but *behind* her. By jumping ahead of herself on *The Stream*, her future has, in essence, become her past. Does that make sense?"

It actually *did* make sense, but it staggered the

imagination. Now, it was time to address the dilemma that this logical distortion of the past and future had produced. "I'll leave the science to you," Henri said, "but what about the ethics? What should we do now? If you can somehow figure out how to send Nicole back to 1876, you'll be returning her to a place where she'll end up being trampled to death. We *can't* do that to her—I won't allow it." Henri sat back in his chair and crossed his arms, waiting for the rebuttal—which came, of course, from Susanne.

"If Nicole returns to the past, she won't necessarily die," his niece declared.

"And you've concluded this—*how?*" He met Susanne's gaze with an equally unwavering, simmering one.

"She'll remember," Susanne replied, as if this assertion was incontestable. "She'll have her memories to warn her and because of them, she'll change her plans and won't end up meeting Edmond at *Place Pigalle*. As a result, no one's life will be lost." She shrugged and smiled, probably thinking her victory had been won. "It's very simple, really. Nicole can return safely."

"I thought of that, too," Nicole said; "but what if I *can't* remember?"

"Why *wouldn't* you?" Susanne countered, her voice edgy.

"I was just thinking that maybe I wouldn't *have* those memories yet, if I return to the past *before* my death happens."

"That's ridiculous," Susanne smirked. "Those memories are *permanent* now, whether you're 'here' in a place where you were never intended to be, or back where you belong, going about your

412

business in 1876."

Henri cocked his head, looking inquisitively at John. "Dr. Noland?"

"It's impossible to know for sure, but I have to say that Nicole's point is well taken simply from a 'time-space' perspective. If she travels back to a time-point before her death in 1876, she might not remember any future events since they have not happened yet, inclusive not only of her own death but also everything that she has experienced so far in the here-and-now of 2011. But beyond that, there are potential astrophysical consequences of travelling through a *Time-Tunnel* that need to be considered as well.

"Like what?"

"You see, the electromagnetic force of a *Virtual-Hole* interacts potently with neurons in the brain, and could very well erase recollections in Nicole's memory center of everything she has experience, or remembered, while she was in 2011. Since we can't get into our time-traveling rodent's 'heads' to know what they do or don't recollect about the moments they've spent in the future, we can unfortunately only speculate."

Susanne's lips compressed, but she didn't say a word.

"It's not just about me." Nicole closed her eyes in what appeared to be an effort to compose herself. "It's really Edmond I'm worried about. My heart tells me I have to go back, to save him."

"But wait a minute, Nicole," Henri said. "If you're not there on that day in 1876, Edmond won't see you across the square and he'll have no reason to run in front of the carriage. If you stay here,

Edmond might actually be *safer* than if you return."

"Not necessarily," Susanne said heatedly, sounding as if she had found her second wind, most likely as a result of Nicole's 'I must return' mantra which just so happened to match Susanne's. "What if Edmond sees someone who *looks* like Nicole if she's not there, and runs through the traffic to greet his mother's lookalike? We can't be certain that Nicole's absence will prevent the fatal accident; and if Edmond is trampled by those horses, I should point out that he would not be the *only* person to die."

"I don't follow," Henri said, failing to put two and two together in his efforts to defend his argument that Nicole should stay put.

"Think about it, *Ton-Ton*. Nicole *has* to go back—because if she doesn't and Edmond dies, both you and I will cease to exist. If Edmond isn't around to have children, who in turn will have their own children (and so on, and so on), there will be no 'us'. It's as simple as that."

Henri grudgingly had to admit that Susanne had a point. He looked over at John, who nodded his acknowledgement. "I'm afraid that Nicole and Susanne have won the argument, Henri. If I can figure out how to send Nicole back safely, I am obligated to do it in order to keep the *Stream* of time flowing on in its intended course, to avoid exactly this type of life-and-death repercussion. My primary concern is making sure Edmond doesn't die because the Bruante line depends on it."

Henri opened his mouth to object, but stopped short when John interrupted him with an index finger raised. "*But*...I think I can achieve those goals without sacrificing Nicole's life," the scientist declared.

Now that was more like it, Henri thought. "How would you propose to do that?"

"I was thinking that we could use the obituary."

"How?" Susanne asked.

"We can send her back with it."

"Seeing something like that would absolutely terrify her," Henri said.

"That's the point." John grinned and Nicole looked at him with raised brows.

"What you're saying is that if Nicole sees her own death notice, she would be sure to avoid the scene of the accident. Are you proposing we put a copy of it in her pocket, or something?" Henri asked.

"Why not?"

Henri bit his lower lip and then nodded his agreement. He had to admit that it just might work.

CHAPTER THIRTY-SEVEN

Now that it was settled, Henri gave his great-niece a look that said 'truce', which Susanne countered with a look that said 'sure, but I still won'; while John's look reflected nothing short of deepening worry. "I hadn't planned on having a life-and-death deadline to contend with."

"How do you mean?" Henri asked.

"Well, today is June seventh, which means we only have eleven days to get Nicole back to 1876 before the incident at *Place Pigalle* occurs on June eighteenth."

"Wait a second," Henri said. Science (or science-fiction, for that matter) had never been his strong suit, so he would need the 'expert' to clear up his confusion. "Why does the date over here matter at all? Can't you just 'insert' Nicole wherever you please, in her original 1876 *Time-Shell*?" At Susanne's urging, Henri had watched John's press conference from June first on *YouTube*, so he could at least 'muddle-through' (kind-of) when it came to basic concepts and terminology.

John shook his head. "No, I'm afraid not. If I can figure out how to send her back, Nicole's entry point into her native *Time-Shell* will most likely be governed by two related principles: the first called the *Rule of Chronologic Symmetry,* and the second known as the *Rule of Recollection*."

"You'll have to explain, for us 'non-scientist' types," Susanne interjected—a sentiment that Henri heartedly seconded with a nod or two of his head.

"Well, our scientific equations predict that

416

when a *Virtual-Hole* forms between two disparate *Time-Shells* that have been lined up one next to the other by a buckle in *The Stream*, the entry-points on each end will correspond predictably so that the month, day, hour, minute, and second will match exactly; but the *year*, of course, will be different. This is called 'chronologic symmetry'. The law of 'recollection', derived from some other equally-complicated formulas, postulates that after a *Virtual-Hole* has been created for the first time between two *Time-Shells* centered on a *Common-Object*, they will 'remember' each other. As long as identical 'conditions' exist leading to re-connection, those exact two *Time-Shells* will always find each other again, and they will align along a parallel chronologic timeframe. For instance, if three weeks has elapsed 'over here', the same three weeks have also elapsed 'over there'. This means that when the *Virtual-Hole* is re-created, an inadvertent passenger like Nicole would find herself back in her native *Time-Shell* in a different year entirely: 1876, but on the same calendar date."

"So, let me get this straight," Susanne said. "Right at this very moment, time is flowing in parallel here, in our present *Time-Shell*, and in Nicole's ex-*Time-Shell* in 1876?"

"Exactly." John looked at his watch. "Right now it's 3:16 p.m. on June eighth *here*, so it's 3:16 p.m. on June eighth *there* as well. Now, using the *Rule of Recollection*, where, exactly, do you think the connection from our *Time-Shell* to 'elsewhere' would end up, if we created a *Virtual Hole* beginning on our end right now using the same *Common-Object* from the first connection?"

417

"In Nicole's 'ex'-Ti*me-Shell*, as Susanne put it—in 1876," Henri said. He seemed to be getting it now.

"More specific," John prompted.

"3:16 p.m. on the eighth of June in 1876," Henri answered.

"Correct."

"You've given us some good news and some bad news," Susanne offered sullenly. "The good news is that if you can figure out how to return Nicole to 1876, we can be relatively sure that she'll get back to the right place, if your mathematical calculations are correct—"

"But the bad news," Henri finished, "is that you only have eleven days to work out a way to do it."

It would be tight—very, very tight—and the worried look on Dr. John Noland's face told Henri that Susanne's American houseguest was thinking the very same thing.

CHAPTER THIRTY-EIGHT

John's mind raced as he tossed and turned in his guestroom bed that night. It would be difficult but not impossible to meet the soon-to-be-ten-day deadline, with the main barrier to success being the overseas shipping constraints for any required laboratory-materials that he might need. There was always overnight mail but the problem is that in his experience, across-the-Atlantic deliver was never really 'overnight' but in reality many days, at minimum. Talk about cutting it close; *this* one would definitely nick the skin.

He had to give himself credit, though. He had played the detective quite well out there in the dining room that afternoon; and with the information he was in the process of gathering, he felt certain that his solution would be the correct one. Nicole had been extremely cooperative— *definitely* a big plus, answering all of his questions calmly with thorough descriptions and some particularly well-placed insights.

John had discovered early on that Nicole was something special: an incarnation of Susanne with nothing but physical appearance in common with her twin. Nicole was levelheaded, Susanne was mercurial; Susanne was egotistical, Nicole was instinctively kind and reliable. The back-and-forth list went on and on, like a see-saw. John's infatuation with picking out the differences was the major cause of his early morning insomnia.

Nicole had surprised him with her insistence on returning home, despite the uncertainties and

419

dangers involved in doing so. Going back meant risking death, both as a result of the process involved in getting there and because of what might very well transpire after she arrived; yet, Nicole was still resolved to do it.

As John thought about it some more, he suddenly realized that Nicole was actually willing to sacrifice herself for Susanne, indirectly. Why? Because by saving her son, Nicole would in turn be saving generations of Bruante family members, right down the line, leading eventually to Susanne: the ultimate beneficiary of Nicole's self-sacrifice. John knew that Susanne would never dream of doing the same for Nicole, if the tables were turned. Despite their genetic connection and shared good looks, these two women were very different people. John had quickly become enamored—intellectually, he kept telling himself—with Susanne's mirror-image.

He thought back to his interview with Nicole taking place yesterday at the dining room table, whereby he had sensed as much about her as he had learned about her time-and-space predicament. "Can you describe exactly what you remember, right before you ended up in the gallery?" he had asked her.

"The painting turned into a white, hot empty hole that sucked me in, from behind."

"Before that." He was trying to identify the stimulus for the *Virtual-Hole's* creation. If it had happened once on that side, he could make it happen again on this side—but he would have to learn what had produced the connection between the two *Time-Shells* first.

"I posed for my boyfriend—René, that entire day," she explained, "just as I had done every *other* day for about a month beforehand. You see, he was a sculptor, while his brothers worked in different mediums. Jean was a painter, and Martial was a photographer." At the mention of René, she teared up; and John's heart went out to her.

Susanne had filled him in on Nicole's professional and intimate relationship with the middle Caillebotte brother earlier—a strange art-world coincidence given her brief artistic involvement with the famous older brother: Gustave, as a subject many years before for one of his only two female nudes; and her many-year association with another just-as-famous Gustave: the father of Realism, Courbet. 'Jean', as Nicole referred to him, had fathered her child: Edmond, conceived after she had posed for a slew of explicit paintings not only for Courbet, but also for a long list of Realists and Impressionists, being the premier un-named nude model of the era. Given her anonymous reputation, no wonder her love interests were carefully 'culled' from that particularly fertile artistic bed.

"I'm sorry about René," he had told her; and he really was. A woman like Nicole deserved, if nothing more, to be happy in love. He had learned, from Susanne as well, that during the years Nicole spent as Courbet's lover she had been less-than-content.

She had wiped her eyes with the back of a hand. "You are very kind, John."

For some reason, hearing her call him by his given name, which gave the impression of intimacy, made his heart beat double-time. "I know it's painful to recall, Nicole," he managed to say over the pounding rush of blood in his ears; "but *after* the modelling, and immediately *before* the painting opened up, did you and René do anything...*else*?" He knew very well what they had probably been doing and it made him feel distinctly jealous, which troubled him; but he needed to hear it from her.

"I took him into my bed, of course—to celebrate. You see, Jean had answered my letter that day, agreeing to the sale of his paintings."

The image of her celebrating with another man really bothered him, more than it should have. He had pushed the feeling away, trying hard to remove the sentiment from what was meant to be a purely objective scientific interrogation. "Exactly when did the *Time-Tunnel* appear during your...um, *activities*?" He felt embarrassment stacked uncomfortably on the jealousy now, making him shift slightly in his seat and concentrate intently on his glass of water on the table in front of him, rather than look her in the eyes.

"We were at the 'peak'—*both* of us finishing, together," she explained simply, with a tone of voice that surprisingly lacked self-consciousness despite the sexual focus of their conversation. He, in contrast, felt distinctly uneasy with the subject matter.

Had the *Virtual-Hole* materialized as a result of Nicole's sexual arousal, perhaps because of a hormone surge during her intimate encounter with René? It was certainly possible; no, make that probable because after all, chronotonin shared an amino acid backbone with a variety of other sex

422

hormones and in rodents at least, copulation increased the time-altering pheromone several-fold. Had Nicole's chronotonin levels peaked with her climax? This would be slightly discomforting to tease out, but it had to be done.

"So are you saying that the *Virtual-Hole* opened at the exact moment that you and René were experiencing your moment of...*pleasure*?" He felt stupid, but not just because of the idiotic phrase he had chosen to describe an orgasm. Here he was, sitting right next to a stunningly beautiful woman, grilling her about the details of her most recent sexual encounter. This was not an everyday occurrence, so how could he *not* feel awkward? The room had suddenly become very warm, and since he was wearing a t-shirt, he couldn't resort to undoing the top button of his shirt to help mitigate the heat.

"Do you mean '*la petite mort*'," Susanne had chimed in as quite-unnecessary clarification, her lips forming a naughty smirk as she walked into the dining room with Henri through the swinging-door, having fixed him something light to eat in the adjacent kitchen.

The comment didn't faze Nicole. "René was a skilled lover so I had a few of those 'little deaths' that night," she said, looking back at John with unapologetic eyes—brown, blended and tinted with swirling green. One thing was certain: Nicole Bruante wasn't shy. This trait, at least, she shared with her great-great-great-granddaughter.

John looked away, trying to make sense of it all. If Nicole had climaxed several times, why hadn't the *Virtual-Hole* opened with her first orgasm, or the second? Something just didn't add up; there simply *had* to be something else. "Was there anything at all unusual about your intimacy that night? Think back. Had you done something out of the ordinary with René this time, that you had not done before?" He swallowed hard, but it couldn't be avoided; he had to ask, there was simply no choice. "Perhaps you tried a different position…or a new technique? Anything at all unusual?"

"There *was* something," she said immediately.

He braced himself for more embarrassment. "What, exactly?"

"We had been drinking—not just wine, but absinthe spiked with laudanum too."

Absinthe and laudanum? That just might do it. "Had you ever consumed those 'extra' beverages before?" John asked, excited by this new information.

"Never," Nicole answered. "The absinthe was very expensive to buy and I could not afford it; and the laudanum—well, I did not socialize with people who could find it. René had plenty of money and surprised me with it, as a special treat for our special celebration."

Extra-potent absinthe, with opium added? That would *definitely* do the trick, if Nicole carried two mutations! What if Nicole had the same sex-linked drug-activated chronotonin gene alteration that his time-traveling mice possessed—inherited two-fold from *both* her mother's and her father's X-chromosomes? If she did, exposure to hallucinogens, like absinthe and laudanum, would accelerate her chronotonin hormone-production by many logs, eventually resulting in sky-high levels above the measly increase induced by the sex alone. That *had* to be it!

Now John could start to piece together the unique scenario that had resulted in Nicole's once in a lifetime (or rather, once in a *Time-Shell*) transposition in time. The usual 'script', written in all the *Time-Shells* located upstream and downstream from Nicole's native *Shell*, had been played-out *without* the absinthe and laudanum; and without those edits, a *Time-Tunnel* was simply never produced. In all of those other *Time-Shells*, Nicole stayed right where she belonged, celebrating with René (and without the 'additives' mixed in with their full-bodied Bordeaux) and dying eighteen days later as a result of her successful attempt to save Edmond from the oncoming carriage. But, in a bizarre deviation from fate's plan, René had somehow obtained the perfect time-travel aperitif, producing a unique event that had taken place in only one *Time-Shell*: namely, Nicole's '*Time-Shell* of Origin'—and *voila*...here she was, living-and-breathing in theirs.

John felt confident now that excessive chronotonin was the stimulus that had produced an electromagnetic deviation at the foot of Nicole's bed in her native *Time-Shell*, which had in turn created a *Virtual-Hole* centered on a *Common-Object*—a painting—connecting Nicole's *Time-Shell* with theirs. Now it all made sense. This real-life scenario corresponded *exactly* with all of his experiments in rodents.

"You say the *Virtual-Hole* opened in a painting hanging near your bed?"

"Yes, the one Jean called *The Origin of the*

World," Nicole had confirmed.

John turned to Susanne. "Were Nicole and René found near that particular painting in *d'Orsay's* exhibit hall?"

Susanne nodded. "Yes, directly across from it."

The electromagnetic energy associated with the *Time-Transfer* must have propelled both Nicole and René forcefully through the *Virtual-Hole*, through the painting and into this *Time-Shell*—the alcove gallery being the entry-point. John rapidly put two-and-two together in his mind…and Henri noticed.

"It looks as if you've come to some conclusions," the elder Bruante had commented. "Would you care to fill us in?"

"Yes, sorry." John turned his chair at the dining room table so that he sat face-to-face with Nicole, so close that he had been tempted to take her hands in his so that the coldly analytical data would be softened into something more direct and personal. He didn't, though. Why? For reasons that were clear to him then, but somehow not so clear to him now, as he tossed and turned in his bed.

"I'm fairly certain you have a 'double'-gene mutation, located on the female X-chromosome, that's over-activated significantly by sexual arousal, but even *more* by the ingestion of mind-altering drugs," he had told her. "The gene alteration, on its own, results in the overproduction of a hormone called chronotonin; but when the levels are increased logarithmically—by ten-times-ten-times-ten—after exposure to certain psychedelic and narcotic substances, the peptide becomes potent enough to open up connections between *Time-Shells*."

The blank look on Nicole's face told John that he was being way too technical. He had to remind himself that the field of genetics was still in its infancy in 1876 and that the discipline of molecular biology wouldn't even be invented for another century. He would have to keep it simple—not because Nicole, an intelligent woman, wouldn't be able to understand it, but because he didn't have the time right now to give her a modern-day science lesson.

"Let's just say that I think you've inherited, from your mother and your father, higher-than-normal levels of a sex-hormone called chronotonin, as well as a unique sensitivity to sex *and* drugs, like absinthe and laudanum. When you over-indulged with these 'medicinals' last week, your body (which already makes more chronotonin than most people's do) produced an excess amount of this pheromone, which was already surging in your bloodstream because of your...uh, *exertions* with René." He had felt his face flush stupidly again with the mention of the 'unmentionable', accompanied by disturbingly vivid images in his mind of Nicole making love to another man while an electromagnetic field formed around her. "The result," he rushed on, "was a tunnel between your time and ours, with something called a *Common-Object* located at both ends." The *Common-Object*, John felt certain, was the painting.

"This *Common-Object*, then, is *The Origin of the World*?" Susanne asked.

"I'm *sure* of it. Extrapolating from my experiments with mice, we'll have to produce a *Virtual-Hole* in that same *Common-Object*, hanging at this very moment on the wall of the exhibit room at *Musée d'Orsay* right here in 2011, in order to return Nicole home to a destination ending under that very same painting hanging on the wall at the foot of her bed, in 1876."

"Do you have any idea why I made it through, while René did not?" Nicole asked, her face going white. "He was horribly crushed, while I escaped without much more than some bruises when I landed, and a nasty scratch from scraping the top of the sculpture, I think. Why did he die?"

"At least in our mutant laboratory mice, the excess chronotonin that they produce functions as a shell that protects them from being injured by the extreme pressures that exist within a *Virtual-Hole*. We call the shell a 'halo.' I think you had a very powerful chronotonin halo surrounding you because you have *two* gene mutations that are capable of being activated when you are exposed to the appropriate stimuli; while René, who lacked even *one* mutation, simply did not."

"Are you saying that only women can generate a halo like Nicole's, and men can't?" Susanne asked.

"Kind-of. All men inherit a Y sex-chromosome, which determines their 'maleness', from their father, and an X sex-chromosome from their mother; while all women inherit their father's *only* X chromosome and one of their mother's two. To put it another way, males have an 'XY' genotype while females have an 'XX' genotype. Because chronotonin is located on the X chromosome (we call this 'X-linked'), women can have one *or* two mutated versions while at the most, a man can only have one. Does this make sense?"

428

They all nodded.

"Okay then. In order to open a *Virtual-Hole* and to survive the journey unscathed, a female must carry *two* gene mutations. A female (or a male for that matter) who only has *one* gene mutation can't open a *Virtual-Hole*, but the higher-than-usual chronotonin levels circulating in these single-mutation carriers can 'protect' them from the crushing energy of the *Time-Tunnel*, should they happen to be pulled into the portal after a double-mutation carrier opens it."

"So, I opened the *Virtual-Hole* because of my 'abnormalities', and poor René got sucked in with me and died because he was 'normal'?"

"I suppose you could say that; but honestly, Nicole—you're as normal as anyone else. It's just that you have unique genetics that have blessed, or cursed, you with certain...*abilities* that most of the rest of us don't have."

He was trying his best to dispel Nicole's impression of herself as some kind of a 'freak'; but Susanne's reaction, which matched Nicole's conclusion except stated more bluntly, certainly didn't help matters much. For Susanne, it was always about Susanne; and this time was no exception.

"Do you mean to tell me that there's a mutant gene in the family?" she had asked with a look akin to repulsion.

"It's not what it sounds like. Mutations are a mechanism by which species change and adapt to an uncertain environment. Many mutations are advantageous, rather than detrimental."

"I need to know whether I have the mutation,

too."

"What does it matter?" he had replied, finding it difficult not to feel irritated by Susanne's unrelenting focus on herself. "Unless using LSD or heroine is on your list of planned recreational activities, I hardly think your mutation status is relevant."

"Look, John, I have the right to know if I'm defective, too."

He sighed, deciding that it wasn't worth arguing with her. Anyway, why not? Scientifically speaking, the genetic penetrance of a naturally occurring chronotonin mutation in a family would be extremely interesting to study anyway; so to satisfy Susanne's personal and his professional curiosity, he would simply send a sample of Susanne's hair follicles, when he sent Nicole's tomorrow. Making arrangements for this was one of the two reasons he had excused himself from the table, stepping out into the foyer and down the hallway a few steps to contact his most trusted senior graduate student in Chicago.

After a few rings, he picked up. "Paul, listen to me carefully. How much TMMP do we have on hand in the rodent laboratory?" TMMP was the abbreviation they used for their injectable and ingestible psychotropic solution—a potent combination of thujone, mescaline, morphine, and psilocybin. Thujone was distilled from wormwood, the active psychedelic component of absinthe, while morphine was an opiate: a modern-day version of laudanum. Both of these drugs had worked on Nicole before, in 1876, so theoretically this four-drug concoction—an even *more* potent hallucinogenic mixture than what Nicole had consumed before—should work even better. If John gave her enough of it, the extra stimulus of a sexual climax wouldn't be needed.

"We have about 50 cc, I think," Paul said. John did the body weight calculation in his head and determined that if he used all of it, that amount (if taken by mouth) should be just about enough to effectively activate Nicole's chronotonin gene mutation and sky-rocket her production of the *Time-Stream* buckling sex-hormone in the bargain. The only problem would be the associated 'intoxication' which would result in complete unconsciousness that could be dangerous. This was the only option, though; they had no choice.

"Could you send me *all* of it, Paul—priority delivery," he said tensely, gritting his teeth, "in a refrigerated biologics container, to the address that I'll give you in a moment." He would have it delivered to Susanne, at *d'Orsay*, where a signature at the time of delivery could be provided by any of Susanne's office staff if arriving on a weekday. This would be safer than risking conveyance to her residence, where there might not be someone to accept it; plus, a museum destination, although not a university, shaded John's unusual request with at least a suggestion of the 'academic'.

"Will you need some needles and syringes as well?"

"Yes," John lied. "Send ten of each, please." His intention was to make Paul think that John needed the solution for an experiment overseas, perhaps at the University of Paris, where injection of the psychotropic mixture into a rodent's tail vein

431

would be required if John was planning on providing a time-travel demonstration. It was much better for Paul to think that John needed the solution for something legitimate and ethical rather than something morally and professionally questionable.

"I'll get that out to you right away," Paul had said. He would have to sign it out, requiring at least two signatures and a departmental stamp of approval, which meant that at the very earliest, the package would be on its way tomorrow. With any luck, the mailing would probably arrive two or three days later, which would still give them a week to spare before their deadline; except that the rapidly approaching weekend would likely cause delivery delays, since 'tomorrow': June 8, would already be Wednesday. He started to sweat. "Is that everything, Dr. Noland?" Paul politely interjected, ready to hang up.

"No, there's one more thing. I'll be sending you something, too…by overnight mail, tomorrow."

"What is it?"

"Some hair samples, including attached skin and follicles, from two female human subjects. I'd like you to run a DNA analysis on the roots using our array of site-specific probes, to find out whether the specimens in question contain 0, 1 or 2 transcription-activating chronotonin mutations. I'd also like you to measure the precise levels of chronotonin in the hair fibers. This is a priority, Paul. As soon as you have the results, scan the analysis printouts and email them to me."

Concurrent with the arrival of the TMMP, the genetic testing would already be in progress and once available, he would have the reassurance of

432

knowing whether his suspicions about Nicole's genetic make-up were true. This confirmation was imperative, before making any attempts to send her back; because it would be a genuine disaster if Nicole didn't really have a chronotonin halo to protect her. He just had to be sure.

"I am thankful that you are interested so much in my safety," Nicole had said later, her formal French already laced with an undertone of familiarity. She and he seemed to connect on an unspoken level—a bond perhaps that was more akin to doctor and patient, rather than man and woman? If he kept telling himself that, all would be well, because anything more than a professional relationship between the two of them could lead to serious problems. The last thing he needed right now was another problem to deal with.

John rolled over and looked at the clock: it read 2:22 a.m., and his mind was still racing. Well, enough was enough, he decided, finally breaking down and digging into his toiletry bag to dig out a sleeping pill which he took with a glass of water, feeling his thoughts slow down almost immediately. As he eventually drifted into relaxation: the certain harbinger to sleep, he felt relieved.

There was no more he could do until the morning, anyway; and so, he finally let it all go and fell into a deep and solid slumber.

CHAPTER THIRTY-NINE

It was funny how rest had radically changed Nicole's perspective on just about everything related to the 'here and now'; but other factors had also helped to tip the scales more towards the positive. Nicole was reassured by the way John had insisted on the analysis of her hair, to be sure she wouldn't be crushed by the energy of the *Time-Tunnel* during her return to the past; and Henri's heroic stance on Nicole's 'staying' (in direct opposition of Susanne's insistence on her 'going') had told her that at least two out of three of her twenty-first century companions cared for her—one of them perhaps romantically, if she was reading the signs correctly.

The look Nicole had noticed on John's face indicated that he might be doing his best to hide the very real danger involved in this crazy notion of sending her back in time: her trip to 'here' repeated but in reverse. The whole thing made her feel as if she were a convicted prisoner *en route* to Devil's Island. If she only had a few days left in this place, it seemed obvious that she should do everything in her power not to waste one second of her remaining time here—and this was the new philosophy that had spawned from the dream-infused ten hours she had just spent under the covers. If a death sentence was inevitable, then she was owed, in a figurative sense, her last meal: three courses transformed into three wishes, if she got her way—involving a person, a place, and a thing.

She slid out of bed and pushed aside the

curtains to her open window with two fingers, feeling the breeze of a clear, sunny day on her naked skin. Yesterday had been all clouds and rain, perfect weather for a day spent inside—but not today. She picked out a pair of trousers and slipped them on, still not quite used to the feel of fabric so tight about her legs, since women of her time always wore skirts or dresses. She found a turquoise t-shirt, a slightly worn cast-off, most likely from Susanne's past—perhaps even from her 'college days', as Susanne put it, when she had been dating John under the false pretense of sincerity. After slipping it on, she grabbed a comfortable looking pair of green-and-blue shoes that would serve her quite well, she thought, on her day's adventure outside.

When she ventured out to the dining room, she found John busy with some strands of hair, which he was carefully placing inside a small black cylinder, no taller than his thumb, with the letters K-O-D-A-K printed on the side. Susanne was sitting across from him at the table, rubbing the top of her head with two fingers. "That hurt," she complained.

John shrugged. "You're the one who asked to have your hair sampled." Nicole watched him write Susanne's name in red on a slip of paper and tape it securely to the side of the little black tube.

Nicole pulled out a chair, moving it over so that she could sit right beside him, just as she had yesterday. "You'll want mine next," she stated, tugging at four or five strands at once. She was used to doing this, since Jean had needed many strands of her hair to imbed in his erotic paintings of her. She grimaced slightly at the first try, then pulled harder—her scalp holding tight until finally she held her hair with attached roots between her thumb and index finger.

John offered her an empty black bottle, sliding it with the back of his hand over the tabletop toward her, their hands touching—his intention, no doubt. She inserted her hair into it and slid the container back to him, repeating the touch but letting her fingers linger meaningfully. He looked in her eyes for more than a moment, searching her very soul it seemed; then averted his glance, snapping on a cap and preparing an adhesive label for hers. It didn't take him long to attach the identifying slip of paper to the side of the specimen bottle, placing it almost lovingly next to Susanne's on the table in front of him when he had finished.

Susanne had gone to stand in front of the window that looked out onto the street in front of the building. "The surveillance car is gone," she commented. "They're tailing Henri instead of me, now."

"That's good," John said, "because we don't want the police in tow when we attempt the *Time-Transfer* next week."

Susanne nodded. "Very true. Henri can be our decoy." She turned away from the window and came back to the table, sitting down again across from Nicole and John. "Speaking of Henri," she continued, "he called a little while ago. The DNA results from our recent trip to the museum are back, already. The hair samples from the three paintings, *plus* the strands Henri recovered from *Waking Nude Preparing to Rise*, are all perfect matches to Nicole's." She had a big smile on her face, and it was obvious that she felt as if she were only a small step away, now, from her much longed-for recognition as the woman who proved that the 'model singularity theory' wasn't fantasy, but fact.

John turned to Nicole with a smile. "I'm not sure you realize it, but you've been immortalized. Your youth, your beauty, your spirit—preserved as images in those paintings; and now your genetic imprint in the form of your DNA, will live on forever imbedded in the canvases."

"Except that she's anonymous," Susanne said harshly. "Nobody will ever know her name."

"Who cares?" he replied with a shrug. "A name is just an arbitrary designation that has no bearing on who a person really is. Nicole is famous, in my book, even if no one ever knows what people called her when she lived and breathed." He turned back to Nicole. "Those paintings are your legacy. The artist left behind his signature, but you've left behind something *alive*; something that no one will ever forget. People will remember you—your body, your face, and your gestures—long after they return home from their visit to museums all over the world. You're the star in all of these paintings, Nicole—*not* Courbet, Caillebotte, Degas, Lefebvre, Renoir, or Manet."

Nicole had never thought about it like that before; and apparently, neither had Susanne. Before, she had looked elated; but now it was as if the air had been let out of her balloon. Susanne wasn't the type of person who liked being nudged out of the limelight. Yes, her theory might make her famous as an art historian, but she would never be able to take credit for Nicole's role as a direct contributor to art history.

Susanne got up, eyeing Nicole with a touch of jealousy in her eyes. "We'll get you back on the posing palette soon, if all goes according to plan. You'll have years of nude modeling ahead of you as a nameless celebrity, after you've returned home—as long as you avoid those horse-drawn carriages." She turned to John. "I'll be at work all day. It seems best if we give the impression of 'business as usual'...don't you think?"

His response was a curt nod, as he busied himself again with the sample bottles and mailing envelope, all the while looking at Nicole—preoccupied with her it seemed rather than the task at hand. "When your time-travel potion arrives, I'll sign for it," Susanne added unnecessarily, annoyed that she was being ignored and virtually begging for some attention, it seemed.

"It obviously won't be coming today," John added, his tone edgy. "Paul hasn't even mailed it yet."

"That's not what I meant," Susanne retorted; "you didn't let me finish. When it comes, do you want me to bring it back here?"

"Oh, right. No. If you can store it someplace safe at the museum, it would be better to keep it there, since we'll need it on-site for the *Time-Transfer* next week." Nicole had noticed that today was *Wednesday, 8 June*—the date glowing red like a dire warning on the face of Susanne's 'cell phone'. They still had ten days before the deadline to get her back; but John seemed extremely worried about the quickly approaching weekend, which he feared would delay the 'air-mail'.

She had learned that they had amazing flying machines here called 'airplanes' which could carry people and deliveries very quickly—sometimes in only a day or two. It was mind-boggling to think about, but by now she had gotten used to being stupefied by the 'futuristic' (for lack of a better term) technology confronting her at every turn. Regardless of how the time-traveling medicines and the information about her genetic make-up got here, the sooner the better, she couldn't help but think; because she didn't want to jeopardize her Edmond by cutting it close. She shivered to think that if anything went wrong, she might arrive too late to save him.

"I'll lock it in my desk drawer, whenever it comes," Susanne proclaimed.

"Very good. I'm thinking Monday or Tuesday, at the earliest."

Susanne nodded coldly, picked up her handbag and exited out the door without another word. John turned to Nicole, the expression on his face looking visibly relieved to see Susanne go, and spoke to her gently. "I'll send off the hair samples immediately so Paul can get me confirmation of your chronotonin status ASAP. Once we're certain you'll have a protective hormone 'halo' surrounding you when we try to send you back, I'll feel much more comfortable moving forward with our plan."

John told Nicole that he was hopeful they would have the results and the 'drugs' in hand by early next week, prior the 'drop-dead' day, as Susanne so crassly put it, of Saturday June eighteenth. He hoped to avoid a 'down to the wire' situation, sending Nicole back early next week if possible giving her a four to five-day safety buffer, depending of course on the mail delivery. They would access the museum just after midnight on 'D-day' (standing of course for '*d*rop-*d*ead'-day but also meant as a witty reference, Nicole learned, to a famous military operation occurring sometime in the middle of the twentieth century), with Susanne 'handling' the security guard immediately prior to the send-off.

"There's no way I'm going 'all the way' this time," Susanne had declared, when they were discussing the plan earlier. "After that last fiasco, I'm going to make sure the night guard is out cold—*period*."

John didn't seem at all surprised to hear about the 'extreme measures' Susanne had used during the first museum adventure. "It's just sex," Susanne had said—making it clear that to her, intimacy was nothing more than a means to an end. John shook his head, saying: "I could never view it that way," which made Nicole's heart soar. She wanted something meaningful, too; and even if nothing happened between her and John, simply knowing that the lover of her 'dreams' shared her own strongly-held viewpoint made her heart soar.

"I'll use your sleeping pills," Susanne went on, "dissolved in a snifter of brandy." And how would she get him to drink it? By offering the somnolent-laced cognac as a pre-coital aperitif, of course—the actual act aborted long before it could even begin. The nightshift officer's drug-induced stupor would last into the next morning, when his relief shift would find their confused and disoriented colleague just waking up at his desk, slumped over the deactivated alarm and video monitor systems and that had been shut off hours earlier. Susanne knew that she could pull it off, no problem. "No man in his right mind would *ever* turn me down," she bragged; and judging from her screaming success just two days earlier with one of these 'right-minded' men, Susanne's confidence was admittedly justified.

As the door clicked shut behind the exiting Susanne and John stood up to box up the two specimen bottles sitting side-by-side on the dining room table, Nicole decided that now was the perfect time to start working on her first wish.

"I will be coming with you, John, to post the specimens," she announced, deciding that it would be best not to give him a choice in the matter. "Afterwards, you and I will take a side-trip. All right?"

His azure eyes gazed back at her, unsure. *This isn't wise*, they seemed to say, but she didn't care. She was a condemned woman, and she was determined to have her way.

"I plan on going on this journey today with you. I *need* this, John," she explained. "It is very important to me." There was something between them—there had been, even from that first moment their eyes had locked in the hallway when Susanne had shown John to his room, opposite hers, yesterday. He had understood her then, and he understood her now. There would be no need for any further convincing.

"All right," he agreed. "And where will our side trip take us?" He seemed a bit sad, as if in agreeing to whatever it was she had in mind, he was resigning himself to heartache. She would be heartbroken too, but clearly recalled a quote written by a British poet whose name escaped her, that her father had read to her once when she was just a little girl. '*Tis better to have loved and lost than never to have loved at all.*' The sentiment had stayed with her all of these many years and she would invoke it now, in *Papa's* memory, in the heartfelt pursuit of her three wishes.

"To Montmartre. I would like to see it, here and now, before I leave." The 'place', in her wish list from this morning, was almost certainly hers, now, for the asking—John would never deny her. Later on, she would have the 'person', and then the 'thing'. She would enjoy that last item the most: the bittersweet conclusion to her final request before her day of reckoning.

It didn't take them long to mail the specimens at a nearby DHL office, with certified priority delivery to Chicago. John seemed to know all about the awe-inspiring underground rail cars that the people here called *Le Metro*, so she followed him, taking the first opportunity to grab his hand so that he could guide her through the crowds—a convenient excuse for contact that he didn't question (and that he didn't seem to mind at all, either).

On the train, they stood close, a steel pole between them on the crowded car, their fingers and shoulders touching as they steadied themselves against the rocking and swaying motion of the first dozen stops. The car lurched, and he held her, briefly—his hand on the small of her back, his fingers on cotton with heated skin underneath, his hip a perfect fit on the adjacent curve of her waist. At their stop, he held her hand again, and she grasped his fingers tightly as they crossed the threshold from car to platform.

He led again, and she followed. They were inseparable, just as she wanted it, with her palm in his as they navigated the sea of people until they found the train they needed. The car wasn't crowded, so they sat on the bench in front, her thigh against his, both of them willing; her foot, eventually, crossing under his, making gradual headway toward the transition from awkward to perfectly natural. At *Station Abysses*: their planned destination, they took the stairs, two hands joined now, his behind and hers in front, as they climbed what seemed an endless spiral that twisted up and up from the buried tunnel of underground tracks, through the rock and soil of the highest city hill, to finally emerge at the top and onto a cobblestoned square in Montmartre.

They were both out of breath, so he took her hand again with a touch that hinted at something different evolving now between them, pulling her gently onto a bench next to him, cool and warm at once beneath the shade of a towering tree. They faced a church, its facade a smooth expanse of brown-finished concrete.

"There was no church here, in my time," she said quietly. "It was a field."

He got up, and she followed, walking together down the stone grade, just two dozen steps or so until they stood arm in arm in front of the church. "*Église Saint-Jean-de-Montmartre*," he read from a plaque. "Construction began in 1894."

"That was long after my time," she said.

"After your time," he said pensively, "but well before mine." How bizarre, to think that they had been separated by more than a century until a natural occurring anomaly in her physical make-up had caused this unnatural flip-flop, allowing her to be standing here next to him in the far distant future. In two days she might be walking past this very spot again, in a time when it was just an empty field rather than home to a church. It was strange to think about this and stranger still to think that time existed at this very moment behind and ahead of them, an infinite and perpetual stream.

"Did you live around here?" he asked, his voice hushed.

"*Oui*, at the top of this hill," she replied, pointing.

"Come on, then," he said; so they passed through the courtyard and up ten-stairs-times-ten, following the sidewalk around the curving ridge toward *Place du Tertre*, passing houses and stores and restaurants on their way to another street. Two blocks further and they were finally there, standing in front of a renovated three-story building with flower-wells in front of each open-shuttered window. The sign on the mailbox read, "*25 Rue de Ronsard*."

"This is where I lived, in the attic room." A window located below the triangle of the roofline had looked tiny then—and it looked tiny, now.

"Would you like to go in?"

"No. I will be back here, soon enough."

The sun felt warm on her face and chest, just as she imagined his body would feel, lying next to her on those cold and lonely nights, up there below the rafters. This was something they would never have together—at least not up there. She turned to face him, taking his two hands in hers, intending to kiss him. But he stepped back.

"We can't—" he began.

She gazed intently, and sadly, into his eyes. "We already have," she replied.

"But you'll be leaving, soon."

"That is exactly why we should."

Her wish would be granted. The 'place' was hers, and now the 'person'; and tonight, she would have the 'thing'.

CHAPTER FORTY

Susanne had painted herself into a corner, but it's not as if she had had any real choice in the matter. She had offered Marcel this partnership out of desperation, cutting him a sliver of the pie in order to save the rest of the whole for herself. That was a sacrifice that couldn't be avoided, but one that still left her seething.

The thing that really got to her is that she had only herself to blame. She had been too cocky, settling for shortcuts when a tiny bit of extra effort would have done it, putting her in first place and landing her in the winner's circle alone, rather than tied to a freeloader who would end up taking part of the credit—*her* credit—for years and years of hard work. But if she hadn't handed Marcel the shared trophy, he would have ruined everything. In fact, she might have been walking at this very minute down a hallway whose walls were decorated with bars and locks instead of oil and watercolor paintings, if she hadn't pulled Marcel off the warpath and into her confidence.

In the very-early morning after her close call at the museum, she'd met Marcel as promised at their usual hotel room, many hours before she would have to drive in the rain to pick up John at *Gare du Nord*, right after lunch. Marcel had had the authorization paperwork with him, of course, but it was only after his other needs had been met that they'd sat, naked, on the edge of the bed to legitimize her illegal sampling escapade. She had expected to sign two copies, but he had brought only one.

"We'll make an even exchange," he had said. "When you give me the DNA results from the hair extractions, I'll hand over the proof that what you and your uncle did wasn't an act of international vandalism. Until then," he had said while folding the papers neatly and slipping them with finality into the front pocket of his jacket, still draped on the back of the hotel room loveseat, "these papers don't exist. As far as I'm concerned, we never signed them. I'll destroy them and turn you in to the authorities if you don't hold up your end of the bargain."

And she had no reason in the world to doubt him. Marcel was as driven to succeed as she was. He had taken every opportunity, in phone call after phone call, to remind her that he was dead serious. Since their early morning appointment yesterday— all business for her, but business and pleasure for him, the fun and games transpiring both before and after their signatures had dried on the authorization paperwork—Marcel had been nothing less than obsessed with getting the information that Susanne now held in her hand.

Well, here it was: a copy of Henri's faxes of this morning, nine or ten pages at least, filed away nicely in an official-looking folder; and in just a few minutes, the unrelenting Marcel Lauren would have what he wanted—but Susanne would too. Avoiding a prison term would be a very good thing indeed; and if she could do that and still enjoy the accolades from the confirmation of her theory, all the better. It had even occurred to her that if she played her cards right, sharing the credit with Marcel might actually

447

pay off with more of a jackpot than if she had succeeded in gambling 'solo'. Marcel's role in proving her 'model singularity' theory would undoubtedly land him a promotion; and with the *d'Orsay* director's chair empty, she would be perfectly positioned to slide right into it. Susanne might still come out on top, as she usually did—her favorite, and customary, position in both business and pleasure.

Marcel's office was not in the back hallway with all the others, but on the other side of the museum—a three-room suite behind and adjacent to the front lobby, equipped with every convenience, including a very pretty administrative assistant whose job description, Susanne felt fairly certain, included duties that the sexy blonde shared with the dark-haired and even sexier Assistant Director of Acquisitions and Special Exhibits. That didn't matter—all good, and perfectly fine because it's not as if Marcel actually meant something to Susanne. In fact, it would be better for everyone involved if he had someone else's shoulder to cry on when Susanne eventually put a stop to their late-night and early-morning rendezvouses.

As soon as Marcel vacated his office, Susanne would summarily vacate their mutually convenient arrangement. As the new Executive Director, she'd also send the overly accommodating secretary packing. She couldn't wait.

She had taken a shortcut through the special exhibit galleries from her office in the back hallway, which was located about midway down the corridor, quite near to the employee-only door that led into the last display-room. This meant that she had to

448

pass painting after painting (and a few explicit photographs, too) of Nicole. She kept telling herself that it didn't really bother her, but it did. She stopped for a moment in the second room, in front of a particularly seductive Jules Joseph Lefebvre piece called *La Vérité*, painted in 1870, that depicted Nicole's full-frontal nudity in a way that could only be described as breathtaking. She stood upright, gloriously nude—her right arm pointing skyward and holding a beacon-like light, while her perfect breasts (beacon-like in their own right) pointed toward the viewer, nipples a hard-and-tight focus-point of the highly sensuous pose.

Susanne had modeled an almost identical scene once, in her freshman year at the University of Paris, but with both arms extended up and cradled behind her head, in a way that accentuated the sexy figure-eight of her interchangeable-yet-superior nudity much more successfully than Nicole's pose ever could. Susanne had also angled her right leg out rather than in, an ingenious personal touch that had opened her up ever so slightly, so that a soft and delicate fold of pink had become the central focus of *her* painting, rather than naked bosom. Now *that* was the way to do it, in her opinion. If it had been Susanne instead of Nicole, all of these paintings would have left their indelible mark on erotic art-history, *not* just the banned and shocking (for its time) Courbet hanging in the alcove room—the only *truly* controversial masterpiece in the whole lot…if you excluded the Caillebotte 'bodyscape' photographs.

Now *those* pictures were more like it, and right down Susanne's alley. Some of the viewpoints and angles were just as shocking as *The Origin of the World*, or more—especially given the 'manicured' intimate subject matter, which Susanne felt certain had occurred at Martial's insistence and with plenty of resistance on Nicole's part. The result was a full-view detail of every sensual crevice, but created with artistic thoughtfulness and using light and shadow to full creative advantage. The result was nothing less than awe-inspiring, and would have formed the basis (if not 'lost' under lock-and-key in that secret closet under Gustave Caillebotte's staircase) for the erotic art-photography genre.

How Susanne wished that she had been the model for this ground-breaking photo-set; because if she *had* been, she would have never settled for 'model unknown'. Susanne Bruante would have changed the history books by refusing to remain nameless, for sure—allowing her identity to be announced far-and-wide, even in the newspaper headlines if necessary. This would have been no different than modelling openly, without compunction and no self-consciousness whatsoever, as she had done while an undergraduate—facing faculty and co-students alike after they had seen her, unapologetically and magnificently nude, without ever thinking it necessary to conceal her identity. Not that 'anonymous' was even possible in a place where she worked and studied, known universally to everyone as the erotically-compelling visual-arts major while at the University of Paris; or the sexy exchange student from France when she was in Chicago who, as it turned out, was more than willing to bare it all like the uninhibited celebrity that she was. Fame was in her nature; and if her unmatched body could gain her the recognition she yearned for and deserved, then so be it.

Susanne couldn't help but think about what John had said this morning about the 'subject matter' of a piece of artwork, and the crucial role the artist's model played in a painting's legacy. She had of course thought the exact same thing herself, on more than one occasion and more-or-less applied to her own personal situation. Susanne had always enjoyed seeing her beauty immortalized—her incomparable body, nude and exposed, captured forever on canvas, her image burning itself into a viewer's memory after being viewed and admired at an art exhibit…somewhere.

'Somewhere' was the word that spelled out the problem, she realized. The student artists who had painted Susanne were 'nobodies'; and *because* they were unknown, those paintings of her had ended up in attics, in basements, or in some flea market rather than hanging in a collector's living room, or on the wall of a noted art museum like *d'Orsay*. 'Somewhere' was nowhere; and *that*, in a nutshell, was the issue. *Real* artists—men and women with reputations behind them—had painted Nicole; and therefore Nicole's image (not Susanne's) would be admired by millions of people in places like this, for centuries to come.

Nicole would live on forever, specifically because she was Courbet's model (and Manet's, and Renoir's, and Lefebvre's, and Cassatt's); and *not* because of her aptitude for the nude pose, or the way her flawless body (a duplicate of Susanne's) seemed to lend itself so naturally to paint and brush. With the right artist, Susanne could have easily been another Nicole, but better. She shrugged. Out of sight, out of mind; and by the same token, out of my apartment and out of my life. A misplaced ancestor who belonged in a different time may have outdone Susanne in the nude modeling arena, but if all went well, this particular nineteenth-century beauty queen would be returning to her own pageant after midnight a few days from now, depending on when the materials for her send-off arrived. When Nicole was gone, all would be well.

She kept moving, through the largest special exhibit gallery and out to the catwalk, making a right and heading down the hall that overlooked the sunken level of the museum, over to her left, eventually finding herself in the lobby, opposite the security desk on the other side. The museum had just opened, and a thin line of people had already formed along the wall, behind a row of roped-off posts near the door. Susanne headed across the lobby, smiling pleasantly at the guard, a youngish officer with short brown hair and a small silver earring in his left earlobe.

"Bonjour, Rousseau," she said, calling him by his last name and wondering if it would be him on the midnight shift on the night of the time-transfer, or another one of her many *d'Orsay* security team admirers. It made no difference, really, since they all wanted her—each and every one. A sway of the hips, a suggestive word or two, a light kiss that promised more, perhaps; and finally, some heavily spiked brandy is all it would take to eliminate the first barrier to Nicole's final departure. No worries, she thought—most men were putty in her hands; and *these*—well, if Pierre had bragged (as she was sure he had) about his 'conquest' from the other night, then all of them would be malleable as clay. After she had finished shaping the security-guard of the evening (soft-molded-to-hard in her seductive fingers) Nicole would be history: literally and figuratively.

Rousseau nodded, watching Susanne lustfully as she passed by, his eyes on her breasts and his thoughts up her skirt, no doubt. She passed through a set of double doors to the right of the security control room, which led her into a short back hallway, immediately in front of a sign marked "Executive Director." There was no reason to knock, since the first line of defense would be sitting prettily just inside, behind a desk that was intended to field interceptions if need be.

"He's expecting me," Susanne declared, hardly looking at the woman who undoubtedly thought of herself as competition, but wasn't. Denise was wearing more make-up than usual, and her coifed hair looked as if it had just been professionally set. She was one of those women who felt compelled to work at her beauty, even though she would still be striking without the lipstick or blush. The girl probably lacked self-confidence, a character trait that seemed completely foreign to the ever-confident Susanne. A touch of color on her lips and cheeks was all Susanne ever needed to wrap up her package for her next lucky victim, and next week would be no exception.

Susanne pushed open the door behind Denise's post, ignoring the platinum blonde's vocal objections and stepping into the dimly lit sitting room adjacent to Marcel's office. He had left his door wide open, so she walked in. He was sitting at his desk, but started to get up when she came in.

"Don't bother," she said, walking around the desk to half stand and half sit on the edge of the mahogany desk, next to his chair. She made as if to hand him the folder containing the DNA analysis, but then pulled it back with a snap of her wrist when he reached out to take it.

"Not so fast," she chided. "We had a deal, remember? You give me the proof of your authorization, and I'll give you this copy of the matching hair samples."

"No problem," he replied with a shrug, pulling out his middle desk drawer to retrieve a folder of his own. "Here you go."

They made a simultaneous exchange. Now Marcel had what he wanted, and Susanne did too— the proof of pre-authorization for the 'sampling', which she would keep in her possession in case anyone came at her with accusations of wrong-doing. It was done, for better or for worse; so now may the gold and silver rain down on them both.

He opened the folder, thumbing through page after page of matching DNA sequences, followed by a summary sheet explaining that all the hairs— three from the gallery samplings, one from *Waking Nude Preparing to Rise*, and some strands from her great-great-great grandmother's 'brush'—were identical. "Good work, Susanne," he finally said, straightening the edges of the miniature stack of papers on his desk before putting them neatly back into the folder. "Our little discovery will change the face of Impressionist art-history forever."

"You're holding my life's work in your hands,"

she replied. "Handle it with care, Marcel."

"Of course I will." He smiled, and she decided it would be fine; everything would be fine. "We'll announce it together," he added, "sometime next week, as partners. All right?"

"As partners." Although the words almost stuck in her throat, that's exactly what they were. For better or for worse, she and Marcel Lauren were partners, but their 'marriage' of convenience wouldn't last. She would get her annulment as soon as the 'pronouncement' was made.

"Partners," she said again, slipping her shoe off and putting her bare sole directly on his lap, her toes in his hardening groin. *Partners, my foot.*

CHAPTER FORTY-ONE

By the time they crossed the courtyard behind Susanne's apartment together at the end of the day, John had come to an important realization. Over the course of the past twenty-four hours, he had been able to shake off whatever 'hold' Susanne's memory had had on him, because a healthier revision of the 'memory' itself had magically materialized right in front of him.

He had remembered Susanne in a certain way, semi-denying all of her deficiencies and magnifying all of her positives, to the point that his recollection of her, stored away in his head for nearly twenty years, was nothing more than an idyllic fantasy. From the outside, Nicole was Susanne, just as John remembered her; but from the inside, she was without a question everything the real Susanne was not...and ironically, everything that John's infatuation had tried to impose, artificially, onto his recollection of his college 'sweet-heart'.

He had wanted *this* Susanne; *this* memory that had unbelievably taken shape into a real person named Nicole, who was akin to a Realist's line-and-brush masterpiece which stood head-and-shoulders above an Impressionist's vague and blurry representation of what love should *really* be. John would happily take today's Courbet and toss away yesterday's Seurat, because now that he had the real thing, why settle for the Pointillist version?

Strange, how it had taken someone from the past to give John closure on his *own* past. Nicole was a woman who didn't belong here; a woman who had come from a place and time that no longer existed; a time traveler whose very existence in the 'here and now' had been enough to make John see that he needed to start living in the 'here and now' as well, instead of haunting those days that were long gone—his life consumed by a past memory that wasn't even accurate.

When Nicole had announced that they shouldn't hold back, he had felt ready to soar; yet he wasn't quite ready to throw the door open and let his heart fly out. This was all very confusing, logistically and emotionally speaking. That's why he hadn't kissed her when she had made her move in front of her Montmartre apartment.

He had *wanted* to kiss her—desperately, in fact; and he should have. Nicole had given her argument, and John had been convinced, but then the perfect moment had somehow passed and he had decided that he shouldn't push it…just yet.

They had strolled together instead, hand-in-hand, up the street from the house where she had lived in 1876, to the top of the winding hill, and finally into the bustling activity of *Place du Tertre*. The square was lined with artist vendors—some with true talent, sitting quietly next to their displays of nudes, landscapes, or portraits, while others seemed no better than gypsies, loudly soliciting the crowds of tourists in an attempt to sell their worthless wares. They had passed an oriental artist who was sketching a truly mediocre caricature of a little boy, while in the next stall an old Frenchman wearing a black beret sat on a metal folding chair, waiting for someone to buy one of his truly breathtaking nudes.

"It was not like this here, in my time," Nicole said, clearly disappointed. "All of the artists who painted in this square when I lived in this place had a gift."

It was true that Picasso and Utrillo, among others, had painted in *Place du Tertre* in the late 1800s. "There aren't many artists like that anymore," John replied. "The Impressionist movement produced a surge of talent that hasn't been paralleled since. It must have been amazing to live here, back then."

He realized as soon as he said this that he had used the past tense, when he should have used the present. Nicole *did* live here, and his heart sank when he remembered that she would be returning to this very place in his past—in *her* present, oddly enough—one night very soon, next week.

"Come on," he urged, pushing the thought aside in favor of the moment. "There's a famous church up here that I've always wanted to see." They passed together through the square and rounded the corner. There, soaring above them, stood the huge, shell-white domes of one of the most renowned basilicas in the world: the beloved *Sacré-Cœur de Paris*.

He heard Nicole gasp. "They finished it, then," she murmured. "They had just started construction when I left." She turned toward him. "I would like it very much if we could please go in."

"I must sketch you first," a voice behind them said, "if your husband will allow." They turned to see an older man in the stereotypical black beret of the Parisian artist.

Being called Nicole's husband made John

blush; but Nicole, on the other hand, didn't seem to mind at all. "Will you let him draw me, husband?" she asked, a twinkle in her eye. He nodded, trying very hard not to look as awkward as he felt. "My husband says yes," she declared, laughing, and John couldn't help but laugh, too.

He watched over the artist's shoulder as the man began sketching Nicole's exquisite face on his drawing pad. She sat perfectly still on a small ledge of stone supporting a wrought iron fence that surrounded the perimeter of *Sacré-Cœur*, with her legs crossed—a professional herself in the fine art of figure posing. After ten minutes or so, John dug into his front pocket and produced a few bills of paper currency. He handed the money to the surprised artist while at the same time taking the pad and pencil from his hands.

"But I am not finished!" the artist objected.

"I would like to finish it," John stated. "Is the money enough?"

The artist fanned out the bills in his hand, counting quietly to himself. "*Oui*," he finally concluded, smiling broadly. "Now, we will see what you can do!"

John started sketching; and now the street artist stood behind him, watching with curiosity as John put the charcoal pencil to paper.

"I did not know that you could draw," Nicole said, resuming her pose after stretching her legs for a second or two.

"I was very good, a long time ago," John replied. It was ironic, really, that Nicole was wearing the very same shirt that Susanne had worn, that night when John had sketched her in the coffee

459

shop on their first date, sitting in front of the fireplace with the steam from her cup of cocoa brushing pale and hot on her neck and face. He took his time, just as he had then, looking up at a memory of turquoise, the very image of 'past-become-present', no longer fading but bright, Susanne replaced by Nicole; and then back down at the paper, over and over again, until finally, more than half an hour later, he had finished.

The sidewalk artist clapped his hands. "*Fantastique!*" he said. "Very well done, indeed, *monsieur!*"

Nicole broke her pose, and John walked over to sit down beside her on the wall, the drawing pad face-down on his lap. She touched his arm. "May I see it?"

He turned the pad face-up to show her the portrait. The outline of her face had been framed by the street artist slightly off center and upwards, which had left John just enough room to drawn in her neck, shoulders and chest, and fill in the details—the rich expressiveness of her eyes, the delicate angle of her nose, the inviting fullness of her lips, and the high almost royal ridge of her left cheekbone. In place of steam and wisps of smoke and flame, John had substituted ivy, behind and around, climbing softly as a background to Nicole's perfect shoulders. The other picture's fire had burned out, while this drawing teemed with the new growth of spring, offering hope and a new beginning. If only Nicole could stay, and give him the love that he had lost before and had now seemingly regained.

"It's beautiful, John. May I have it?" she asked.

He had kept his sketch of Susanne as a hoarded memento that sat at the bottom of a dresser drawer, a painful and unhealthy reminder of his heartbreak. This drawing, he decided, would have a very different fate. "Yes," he replied; *yes,* he thought, *it would go with her.* Nicole asked him to sign it, and so he did, ripping it off the artist's pad and handing the remaining sheaf of blank paper, along with the charcoal, back to its waiting owner. Then he folded his drawing, again and again, until it was small enough to fit into the back pocket of Nicole's pants. "Perhaps you will remember me, when you see it."

"I will remember," she said, her brown eyes tinged with green gazing into his sad and lonely blue ones. He would remember, too.

They had approached the basilica from the side, by way of *Place du Tertre*; now they walked around to the front, looking down at the seemingly endless cascade of stairs that began at the foot of *Sacré-Cœur* and ended at the base of *Butte Montmartre*. Turning, they climbed the bright white steps of *Sacré-Cœur* hand-in-hand, after pausing for a moment at the foundation stone, which had been laid in 1875. "A small chapel was consecrated here in 1876," she explained, "for people to use while the church was being built. I came here often."

"Do you believe in God?" he asked.

"Of course I do," she replied. "He brought me to you, did he not?"

Yes, he had; and one sad day next week, he would send her away.

They reached the top of the stairs, where a greeter handed them an informational brochure, instructing them in a whisper to respect the sanctity of the vestibule and refrain from taking photographs. Inside, John felt the presence of something unquestionably spiritual, permeating the travertine stone, the glass, and the marble—even the air itself. Nicole lit a candle, so he did too, and with eyes closed, he prayed—for what? Without even thinking, he had prayed for something lasting between them, for something durable and meaningful, for a bond that comes only once in a lifetime. He had prayed for something that could never be, because she was leaving. He had prayed for love.

The narrow stairs leading to the top of the dome were open, so they walked one behind the other up to the observation deck, where they had a view of all of Paris sprawled below them at the foot of the ancient *butte*. "This is my city," she said quietly. "It does not matter what the year on the calendar says." She turned to view the cityscape from a different angle, when something caught her eye, over to the right. She frowned and pointed. "That was not there, in my time. What is it?"

"It's the symbol of Paris, *La Tour Eiffel*. It was erected in 1889 as an entrance arch to the World's Fair." John smiled, sadly. That was thirteen years after Nicole died. "Do you like it?" he asked.

"No." She made a face. "It is ugly."

"Some people think it is very beautiful—especially at night, when it comes to life with thousands of tiny lights, like stars."

She seemed willing to accept this possibility. "I would like to see it, at night. Perhaps it could be beautiful, with lights."

Yes, it was beautiful; and she was too. He

wanted to hold her—to wrap her in his arms and tell her that everything would be fine. But that would be a lie. Yes, he might be able to get her back to 1876 safely, but then she would be gone, and each of them would be alone on either side of forever.

They left the church, hungry since it was almost 4:00 so they shared some cheese, a baguette of bread, and a bottle of wine at an outdoor *café* halfway down the hill toward the *Abysses* Metro stop. Then, slightly tipsy, they carefully descended the same stairs they had climbed well before noon and successfully renegotiated the Paris underground back into the heart of the city. It was a short walk from the station to *Avenue Georges V* and although Susanne's house was no longer under surveillance, the back entrance still felt safer. He had been carrying the keys to the gate in his pocket since Nicole had no use for a purse, so he got them out, poised and ready; but she stopped him, just before metal slid into metal, with her hand on his.

"Thank you, John."

"For what?"

"For today. It was—"

"Incredible," he finished. And now, the time was right. He pulled her toward him, and the kiss was incredible, too—long and lingering, going on and on as if time itself had stopped. He wished it would. This was the answer to his prayer; *she* was the answer to his prayer. But soon she would be gone, and it would all be over. He tried to pull away, thinking it would be best to stop, but she held him close. Her lips on his spoke a wordless argument that he simply couldn't resist.

"The drawing of me...the one that you gave

me," she finally said, her lips still touching on his.

"Yes?"

"It is not enough."

"What do you mean?"

"You must prepare another one," she insisted.

He didn't understand. "What's wrong with the one from Montmartre?"

"It shows only a small part of me," she said. "I am more than just a face and a neck. Come upstairs, and I will show you."

She led, and he followed, up the stairs and into the empty apartment. He found a drawing pad in Susanne's desk drawer and a set of old charcoal pencils. When he had confirmed that he had what he needed, she took his hand again, pulling him with silent understanding, no need for words, down the hallway and into her bedroom. Her bed was unmade, the blanket pulled down, the top end folded over the bottom and resting partly on the floor, the sheets creased and furrowed from last night's sleep, when her naked skin had rested on burgundy silk, a scene that was easy for him to imagine, and one that he would witness again in just a moment.

She slid out of her shoes, the beginnings of nudity drifting from her toes over the smooth arch of her feet, onto elusive ankles and up the subtle swell of calves and the secret whisper of beckoning shins. Buttons in front were easily opened revealing white, tan, and pink—gladly uncovered, anything but shy; and then her blouse joined the pants on the floor, turquoise tumbling down on rumpled beige with a sigh, right there at his feet—and it was done.

Nicole climbed onto the sheets, her eyes

looking into his: brown and green and warm and close. She slid on her back, up and smooth—a reclining nude against a pillow, her right shoulder propped up ever so slightly, arm extended down on that side, pushing urgent and close against her body, right under her breast, lifting it upward, aching soft and firm. Her right arm reached out across her navel, breathing in and out against skin and muscle and ribs, a hand resting palm-down on the opposite hip, legs bent over to the right and together, dual lines of long and trim desire. At the other end, she had turned her head to the left, pillowed in the crook of the opposite arm, eyes closed, enjoying some private ecstasy that he must capture on paper. And he would; he knew that he would.

Wordless still, he drew, and she posed—artist and model, his past and her present, taking him back in time almost twenty years to the studio in Chicago, where he had painted a similar body, a different person…the wrong one—one that he had mistakenly thought was right. Nicole: this biologic enigma, was the right one, a treasure that he would have to return—soon, too soon; God's gift and fate's curse, both at once. He had found her, only to lose her. How would he survive? How in the world would he survive without her?

When he was done, he tore the paper from its pad, folded it once, then twice, and then again, and placed it on her nightstand.

She opened her eyes. "Can I see it?"

"When you get there," he said. "Take it with you, and look at it then."

He started to get up, but she reached out, taking him by the arm and pulling him toward her, gentle and forceful at the same time. They kissed again; and while they did, she unbuttoned his shirt, pulling it off his shoulders, her breath quickening in his mouth as she undressed him. He helped her open his pants, his fingers on hers, reaching down to free him with a moan and a palm against his hidden skin, urged on with tongue and lips. In a moment, quick and pressing, his clothes were at his feet joining hers on the floor; and then, with her on top, her softness yielded while his hardness strained powerful and intent against her, and inside her.

There was no need for words; their shared voice was primal and transcendent, all at once. Her breath was shallow, and his was panting, as he moved out from under her, and around to behind. Her skin, moist and warm, burned like fever in front of him, his lips in her hair and his mouth on her neck, melting and melding in a blended flame, wick and wax and dripping heat. His cheek touched hers with rough-on-smooth, her back arching, twisting around to urge him back down, his tensing muscles no longer behind her but alongside and in front. She shifted to face him, her breasts pressed moist against his chest, her leg draped over his, vulnerable and open, her wetness like tears that streamed down onto cheeks and open lips. Time, like her river, flowed forward and backward—down and down, and up and up, finally reaching that pinnacle, her moment and his together, more than a shudder and a cry, the past and present and future combined.

"*Mon Dieu*," she whispered, trembling.

My God, he echoed, shaking. What had they done? And how would he survive? How in the world would he survive…without her?

466

PART IV.

THE LAST FEW DAYS
JUNE 14 – JUNE 18, 2011

CHAPTER FORTY-TWO

By now, Henri was used to being tailed. For the past seven days, a police car had been parked on the street outside of his house 24 hours a day, and wherever he went (always on foot, his usual way of getting from one place to another) one of the two assigned officers sitting in the surveillance vehicle would get out and follow, keeping a safe distance back, usually a half-block or so behind, trying to blend in with the other sidewalk pedestrians.

They thought he hadn't noticed them, but he was more perceptive than most people. Although Henri had had no further face-to-face visits from inquiring law enforcement officials, the constant presence of *the 36* out there was more than a little disconcerting. He had willingly given his DNA sample and fingerprints to Inspector Crossier last week; and the results, by now, had most certainly returned—along with Claudine's. He fully expected the able homicide detective had been disappointed on both counts; so where would she point her investigative gun next?

It was Henri's job to ensure that he was still the main target, even if his 'biologic material' had not been found in an incriminating location, so as to draw the fire away from Susanne, Nicole, and John while they attempted the *Time-Transfer* tomorrow night at the museum. It wouldn't do for H.G. Wells and company to have a police escort accompanying them to the final chapter in this bizarre, real-life version of a science fiction novel. Henri had agreed to serve as an on-going distraction for Crossier, who was probably scratching her head at this very moment sitting at her desk at *the 36,* as she re-reviewed the Bruante DNA analysis print-out which had of course failed to place his or Claudine's genetic material at the murder scene.

As far as the repeat 'brushings' for fingerprints, he had been extra careful while collecting the samples from the painting just over a week ago, making sure that he did not leave his 'mark' behind at the 'crime-scene'; but his prints had certainly be discovered on the damaged Caillebotte sculpture, its pedestal, and the outside of the cleaning chamber since he had handled all of these things in the process of restoring the unfinished piece of artwork and installing it in the special exhibit room. This would implicate him in the 'crime' but of course wouldn't prove anything, since his job required 'contact'…and there was no crime in that.

It had been somewhat tense up there earlier this afternoon, on the *deuxième étage* of *14 Avenue Georges V.* Henri had been sitting on the living room couch, sipping the *café au lait* Susanne had served him. John, mini-laptop balanced on his knees, sat on a leather push-back chair, reviewing the DNA and chemical analysis read-outs that his graduate student in Chicago had just scanned and emailed to him. Lost in ultra-focused concentration, John had scrolled up and down the pages of his downloads until he was satisfied (or maybe dissatisfied?) with the answer.

"Well?" Susanne had inquired irritably, navigating around the coffee table and sitting down on the couch next to Henri while Nicole, perched nervously on the edge of a matching loveseat to the left of the sofa, reminded Henri of a wrongly accused defendant awaiting the jury's contentious decision. "Am I a mutant, too?"

Of course it was always about Susanne. Henri couldn't help himself. "We're more interested in Nicole's genetic status at the moment, *ma chére*." Susanne shot him a look that could kill, but Henri didn't care. "What's the verdict, professor? Will Nicole be able to make it through another *Virtual-Hole* leading to the past without getting crushed?" This was the bottom line, after all. Henri wanted to be certain that Nicole could safely reach the other side, a concern that he knew John shared as well—because if Nicole couldn't make it back unharmed, Henri knew *exactly* where he'd be spending the rest of the day. It wouldn't take that long, really, to convert his attic bedroom in *Saint-Germain-des-Prés* into an apartment of sorts for an unexpected but permanent houseguest.

"Nicole is something we call a homozygote, and Susanne is a heterozygote."

Henri had heard Nicole's quick intake of breath. "What does that mean?" she had asked, locking gazes with John; but it seemed clear to Henri that the glance passing between them was far more personal than professional. When it came to matters of the heart, Henri was never wrong; and *this* time, it didn't take a mind reader to see that John and Nicole had made a deep connection, probably on more than one level, that they had likely been cultivating while living under the same 'roof', bedroom-facing-bedroom from across the hall, for the past week.

Henri, a true romantic, couldn't help but smile to himself. *L'amour* was a beautiful thing, transcending boundaries of every kind, ranging from the social to the geographic; but Henri felt fairly certain that *this* romance, if that's what he was seeing, would go down in the record books as the first long-distance relationship separated by time.

John looked down at his computer screen, visibly troubled—by what he saw there? No, it wasn't that at all. Susanne was probably oblivious to the emotions that showed so clearly on John's face, but Henri wasn't. Henri was certain now…there was no question about it. John was in love, and what he had to do tomorrow night would result in heartbreak—mutual, it seemed. What a tragedy that two people would find love, only to have to say goodbye before they had a chance to really say hello.

"Well," John began, valiantly all business now, "Nicole inherited one chronotonin alteration from her father and another from her mother: a 'Double-X' chromosome mutation situation. We call an individual with two mutations for a particular gene a 'homozygote', and individuals with a single gene mutation a heterozygote."

"Does Nicole have the chronotonin mutation that you thought she would have?" Henri inquired.

"Yes; she has the same sex-linked transcription activating mutation as our laboratory mice have, making her ultra-sensitive to psychotropic and narcotic agents," John confirmed. "When Nicole ingested absinthe and laudanum, her chronotonin levels hit the roof, and that's what opened up the connection between her *Time-Shell* and ours."

"What about me?" Susanne inquired, crossing her arms impatiently. Henri could see that all she really wanted was for John to cut to the Susanne-specific chase.

"Let's put it this way," John replied. "There's no genetic reason to think that you and magic mushrooms shouldn't get along famously. You have the same mutation, but only on *one* of your two X-chromosomes which means you aren't capable of opening a *Virtual-Hole*, even if you took incapacitating amounts of mind-altering drugs."

Susanne got up from her seat, visibly satisfied with the result. "It's settled, then," she proclaimed, addressing John. "Nicole should be able to get back to 1876 safely, and if all goes well with our little going away party tomorrow night, we'll be wishing her *bon voyage* shortly."

For a fleeting moment, John looked as if he had been stabbed in his gut with a knife—and Nicole? Her face had turned a shade paler. "Theoretically, Nicole should be safe," John said, "but we're not talking about a mouse here. What we're proposing has never been tried on a human before. There might be dangers and risks involved in the process that none of us has anticipated."

Was John having second thoughts? If so, the personal was winning the tug-of-war with the professional.

"We have a deadline to consider," Susanne

471

reminded him—although she didn't have to. Nicole had arranged to meet Edmond on the third Sunday in June, 1876—which on *that* year's calendar was the eighteenth. The eighteenth, on *their* 2011 calendar, was this coming Saturday—fast approaching, merely four days from now. John's international 'package'—delayed, as expected—would arrive tomorrow morning, on Wednesday (according to tracking information); which meant that if they could successfully send Nicole back after midnight tomorrow night, in the early a.m. hours of Thursday June sixteenth, Nicole would have barely two days to spare before the potential June eighteenth tragedy.

"There's no turning back now," Susanne added. The lines of her face had hardened with the determination of self-preservation because Susanne's, *and* Henri's, very existence, in all likelihood, depended on Nicole's successful return to the past in order prevent Edmond from dying.

"I know the risks," Nicole spoke, calm and stoic. "I'm going; and I'm going tomorrow night." Nicole was determined, too—Henri knew the look. There was no further discussion.

Henri knew that when John's sixties-style psychotropic admixture arrived tomorrow, that Susanne would sign for it, locking it safely in her desk drawer at the museum. It would be important for Henri to keep the police busy while his niece functioned as master of ceremonies at *d'Orsay*; and that's what he and Susanne had spent some time discussing over a second *café au lait*, in the relative privacy of Susanne's dining room. It seemed quite unnecessary to pull John and Nicole into this particular dialogue, since it did not involve either of them directly; and anyway, they had both seemed quietly grateful for the opportunity to spend some time alone together, just across the foyer on the couch in the living room.

At this very moment, the unlikely but well-matched (in Henri's opinion) couple sat knee-to-knee, conversing in discreet whispers about their impending separation, no doubt. Susanne, in her usual self-absorbed fashion, seemed to either have no clue that her ex-boyfriend and her lookalike ancestor had in all likelihood become romantically involved; or else she just didn't care.

"I'm sure Claudine's DNA results are in, along with my own," Henri had said. "Without objective proof linking either myself or your cousin directly to the body, the inspector might be tempted to abandon her theory—if she hasn't already."

Judging from Crossier's line of questioning the other day, Henri had deduced that the homicide detective now believed that rather than Henri killing his gay lover in a premeditated fit of jealous rage, that he had killed Claudine's pimp, or maybe her drug supplier, in a show of protection towards his wayward niece. So far, Henri had functioned as a very effective decoy: a role that he might not be playing much longer if the crime scene evidence didn't point at least a circumstantial finger his way.

"That would not be good," Susanne said. "We need to keep the police focused on you, at least until our misplaced relative goes back home. I don't want them following us to the museum tomorrow."

"Do you have any ideas?" he had asked her.

She smiled; of course she did. One thing about

Susanne is that she always had a plan. "Remember when this place was being renovated, and I stayed in your spare room for a few months?"

He nodded; how could he forget? He loved his niece, but she wasn't the easiest person to live with. Well, that wasn't exactly true, since it wasn't really her that he had had a problem with, but the endless phone calls from hopeful admirers, and her frequent overnight absences to sample the short list. He didn't know how she could keep them all straight in her head, although her smart phone seemed to have a special program to do just that. "Of course I remember," he answered. "In fact, I still think I have some of your clothes in the guest room dresser."

"That's exactly what I was thinking about, *Ton-Ton*."

"What, your clothes?" He didn't get it at first, but then it hit him. "The woman that I left behind in the museum—the one that I killed for—was naked," he rationalized out loud. "I wonder what happened to her clothes?" he had asked, keeping in perfect step now with his wily niece.

"You took them, obviously; and now, you're worried that the police might find the evidence you absconded from the crime scene, if they ever decide to search your house."

"I think it's about time for me to get rid of them, don't you?"

"Absolutely. Remember, there was a struggle," she said, improvising. "Dirty them up a little bit before you toss them away in a dumpster somewhere, in full view of the gendarme who is following you. Try not to pick the pricey stuff,

474

though. There should be plenty of non-designer options in your guest room dresser."

He would go a step further than that. Susanne agreed that it would be a nice touch for Henri to throw in some of his own clothes as well, bloodied here and there by a cut on his leg or his arm, maybe, that he could easily inflict on himself with a pair of scissors or a kitchen knife. And then, the *pièce de résistance* would come in the form of a heavy mallet, one of the many tools of his trade, and one that could have easily caused the right type of head trauma, if applied forcefully, metal end first, against someone's skull.

These finds, hauled out of the trashcan by the excited police officer and wrapped up nicely in plastic bags with twist-tie bows, would keep *the 36* busy for at least a day or two and would, in turn, keep Henri in the spotlight until at least the weekend. By then, Nicole would be gone and John would be back in Chicago. It wouldn't matter, then, what the police did; but now, Susanne and her all-star cast needed to keep the authorities out of their business. This drop-and-run piece of play-acting seemed a perfect way to do just that.

So Henri had left, intent on preparing the phony evidence tonight, in order to execute his next assignment first thing in the morning, during his usual bright-and-early constitutional; and now, after almost losing his 'tail' inadvertently at the last busy intersection—he on-foot and his pursuer in a grey Ligier microcar this time, he had arrived back on *Rue du Bac*, rounding the corner to approach his house, visible now, less than half a block away.

After a half jog up the stairs that gave access

from the outside to his *premiere étage*, Henri let himself into his upstairs flat through the side door.

There was no time to lose. Henri picked one of Susanne's outfits from the dresser drawer, tearing the hem of the skirt and the collar of the blouse and soiling them on the tiled kitchen floor before throwing them into a garbage bag with a pair of her shoes. Then he moved on to his own bedroom, choosing some worn pants and a fading denim shirt, along with an old pair of work boots that he had been meaning to throw away for months now, anyway. His arm would bleed more than his leg, especially if he made the slice over one of the lines of blue that tracked up and over his biceps; so, with his eyes closed, he pressed the blade into his skin, letting his blood stain the throwaway clothes that he had placed on the table, right under his arm.

It all looked wonderfully incriminating. When the police actually analyzed the spatter, however, they would discover that the blood did not belong to their victim. Rather, they would determine it belonged to a careless art restorer named Henri Bruante, who would explain that he had accidentally cut himself with a razor-sharp planer while re-surfacing a frame.

He took the inside stairs down to his ground floor workshop, where he picked a large mallet, the perfect crime weapon dissembler, and dropped it with a thud into the bag. Along with the clothes and shoes, it completed his collection. Now he would be ready for a nonchalant walk at the crack of dawn, past the surveillance car to find a public trash can on the street—not the small one on the corner, which was usually full to overflowing anyway, but another one, a larger dumpster located six blocks down and three blocks over. It would work out perfectly, his guilt magnified by distance—the farther, the better—and by the time he returned to his house, the CSI team would be swarming around the garbage container and picking through the evidence.

He had a fairly sound sleep, waking at his usual time, just as the sun came up. Pushing a curtain in the front-facing window aside, he saw that the minicar from yesterday had been replaced overnight by the usual white Citroen, idling already in anticipation of Henri's usual routine. A short while later, he had made the trip there and back without a glitch, delivering his package to the dumpster while the unmarked police-car followed indiscreetly behind with its occupants taking note. Now that it was done, mission accomplished, he felt much better. Back in his living room, he poured himself another cup of coffee and settled into his favorite easy chair for a few moments of down time. Remote in hand, he switched on the television, already tuned to *France 3*, his usual viewing preference. It took a moment or two for the cable box to boot up, but when the screen flashed on to breaking news, he couldn't believe what he saw.

A press conference, televised live, was taking place in front of *Musée d'Orsay*, of all places; and the star of this particular headline piece was none other than Susanne's executive director, Marcel Lauren.

"The results of the hair analysis are definitive," he was saying. "Now, thanks to modern technology, we have DNA evidence that supports my theory that a single model posed for this wide variety of nude, nineteenth century masterpieces."

"Monsieur Lauren," a reporter asked, "how did you discover the hair embedded in these paintings? Were you following a lead from historical documentation?"

"I astutely noticed the hair, subtly poking out in the most famous erotic Courbet nude: *The Origin of the World.* That's when the idea came to me, so I authorized an art restorer to retrieve a hair from each of three paintings. Add to that a letter discovered by one of my subordinates hidden in the back of an unsigned piece, which also harbors an identical hair match—and *voila*. I think we now know the identity of this 'singular' model and her name was Nicole Thérèse Bruante."

This was bad—*very* bad. Lauren was trying to pass off Susanne's theory as his own, and he was succeeding! But there was more.

"Our sources tell us that this find has already resulted in your confirmed nomination to the Ministry of Culture. Is this rumor true?"

"I'm not at liberty to say," he replied, but the smile on his face could only mean that he had already signed his contract.

"If you were to speculate," another journalist said, "who would replace you as executive director of *Musée d'Orsay*, if you happened to receive this appointment?"

"François Bertolette," Lauren replied without hesitation. "He would be my *only* choice, when my position at *d'Orsay* needs to be filled."

Henri sighed. This turn of events would devastate Susanne, whether she admitted it or not.

478

Even the woman of steel might break, once she got wind of Marcel Lauren's betrayal. There would be a confrontation, of course—Susanne was not the type of person to take a set-back like this lying down. But what good would it do? Lauren would now be viewed as the mastermind behind the explosive model singularity discovery, and the media—whose memory was always strikingly short when it came to things like this—wouldn't remember that Susanne had originally floated the theory, even though she had given a poorly attended presentation about it on opening night. Marcel would be the one to reap all the benefits, while 'his subordinate' (he hadn't even had the courtesy to mention Susanne by name) stood by with her fists clenched and raised, but with no muscle behind her punches.

What could Susanne do, really? She could threaten to expose him as a cheat and a liar, but it would be her word against his—and whom would the public believe: the executive director of *d'Orsay* (a man with an impeccable reputation to back him) or a hotheaded assistant director with arguably questionable motives, making wild accusations against a boss whose position she clearly coveted? The train had left the station; in fact, it had already gained enough momentum that it couldn't be stopped, no matter what Susanne threatened to do.

In Henri's opinion, Susanne stood helpless on the tracks. If she didn't get out of the way fast, the oncoming rush of the inexorable would flatten her, once and for all.

Well, somebody had to tell her, so it might as well be him. Henri picked up his cell phone, letting his speed dial call her mobile. It only rang once before she picked up. "Susanne, it's Henri," he announced. He took in a deep breath. "Turn on your television and tune to *France 3*—and please, don't shoot the messenger."

CHAPTER FORTY-THREE

It was time for them to send Nicole away; and although she should have felt elated, she was furious instead, and it had nothing whatsoever to do with her great-great-great grandmother's send-off.

As she pulled her light-blue BMW into the underground parking lot at *d'Orsay*—with John in the front passenger seat, quiet as can be, and Nicole in the back, equally silent—Susanne just couldn't get a grip on her anger, try as she might. She had confronted Marcel face-to-face, immediately after talking to Henri this morning. She had driven directly to the museum, catching him just as the news vans were pulling out of their parking spots.

She had intended to make a scene, but with no one around to see it, her energy would have been wasted; so behind closed doors instead, she had found herself trying to open a hole in a brick wall with a wooden stick. She kept replaying the interchange in her mind, a mostly one-sided rage against the smug Marcel, who barely reacted to her threats and assurances of retaliation. She said she'd expose him; he replied that no one would believe her. She swore she would ruin him; his answer was, "Go ahead and try." She promised to call his wife and tell her about their affair, but he responded by looking back at her with contempt, informing her that his wife, and everyone else, already knew—and had known for months.

Susanne threw the terms "academic plagiarism" and "intellectual property" in his face, but he had only smiled. When she mentioned "sexual

481

discrimination," he had actually laughed out loud. He'd be singing a different tune, she predicted, when a lawsuit instead of an irate and fuming mistress slapped him in the face. She had stormed out of his office with her hand stinging and her indignation seething. The whole thing was outrageous, and she would get her revenge.

Finding an attorney wouldn't be hard, but the fight would be, potentially. The model singularity theory had been the topic of her master's thesis of course, so at least there was something in print, albeit only a department copy, on file somewhere in the stacks of the University of Paris. Copyright laws might not apply to a student's scholarly research piece, though, which was really just an extra-long essay, submitted in exchange for a lettered degree.

Besides, there hadn't been anything of true substance in those pages. Her thesis had been nothing more than an intriguing hypothesis, backed by no hard evidence whatsoever despite reams of conjecture detailed in footnotes, appendices and her bibliography. It would matter little that in the end, her studious premise had turned out to be true, 'manhandled' by someone more astute, it would seem, if Marcel's lies were taken at face value by the gullible press and their even more gullible readership.

And what about the sexual discrimination angle? She wouldn't get far with that one, since François Bertolette was as qualified as she was for the executive directorship (if not more, it pained her to admit), and there were two other women on *d'Orsay's* leadership staff besides Susanne who would be equally pissed that they had been passed over as potential candidates for the position. A legal battle wouldn't be easy, but what other option did she have? It's not like she could just pick up and start her life over again somewhere else. She had repeated these agonized thoughts to herself for most of the evening as she sat at her dining room table with a bottle of cognac in front of her, weighing her nonexistent options. Her tentative conclusion was that good things were worth fighting for—and she was a fighter.

She wouldn't be popular, though; she would be earmarked as the troublemaker who had eaten sour grapes and who was now on a mission to bring the grocer to his knees. Could Susanne really stay at *d'Orsay* and function productively in that kind of environment? She would be a woman scorned; a loser whose own stubbornness would not allow her to step out of the ring gracefully, forced by her very own character makeup to flaunt her rejection for all to see, instead of her body—a foreign concept, and one that she couldn't help but dread. She was strong, though, a woman who always had a plan; and right now, her plan was the better of two (or more) evils.

Stealth was no longer necessary at least as far as she was personally concerned since her 'blip' was now off Crossier's radar, having been replaced by Henri's; but she needed to make sure that Nicole and John were not seen. "Get down, both of you," she ordered, approaching the front-of-museum garage access and waving her magnetic key-card conspicuously in front of the reader. She drove down the sloping concrete tunnel and a moment after her entry, heavy machinery lowered the curtain of metal behind her with an odd finality, as if to say there was no going back.

She had to admit to feeling trapped. The only world Susanne had ever known—back there, up the ramp, and on the other side of the cold aluminum garage door—no longer existed. Adjusting to the new reality that awaited her would be a challenge. But she was up for a challenge; she always was. *This* Bruante was tough as nails, and she would never change. If that way out, behind her, was blocked, then she would just have to find another exit. The world on the other side of the *front* door, instead of the back, would be better than her old one because when one door closed, another one opened, as they always said; it's just that she liked what was behind door number one, and it was a shame that she had lost it in the way she had.

Try as she might, Susanne's attempt to think positively was having a meager impact on her anger-management problem. She sped erratically through the empty parking lot with squealing tires, pulling into her designated space with a screech. She heard some nervous murmurs from her stowaways, huddled together on the floor of the backseat as the car jolted to a halt.

Susanne had one foot out of the door before even killing the engine. "Both of you stay put," she instructed through her open door. "Don't even think about moving because, as we discussed, the four corner-cameras are trained on every inch of this place. They'll be able to spot you through the car windows if you show your faces. I'll come back down to get you after I deal with the security guard and shut the surveillance and alarm systems down."

484

She had locked up John's elixir: the one that would intoxicate Nicole, in her desk drawer right after signing for it this morning; so she planned on taking a detour there to collect the 'dope' after delivering a different kind of 'dope' to the night duty officer. Then she would return to the garage and retrieve the man and woman of the hour, so they could get this over with. She hoped the procedure wouldn't take too long, because she simply needed to put this all behind her, and quickly.

Susanne took the staff elevator up and headed down the walkway to the left, retrieving a pint of spiked brandy and some bright red lipstick from her shoulder-purse as she walked. At the other end, she stopped for a moment to freshen her painted lips, pressing them together to even out the color.

She had dressed specifically for tonight's deception, in spiked black heels and an ultra-short party dress, cut low on top and riding up obscenely high down below. She made a dramatic entrance into the front lobby, giggling as she steadied herself with one hand against the wall, zigzagging on precarious heels to finally arrive at the security desk. This time, the night guard was a guy named André. *Perfect*, she thought; he would make a very easy mark being one of the premier members of her 'at-work' fan-club.

She leaned on the counter, directly across from André. "I'm so drunk," she slurred. "I never get like this!"

"I, uh—well…oh my," he stuttered. He struck her as a poor excuse for an attack dog: one that would be easy to subdue with Susanne's particular

485

cut of meat.

"I'm finished, André," she confided, following her script perfectly. "Ruined. My personal life is an absolute mess, my career is over, and I have nothing left to look forward to. What the hell," she declared, raising the bottle in the air. "I might as well drink and be merry." She eyed him suggestively. "There's nothing companionship and a bottle can't fix, they say. Care to try?" She moved toward him but slipped, catching herself by grabbing the edge of the counter, a nicely executed touch. "I'm so clumsy. It must be the heels."

He gulped, and his eyes grew wide. "Perhaps you need to sleep it off, Mademoiselle Bruante," he said, getting up from his chair and moving around the security station to help her. "I can't leave the museum, but I could help you over to your office so you can rest on your couch."

"I'll let you help me to my office, André, but sleep wasn't exactly what I had in mind." He was next to her now, and he startled when she threw her arms around his neck. "I came here looking for you, and I guess I found you!"

"But Mademoiselle Bruante—"

"Call me Susanne, please." She leaned forward, so that their lips were almost touching. "You're cute. I've always thought so." He glanced down to examine her cleavage, and a few beads of sweat started to form on his brow. It was working; she had known that it would.

"You came here tonight, to…to find *me*?" he stammered, incredulous, but she noted that he did not back up.

"*Mais oui*! You're just what I need right now,"

she cooed. She kissed him full on the lips, with plenty of tongue thrown in to make sure her offer hit home. He put his arms around her, but when he tried to pull her close, she put both hands on his chest and pushed him away with a playful smile.

"First you need a drink. If I'm a little bit tipsy, then you should be too!"

He nodded—ready, it seemed, to agree to anything just to get her in the sack. She still had the flask (more sedative, really, than brandy) in one hand. She held it to his lips, so very helpful—tipping it up just enough to give him the first powerful dose.

"That's strong," he said, swallowing hard and shivering as the tranquilizer-in-disguise hit his stomach.

"You'll need a bit more to catch up with me," she said.

He nodded again, as docile and compliant as a pet dog, taking the bottle from her hand and swigging almost all of it down.

That should do it, she thought, but how long will it take for the drugs to do their job? She might have to show a lot more skin before the sleeping pills finally kicked in. No problem, she thought, turning around and pretending to fumble with the zipper on the back of her dress. "Could you help me with this, André?"

"Yes, sure, come here." His speech already sounded slurred and his eyes looked glassy.

That was fast, Susanne thought. This time, in contrast to last, she wouldn't even have to bare it all for the sake of science, let alone take it all the way.

"I feel… dizzy," he said.

"Because you drank it too quickly, silly." She took him by the arm, guiding him around the security island and easing him back into his chair. "Rest here a minute or two, and then we'll go down the hall for some real fun and games."

"Fun…" His smile was drugged, his eyelids heavy.

"And games," she finished, pushing the chair forward on its wheels toward the desk.

"So… sleepy." He folded his arms on the table, laying his head one-ear down on the flat surface. "Sleep," he mumbled, and in a matter of seconds he was out.

It was time to get down to serious business. She leaned over the now-unconscious André, her all-but-naked breasts dangled invitingly on the flat of his cheek—a most amusing 'tease' which in normal circumstances would arouse even the most tepid of quarries but not this one, who was dead-to-the-world; while with an outstretched arm she de-activated the video cameras and artwork-connected motion-detectors by tripping two switches on the tabletop with a well-manicured finger. Through all of this André remained oblivious to the lost opportunity literally staring him in the face. Straightening up again, she watched satisfied as the monitors all went dead; and now that her task was complete, she would make a beeline to her office to collect the *Time-Transfer* concoction, and then back down the elevator to the garage to collect the *Time-Transfer* participants.

She crossed the lobby, using the access door on the other side of the ticket counter that led to the administrative hallway, running parallel to the left catwalk but behind the sets of galleries including special exhibits. Her office was located about halfway down the passageway, closer to the lobby entrance where she stood than to the emergency exit at the far end—not really that far, but a destination that she would reach more quickly walking on bare feet; and time was of the essence if she wanted to change her situation 'pronto'. She slipped off her high-heels, letting them dangle on a finger while she padded quickly to her office, throwing the ever-unlocked door open and tossing her shoes onto her office couch in one motion; then using the tiny key hidden in the pocket of her purse to open her desk drawer. She expediently retrieved the clear liquid: colorless and bland, looking so deceptively innocuous in its graded glass flask, the meniscus curving upward on either side. Was it odorless and tasteless, or pungent and bitter? Susanne would never know. She had the wrong 'number' of gene mutations: one rather than two (or the *right* number, depending on how you looked at it) so she wouldn't be the one to sample John's specially manufactured pick-me-up. Nicole would; it was *always* Nicole.

She descended on the 'lift' to the garage, calling out: "let's go" impatiently, her voice echoing into the vast emptiness of the cavernous basement lot which at present was empty except for her solitary car. Nicole and John exited each from opposite sides of the back-seat in response, stretching their cramped legs and walking briskly, close together, to meet Susanne who was holding the elevator door open with one hand as she waited. Next it would be on to the alcove gallery for a solemn assembly underneath and opposite *The*

Origin of the World for the *Time-Transfer*. Well, two out of the three of them would be solemn; but she, for one, wouldn't be crying because tonight would mark the start of a new beginning—the old discarded for the new, the future uncertain but still stretching ahead, a world of challenges she had not asked for but would embrace nevertheless. It would all be better with the *Time-Transfer* behind her. She couldn't wait.

She looked at her watch: 1:15 a.m.—right on schedule. John had better be true to his word. He had said he felt fairly certain that he would be able to open the right connection from this time to the other, using Nicole, her two mutated chronotonin genes, and a bottle of his magic potion—but not without risk. *Danger be damned*, was her motto. It stood to reason that if Nicole had traveled safely from the past into the future with a so-called 'chronotonin halo' surrounding and protecting her on the way here, that she would have no problem making the same trip in reverse—a reasonable theory that would be tested very, very soon when they sent Nicole on her way with a one-way ticket out of sight, out of mind, and out of Susanne's life.

As the three of them exited the elevator together, John and Nicole held hands. Susanne had suspected that something was going on between them long before yesterday, when she had noticed John trembling when he had folded the copy of Nicole's obituary, slipping it carefully, even intimately, into the back pocket of her jeans...and this proved it. There were other clues, too—for example, the way Nicole's eyes had glistened with emotion when John had pledged, in almost marriage-vow solemnity, that he would get Nicole back to her own *Time-Shell* safely; or how he had touched her just so, his arm around her waist, taking her hand in his to help her into the car just a little while ago, when they had left Susanne's apartment together. She wouldn't be surprised if they had been spending every night together this past week, sneaking across the hallway in the midnight silence enjoying a carnal secret that, little did they know, was *anything* but clandestine. Of course Susanne knew; and frankly, she could care less.

All of these things added up to one thing: a problem for them that didn't concern her in the least—unless, of course, their little romance got in the way of tonight's big adventure. The hand holding 'thing' might be cute, in some people's book, but sickeningly sweet in Susanne's...and surprisingly distracting. Yes, she had to admit that it bothered her; but she refused to waste time on a misplaced emotion that she forced herself to dismiss, telling herself that she couldn't afford to lose her concentration on a pair of lovebirds who were apparently 'getting some' while sharing captivity in the same cage. Let them flaunt their little love affair for the next 30 minutes or so; because by two a.m. at the latest, all of this would be nothing more than ancient history, to be shelved right next to John's one-sided infatuation with 'yours truly' when they were in college together.

They navigated to the far-side catwalk, and then into the first special exhibit gallery; and there she was, hanging on all the walls...not only in this room, but in the next and the next and the next. It was nothing short of infuriating to see images of the renowned yet nameless Nicole plastered everywhere. Susanne could have done that nude modelling gig a thousand times better, and out in the open, to boot. Whereas Nicole hadn't had the guts to reveal her identity then, or now, 'Susanne Bruante' would have been a household name, in real time, had she been given the same opportunity; because *she* was bold and unapologetic where Nicole was meek and self-effacing. Now *that* was something to daydream about.

The witching hour was fast approaching. She handed John the flask and then turned on her barefoot-heel, leading the pair into the alcove room without looking back. She would *never* look back, because everything important to her lay straight ahead, right in the center of *The Origin of the World*: looming like salvation itself, right there in front of her. She stood with arms crossed, feeling like judge, jury and executioner rolled into one as she took a moment to examine Courbet's explicit depiction of Nicole's genitalia, which honestly looked indiscernible from her own. "Where is that birthmark you keep raving about?"

"*Ici*," Nicole said, pointing just to the right of her labia where the pink fold bordered on creamy-white skin, in an area obscured completely by pubic hair.

"*I* can't see it," Susanne remarked.

"It is naturally hidden by hair of the same color."

"Do we have to do this now?" John chided; and of course he was right. This was really *not* the time for petty physical comparisons when the 'defective' model was about to be returned to the manufacturer anyway."

"Alright, alright," Susanne conceded. "So, how should we do this?"

John had called the erotic painting a *Common-Object*: the focal point where the *Virtual-Hole* would begin and end; an energy tunnel that would open for a homozygous time traveler, taking the luckily-mutated individual in from this side and spitting her out at the other. The whole bizarre process could be likened, really, to an astrophysical imitation of human procreation, beginning with the portal's activation (replace this with sexual arousal), followed by physical entry into the *Time-Tunnel* (think about it as 'male-entering-female'). The time-traveler's journey was much like an embryo's— conceived in darkness, but eventually born into light; ejected through an electromagnetic, supernatural 'birth canal' and finally arriving, disoriented and confused, into a strange, new world rife with danger…and opportunity.

Would it hurt? How would the *Time-Tunnel* look, and how would it sound inside? Would the journey be rapid or slow? These were questions only a time-traveler could answer; and at the moment, there was only one person in this room who could open up the portal and qualify as one of those.

John held up the flask, studying it, his sadness undisguised as he finally got around to answering Susanne's logistical question. "Nicole needs to be near the *Common-Object*. After she drinks the TMMP, you and I will need to step back—*way* back. Otherwise we'll get sucked into the *Virtual-Hole*."

"Should I lie down?" Nicole asked. Susanne saw that the younger version of herself wouldn't meet John's eyes. This would be difficult for her, and for him. *C'est la vie.*

"I'm not sure it matters much, but I would say that you should try to reproduce your positioning from two weeks ago—if you remember; just to make sure you're pulled smoothly into the *Time-Tunnel* from exactly the same angle as you were before."

"I was on top," Nicole answered quietly, "with my back-side towards the painting." Now *this* might be awkward. How would the good Dr. Noland handle this kind of ultra-personal information?

"You should kneel on your haunches, then, as if straddling your...*partner*—directly in front of *The Origin of the World*, but facing backwards." John flushed, but to Susanne's surprise, only slightly. She thought she knew how to rattle him and have some fun at the same time.

"If you want to duplicate the situation precisely, don't you think she should do this naked?"

His flush deepened but he kept his cool. "There's no scientific reason to believe that her clothes will interfere with the chronotonin halo. Have you heard of 'nude mice'?"

"Sure. Aren't they genetically altered to make them bald?"

"Yes and no. They have no thymus, which weakens their immune system so they don't reject experimental organ transplants. A 'side-effect' of having no thymus is lack of fur so that's why we refer to them as 'nude'."

494

"So?"

"Well, we've sent nude and 'non'-nude chronotonin-mutated mice through a *Virtual-Hole* and it doesn't matter one bit if they are 'wearing' fur or not. Body hair (otherwise known as 'fur' in mammals with a lot of it) represents the equivalent type of barrier between skin and environment in a rodent, as clothes do in a human. Plus," he added, "where would we 'stash' Nicole's obituary if we don't have a pocket available to use?"

She laughed out loud. "I was only being facetious, John. You're so damn serious, sometimes." She would hate to see his reaction if she had gone a step further, suggesting that Nicole replicate her previous state of sexual arousal to insure the success of tonight's efforts.

John glared at Susanne, the non-verbal reproach clearly stating: 'this is no time for joking around'...*especially* involving the good-doctor's love-interest. In fact, he was gripping the flask defensively, giving Susanne the distinct impression that in the end, he might actually decide that he would keep it, rather than giving it up for Nicole to drink. "You'll have to take it all, Nicole. The amount of hallucinogen in this bottle should be just enough—" (He paused for a moment, and it seemed to Susanne that he was engaged in an inner struggle to rein in his emotions) "—to send you back."

His voice quavered; and in a second, she predicted, so would his will. She had actually expected as much, this being one of the main factors in her decision to be present to supervise the procedure's execution, rather than elsewhere— otherwise engaged with the night security guard, as

495

she had been the last time they needed to make an after-hours visit to the museum. For the job to get done, it seemed crystal clear that Susanne would have to do it herself. "I'll handle this," she said, snatching the bottle abruptly from him.

"But—"

Susanne now had possession of the bottle. "Wait over there, John." It was a command, not a request. "I'll join you in a minute, as soon as she drinks it."

He stood there numbly, his feet rooted to the floor, unresponsive to her orders. Maybe a gentler approach would be needed to convince him to step back. "Look, I know what's going on here," she said, trying to lend a note of kindness to the hard edge in her voice. "Even a blind man can see that you're too close to this. You need to let me do it, because you won't be able to."

John stepped toward Nicole, but Susanne stood in his way. "No goodbyes. It will only make things more difficult—for *both* of you."

"If it works, it will work fast," John warned.

"Don't worry, I'll move away quickly."

He looked past Susanne, over her shoulder, at Nicole. "When you get to the other side, stay away from the painting, or else you might ricochet back. And remember what I put in your back pocket. Don't go to *Place Pigalle*! Promise me, Nicole, that you'll remember. *Promise* me!"

"I promise, John." Nicole's voice barely rose above a whisper. "I promise that I'll remember. I could never, ever forget…" Her words trailed off, and she looked at John with a depth of feeling that Susanne realized she herself had never known for

496

another person.

The feeling almost got to her—*almost*. Susanne shook herself loose from the emotion and reminded herself that this had to be done now! She simply couldn't—correction, *wouldn't*—let these star-crossed lovers waste any more time and risk losing the opportunity to correct 'time's mistake'. Susanne handed John her purse not only to give him a purpose, but also so that her hands, unencumbered, could concentrate on the task at hand—giving him a gentle, one-handed push toward the alcove-threshold. "Here, take this and go stand in the archway over there. I'll join you in a minute."

"If she starts to ricochet back and forth, that would be a disaster," he said in her ear, so Nicole wouldn't hear. "I hope you realize that if that happens, we'll have to destroy the *Common-Object*—Courbet's painting—after Nicole's second trip back to the past. That would be the only way to break the cycle."

Susanne waved him away. It would be a shame to destroy a masterpiece, but it would never come to that. John was just fretting unnecessarily, as usual, and the last thing they needed at this crucial juncture was something else to worry about. "One thing at a time, John." She had to physically turn him toward the main catwalk and give him another gentle shove. "Go stand over there, please." He hesitated but finally complied with her shoulder-clutch in hand.

Now that their modern-day Romeo was out of the picture, she would have to deal with Juliette. "On your knees and facing backward, Mademoiselle," Susanne told her, realizing but not caring that her instructions sounded lewd. "Assume the position"

Nicole squatted in front of the painting, and Susanne handed her the opened flask, moving around to stand by her right shoulder which positioned Nicole eccentrically between Susanne (right next to her) and John (far, far away). "You must drink all of it."

"I know," Nicole said, her voice flat. She raised the flask to her lips, and in one swig, it was gone. This girl knew how to down a shot. Susanne breathed a sigh of relief. It was done. *Finally*, it was done.

And now it was time for the fireworks. Let the show begin.

CHAPTER FORTY-FOUR

It tasted more sweet than bitter, in stark contrast to the moment. Nicole, just a few feet from the painting leering at her from behind, tried to imitate her sexual position with René underneath her, in an attempt to minimize the variables involved in opening up another *Virtual-Hole* leading from here to there. She felt ridiculous straddling an invisible lover fully clothed, on her knees and with her palms laid flat on the cold wood floor in front of her as John looked on from afar, and Susanne stayed close—right next to her, in fact, like some kind of perverse '*madam*'-of-ceremonies in a place of particularly-ill repute. Nicole could almost imagine the whip in Susanne's sadomasochistic hand, just inches from her crouching body near her right shoulder.

Make no mistake about it: Susanne had not chosen her role as some kind of self-appointed *Time-Travel* expeditor out of any love or concern for her relative. There was measurable danger involved in remaining at Nicole's side, but Susanne obviously had concluded that this risk was greatly outweighed by the potential benefit. By hovering over Nicole's left shoulder, Susanne could ensure that the soon-to-be time-traveler had taken all of her medicine: every single drop; and Nicole had the distinct feeling that if Susanne could have poured the elixir down her throat, causing her to sputter and gag as it went down, she would have done so gladly.

Nicole had decided to save the impatient

Susanne the trouble. She had taken it all down, in one gulp—not so difficult to do, really, since there wasn't much liquid in the small container to begin with. The TMMP, as John had called it, burned warm in her throat, seeping quickly into her bloodstream—almost instantaneously, in fact—and the rapid ingestion led to immediate results. Nicole, having been there before, knew exactly what would come next.

In a state of delirium already, Nicole looked down the front of her loose-fitting blouse at her breasts, both of them falling forward, nipples hard and tingling, pushing hot against the fabric—a sensation that rippled outward in electric static to activate every nerve in her body and every pore of her sweltering skin. The burning heat, generated from inside her somewhere, made her genuinely wish that she was naked; but the tactile sensation was nothing compared to the visual.

Her breasts were actually *glowing*: the left one shimmering pink, containing dizzying whirls of spinning blue; the right one pulsing and burning insanely, a deep green touched with patches of black. Her distorted focus, hazed and steamy, moved from her breasts down to the floor; and with odd detachment, she saw herself in duplicate. One version, vaporous and ethereal, was floating up above the other: an earthly shadow far, far below—crouching, vigilant and trembling, on the floor with Susanne standing like a guard at her side. The paintings, from her new vantage point up here, were all at eye level, including the one directly in behind her—the one that looked so very familiar.

This had happened to her before, hadn't it? It

was hard to recall. Her thoughts were scrambled now, racing forward and retreating back; but she remembered a bed, and a man, and a painting—*this* painting, the surface as indistinct then as it was becoming now. Those were her legs, parted ever so softly, right behind her she could see, as she craned her neck to peer over her left shoulder; but in between, at the place where pink flesh stared back at her, partially concealed by the curls of hot brunette wildness, she saw something swirling, bright and awful—whiter than white, starting out small but growing in terrifying increments…a slowly expanding consumption of glaring heat.

In a moment the painting would be gone; she remembered now, all too well. The hole would start pulling, just as it had before, and she wouldn't be able to stop it. When that happened, all would be lost—*she* would be lost, falling and falling into nothingness, searing white turning to frigid black, leading God knows where.

Nicole looked down again. Things had changed: she wasn't down 'there' anymore, but up 'here' instead, her body joined with her soul, an inevitable communion filled with meaning, a signal that meant it would happen rapidly now, the first step in the dreaded consummation, the beginning of the end.

Time had slowed, though, just as it had before. Once again, her skin burned and burned, hotter and hotter, as if she herself were some kind of living fire surrounded by a cloud of heat that John's elixir had ignited by its interaction with her unique body chemistry, emanating outward in a protective shell that she now knew would prevent her from being crushed within the *Virtual-Hole*. A split second, once again, could easily last a minute; one heartbeat was more like ten; a single breath was almost half a lifetime. It was all so slow and sluggish, seemingly unstoppable.

Nicole watched the painting of herself as if out of eyes looking from the back of her head, right there behind her, gradually become a blur of unfocused flesh and skin, in slow motion—a collage of pale tans, whites, and browns; a disrupted kaleidoscope of melting paint; a cloud of swirling colorful mist; and finally, a bright white maelstrom, spinning with screaming and broiling wind, leading directly into a void of nothingness that pulled and pulled and pulled. Nicole was slipping backward—she couldn't stop it—and in a moment the white heat would turn to cold black when it sucked her in, just as before. The hole would consume her—this is what it did, and that was exactly what it was doing, now.

Nicole anticipated the slide behind, inching toward the lip; but before she started to 'fall' she noticed the hint of movement, off to her right side. She knew it must be Susanne beginning to inch passed and around her toward safety—away from Nicole, away from here, and away from the sucking power of nothingness, which stretched ahead. But that didn't matter—*Susanne* didn't matter. Why? Because ahead and behind, an illogical dichotomy, was Nicole's world, just as the hole demanded. *Come to me*, the hole seemed to say. *Come to me, I'm right here. Come to me, come to me...*

But then she felt a body-jogging impact—maybe her right shoulder hitting the edge of the

Time-Tunnel; or that side of her chest scraping the brink, perhaps? Had this happened before? Possibly, but maybe not; she couldn't decide. And then, she found herself, suddenly, looking ahead and behind, both at once, an impossible feat made possible—made *real*—by her psychedelic eye. Was she falling backward or ricocheting forward? Was she being pulled in or pushed out? Nicole felt too confused to know.

Her thoughts, and the sights and sounds around her, tangled together in jumbled chaos—deafening, yet muted. It was wrong, yet it was right; it was right, but also wrong—tumbling and spinning, back and back and back, moving forward perhaps; but then again, no. The past was behind her, but the future was too. It all made sense, but none of it did, until she fell onto something hard, her head crashing into dizzying reds and blues and yellows and greens…and whites; *explosive* whites, burning and searing with pain in the back of her head, where her 'eye' couldn't see. Was this real? It *had* to be, but it wasn't; it was, but it couldn't be. The paradox was in her mind—that was it! *It's all in my mind*, she thought. *It's all in my mind.*

Come back, the hole seemed to scream. *Come back, come back*!

She *was* back, she suddenly realized. She went in, then she came out; she was 'there', but now she was 'here'; she had gone, but now she was back. As the entire world around her faded from white to the all-consuming nothingness of black, she realized that it was over…and she was back.

CHAPTER FORTY-FIVE

When the time for action finally came and her ex-lover had found himself unable to act, Susanne had stepped in to take control. She had reacted perfectly and thank goodness she had because now, it was finally over.

It hadn't taken long for John's compound to work. Susanne had seen Nicole's face turn very pale, very quickly, which was Susanne's signal to squat on sprint-ready legs and look for the signs in the painting that the *Virtual-Hole* was beginning to form. She warned herself again, for the twentieth time, that she needed to be careful, staying so close to the action because it just wouldn't do to have the wrong Bruante sucked in. That would ruin everything, throwing a wrench into the gears of her plan—the one that she had spent so much time, recently, conceiving.

John kept yelling warnings, over there by the threshold, but Susanne couldn't care less. He wasn't the one whose life depended on a successful *Time-Transfer*; so he could scream until he was blue in the face, and Susanne would just continue to ignore him. Susanne was staying, there would be no argument, until the moment she could be sure that the right person was precisely where she had to be, at the right time.

She had kept her eye intently focused on the painting, because this is where Nicole had said the *Virtual-Hole* had formed before, back in the past when her mutated genes had been hyper-activated by *another* potent mixture: absinthe and laudanum, rather than TMMP. The former mind-altering concoction had been happily provided, of course, a long time ago by her nineteenth century lover: René Caillebotte (*another* family relation in their famous heritage, believe it or not); while the latter had been unhappily furnished just a minute ago by her twenty-first century one, standing right there ringing his hands, across the room waiting nervously in the archway between alcove room and exhibit hall.

René had definitely been in the wrong place at the wrong time, with no forewarning of the sucking force that would drag him backward to his death, since he didn't have a chronotonin halo to protect him from the crushing force of the *Virtual-Hole*. There's no way that would happen to her, since Susanne's vigilance, her shrewdness, her strength of will...*and* her inherently resilient makeup would surely protect her. She, for one, always ended up on top; and *this* time especially, she would be extra-certain that her perfect timing would put her in the right place at the right time. She was no René: a man who sadly hadn't measured up; she was Susanne Bruante...and Susanne Bruante always won.

The scarcely discernable undulation on the surface of the painting had started between the image's realistically-depicted legs. It was barely a ripple, but still enough for Susanne to know that it was starting. After only a split second, the agitation grew—a circular whirlpool now; and if Susanne didn't move fast, it would be too late.

It all seemed to happen in slow motion. The void centered in the middle of the painting grew and grew, consuming the piece of artwork and the wall where it had been hanging until all that remained was a panel of solid mist. As if by magic, Nicole was no longer crouching on the floor by Susanne's side but hovered in the air instead, levitated by a magnetic force that had raised her up and would momentarily pull her in, feet-first. Moving fast yet slow, Susanne's next step relocated her intentionally closer to Nicole rather than away while the swirling maelstrom, screaming silently behind her and to the left, was quickly gaining strength.

She would easily be able to execute her plan, she thought, since milliseconds seemed to drag on like hours due to the bizarre distortion of time by the *Virtual-Hole*. Nicole, helpless and weightless, hovered at the lip of the void and started to move backward, in virtual slow motion. At this crucial instant, Susanne made the necessary impact, her hands and her full weight behind her, against Nicole's right shoulder and chest. The sucking pull of the hole was only just beginning, so the shove (forceful by necessity, intended to counteract the magnetic back-pulling draw of the Time-Tunnel) sent Nicole tumbling and spinning through the air, forward and angled left a perfect thirty-degrees or so, towards John; finally landing with a thud and a roll, literally at John's feet—precisely where he was standing, eyes wide with surprise, on the threshold between the two rooms.

Physically removing Nicole came first; and next she must deal with herself, and quickly— because staying here was simply not an option. She had to act fast. With Nicole's chronotonin field abruptly disconnected from its *Common-Object*, the hole would conceivably close very quickly—a theory that seemed to be playing itself out in real-time because the vortex was growing smaller, and smaller, and smaller; and in just a moment, she wouldn't be able to pass through.

Her forceful displacement of Nicole had situated Susanne a good ten feet or more away from the shrinking wall of mist—so she turned away from John; turned away from d'Orsay; and turned away from everything 'old' in present-day and toward everything 'new' in the forgotten past. She belonged in Bohemian Paris; belonged in 1876; belonged in an artist's studio, posing nude for one Impressionist after another, immortalized on canvas *and* on photographic film...because *yes*—she had figured it out, only recently. It was *her*: Susanne Bruante, and *not* the timid-by-comparison Nicole, whose body had been portrayed so boldly in Martial's ultra-explicit bodyscape set.

What did she have here? What was she leaving behind? *Nothing.* On the other side of that *Time-Tunnel*, she could start her life over again as the most unforgettable erotic model the world would ever know—leaving as her *own* legacy the very same paintings and photographs, hanging at this very moment on the special exhibit walls around her, that Nicole had so vehemently 'denied'. Flawless (*no birthmark*) and bare (*not even a hint of stubble*) could only mean those photos depicted Susanne, *not* Nicole—a foregone conclusion that eliminated failure, entirely, as a possible outcome of her impending time-traveler's journey. Those photographs were proof-positive, long before *and* after the fact, that Susanne was destined, without a single question or a smidgeon of doubt, to succeed.

With the fire of foreknowledge propelling her, Susanne dashed forward, ran into the jump, closed her eyes and made the leap of faith that would take her far, far away. The energy closed in behind her—launching her forward, pushing her along on the crest of the electromagnetic wave, into and through the empty void; forward and backward, ahead and behind, into the past but toward her future, once and for all. She knew the hole was closing, a black shadow following closely, disaster barely averted. She felt the hole around her, too, but soft, not hard. Susanne had her own chronotonin halo, after all—not as strong as Nicole's, born from one mutation not two; but strong enough, it seemed, to do the job. Without it, she would have certainly been crushed by now; but look at her—she was fine. Susanne Bruante was *always* fine.

As she tumbled and fell, down and down, and up and up, she would have patted herself on the back if she could have. When it had finally been time for action and someone had needed to take control, she had reacted perfectly; and in a moment, it would all be over.

Whiteness surrounded her, in front and to the sides, but not behind; and then, just as Nicole had described, it turned suddenly and completely black.

Finally, it was over…and she was gone.

CHAPTER FORTY-SIX

It had happened so quickly that John didn't have time to react. The painting first, and then nearly the entire wall, had suddenly turned to swirling mist; and in less time than it had taken for him to blink, Nicole was lifted up and backward by the interaction of her super-charged chronotonin halo with the oppositely charged magnetic field of the *Virtual-Hole*. Susanne, in the meantime, was in the process of doing the unthinkable—namely, removing Nicole physically from her essential position right in front of the *Common-Object*, backside facing the evolving, swirling portal. After the confusing action was over, John realized that the hole had promptly snapped shut, but not before Susanne had dived into the void herself. Nicole lay on the floor in the middle of the gallery, motionless.

John felt fairly certain that Nicole had sustained a blow to the head (he had actually heard the thud) and he prayed that he wouldn't have to deal with a serious concussion on top of everything else. Nicole was still exuding a very potent chronotonin halo, and there were countless of other *Common-Objects* hanging on the walls all around them. In her current state, Nicole was a living and breathing super-inducer: a walking stimulus for the formation of another *Virtual-Hole* if she passed close enough to a piece of artwork that could function as a Common-Object, at least for the next twelve hours or so unless John could get the remaining unabsorbed TMMP out of her system, and fast. The last thing they needed was for Nicole to open a hole underneath a Van Gogh, for instance, sucking them *both* in and transporting one living and one dead time traveler directly back to Vincent's back yard in *Arles*, circa 1888 or 1889.

John's mind raced as he knelt down at Nicole's side, who was lying at his feet. Susanne had taken a big risk, relying on her one mutated chronotonin gene to protect her from being crushed by the tremendous pressures created by the magnetic field distortion within a Virtual Hole. Traveling through the *Time-Tunnel* without the ultra-high levels of chronotonin that a homozygote harboring two mutations (like Nicole) could produce was dicey, at best. John wondered if Susanne had even been able to make it past the borders of their present-day *Time-Shell*.

It was sad, really. It seemed hard to believe that Susanne's life here, in 2011, had been bad enough to trigger this kind of extreme measure; but he could certainly understand how devastated she must have felt when her boss took the credit this morning for her life's work. With her career in shambles and no husband or children to offer her emotional support, who wouldn't leap at a chance to start their life over again in a new and exciting place? Granted, most people would choose a fresh geographic start rather than a chronological one, but Susanne had always marched to her own drummer. *Godspeed*, he thought. In the end, if she made it to the other side safely, Susanne would come out on top. She always did.

Now it was time to focus on the problem at hand. He gently turned Nicole over from face-down to face-up, supporting her head and neck as he did so. There was no blood (*that* was good, at least) and she was breathing, slow and steady. He put a finger on her wrist to check her pulse, which felt strong and even—*another* good sign.

"Nicole," he said, bending over with his lips near her ear. "Can you hear me?" Her head moved, almost imperceptibly. Yes, she had heard him! "I'm going to get you out of here, but you're going to have to help me, by holding on to me with your arms around my neck. Do you think you can do that?" He could easily handle 115 pounds of semi-conscious weight, but the same amount, totally unconscious, would have been a different story entirely.

Nicole nodded again, and this time, she even opened her eyes. "I feel… sick," she said, her voice thick and slow.

Perfect, he thought. If she felt nauseated already, he wouldn't have to encourage her to empty her stomach with a finger down her throat. But here was not the right place for that. If she could just hold on until they got to the underground parking garage, a drying puddle of vomit on the concrete floor, off to the side and in the corner somewhere, would attract much less attention than the same kind of thing up here. "When we get downstairs, we'll handle that," he promised. "Can you keep it down for just a few more minutes, until I can get you there?"

"*Oui.*" She closed her eyes again, moving her lips as if she were talking to someone. She was hallucinating—big time, no doubt. The combination of psychedelics and narcotics she had ingested was enough to produce a soaring trip which would soon lead to blissful unconsciousness unless he could prevent the remaining mixture in Nicole's stomach from being absorbed. God knows where her mind was right now, but it certainly wasn't realistically engaged with her present situation.

Slinging Susanne's hand-bag, which contained keys and other essentials, over his head and across the opposite shoulder, he lifted Nicole, one arm under both legs and the other around the small of her back. She wrapped her arms around his neck and laid her head on his shoulder—so vulnerable, so grateful, and so completely deserving of his love and protection. It felt wonderful to have her back like this, and he swore that he would never, *ever* try to send her away again. He decided, at that very moment, that he had no scientific obligation whatsoever to get Nicole back to where she had come from.

Why? Because destiny, he rationalized, had intended to send her here; and that same hand of fate, just a few short minutes ago, had unequivocally prevented him from sending her back. If this wasn't a sign, what was? It felt right; and as far as John was concerned, Nicole had ended up exactly where she belonged—which was right here, in *Musée d'Orsay*, on Thursday the sixteenth of June in the year 2011, at precisely 2:09 a.m., cradled in his arms.

But what about the Bruante line? They would survive—John's intuition told him they would. Susanne had gone back, hadn't she? And like it or not, by choosing that path, she had taken on the role of Nicole's surrogate: the protector of her own bloodline. It was pretty simple, really. Susanne

512

would feel compelled by her own need for self-preservation to save Edmond—because if she didn't, all of his direct descendants, including Susanne, would cease to exist. John wasn't sure how that would work, exactly, but whatever the mechanism, Susanne would not want to be part of that particular time-space experiment.

With Susanne's purse hooked on an elbow and Nicole reclining across his arms, John made his way carefully down the middle of the exhibit hall, keeping as far away as possible from the paintings on either side. As he exited the room and moved onto the catwalk, he realized that the museum was littered with landmines: not just paintings, but sculptures, and furniture, and antique decor—*all* of them potential *Common-Objects* by virtue of their age; and *all* of them prone to the stimulating effect of the intoxicated electromagnetic "deviant" he held in his arms. One false step and it would all be over. But somehow he got past them all safely, at last stepping with his lovely burden into the elevator again, but this time going down.

As it turned out, Nicole didn't need to crouch in a corner of the garage once they got there to rid herself of the remaining TMMP. There was a large trash bin next to the elevator, so John eased her down carefully onto unstable legs for the purging, supporting her with one arm around her waist and the other on her shoulder. After a few successful retches, he lifted her up again, carrying her across the parking lot to where Susanne's solitary parked car waited, ready to take them home. Gaining entrance with the electronic key that he dug out of Susanne's purse, he laid Nicole gently on the back seat and hurriedly slipped into the driver's seat. He tipped his rear view mirror down, choosing just the right angle so that he could keep an eye on Nicole resting in the back while he drove.

He knew where to go—it wasn't far. Twenty minutes later, after navigating the deserted streets of a sleeping Paris, he pulled up at the curb in front of Susanne's condo. When he helped her out of the car, he found that Nicole could walk—kind of, with more than a little bit of assistance. Although there was very little risk of running into neighbors at this early hour, John wasn't worried even if they did. Nicole could easily pass for a drunken Susanne, being helped up the stairs, one tenuous step after another, by her caring American houseguest…and boyfriend.

Inside, it didn't take long to get Nicole out of her clothes and into her bed. She was his beautiful and irreplaceable 'nude reclining': a living and breathing legacy from the distant past; a temporary visitor materialized quite by accident in the here and now, whose visa had just been stamped '*permanent*' by the official hand of fate. She would sleep off the effects of the TMMP; and even now, her blood levels were probably approaching normal as she dozed—his one and only: the one that *didn't* get away.

He would join her there shortly, lying next to her and wrapping his own naked body gratefully around hers; but first he had a phone call to make— Susanne's last promise to the other involved party in their endeavor, and one that John intended to keep.

'*I'll phone you as soon as we get back,*'

Susanne had said, speaking into her cell phone just before the three of them had left for the museum. The absent, elder Bruante was probably sitting at this very moment in his easy chair, waiting for word that all had gone exactly according to plan.

He pulled Susanne's phone out of her purse, and found Henri's number in her contacts. Then, when he touched the screen to make the call, a voice at the other end answered after only one ring.

"Henri, it's John," he announced into the phone receiver. "We need to talk. There were... *complications.*"

CHAPTER FORTY-SEVEN

'*There were complications,*' John had said, jumpstarting their phone conversation a few hours ago—Henri's phone ringing only once before he answered it, sitting awake in his favorite armchair waiting for the call. He and John had decided that they would re-group at Susanne's apartment at 8 a.m., to give them all a few hours to sleep; and now he was on his way, the police following behind, still tailing him but on foot this time. It seemed the portly gendarme had decided that some exercise would do him some good, for a change.

Yes, it was a problem that Susanne had 'disappeared', but he and John had come up with an explanation that would satisfy just about everyone. The diligent Inspector Crossier would not be happy—but too bad. After all, it wasn't as if Susanne was a full-fledged suspect in the case, given the lack of evidence linking her in any way, shape, or form with any kind of wrongdoing. Besides, Susanne hadn't been given any official instructions by the authorities to stay in the city (or even in the country, for that matter) during the ongoing investigation.

The police would just have to deal with Susanne's spur-of-the-moment decision to relocate to the United States with her American boyfriend. It would be their problem, not Henri's, to get Susanne back to Paris if need be—but it would never come to that. There was no doubt about it; the *d'Orsay* 'double-murder' would end up as a cold case, because no actual homicide had been committed in the alcove gallery two weeks ago. When more time passed and no concerned family members or friends came forward to report John Doe as missing (which would happen around the same time that the accumulated evidence had failed, once and for all, to add up), the hype would die down and the case would be shelved.

Of course, Henri's fingerprints, or his DNA from hair or skin, would be discovered on the outside of the restoration machine *and* on the Caillebotte sculpture with overturned pedestal—an expected consequence of working with those pieces; but without *his* biologic material on either victim (and without John Doe's DNA-imprint inside or outside the pressure machine), the authorities would not be able to link Henri to the murders and they would be obligated to drop him as a suspect. The case would die, and all of the nonexistent evidence would be boxed up and shoved into a corner of the storage basement of police headquarters and summarily forgotten. Give it another month or two at the most, and that would be that.

The pressing question, at this particular moment, was whether the police would want to question Susanne today. That all depended, Henri rationalized, on whether the night guard from last night, a fellow named André, had woken up before or after the morning shift came in. If he had regained consciousness before his colleagues clocked in to relive him, logic dictated that he would have scrambled to reboot all of the museum's surveillance systems—the ones Susanne had disarmed after her smoothly executed charade—and do his best to cover up his several-hour absence from the land of the diligent.

In this scenario, André wouldn't *dare* mention a word about Susanne, since keeping quiet would mean the difference between gainful employment and waiting in line for *l'allocation chômage*. His recollections of the night's fun and games might be somewhat hazy anyway, since the brandy had been heavily laced with a dizzying dose of sedative. At any rate, accusing the Assistant Director of anything more than making a friendly stop at André's desk on the way to her own office might land him in more trouble than he was in already. It would be her word against his, so keeping his mouth shut would be the most expedient way to make it all go away.

Henri hoped for this outcome, because if the police came knocking on Susanne's door, the striking physical resemblance between his niece and Nicole would not be enough to fool the astute Crossier. Nicole's speech and mannerisms were all her own, so there would be no way, in this world or any other, for Nicole to pass herself off as the absent assistant director in the company of people who had met and actually knew Susanne.

Henri had not been as surprised as John that Susanne had opted for a one-way ticket elsewhere. Yes, the trip from here to there was risky, but if Susanne had made it, Henri had no doubt that she would use what she knew about the future of Impressionism to position herself just so, as the *prèmiere* nude model for all of the big names. He wouldn't be a bit surprised if, a few years from now, a previously undiscovered cache of Renoir or Degas nudes magically surfaced, featuring none other than the famed Susanne Bruante herself. She might even find a way to get her name, along with her naked physique, into the history books. Leave it to Susanne. If there was a way to make her mark on posterity, she would find it.

Henri agreed fully with John that Susanne would make it her first order of business to ensure Edmond's safety. If Edmond died, so would Susanne—theoretically, at least; and so would Henri, for that matter. No one, including John, could say if Edmond's descendants would cease to exist at the very moment that Edmond died, or if the impact of the boy's demise would be delayed the twenty-odd years that it would have taken him to have children of his own given the parallel flow of time between their *Time-Shell* and Edmond's.

For Henri, the one and only important moment of truth would occur at twelve noon on Saturday, June eighteenth: two days from now. As long as he made it past this milestone, he couldn't care less about the next one, two decades down the road. By then he would be an old man, if he lived that long, and it wouldn't really matter if he existed or disappeared when he had already lived his best years anyway. Susanne, on the other hand, had much more at stake, since she was still young. Rest assured, she would make sure that Edmond made it, because her own life depended on saving the four-year-old version of her great-great-grandfather.

Henri climbed the front steps to Susanne's apartment while the policeman who had been following him stayed back, stationing himself unobtrusively on a sidewalk bench just a few doors down. Yes, Henri was taking a risk by leading the police here; but then again, there was something to be said for making things look normal. The gendarmes had made the trip from Henri's house to Susanne's residence and back more than once over the past three days, so another visit paid by a loving uncle to his niece did not seem out of the ordinary. He wouldn't stay very long this morning anyway—just long enough to work out John and Nicole's escape plan.

John buzzed him in, and a moment later Henri found himself sitting in the living room on the couch, while John paced back and forth.

"How's Nicole?" Henri asked.

"She woke up at five or so, totally lucid. I filled her in, and now she's asleep again. She's drained, but that's to be expected. She'll be fine."

"How did she react when she realized she was still here, and not there?"

"Worried—about Edmond."

"That's understandable," Henri said. "She's a concerned mother. But I think Edmond will be fine, as long as Susanne made it back."

"Or even if she didn't," John added. "If Nicole's a 'no-show' for her visit with Edmond, I think the chances are slim-to-none that Edmond will run in front of that horse-drawn carriage. He was excited to the point of distraction when he saw her, leading to the accident; but if she's not there to elicit that reaction, my best guess is that he'll just turn around and go home."

We'll see, Henri thought; in two short days, we'll see. "Did you tell Nicole about our plan?" he asked, changing the subject. There was no point in belaboring the Edmond quandary, because what would be would be. There was one positive, though, in all of this: namely, if Henri suddenly ceased to exist at noon on Saturday, it would probably be quick and painless. Here one second, and gone like a puff of smoke the next—who could ask for a cleaner end to it all?

"Yes, I told her what we have planned, and she's on board."

Of course she was! Nicole belonged here, and she belonged with John. The two of them were in love (even the self-consumed Susanne had probably noticed it); and this romance definitely wasn't one of those flash-in-the-pan affairs—it never would be. Henri had a knack for spotting the real thing, and this was it.

"Did you find Susanne's passport?" Henri asked.

"Yes," John said with a smile. He walked over to Susanne's desk, pulling open the front drawer to retrieve the document. "It was right where you said it would be." He held up the passport triumphantly. With his free hand, he gathered up Susanne's purse and carried it to the couch. After setting the passport and the purse on the coffee table, he settled down with a satisfied grin next to Henri. "You were right about the drawer key, too. It was in a zippered pocket, right in here," he said, patting the shoulder-clutch.

"Told you." If nothing else, Henri knew his niece. Just as he had hoped, it looked like the good Uncle Henri would be an invaluable 'inside' contact in their evolving relocation plot. He was glad.

"Have you booked the flight?"

"Yes, we leave today, just after one o'clock."

John wasn't wasting any time, and Henri

agreed completely. It was best to get Nicole out of here, as quickly as possible, before friends, employers, and homicide detectives started making their inquiries; and long before the witching hour, at noon on Saturday. It was best that way, really. No need upsetting Nicole unduly with the disappearance of a certain family member, if their worst-case scenario came to pass. Nicole might mourn a little for Henri, but her more devastating loss, logically extrapolated from Henri's sudden demise, would have occurred exactly 135 years in the past, to the exact minute and second. A mother should never lose a child, and Henri prayed that Nicole's new life in the modern world would not be saddened by this kind of tragedy.

"I hope Nicole understands that she will need to truly become Susanne," Henri said. "She should use Susanne's credit cards, write checks from her checkbook, and even assume her name. I'll take care of Susanne's bills, from this end; and in a year or two, we can sell the condo. I don't think the two of you will be coming back here anytime soon."

"We'll stay in Chicago," John said with a nod. "My life is there, and if things go the way I hope they will, Nicole's new life will be there, too. Anyway, she can't stay here. Too many people know Susanne in Paris, so there's no way Nicole would be able to pull off the masquerade for more than a few days if she stayed."

"Agreed."

"Will you take care of Susanne's resignation?" John asked.

"I already typed the letter and forged her signature. I'll drop it off at the museum as soon as you leave."

"So, I guess that's it. We seem to have all the bases covered." John dug in Susanne's purse and retrieved her ring of keys. "You'll need to get in here, every so often, to check on things—and then there's the question of what to do with Susanne's car. Why don't you keep it? Instead of 'hoofing' it, you'll finally have some wheels to get you places."

Henri took the keys, looking at them skeptically. "I'll probably sell the damn thing. There's no place my legs can't get me in this city." Henri held out his hand, and John shook it. "You're good for her, John. Keep her safe."

"I will." John looked Henri in the eye. "And you stay safe, too."

"I'll try." These were meaningless words, really, because Henri's safety rested in someone else's hands entirely, and that person didn't even live in this century anymore.

"I'll give you a call when we get to Chicago," John promised.

"I'll be waiting."

God willing, he would be waiting.

CHAPTER FORTY-EIGHT

It was June eighteenth, which meant that just shy of three weeks had passed since Inspector Michèle Crossier had been assigned the role of lead investigator in the *d'Orsay* murders. By now, she had hoped to have solved the perplexing case; but unfortunately, she was no further along on the road to solving the case than she had been in the early morning hours of June first.

Every one of her leads had taken her down a path to a dead end, including the promising-looking bag that held clothes and a metal framing mallet— the bag that Henri Bruante had deposited in a nearby garbage can (intentionally 'planted' it seemed) for her men to find. Why he would do that was beyond her. The blood they had tested on Monsieur Bruante's work clothes matched with his own DNA sample, *not* the victim's; some hair they recovered from the woman's blouse and skirt belonged to Susanne, *not* Claudine; and the art restoration tool came up completely clean of biologics, which meant that it hadn't been used as the ancillary murder weapon, along with the sculpture, to kill the night security guard.

Still, Michèle believed that something vaguely resembling her sadly disorganized theory involving perverse prostitution, pimps, drug-bosses, a jilted gay lover, and family loyalty had transpired in *d'Orsay's* basement; it's just that she didn't have one iota of evidence to prove even one small part of it. Claudine's DNA didn't match the hair or the secretions on the victim's genitals, and neither did

Susanne's; Henri's DNA was nowhere to be found on either of the victims (although they found his fingerprints, as expected, on the outside of the pressure machine and on the sculpture he had been working on, along with the overturned pedestal); Susanne and Claudine's fingerprints were glaringly absent from the crime scene or the equipment in question; and the 'mystery' victim himself remained unidentified, nameless, and unclaimed by any friends or family. Perhaps all Michèle needed was to look at things from a different angle; but the problem, it seemed, was that all the angles she could think of had already been looked at.

Why had Monsieur Bruante gone to the trouble of packaging up some phony evidence for her crime lab technicians to scrutinize? The elder Bruante had to be involved in this case somehow; otherwise, why would he bother to throw a stick in the wrong direction for the police dogs to fetch?

"Go back and question him again," Deschamps had suggested at their daily lunchtime de-briefing just an hour ago; and that's exactly what Michèle Crossier was about to unenthusiastically do, since the wind had largely been taken out of her sail.

It was drizzling when she pulled up in front of Henri Bruante's home workshop, right behind the surveillance car that had been stationed there twenty-four hours a day for over a week now. She slid out of her red Peugeot, umbrella in hand but unopened, walking up to the driver's side of the white Citroen to get an update from the officer on duty.

"Has he gone anywhere since Thursday?" she asked Foujois, a heavy-set fellow with coffee stains on his shirt. She knew that Henri had walked to Susanne's house early that morning, returning home after only a half-hour or so upstairs with his niece. Then he had gone to the museum in the early afternoon, but only briefly. Michèle had made her own inquiries afterward, discovering to her great surprise that Susanne had resigned her position as Assistant Director of Acquisitions and Special Exhibits, in a letter that Monsieur Bruante had hand-delivered for her.

Michèle felt certain that Susanne's decision to quit her job stemmed from the Executive Director's press conference, televised live from the front of *Musée d'Orsay* earlier this week. It must sting in the most humiliating kind of way, to have your erstwhile boyfriend make a discovery that should have been yours—but the first one to the finish line wins, as they say, and Marcel Lauren had definitely gotten there first.

"He hasn't come outside since Thursday's outings," the other gendarme, a thin and wiry guy named Godessart, answered; "not even for his usual morning constitutional." Michèle knew, from the phone debriefings, that Godessart had pulled the short straw on Thursday, following Henri Bruante on foot—back and forth, and back and forth again, on both his morning and afternoon excursions. For a man in his sixties, Henri's legs, and his stamina, never seemed to tire. But why hadn't he come out for his usual morning exercise, the past two days? She shrugged, concluding that maybe he was feeling under the weather and just not up to it.

"He's inside right now, I assume?" From where she stood, everything looked dark and quiet through the windows, both upstairs and down.

Foujois shrugged. "He went in Thursday at around 2:15, right after his walk back from the museum. Those two doors are the only way out." He nodded toward the front and side entrances. "Unless he magically made himself disappear, he's in there."

It was raining steadily now, so she opened her umbrella. "Good work, boys. Keep it up," she said; but in all likelihood, they wouldn't remain parked out front for very much longer. Unless something unexpected came out of her interview with Henri today, the 'tail order' on *this* particular Bruante would soon be cancelled. There was simply no point to it anymore.

Michèle crossed the street, stepping carefully on the wet pavement and arriving a few seconds later at the business entrance—the one that gave access to Henri Bruante's art restoration workshop. She peered in through the adjacent picture-glass window, under the sign that said *CLOSED*—odd for a weekday. She made note of a covered painting sitting on an easel off to the side, a long table cluttered with frames and tools, and an alcove in back that the elder Bruante apparently used for drawing and painting, judging from the handful of partly finished canvases there. The place looked dead, with no sign of its owner.

She decided to ring the bell anyway. After three tries, all of them resulting in no response, she made her way from the front of the house to the side, climbing the stairs that led to the *premier étage*. There was no bell up here to ring, so she knocked— a few light taps to begin with, but then louder. She tried again, and again until she was starting to think that maybe he wasn't there after all.

She looked over her shoulder, which gave her a perfect view of the unmarked police car, to glare meaningfully at Foujois. Henri Bruante had probably slipped out unnoticed. If she found out that the surveillance officers had either left their post or had fallen asleep on the job, she would have both of their badges. She turned to leave, her temper well on the way to boiling; but that's when Henri opened the door.

"Hello, inspector." His greeting was pleasant, unstrained...and accented with sniffles. He didn't seem at all surprised to see her—his all-too-familiar reaction to all of their dealings so far. "I'm sorry to keep you waiting, out here in the rain. I was sleeping. You see, I have been very busy, these past few days; plus, I seem to have contracted a cold."

She nodded. "I'm sorry to disturb you..."

"...but you have some questions for me, I'm sure; or else you wouldn't be here." He smiled benevolently at her through slightly injected eyes, due to the cold—almost like an uncle would to a niece. Well, they *were* related, after all—on the Caillebotte side. Should she bring their family ties to his attention if the opportunity arose? Her professional half said 'no' while her emotional half said 'yes'; so what would tip the balance? *A career-making case that's rapidly turning cold*, she thought. "Come in, please, out of the rain, and we'll talk." He stepped kindly to one side and let her in.

She closed her umbrella and leaned it against the wall by the door as she stepped into a small dining room, where she saw a table cluttered with papers. "Pardon the bachelor's mess," he said, leading her through the first room and into a second. He motioned hospitably toward a couch and an easy chair. "Take your pick. Could I get you something to drink?" He acted as if he had nothing to hide, which made her wonder what, exactly, he was hiding; but did it even matter now?

"Thank you, monsieur, but not this time. This shouldn't take long, really."

She took a seat on the couch, while he sat across from her on the chair. "How may I help you?"

"You dropped off an interesting bag of 'trash' for us a couple of days ago. Would you mind telling me why you felt the need to dispose of some ripped and bloodied clothes, along with a perfectly good framing mallet, in a garbage bin six or seven blocks from here?"

"So that's where my mallet ended up!" His tone of voice sounded convincingly surprised. "It must have gotten mixed in with the clothes when I put them down on my workbench to sort."

"So, you didn't mean to throw it out?" She didn't believe him for a second, but she played along with his ruse anyway.

"Of course not. That was one of my better ones. I was just about to order another. If you still have it, would you mind returning it to me?"

She ignored the request. "Why did you dump the bag so far from your house, Monsieur Bruante?"

"The small can on the corner was full, so I took it to a bigger one a few blocks away. It's not that far; anyway, I enjoyed the walk."

Enjoying the walking part was true, at least.

Henri Bruante went everywhere on foot, as her surveillance officers could attest. "We found your own blood on the work clothes," she said.

"Yes. I'm afraid I cut myself with a sharp planer, resurfacing a frame." He pulled up his sleeve, and showed her a rather nasty cut on his biceps. "I was holding it rather awkwardly in the crook of my arm—the price one pays sometimes for working alone, without an assistant." He shrugged. "I could have tried washing them, but the clothes were old anyway, so it was simpler to just throw them away."

He seemed to have an answer for everything. The last question she had for him might be more difficult to explain. "We found Susanne's hair on the women's clothes. Why did you throw away one of your niece's outfits?"

"She stayed with me for a few months when her condo was being renovated, and she left some clothes here. She took everything back to her apartment a few weeks ago, except for those."

"They looked pretty ragged," Michèle commented, raising her eyebrows. "Normal wear and tear?"

"Not exactly." He smiled. "What Susanne and her friends enjoy behind closed doors is none of my business; but let's just say she likes it rough. That's not my idea of a good time, but, to each his—or her—own."

Michèle gazed at Henri with a mixture of undisguised skepticism, and defeated resignation. "And you expect me to believe all of this?"

"Why wouldn't you? It's all true." He leaned forward in his chair. "You police always try to look for hidden meaning in everything. It was just a bag of throwaway clothing—nothing more, nothing less."

"So when I question Susanne about her clothes and her sexual idiosyncrasies—when I pay her a visit later today—she'll tell me the same story?"

"She would, if she were still in Paris for you to question."

Had Susanne taken a little vacation to re-think her washed-up career? "I know about Susanne's resignation," Michèle countered, "and I don't blame her for wanting to get away for a few days to get her head together. Where is she, and when will she be back?"

"She's in Chicago with her fiancé, probably picking out her wedding ring as we speak."

"Fiancé?" Michèle stared at Henri, who was grinning at her, as if daring her to think of a snappy comeback.

"Yes—Dr. John Noland. I think some of your gendarmes met him, *n'est ce pas*? Surely they told you that he was visiting."

"Well, yes; but I had no idea they were engaged." Could this part of Henri's story possibly be true? "It just seems rather—sudden."

"Not at all, inspector. She and John have had a long-distance relationship for quite some time, now. In fact, they've been discussing marriage for years. They were college sweethearts, you see."

"But what about Susanne's *other* boyfriend?"

"Do you mean Marcel Lauren, *Musée d'Orsay's* Executive Director? Susanne's boss?" Henri laughed. "Yes, they were involved, but never seriously—for *either* of them, I believe. Susanne's special arrangement with her employer meant nothing to Susanne or to John, if he even knew about it. Susanne is very open-minded when it comes to this kind of thing. John is, also. As I said before: to each his own."

What could Michèle do? Absolutely nothing. Susanne had not been ordered to stay in Paris. She had never been arrested, and she wasn't even under police surveillance anymore.

Henri got up and wrote two phone numbers on a piece of paper. He handed it to Michèle from across the coffee table with a pleasant smile and then sat down again, dabbing his nose with a tissue. "You can reach her on her cell phone—or John's, if you'd like. I'm sure she'd be more than happy to talk to you."

Michèle sighed. There was nothing more to say. The guiltless Susanne had skipped town; the virtuous Claudine would get off scot-free; and the eager-to-help and ever-truthful Henri would go on restoring paintings and disposing of bloodstained clothing to his heart's delight. Michèle was finished here, it seemed; but as she got up to leave, she decided to give it one more try.

"What *really* happened at *Musée d'Orsay* two weeks ago?" she asked. It was worth a shot; maybe a head-on approach would make him talk.

He gazed back at her thoughtfully, as if quietly weighing the pros and cons of leveling with her. Finally, he seemed to come to a conclusion, so she sat back down. The question was whether truth or lies had just won the silent debate.

"You won't believe this," Henri stated soberly, "but the naked woman in the gallery that night three weeks ago was a time traveler, who was transported through *The Origin of the World* with a companion. He died on the way here from 1876, but she survived. The night guard was an innocent bystander, who was standing in the way and was accidentally killed when they 'arrived'."

She was surprised only by the absurdity of his lie. She should have known. Next, he would be telling her that the woman was Courbet's mistress, or maybe even the very same anonymous nude model featured in Susanne's special exhibit; and that John Doe was an artist (perhaps even someone famous, like one of the Caillebotte brothers) who was using her to pose for his latest painted, photographed or sculpted creation.

"Thank you for your honesty, monsieur," Michèle responded with cold sarcasm. "If you could get me in touch with this nineteenth century time traveler of yours, maybe she would be willing to answer some questions? I'm sure she'd be able to clear up everything, and then I'd finally be able to close my case."

"I'm afraid you just missed her," he responded, deadpan. "You see, she's gone back…" (he hesitated, seeming to choose his words carefully) "…to the time in which she truly belongs."

Enough was enough; but as she started to get up, ready to leave, she realized that she no longer felt irritated, but literally numb; resigned to her failure and unwilling to continue beating her head against the wall. She was weary—of the clues that didn't add up; of the pressure from Deschamps to solve a case that was looking more and more like it was thoroughly unsolvable; and of certain condescending relatives that seemed to enjoy making her look like an idiot.

Henri touched her arm—his manner kind, gentle...fatherly. "Don't go yet," he said. "I'm not trying to make fun of you." At any other time, or with any other person, she wouldn't have believed him; but his soft, no-nonsense tone and the forthcoming look on his face made it seem that he was sincere when he said that he wasn't ridiculing her. Whatever his reasons for telling her such an outrageous tall-tale, she found herself truly believing that it wasn't out of spite or a desire to paint her as foolish or gullible.

She settled back down in her seat, returning his gaze a little bit sadly. Now was as good a time as any to reveal their common ancestry, since she would be resigning from the case at the earliest opportunity anyway, eliminating the potential conflict of interest that staying on an investigation into her very own family represented. "Let's let sleeping dogs lie, whether they are resting in this century or another," she said. "If you're in touch with her, though—give her my best regards...from one cousin to another."

She thought his face would register some modicum of surprise; but instead he smiled broadly, in a way that told her he already knew about their common family ties. "I was always against the way they treated your great-grandfather: Jean. I knew him, you know. His sister: your great-great aunt Genevieve, was very much like mine. Joelle was equally unforgiving with her son (my nephew, and Claudine's father: Jacques), if it's any consolation."

She stared at him in disbelief. "How did you

know we were related?"

His eyes twinkled. "*Your* branch of the Bruante-Caillebotte family tree that I left out on the table, that day you came to question me, may be incomplete; but I have plenty of others that illustrate the Caillebotte-Crossier ancestral line in full detail…and it leads directly to *you*, my dear."

"So you left the family tree out for me to see?" She thought about this for a few seconds, and then asked: "Why did you want me to know?"

"It was the right thing to do. I didn't think it was fair for you to be kept in the dark about such a strange coincidence. You *needed* to know that the case you seemed so intent on solving involved your family relations."

"Did you think that would influence me?"

"Of course—but not in our favor. I wouldn't blame you at all, if you were bent on revenge; but fair is fair. You can't pick your relatives, as they say."

This was actually admirable, and gave her even *more* justification for resigning her lead. She got up, putting her hand out to shake his. "Don't be ridiculous," he said, pulling her towards him in a hug that only an uncle can give. "We're family…remember?"

She walked to the door, feeling more satisfied in failure than she thought would have ever been possible. With her hand on the latch, she heard Henri call after her.

"Michèle?"

She looked over her shoulder, across the dining room to where he stood on the threshold of his sitting room. "What is it, Monsieur Bruante?"

"Keep in touch," he instructed; "and *please*," he added, "call me *Ton-Ton*."

Made in the USA
Monee, IL
11 April 2021